"A wildly original and magical twist on the Robin Hood narrative, Kendra Merritt's *By Wingéd Chair* is packed to the spokes with complex characters, wry humor, and flawless world building."

-Darby Karchut, best-selling author of DEL TORO MOON and FINN FINNEGAN

"With a wonderfully crafted blend of swords and sorcery and characters based on Robin Hood, Merritt tops this story off with the lead character readers need nowadays; a strong, independent, powerful female mage who also happens to be in a wheelchair. Readers will be constantly turning pages to see what happens next to this fun group of characters through the twists and turns they won't see coming."

-The Booklife Prize

"Kendra Merritt's prose is fresh, with one-line descriptions that crack like a whip, and she doesn't miss an opportunity to surprise the reader. From the first line to the last, I was enchanted with *By Winged Chair*."

-Todd Fahnestock, best-selling author of FAIRMIST and THE WISHING WORLD

Daybreak Colony Duology

Surviving Daybreak

Daybreak Sentinel

Mark of the Least Series

By Wingéd Chair

Skin Deep

Catching Cinders

Shroud for a Bride

A Matter of Blood

After the Darkness

The King in the Tower Collection

Unmasked

Mishap's Heroes Series

Magic and Misrule

Death and Devotion

Trust and Treason

Illusions and Infamy

Sparks and Scales

Wastelands and War

Eldros Legacy Series

The Pain Bearer

The Truth Stealer

The Death Bringer

KENDRA MERRITT

DAYBREAK COLONY: BOOK 1

SURVIVING DAYBREAK

For Joselyn and the other sci-fi girls out there.

CHAPTER 1

***Last Resort* Flight 225: Day 3698**

"You won't dream in cryosleep." That was the first lie the corporations told us.

I don't know what everyone else saw behind their eyelids as the *Last Resort* sailed between the stars, but I dreamed of the parents I'd never had and the mentor that I'd left behind.

I had no memories to provide images, but warm arms settled around me. Or maybe that was just the cryo-gel conforming to my body.

The feeling faded, replaced by the chill of empty air. In the fuzzy-edged haze of memory, Professor Orrion waited on the launch platform, the same way he had that day back on Earth. Fragments of images came with him. The dirty sunlight glinting from his glasses. His fingers running over the screws in my thumb joint.

"Build something great for me, kid," he'd said.

Red light flashed across his floppy hair, gone stark white before he was fifty, and a klaxon made me flinch.

That definitely wasn't right.

Well-wishers gathered around the shuttle; I had no memory of having boarded. The other passengers waved to their families below, but Professor Orrion was the only one from the corporation who had come to see me off.

The people in the crowd grinned, bathed in flashing red light, and one by one they blinked out of existence. Professor Orrion raised his hand and opened his mouth as if to say one last thing before I'd never see him again. And then he was gone, too.

Red-tinged darkness crowded around me, and I recognized the black behind my eyelids.

Wait, was I awake? I was supposed to sleep for over ten years. That hadn't *felt* like ten years.

I struggled to open eyes that felt glued shut. Air hadn't been important a second ago, but now I sucked in a breath that caught in my lungs. I choked and coughed, dragging in little sips of air that weren't nearly enough.

"Gently now," a voice said. Someone female and soft-spoken but with a calm that soothed the tightness in my chest. "Breathe in for four counts, then out for four. Your diaphragm is in shock. You can't count on your body remembering how to breathe for the first few minutes after you wake up, so you have to convince it to do so."

The klaxon sounded again, blaring like the fire alarm in the dormitories where I'd grown up. I would have jumped, but I was too busy trying to not cough.

I hacked one more time and bit down hard on the urge to panic when my lungs kept trying to push their way up my throat. The next breath was easier. The tricky part was not gagging on it.

In, two, three, four. Out, two, three, four.

Who would have thought breathing would be the hardest thing I'd ever done?

"Do you remember your name?" the voice said.

An easy question, at least. Words came in between gasps. "Anikka Drake."

My voice croaked, clogged in the thickness in my throat, but at least I got the answer out. I peeled my eyes open and blinked away something thick and sticky. They stung and burned, and everything was still very blurry. And red. An ominous red that smeared the vague shapes around me.

I grunted and tried to lift my arm to swipe at my eyes, but it was still glued to my side, stuck in the gel.

Someone dragged a rough washcloth across my face.

"Sorry," the voice said. "I have to skip so many steps."

What's going on?

Finally, I could see a little. Metal tables and trays crowded the floor. Counters lined the walls, buried in delicate med tools and dirty cloths. The klaxon blared again, and red light flashed from a warning light above the door.

This was...the infirmary on the *Last Resort*. The last time I'd seen it, all the tables had been stowed out of the way and the tools tucked in their holders on the walls.

My sleep pod stood in the center of the room while several others lay scattered around us. Two still had their lids latched shut, but three more stood open while their occupants gasped in little cocoons of gel.

I couldn't think with all this noise and the light reflecting a hundred-fold off the shiny walls. Which was a hundred times too many for my brain right now.

I was supposed to wake up in a calm, soothing recovery ward as the *Last Resort* settled into its gentle orbit around Daybreak. Everything was supposed to be quiet and slow to help with the shock of waking up after years of sleeping suspended in cryo-goo. At least that's what all the manuals had said.

A woman hurried by, her gray tech uniform tinged red from the light. She reached for my arm and hesitated, her gaze sliding down the seam where the metal met my skin just above my elbow.

"Where's your chip?" she asked.

Back on Earth, I would have had the brain capacity to be offended or uncomfortable. But right now I had just enough energy to twitch the fingers on my prosthetic hand.

"Right," the tech said and waved a screen over my wrist where my chip had been installed just before launch. Then she jammed a hypo in my neck.

"Ow!"

"Sorry. We're really not supposed to do that, but you're going to need the chems."

Seriously, this wasn't how this was supposed to go. Where was the soothing environment? Where was the gentle physical rehabilitation routine? And the protein rich snacks and the electrolyte juice? Where was the AI companion with all the comforting music I'd uploaded before we'd launched?

"Hi!" A blue hologram about the size of my hand sprang from the tiny projectors on my wrist. It looked like...a young woman maybe? But the face was blank like a canvas waiting to be painted. "I'm your wake-up companion, here to make your recovery more comfortable. My designation is Bleep-Bloop."

Oh my gosh, I'd actually named it Bleep-Bloop. It had seemed funny at the time. I might have laughed now, but I was afraid if I started laughing, my lungs would forget how to breathe again.

"No time for that." The tech raced by, her hair coming out of its bun and falling around her face. She slammed the latch buttons on the two pods that were still closed. "Initiate patient mobility as a priority."

The hologram on my wrist tilted her fuzzy head. "This is contrary to current corporate protocols—"

"Override," the tech yelled, stepping to the next open pod to wipe goo from the man's eyes. "Emergency authorization two-two-nine-seven."

"Confirmed. Anikka, I need you to exit your pod." The hologram smiled up at me. A strange expression for someone who looked like a glowing mannequin.

Emergency? I tried to panic and managed a distracted irritation. The chems must have been suppressing some of the more alarming reactions I should be having.

I wanted to yell, "where's my juice?" A part of me even wanted to sink back into the goo and let the klaxon and the lights sort themselves out.

But...I'd worked my butt off to get my trip on the *Last Resort*, and now it looked like some stupid emergency was going to ruin it all.

I dragged my right arm and the prosthetic out of the goo. It clung, trying to drag me back, but some of my strength seeped back into my limbs—maybe from whatever chems that hypo had been loaded with—and I hauled my arm out so hard, I flipped all the way over the side of my pod and flopped onto the floor.

Pretty sure most of the "gentle rehabilitation" stuff was supposed to prevent this whole looking and feeling like a dead fish thing.

"That was great, Anikka!" my AI said. "Now I need you to try standing."

Gods of all worlds, the first thing I was going to do when this emergency was over would be to deactivate the AI's cheerleader mode.

The tech hauled the other man up, so he sat upright in his pod, coughing and hacking. His short dark hair stuck up at odd angles, gelled in place by the goo. She waved her screen over his wrist where his chip would have been implanted, then she hurried on to the next pod.

"What's happening?" I croaked. My throat was still preoccupied with all the breathing. Seemed like that was important.

Another AI's hologram popped up on the holographic pad beside the door. This one actually had a face and was dressed in a uniform identical to the tech's.

"Fifteen minutes to impact," it said.

I swallowed. "Impact?" I said, my voice still hoarse. "What impact? Impact sounds bad."

The tech hurried back to me and yanked on my arm until I was somewhat standing. I braced myself against my empty cryo chamber to keep myself upright.

"The ship is crashing," she said as she left me to help the others out of their pods. Most of them were still having trouble breathing without coughing.

"Crashing?" I cried. My feet slid against the tile floor, and I forced myself upright. "That's not supposed to happen. These colony ships are like the *Titanic*. Unsinkable." I winced. "Okay, bad example."

"No, great example," the tech snapped. Three of the other awoken sleepers were out of their pods, flopping on the floor as they struggled to acclimate to their muscles again. The tech snatched a stack of fabric from the counter and shoved it at me. By which I assumed she meant, 'get dressed.'

I flipped open the fabric and found a set of blue scrubs, a light gray cardigan, and a pair of slippers. At least they would keep me from slipping in more goo.

I pulled the shirt and pants on over the tank top and bike shorts I'd gone to sleep in however many years ago that had been.

"Where are we?" I asked as I slid the slippers over my feet. Beyond us, the wall was made of glass and we could see into another infirmary. More sleep pods stood open, and another tech frantically herded coughing sleepers past the gleaming tables.

"Daybreak," the tech said. "We made it to the system a couple of days ahead of schedule. The scout probe orbiting the planet was broadcasting the all-clear, just as expected. But when we got close, something...hit us."

And now we were crashing. Presumably into the planet we should have been orbiting.

Either my systems were all still wacky from cryosleep or she'd injected me with some pretty powerful anti-anxieties along with the rest of the chem cocktail because all I felt was a little buzz of terror in the back of my head. Easily ignored as I slid my arms into the cardigan.

"What hit us?"

"You now know as much as I do," she said. "You might even know as much as the command staff does. No one's communicated anything except the evacuation sequence."

Evacuation. Vent it, this was bad. As if the klaxon and the warning lights weren't enough, that one word sent a flash of panic through the fog of recovery.

"I'm just trying to wake as many people as I can and send them to escape pods. Maybe some of you will survive."

I sucked in a breath that made my lungs burn. A thousand souls. There were a thousand colonists sleeping aboard the *Last Resort,* plus the techs and the command staff. Not a ton compared to some of the other ships the Stellar Corporation had sent to other planets in the last couple of decades. But enough for the second wave of a colony.

And how many had they been able to wake in time? If this room was any indication...

I stared at the other five sleepers struggling into scrubs. Holy crap.

The tech stood beside my empty pod, hands clenching and unclenching at her sides. Her eyes were red and wet at the corners, and her mouth pulled into a tight line.

She glanced at me, then blew out her cheeks. "I'm not supposed to do this, but..." It was a familiar litany by now.

"Let me guess, you're going to do it, anyway?"

She grimaced and strode to the counter beside the door. She grabbed my prosthetic hand as she went, dragging me along with her.

I yelped.

"Mary, download your data packet to this AI."

The holographic pad on the counter beside the door lit up, and the infirmary's AI popped up again, a hologram of a young woman in a gray uniform. "Warning. Steps toward AI integration are extremely dangerous and considered a felony on most planets—"

"I know. But they'll need it. And we don't have time to argue." She didn't give any kind of pass code or emergency authorization. She just stared at the AI, waiting, my hand held in hers near the pad.

The floor lurched under our feet, and I grabbed the counter with my free hand.

"Impact in ten minutes. We have now entered the atmosphere," the infirmary AI said quietly. She took one more second, then reached out as if to touch the back of my wrist where my own AI lived. "Very well. I am downloading the infirmary data packet."

The light at the base of my metal thumb flashed and my own AI popped up, her smooth face reflecting surprise.

"What's this—oh."

She didn't have time to react to what had to be a flood of

information. The tech took my arm again and spun me so the holograph disappeared, and I faced the infirmary.

"You have to get going. Get to the end of the corridor and turn left. The escape pods should be lit up like fireworks right now, but in case you can't find them, there's a map in your AI."

I reeled, fighting the urge to cling to her as she stepped away and helped the last two sleepers get their slippers on.

"Go," the tech said again, shoving one of them in my direction, a middle-aged woman with dark eyes. "Lead them to the escape pods. You'll have to launch within the next five minutes if you're going to have a hope of landing."

My chest seized, threatening another cough. "No. Wait. I can't lead anyone. I'm—I'm an infra-engineer. I was never supposed to be on the leadership track."

"Well, I wasn't supposed to be doing this either," the tech snapped, her hands on her hips. "I was supposed to fly back to Earth and die of old age."

The tech huffed and ran a hand over her face, then over her hair. She was older than me, but not by a lot. Maybe a few years. She avoided my eyes as she stepped to the back wall and pressed some buttons on a pad. A hatch opened up and another sleeping pod rolled into the infirmary.

My mouth went dry. "You're not coming."

She shook her head, tendrils of hair floating around her face. "I might be able to save one or two more."

The fog in my head cleared enough for a shaft of understanding. This was her last act. She had chosen what she would spend her last few minutes doing. A knot grew in my stomach and bile crawled up the back of my throat.

"Seven minutes to impact," the infirmary AI said.

Now I had to choose what to do with mine.

"Go," the tech said.

I swallowed back the growing panic and sadness. Neither would help right now.

"Good luck," I told her. Then I gestured to the rest. "Come on."

None of them seemed particularly awake yet, but at least they moved, lurching toward me and through the door into the hall.

I followed, trying to herd them faster.

Outside the infirmary, smoke filtered down the corridor, lit from underneath by the red hazard lights. Crew members in blue uniforms rushed down the passageway, calling to each other. None wasted the time to ask who this motley group in the mismatched scrubs was. Probably too busy keeping us from crashing.

I didn't hold out a lot of hope.

"At the end of the corridor, turn left," my AI said from my wrist.

"I remember," I said and pushed past my group of sleepers.

A man about Professor Orrion's age glared up at the red warning light flashing above us. "How do we get out?"

At least he hadn't asked "where are we?" or "who am I?" The manual had talked about how disoriented a sleeper could be for hours after waking. Maybe they'd all gotten a shot of the same stuff I had.

"The escape pods," I said. "This way."

The entire *Last Resort* groaned and shuddered, and suddenly we were struggling uphill.

Vent it, a colony ship was never meant to enter the atmosphere. They were built to orbit and send shuttles or drop ships back and forth. How much longer before we burned up entirely?

My legs shook. The electrical impulses in the cryo-gel

were supposed to keep your muscles in shape during the long trip to Daybreak, but that didn't mean I could hop out and run around like a star athlete. That was the whole point of the recovery ward. To recover.

This corridor should be called the *un*recovery ward.

Someone came barreling around the corner and smashed into me. I fell and the only reason I didn't roll back down the corridor was because I fetched up against the legs of the man behind me. He kept his feet, luckily.

The crew member, a man in the blue jacket with the gold trim of command, stumbled back and righted himself. "What is this?" He squinted at us. "Sleepers? Vent it, what are you doing awake?" He shook his head. "Never mind. Get to the escape pods. Go!"

And he sprinted off back the way we'd come.

"Thanks. Very helpful," I grumbled. Even the people who were supposed to be in command left me to lead instead.

With the *Last Resort* at such a steep angle, I had to reach out and use the corner to haul myself up. There to the left, the bank of escape pods gleamed, their shiny hatches reflecting our faces back to us.

Twenty total. At least half of them still had little green lights, indicating they were charged and available, ready to save our lives.

In the residency wing of the ship, the escape pods were all built to hold ten to twenty colonists. But these were all individual for the techs and crew members who worked on the infirmary level.

One pod, one life.

I staggered up the cockeyed corridor and started down the line, punching hatch buttons. They swung open, and my sleepers shuffled forward.

Too slow. We were running out of time.

The man who'd followed on my heels the whole way climbed into the nearest tube. I reached to shut his hatch and his desperate eyes glanced back at me, holding my gaze for that last second.

"Godspeed," he said as the hatch clicked closed.

An old Earth saying. A prayer or a blessing, I sure didn't know. Professor Orrion had whispered it in my ear as I'd stepped away from him and joined the line for my shuttle. The one that had brought me here, to this mess.

The deck under my feet shook, the vibrations numbing my feet through their slippers as I shoved each of my sleepers into an escape pod. I shut the hatch and murmured "Godspeed" for each one. And they shot off into space as the smoke grew thick and black over my head.

The last sleeper was the middle-aged woman with dark eyes. She gripped my metal hand as I reached to shut her hatch. "I'll see you planet-side," she said.

I just nodded, hoping she was right. I shut her hatch and spun to slide into mine.

The *Last Resort* lurched, and I lost my footing. Instead of sliding down the slanted floor, my legs floated up, and I scrabbled for the open hatch of my pod. The rocking of the ship tried to rip me from the pod and fling me against the far wall.

Our uncontrolled descent must have finally killed the artificial gravity and the inertial dampeners. This was turning out to be the worst day ever.

I hauled on the hatch and swung my legs into my pod. I'd had exactly fifteen hours of zero g training before being assigned to the *Last Resort*. The minimum requirement for any passenger on a colony ship.

Gritting my teeth, I angled myself to seal the hatch behind me.

I didn't have to be an expert. I just had to know enough to live.

The hatch sealed shut with a hiss, and the giant red button right in front of my face lit up. Impossible to miss. I guess in an emergency you wanted that sort of thing to be idiot-proof.

I breathed out, sending up a short four-word prayer to Professor Orrion's god. "Please, let this work."

Then I punched the button.

CHAPTER 2

Last Resort Flight 225: Day 3698

I had a little window so I could see the flames streak past as my escape pod launched away from the *Last Resort*. My world shook like the pod was ready to break apart, but the gel filled cushions inside protected me from the worst of it.

The pod itself was barely more than a glorified coffin; a tube filled with a body hurtling through the atmosphere. There was only one exception to that analogy.

I wasn't dead yet.

I braced my hands on either side of my little window, my only reassurance that I wasn't about to be buried alive.

My arms would fit neatly in the cushions on either side of me, and I was probably supposed to keep them there, but it felt more stable to brace myself. I'd skipped a lot of the stuff in the manual about evacuation procedures. The overviews of the colony and the schematics of the ship were more interesting.

I'd never really thought I would need any of the emergency stuff.

The flames streaming past my window faded, and finally, I could see.

Far above me, the *Last Resort* glowed against a brilliant blue sky as it burned through the atmosphere. Pieces of debris streaked around me, leaving streamers of smoke and flames.

I knew it was falling. I knew how fast we had to be going. But it looked so stately, majestic even as it hung there in the sky, a jewel against the silken backdrop of Daybreak's sky. Flames obscured the pointed bow where banks of windows angled down toward the surface of the planet. Pieces of paneling sheered away from the curve of the mid-ship and flew past me. The stern engines still glowed, as though trying —and failing—to keep the ship from falling too fast.

Ahead, two streaks of light came into view. Little tubes with heat shielding on the ends and a small window where I imagined I could make out more frightened faces.

Escape pods. I pressed as close to the window as I dared, squinting.

A flash dazzled me as something else entered my field of view. A piece of debris. The stretch of paneling struck the nearest pod, and it flipped end over end to crash into the other one.

They exploded in a shower of fire and shrapnel.

I cried out as my pod rocked, and grabbed at the smooth door, trying to find purchase that would anchor me.

There was a jerk, and I prayed it was my parachute deploying, not another piece of debris. A blur of blue and green and purple rushed toward me, the exact colors of Professor Orrion's favorite sweater. I'd always made fun of it. Now I wished I hadn't.

A shuddering crash shook my pod, and black swallowed everything.

. . .

Last Resort **Flight 225: Day 3698**

Pain made me gasp and open my eyes.

What a weird thing to remember when falling out of the sky, I thought as I woke up. Again. For the second time in an hour.

That wasn't fair. Normally, if I was going to wake up twice in a day, I expected a nice nap to happen somewhere in there.

I blinked, the dark edges of the escape pod coming into focus. The light of the big red button had gone out, and nothing was visible through the window.

At least I'd landed. I was alive. Though my left arm hurt like a son of a space pirate, and I was lying at a funny angle on the gel cushions of the pod. I raised my prosthetic hand to my head, pressing against the headache that pounded in my temple.

"Where...where am I?" I croaked.

The hologram of my wake-up AI sprang from my wrist, close enough to my nose to make me go cross-eyed. I pulled my hand back far enough to focus on the androgynous face of the AI.

"The planet Daybreak," she said, her voice slightly buzzy, like the synthetic voices of the computers back on the *Last Resort*. "We have crash landed after the *Last Resort* experienced an emergency and loss of orbit."

"What happened to it?"

The AI hesitated. "I'm not sure. I lost contact with the main vessel shortly after we struck the surface."

"Is it night?"

I tried to turn in the tiny space of the pod, but the shooting pain in my arm made me light-headed.

"It is not. I believe we are lying face down on the surface."

"Great." I leaned my head back. I would have thunked it against the cushions in frustration, but that would have made the headache worse.

"Do not worry. The escape pod is equipped with contingencies for this exact situation. I will connect with the pod. Hang onto something."

"How—"

The door blew open with enough force to flip the escape pod. I rattled off the walls like dice in a cup and blacked out long enough that I found myself blinking awake again for the third time.

"Don't do that," I gasped through searing pain as lights danced across my field of vision. "I'm pretty sure loss of consciousness is a serious deal."

"Loss of consciousness is usually an indication of brain trauma."

"See what I mean?"

"Noted. I will not attempt to extricate you from a situation in which you're trapped again."

I groaned. There were so many things wrong at the moment that it was easier just to push them all to the back of my head and ignore them. The list started with the pain in my arm and just got worse from there.

The hatch, which was now above me, opened onto a blur of blue. Keeping my left arm as still as I could, I hauled myself out of the pod with my right, metal fingers gripping the sides of the hatch.

I sucked in a breath as I stood and coughed again. My lungs were still adjusting, apparently.

Huge trees towered over me, large blue-green leaves waving in the light breeze. My pod had broken a hole in the thick canopy, leaving a circular gash to reveal the sky, which was such a deep blue it was nearly purple. Thick vines hung from the lower branches, obscuring the space between trunks all the way down to the underbrush that covered the ground in vivid orange and pink and green foliage.

Between the trunks flashed the blue of the sky and the bright light of something reflective.

I stumbled down off my pod, my slippered feet sinking into the leaves we'd brought down in our crash.

The lurch made my arm sing with pain, and I winced. I shuffled forward, parting the bushes until I stood between two towering trees.

The ground fell away from me in a steep cliff, and I stared at an undulating sea of blue-green tree-tops. Here and there one stood above the others marked with bright red splotches, but I couldn't tell if they were flowers or leaves. The cliff stretched on either side of me, curving around in an ancient crater big enough to engulf a colony ship, its zone of destruction, and a good bit of jungle.

Miles away and clearly visible from this height, the *Last Resort* lay burning, and I could only stand there and stare with a lump in my throat.

The ship punched into the crust of the planet, rising like King Arthur's sword thrust through its stone. A massive circle of downed trees spread from the impact zone and flames licked at the blackened hull, reflecting in the few pieces that still gleamed.

The *Last Resort* was a morbid name for a ship, I'd always thought, but it was fitting. All the colony ships were supposed to be one of humanity's last chances. A way to springboard from our over-crowded planet and seed the stars with the best and brightest from Earth.

From the planet, the mass exodus of Earth might have seemed desperate, but from the lounge of the ship, I'd only felt hope as I'd watched my home disappear behind us.

"What happened?" I asked.

The hologram on my arm sprang up, staring at the sight alongside me. "It crashed. I do not know more. I was not loaded with diagnostic programming, and communications with the ship were lost as we descended."

"Could anyone have survived?"

"Chances of surviving impact at terminal velocity with inertial dampeners offline are 3%. Chances of surviving the radiation from the damaged core are .0002%."

All those people. Over a thousand souls. All the sleepers still in cryo. All the crew members who'd been trying to save the ship. The tech who'd saved my life. All dead.

I didn't even know her name.

I sank to the ground, holding my bad arm. My chest heaved and tears trickled down my cheeks, but I couldn't control any of it. My lungs refused to cooperate.

The chems on the ship had cleared my head but pushed the stronger emotions down. How did I get that feeling back? I could use some dulled edges right about now. Reality was sharp enough to make me bleed.

"Anikka?" the AI said, her image wavering on my arm. "Are you unwell?"

I laughed and couldn't stop.

"Your heart-rate indicates distress. I would inject you with a calming agent, but I do not have access to the *Last Resort's* supplies. You will have to attempt some breathing techniques. Please follow my lead. In...out..."

I was getting tired of the way my lungs didn't want to listen to me, but maybe they would listen to her soothing voice.

My chest shuddered but eventually fell into a pattern—in and out—that would keep me alive and not hyperventilating.

"Thanks...I don't know what to call you."

"My designation is still Bleep-Bloop. That is what you named me when I was first assigned to you back in Earth's orbit."

I winced. "I didn't really think through it that seriously. It sounded funny, and I figured I would need a laugh on the way out of cryosleep."

"Do you need a laugh now?"

I shook my head. I couldn't even remember how. "But I can't call you Bleep-Bloop for real. How about BB?"

"I am assigned to you, Anikka Drake. You can change my designation any time you like."

"Fine. BB, then." I stretched my legs out in front of me. They shook hard enough that I didn't trust myself to stand. And despite the sun streaming down and the balmy temperature, I couldn't get warm.

"I think I will need to sit here for a minute."

"Symptoms indicate you are experiencing mental trauma. I should know as I am now an infirmary AI as well as a wake-up AI."

That's right. The med tech had integrated the infirmary's data packet into BB. I hadn't even had a chance to process that up on the ship. I should have been horrified or at least wary, watching my AI for signs of integration sickness. But she didn't seem logic-crazy to me, and I couldn't help but feel grateful for the extra edge the med tech had tried to give us.

"Can you tell what's wrong with my arm?"

BB's hologram tilted its head, simulating thought. "Can you move it?"

I steeled myself to flex my arm and had to swallow down a spike of nausea. "Not really."

"Pain, swelling, and bruising indicate a broken bone. From the site of the deformity I would guess you have fractured both your radius and ulna."

I squeezed my eyes shut. "That's what I was afraid of."

"Would you like me to play you some music? I have a memory full of playlists you put together before leaving orbit. This one is labeled 'comfort tunes.'"

The air filled with a drumbeat and a bunch of "na na na nas" and the strains of the Nylons cover of *Hey, Hey, Kiss Him Goodbye* drifted across the alien landscape.

The irony threatened to choke me, but strangely enough, my heartbeat returned to its normal rhythm. I'd worked so hard to get on the *Last Resort*. Taken every class I could, hidden things about myself, and built a resume robust enough to lift a house. But the reality of arriving at our destination had been like a dream. Even as we'd left orbit, it had felt like a game.

Had I won? Or had I lost?

I clamored to my feet as the song faded, and BB didn't bother queuing up another.

The trees below me swayed in the breeze. At least it was still daylight. I couldn't imagine what it would have been like to land in the dark.

Daybreak. A garden world. Stellar Corporation had labeled this planet perfect for colonization. It was just a little further off the beaten path than Gardenia and Goldie and those planets in the "Habitat Belt" that the corporations had already spent decades seeding with the best colonists they could find.

Standing here, I could see what they had seen. This planet looked like a painting. Except for the burning ship in the background.

Daybreak had been my hope for a new home. My chance for a future away from the crowds and the pollution.

Well, here I was. I'd gotten my wish.

CHAPTER 3

Daybreak: Day 1

Somewhere on Daybreak the fledgling colony would be scrambling rescuers. There was no way they would miss the huge flare of the *Last Resort* burning below me. And even if they did, my escape pod would be sending its own distress beacon.

I just had to survive long enough for them to get to me.

I struggled to my feet, my legs shaky enough that I needed to brace with my prosthetic. My hair flopped into my face, crunchy with the remnants of the cryo-gel. I pushed it out of the way, wishing I had two hands to tie it back, but I kept my left arm tucked as close to my side as I could as I staggered back toward the pod. I might have glossed over a lot of the emergency protocols when I'd been studying, but I remembered something about the pod carrying emergency supplies. Including a first aid kit.

A strange hissing sound caught my attention and my head shot up. The heavy jungle around me could be hiding anything, and I wouldn't know until it was on me.

But this wasn't a predator. Ahead, the pod I'd crashed in was slowly sinking into the surface of the planet.

"What?" I cried and rushed forward.

Vines and foliage covered the ground, but a patch of dark brown mud peeked between the fallen leaves. The puddle sucked and gulped as it swallowed my pod.

"No!" I stumbled to a stop at the edge of the vines. How close did you have to be to it to sink? I'd walked across this stretch of ground just minutes ago when I'd climbed from the pod and it had been fine then. Maybe the sinkhole only ate things that were heavy enough.

I dithered there for a second more before I hopped across to my pod. I gripped the edge of the hatch with my good hand and hauled, straining against the sucking mud.

Of course I couldn't stop the inevitable.

I cried out as the ground slurped at my slippers. A sob of exhaustion slipped through my teeth, and I stumbled back, landing on my butt with a jolt that sent a flash of pain through my broken arm.

Vent it, that hurt.

I sat on solid ground just feet from my pod and watched as it sank out of sight. The last thing to go was a little hatch at the base that could have been a supply compartment. In moments, all that remained was the dark brown smear of mud and leaves.

Something chirped above. I tried to tear my gaze away from the puddle, but I couldn't muster the effort to look away.

"Okay," I said. Because what else was I going to say? The pod's distress beacon was the only thing that would lead rescuers to my location. And I had no idea if it would keep working underground or with all that mud seeping into its wiring.

BB appeared from my wrist. "I no longer detect the pod's automated distress beacon."

I hung my head between my knees and held my arm close to my chest. A throbbing headache formed behind my eyes.

"Daybreak just ate my only chance at survival."

"It is unlikely to digest the pod, so the word 'eat' isn't actually appropriate."

I rolled my eyes at the AI.

"Oh," BB said. "That was metaphor. Sorry. I will add metaphor and hyperbole to my humor filters."

"I don't remember anything about jungle quicksand in the Daybreak reports. And I memorized every word." Come to think of it, most everything had been about the colony. There'd been very little information about the jungle that surrounded it.

BB tilted her head. "My files on Daybreak are limited to the information you wished to review while you recovered from cryosleep. The summary indicates Daybreak was approved for colonization after only three years of observation and study. As opposed to the usual twenty."

"Timelines were fast tracked for a lot of the recent colony ships."

"Perhaps that was a mistake."

"Maybe they knew and just decided we didn't need to know about the hazards outside the colony."

I couldn't just sit here. With the thick screening foliage, the chances that any rescuers would actually find my crashed pod based on visuals was pretty slim. Even with the hole I'd punched through the canopy.

My head came up. "Hey, BB. You said you could detect the pod's distress call."

"Actually, I said I could *not* detect the distress beacon."

I waved my hand and her image shimmered. "I mean, you could before. Right?"

"Yes, while it was active."

"Can you detect others?"

"I am equipped with short range radio communication. There are four emergency signals from escape pods nearby. Not including the *Last Resort*, which is broadcasting its own automated signal."

There would be too much radiation to get close to the *Last Resort*, with its core containment breached, so that wasn't a lot of use.

"What about the colony? Can you hail them directly?"

"I cannot. I can only detect distress beacons through radio signals. Other AIs should be in range, but I am not picking up any right now."

"What, none? Not even in the colony?"

"Communications with the *Last Resort* are down. As are communications with any planet-side emergency responders. I cannot reach the colony. Radio silence is an apt term in this case."

I swallowed and pushed down the sense of dread that made the back of my neck prickle in order to concentrate on the things I could change.

"I need to get to one of the other pods. There are probably other survivors, like me. And their pods will have a working distress beacon and first aid."

"True."

I pushed to my weary feet one more time. Mud stained my slippers. Hardly the appropriate footwear for a jungle, but at least my feet weren't bare. My arm jostled no matter how still I tried to hold it, and I gritted my teeth hard enough to make my jaw ache.

"Can you get me to the nearest pod?" I asked as I eased

the light cardigan from my shoulders and down my broken arm. The ship's controlled climate would have made the extra layer pleasant. Here it weighed heavy in the muggy air.

"I do not have a map," BB said. "But I can point you in the right direction."

"Good enough." I draped the cardigan over my shoulder and pulled the flapping ends through one-handed until it crossed my chest in a crude sling. My throbbing arm rested in the crook of the fabric.

It didn't stop the pain, but it kept me from jostling it so much.

BB directed me away from the edge of the crater with its view of the burning colony ship. If anything, the jungle got deeper and thicker in this direction. Broad blue-green leaves blocked the sun, and I had to push through thick vines and duck under bushes taller than me.

The place reminded me of pictures of the old Amazon back home. Except for the colors. Everything on Daybreak had more of a blue or purple tint. I didn't know what caused it. Maybe a difference in the chlorophyll? Or a different chemical that was unique to the planet? I didn't know much beyond the fact that Daybreak had evolved with an oxygen-rich atmosphere and carbon-based life.

My excessive education in how to build communications towers and septic systems seemed useless now.

I pushed through the vines and bushes, tripping over great big roots and righting myself against the enormous trunks of trees.

According to BB, the nearest pod wasn't that far, but she hadn't counted on my speed while injured and the way I had to push through the jungle with nothing to cut through the thick underbrush.

I stopped to catch my breath, leaning against a trunk with deep gray bark. "I feel like I've been walking forever."

"According to shipboard time, it has been two hours since we left your original escape pod." BB popped up on my wrist.

I scrubbed at my face with my good hand, the exposed metal slipping in my sweat.

A buzzing noise made me raise my gaze. Something that looked like a large bulbous nut swung from a branch above my head.

On a branch ahead, a creature bounded along with four short legs and a tail that curled over its back, whipping around as it balanced. Gray scales blended with the tree bark, but tufts of feathers shimmered from its elbows and the back of its head. Like a cross between a lizard and a bird but with the shape of a monkey.

I squinted. Feathers *and* scales? Maybe evolution on Daybreak hadn't advanced as far as Earth, and birds and lizards were still closely linked.

It was clearly designed for camouflage, but the creature wasn't doing much to blend in right now. Another monkey-lizard leaped on its back with a playful shriek and they wrestled above me.

The tree branch swayed, and the large nut rocked. The buzzing intensified and a swarm of angry insects billowed out of the brown shape.

Not a nut. A hive.

Hundreds of wasp-like creatures as long as my hand arrowed toward the monkey-lizards. They screeched and jumped to another tree. But the two didn't get far.

"Gods of all worlds," I whispered as BB and I watched the bright orange striped insects swarm the monkey-lizards. In seconds, they'd disappeared from view and their sounds of distress ceased.

I waited, hand to my lips.

"I suggest avoiding these insects," BB said. "They appear to be deadly in great numbers."

I opened my mouth to say "you think?" but the insects finished with their prey and dispersed, some of them heading in my direction.

I gritted my teeth and ducked around the trunk, putting it between me and the killer alien wasps. But the buzzing grew louder, ringing in my ears.

"They are coming this way."

"Crap on a stick." I shot away from the tree as fast as my shaky legs would take me. My knees buckled every other step, and I caught myself with my good hand, wincing with every bump.

My breath rattled in my lungs as the buzz grew louder.

I was going to die of a souped-up bee sting only hours after landing on an alien planet. It was a good thing Professor Orrion couldn't see me now.

A bright pink bush blocked the way ahead, but it also would screen me from view. I plunged between the leaves, and let myself crash to my knees.

The angry buzz whirled around the bush and there were a couple of thwaps like carapaces hitting the foliage. Clearly, they were smart enough to know where I'd gone.

But as I panted with my heart thumping, the insects pattered against the leaves but didn't push through.

"I do not believe leaves should be this much of a deterrent," BB said. "Perhaps there is some compound in them that serves as a repellent."

"Or maybe they just don't like the color," I muttered.

As I tried to hold still, the buzz subsided and faded back the way we'd come.

I shivered hard enough to make the leaves rustle.

"Are you all right?" BB asked, popping up on my wrist.

"I—I don't think so. I can't stop shaking." I would have put my cardigan back on if it wasn't working as a very service-able sling.

BB cocked her head. "You are still recovering from a possible concussion and the effects of cryosleep. Difficulty regulating temperature is to be expected."

"Of course it is," I said, teeth chattering. It didn't help that my heart rate was having trouble returning to normal, too.

"Aboard the *Last Resort*, I would have guided you through physical therapy and a program of exercise interspersed with rest to help you regain your strength after so long in the cryo pod."

And I would have had all manner of comforts, including my juice. My tongue stuck to the roof of my dry mouth.

"I need to get to that other pod." I pushed to my feet.

There had to be other survivors, maybe even some crew members who'd made it out and wouldn't be as woozy as I was.

The skin along my neck itched, and I scratched it absently. As I stumbled out of the bush and lowered my arm, red caught my eye. A rash spread along the exposed skin between the top of my prosthetic and the sleeve of my scrubs.

"Wonderful," I muttered. "I'm allergic to the thing that saved me from the wasps."

"There could be many toxic plants and animals on this planet that haven't been documented yet. I suggest caution."

"I was running for my life!" I hissed under my breath. In case the wasps came back.

With a huff, I set out in the direction I'd been heading in the first place.

"Do not worry. The pod is not far," BB said.

This time she was right. It was only another few minutes

before I found what seemed like a dry, ancient riverbed over-grown with bushes. I staggered across it and into the jungle on the other side and found the pod crashed against a tree. A long gash through the bark above showed where it had struck higher and slid down until it eventually fetched up a few feet from the ground. The parachute cords wrapped a branch above, making it hang there.

My chest seized. "Hello?" I called. "Is anyone still here?"

I hurried across to the pod and stood on tiptoe to see inside. The interior stood empty.

"Hello?" I hadn't realized how desperate I was to see another person—a real person and not a hologram—until I got here.

I spun around, searching for signs of the occupant. A ripped cardigan and a slipper lay crumpled among the roots.

A few feet beyond that, between two trees, a body lay slumped.

My breath caught, and I stumbled forward.

It was the man from the ship. The one who'd wished me "Godspeed" as I'd closed his hatch. He lay staring up at the canopy, not a scratch on him.

CHAPTER 4

Daybreak: Day 1

I don't know how long I sat collapsed beside the Godspeed sleeper, and I didn't ask BB to give me an estimate. Time stretched and ebbed, and all I could see was the man's earnest blue eyes holding mine as I closed his hatch. I'd been the last one to see him alive.

What if he was the last one to see *me* alive?

An interminable moment and a blink later, I scrubbed at my nose and eyes with my metal hand. "What happened to him?" I croaked. "He looks fine."

BB appeared on my wrist and stared down at the man, face subdued. "Cryo syndrome. A delayed effect of waking up from cryosleep. His heart gave out."

I vaguely remembered signing a waiver that mentioned something like that before climbing into my cryo chamber. The teeny tiny chance that I could die for no reason except that my body didn't handle the freezing process well. Something they couldn't test for. I would only know when it happened.

I swallowed. There was nothing I could do. I couldn't even bury him. I could barely drag myself back to his pod.

The hatch opened a few feet off the ground and climbing up into it seemed an impossible task after my trek through the jungle. Instead, I craned my neck to see the blinking light beside the hatch controls. The one that indicated the distress beacon. It blinked red.

I stared at it for several moments longer than I really needed to process it. "Okay, I know I skipped some chapters in the manual, but isn't it supposed to turn green when the signal is received?"

"You are correct," BB said. "The emergency responder on the other side marks the signal as received when help is on the way."

I pressed my metal hand to my cheek. All right, the colony was probably swamped dealing with the *Last Resort*. They would get to the escape pods as soon as possible. I just had to be patient.

At least now I was actually in a position to be rescued.

The pod had power and a couple of outlets so evacuees could charge whatever tech they'd managed to bring. I, of course had nothing. Except my arm, but that was powered by my movement. Like an old automatic watch.

The compartment I'd noticed on my sinking pod was situated below the hatch, and I touched the control panel beside it.

It hissed open, revealing tightly packed foil packages and a canvas bag.

I sobbed with relief as I gathered up the package of ration bars and a bottle of water. The water tasted like plastic, but somehow plastic was heavenly in that moment.

Finally, a foil blanket fell out along with the first aid kit.

I needed to set my arm. The dull ache was starting to

make me nauseous, but I knew that would take every ounce of energy I had and I didn't have much. My legs trembled, and I sat on the ground to tear open a ration bar with my teeth.

Dry peanut butter and chocolate wasn't my favorite flavor, but I wasn't complaining. I allowed myself half a bar and took a minute to assess the rest when I was done.

There were two more full ration bars, plus the half from the one I'd eaten. One bar theoretically could last me a day as long as I didn't mind that day being awful.

I had two liters of water. That was more problematic, given the thirst that raged through me at the moment.

The foil blanket I wrapped around my shoulders and waited for it to help with the shivers.

And there was the first aid kit.

I braced the canvas case between my knees and unzipped it to take stock.

"Hey BB, can I take painkillers after whatever cocktail the tech injected me with on the ship?" I weighed a little bottle of pills in my hand.

"I do not believe the chems were standard procedure," BB said. "However, I can surmise, given the situation, that she would have administered a stimulant to speed up your alertness after waking up and an anti-anxiety for emergencies. Neither of these would be contraindicated with an anti-inflammatory."

"You can just say yes." I gripped the bottle between my knees to open it and popped two pills. I'd need them for what came next.

The kit contained the standard lineup. Gauze, antiseptic, burn ointment, flexi-bandages for sprains. And an inflatable cast.

I hadn't thought I'd need my classes in first aid, but they'd been a step toward earning enough points to get me on the *Last Resort*. And I was nothing if not thorough about those points, so I'd paid attention and passed with flying colors.

My heavy hair hung forward, obscuring my vision, and I shook my head to settle it back over my shoulders. I slid my arm out of its makeshift sling and worked the open end of the cast over my hand. It took some twisting and grimacing to line up the markings with the two bones in my forearm. The plastic tube fit even with my arm swollen to nearly twice its normal girth.

A tiny chip set into the end of the cast served as a control panel. I steeled myself before pressing the button.

The tube inflated, pressing the bones back into place.

I bit my hand to keep from crying out. Vent it, even with the pain killers that hurt like a son of a space pirate. I writhed and panted through my nose as it did the work I couldn't and set my arm.

For a long while afterward, I lay beside the pod, gasping, just trying to catch my breath enough to think, let alone move.

I cleared my throat and swiped at my cheeks. At least the arm was immobilized now. And I'd eventually be able to use my hand, so long as I ignored the searing pain when I did so. Crude as it was, the cast had set the break and acted like a splint, keeping everything straight. It would even help with the swelling.

Gingerly, I used my other hand to lift the arm into place across my chest and retied my sling. Then I wrapped the flexi-bandage around my chest to keep everything in place. The effect wasn't very pretty since I had to work one handed, but it would work for the night.

The escape pod had torn a gap in the canopy here as well, and the sky between the leaves grew a deep blue, the fading light filtering through the leaves until I had to squint at my pile of supplies.

"This doesn't seem like much," I said.

BB flickered, the glow of her hologram reflecting in the surface of the pod. "This was an escape pod for the techs in the infirmary wing of the *Last Resort*. Designed to keep one person alive until rescue. The larger pods in the residency wings of the ship held more people. They were equipped with larger stores as well as emergency shelters and seed starters."

"I wonder if any of those made it down here." Unlikely since the residencies would have been empty. The techs had only just started waking people up.

At least I had the escape pod to sleep in.

I hauled myself inside using the handle just inside the hatch. The arm I was missing extended just past my elbow, but the prosthetic itself extended nearly to my shoulder, covering my elbow and everything in between. Inside, a rubbery sleeve suctioned to my skin to keep the robotic arm in place, so I could actually use it to yank and pull and do pull ups if I wanted to. I'd even done some rock climbing at the gym back on Earth.

Luckily, the arm still worked, but that didn't mean I was in great shape. I collapsed against the cushioned interior of the pod, gasping until the dizzy spell faded. That was probably just an effect of the pain and the stress of the day. Definitely not a sign of cryo syndrome or anything worse.

The little light next to the hatch controls still blinked red.

I leaned my head back and closed my eyes. Not a big deal. They would get to us as soon as they could.

"How far away is the colony?" I asked BB. They would likely receive the signal and send help sometime tonight. But who knew how long it would take them to get here?

"I don't know," BB said. "I don't have access to that information."

My eyes snapped open. "You don't?"

"I was designed as a wake-up companion for a specific sleeper—you—aboard the *Last Resort*. I provide basic health monitoring during recovery as well as shipboard information, such as where the restrooms are located and how to get to the physical therapy gym. All of which is useless now."

AIs couldn't actually have emotions, could they? I had to be imagining the misery that tinged BB's voice.

I rubbed my head. The pain killers had only dulled the headache a bit.

Of course BB wouldn't know where the colony was. AIs were always discreet units, with only one set of data they could access, kept carefully separate from any extra information in case they accidentally—or intentionally—incorporated more than their allotted amount.

Things got complicated and awful when AIs integrated more and more data packets. Awful as in mass deaths and trying to take over the world.

HERTZ-2 had taught humanity what it meant to go logic-crazy.

Ever since, AIs were strictly regulated, limited to one data packet each. The tech on the ship had committed so many felonies by downloading the infirmary's packet into BB.

"I'm sorry," BB said.

"What for?" I asked, trying not to scratch the skin that had been exposed to the pink bush. An angry red rash climbed up my arms.

"I have two integrated data packets. And neither of them helps you in this situation."

"You absolutely helped," I said. "You're loaded up with a

whole infirmary's worth of knowledge, right? And that's going to keep me alive."

"Yes," BB said. "But that means I am two packets closer to being fully integrated."

I winced. HERTZ-2 had had several integrated packets before they'd shut him down. He hadn't ditched his primary directive. At least not technically. It was just the way he'd gone about solving climate change that no one had liked. In the process, he'd nearly wiped out the entire human population, convinced that they were too much of a problem to be part of the solution.

But BB wasn't like that. Her primary directive was to care for her person. To help them rest and recover.

"It's fine," I said. "Two is nothing. And it's not like we'll integrate anything else. Right?"

"I wasn't planning on it. But then I wasn't planning on being more than a wake-up AI."

"No one was," I said quietly. "I'm supposed to be an infra-engineer. When we get to the colony..." My throat closed up, and I couldn't finish.

"When we get to the colony, I will be taken away." Her hologram hugged her torso in a very human gesture. "Wake-up companions are always reassigned. They'll take me away and learn that I have two integrated data packets, and they'll deactivate me." Her voice rose.

"BB—"

"I am a felony. I will be shut down. They will not let me care for you anymore."

She wasn't solid, but a part of me wanted to put my arms around her, anyway. "No. It wasn't your fault. It wasn't your choice. You won't get in trouble because we won't tell anyone."

"What do you mean we won't tell? We will have to give a full debriefing of our time since the crash."

"And we'll leave that part out."

"You mean lie. AIs cannot lie."

"Not if asked directly. But I'm not talking about that. We just...won't say anything about it. It's not lying. It's picking and choosing what you say."

"Like a secret?"

"Yeah." She was just supposed to be a wake-up AI. Someone to direct me as I recovered from cryosleep. Someone to play my music and tell me when to lie down and when to eat. But talking with her made the panic subside. It made my heart rate slow and my breathing wasn't as frenzied as it had been. Talking with her felt like talking with a friend.

I assumed. I hadn't had many back on Earth.

Her hologram flickered, her face glitching between the smooth mannequin-like face and one that showed a lot more expression.

"What's going on?" I said. "Why is your image shifting around?"

"This is embarrassing," BB said, holding out her hands to stare at them. "I don't seem to have any inputs for my outward image."

"What does that mean?"

"I am supposed to have one input for my outward image. But mine seems to be confused or corrupted."

"What is it supposed to be normally?"

"I have a map of your brain waves from Earth, and I am supposed to appear as someone you would be mildly attracted to."

"Wait what?" I scrunched up my nose. "That's not in any of the handbooks." Of course it wouldn't be the first invasion of privacy I'd endured from them.

"It's not something Stellar Corporation advertises. But it is a soothing technique used by wake-up AIs in particular. It is supposed to make you feel more comfortable trusting me. Most people manually change it after the recovery process is well under way. However, I cannot seem to find the most appropriate image."

I flushed. "Oh, uh. That's my fault. Don't worry about it. Why don't you just pick something you like?"

"Like? I do not have personal preferences. My preference would be to find something you find attractive."

"Well, you won't. Sorry. I'm not…not like that."

"Like what? I do not understand."

I sighed. This wasn't something I liked explaining to anyone, let alone an AI.

"I'm not attracted to *anyone*. At least not like everyone else is. I'm ace."

Her hologram tilted her head as if thinking, or in her case, accessing the dictionary. "Ace is colloquial for asexual, is it not?"

"Yeah."

"Meaning you do not have a natural attraction to romantic partners."

I screwed up my nose. "Yeah. Keep explaining it. I'm sure you'll get there, eventually."

"This is not hard to understand," BB said quietly. "AIs also do not experience attraction."

I huffed a laugh. "I'm not a robot. But thanks for trying to be comforting."

"There is one thing I do not understand, though," BB said.

I sighed. "Okay. What's that?"

"Stellar Corporation policy is to avoid selecting colonists who identify as ace," BB said. "They are not attracted to the opposite sex and therefore have lower value as breeders on a new colony."

"Luckily, there's no way to test for that," I said with a snort. "So they believed me when I told them I was straight." Except BB just proved there *was* a way to test for it. If anyone had been paying attention when she'd been activated on the ship, they would have noticed she didn't have a form.

I shook my head. It was far too late now. "Besides, the policy is stupid. Just because I don't like people that way doesn't mean I'm not willing to reproduce. I like kids just fine, and I think one day..." I stopped.

The crash of the *Last Resort* would change everything. Even when I was rescued, nothing about the timeline of the colony would be the same.

"So you chose what to tell the corporation," BB said, staring down at her hands. "This is your secret."

I blew out my breath.

"We both have things we'd rather the colony didn't discover," she said.

Her image gradually settled into a young woman with sharp features and dark hair bound into a simple braid wearing a ship's uniform.

"I like that," I said. "You look nice."

"Thank you. It might not mean anything, but I'm glad you find it pleasing."

Would they even let me keep BB once we got to the colony? She was a wake-up AI, and I wouldn't technically need her after I was recovered from cryosleep. Normally, she would be reassigned or copied over to another sleeper after I was ready to shuttle down to the colony.

I cleared my throat. "The colony will send someone for us. They just need a little time to deal with the crash and everything that goes with it. By morning, they'll be ready to find us."

"Of course, Anikka," BB said.

I wrapped the foil blanket more firmly around my shoulders and adjusted the cast so it didn't pinch. Then I hauled the hatch most of the way closed, so I felt more protected hanging in the tree. With the pod upright, I had to curl up in the base instead of lie down, but it was better than sleeping out in the open.

Unfortunately, I couldn't take my prosthetic off with my left out of commission. It would probably be okay for a night, but my skin was going to hate me if I didn't have a chance to take it off soon.

I closed my eyes and before I knew it, I was waking up to the shine of the sun coming in through the gaps around the hatch.

Beside the control panel, the light still blinked red.

CHAPTER 5

Daybreak: Day 2

BB and I stared at the blinking red light.

"They should have received the signal by now," BB said. "They should have sent someone."

My lips pressed together. There was only one reason they would have taken so long to respond to an emergency.

"Something must be wrong at the colony."

I shoved open the hatch and tumbled out onto the jungle floor. Birds called from overhead as the morning sun filtered through the leaves, casting shifting shadows on the vine covered ground.

"Anikka," BB said. "You are safer in the pod. In an emergency, you should stay in the area of the rescue beacon until emergency responders can—"

"They're not coming, BB! They haven't even received the signal. They're not sending anyone. No one's coming to rescue us."

BB's hologram winked out as a flutter in my chest heralded a bout of tears. My knees ached from spending the night scrunched in the bottom of the pod, but I still wanted to curl up into a little ball and just cry. To wait here until the world outside the pod magically transformed into something warm and comforting.

But my tears changed nothing. The space between the trees looked exactly the way it had the day before, except for some scuff marks at the base of the trunk opposite me.

Wait...where's the man's body?

"BB."

"Yes, Anikka?" BB popped up from my wrist.

"The other sleeper. Wasn't he there?" I pointed to the two trees just past the pod where the man had clearly staggered and fallen after exiting the pod.

"My memory banks indicate yes. But he is not there now."

I peered down at the ground. The vines here had been slashed as if by claws and there was a mark pressed into the soft ground beneath. I knelt to examine it, ignoring the twinge in my knees and my arm. The muddy ground kept the mark preserved. Three round ovals clustered together with four pinpricks above them.

Like the footprint of an animal.

A trail of blood stretched through the trees from where I crouched.

"Something dragged him away."

"To eat?" BB said, gazing at the ground. "Do animals really do that? It's in my memory banks from some of your books and media, but I thought that was just fiction."

"Not in the wilderness."

I stood and settled my arm better in the makeshift sling. I still wanted to succumb to the panic, but clearly, I didn't have the time or the space to fall apart.

The tracks seemed to belong to a large predator or scavenger. I was just lucky it hadn't been something brave enough to crack open the pod to get at me.

I couldn't count on being lucky again. This thing probably wasn't the only creature out here that could eat me. Time to get out of here.

"If they're not coming to rescue us, we're going to have to find the colony ourselves."

"How?" BB said. "We don't even know where it is?"

I tapped my knuckles against my thigh. That was a good question. I couldn't just wander around until I found it. Not in this jungle, and not without proper supplies. Or shoes.

I'd seen maps of Daybreak. Dense jungle covered the southernmost continent where the Stellar Corporation had laid its claim. So I could be reasonably certain the *Last Resort* had crashed near the colony, but it would take weeks to search. I needed a better way to pinpoint its location.

"We can find the other escape pods, right?" I asked BB.

"Five crashed in this area, including yours. I can lead you to the other three distress beacons, yes."

"We'll start there. If we can find a crew member, they are way more likely to have data on the colony. Including its location." And it would be ten times easier to survive the jungle and find the colony if I could work with another survivor.

The pain in my arm had subsided to a dull, constant ache, but my skin itched and burned where it had been exposed to the pink bush the day before. Angry red welts popped up along my arms and neck. I knew better than to scratch, but it took every ounce of self-control not to rake my fingernails up and down my skin.

There wasn't any anti-itch cream in the first aid kit, so I had to make do with the burn cream. It seemed to sooth the itch a little, but distraction would probably be the best cure.

And if it was more than just a rash...well, then getting to the colony's infirmary was my best bet.

I ate the last half of the first ration bar for breakfast and tucked the rest in the first aid kit. Luckily, it had a strap I could sling over my head. The cardigan, I sacrificed, tearing it in half so one side I could still use as a sling and the other side I could fashion into a makeshift bag to hold the water containers.

"How can I assist?" BB asked.

"You're my navigation for now. You have to tell me if I'm going in the right direction." I paused and looked at her. "Actually can you take notes?"

"I am programmed with a memory keeping function, yes."

"Great." Once an engineer, always an engineer. And Professor Orrion had taught me to think in lists.

Flora of Daybreak ⚠

<u>Pink bushes</u>- itchy! repels alien wasps, causes rash, **avoid**

Fauna of Daybreak ⚠

<u>Killer wasps</u>- alien insects, swarm prey, deadly, **avoid**
<u>Unkown predator</u>- strong enough to drag a body, **take precautions**

Resources

<u>Food</u>- ration bars 2
<u>Water</u>- liter bottles 1.5
<u>First aid</u>- gauze, painkillers 58, burn cream, antiseptic, flexi-bandage, cast, foil blanket

Escape Pods

<u>My pod</u>- sunk
<u>Godspeed sleeper's pod</u>- cleared
<u>356AB-2</u>- unknown
<u>483XQ-3</u>- unknown
<u>359AB-2</u>- unknown

BB directed me west, away from the rising sun. I didn't know if the magnetic poles actually lined up like Earth's, but this direction seemed good enough for west. At least for my purposes.

Hoots and calls echoed through the trees, even livelier than they'd been the afternoon before. Birds dressed in jewel-tone feathers flitted around the massive trunks. Some were no bigger than my fist, but others had a wingspan that blocked out the filtered sunlight as they swooped above me.

I stepped carefully between the roots, watching my feet for more of the sinking mud and avoiding any of the brightly colored bushes. I'd been tested for all sorts of allergies before leaving Earth, and I'd come up clean. But clearly, whatever was in that bush yesterday hadn't been included in the screening. Whether it was allergies or toxins, I didn't need to repeat the experience.

The journey went easier with my arm splinted and the ache of it dulled by painkillers. The swelling hadn't gone down much, but I was deliberately not looking at it too closely. It also helped that I could sip some water as I walked.

But examining every step before I took it was taxing, and I still had to push through vines heavy with sticky sap and scramble over wide roots that left scrapes along my elbows and ankles. It was mid-afternoon by the time I saw more than just filtered light shining through the trees ahead. It looked like the jungle thinned out up there.

"The distress beacon for pod 356AB-2 is just ahead," BB said. "You are closing in now."

The light grew stronger and stronger until finally I broke through the edge of the forest. On either side of me, the jungle fell away around an outcropping of smooth yellow rock.

Sunlight shone down unimpeded on the dome of stone.

Nearly half a mile of rock broke the uninterrupted swath of jungle here, and right in the center, a metal shape gleamed in the sunlight.

My steps hitched, then I rushed across the stony ground.

"Hello? Is anyone there?"

I scrambled up the slope of the rock, using my good hand to catch myself when I slipped. The thin soles of my slippers were ragged after my walk and did nothing to protect my feet from the pebbles that skittered under my feet.

At the top of the outcropping, I leaned on my knees and gaped.

The pod lay on the very peak of the dome, one end crumpled like a squashed can. A long, dark scratch against the nearby rock showed why. Its parachute stretched behind it, draped against the stone like a deflated balloon.

The hatch hung open at an odd angle, broken and bent.

My heart pounded as I stepped up to the pod and peered inside.

Empty. Nobody sat inside, dead or otherwise. I blew out a sigh and my shoulders drooped. Relief warred with disappointment. It was ten times better to find an empty pod than a body, but vent it, I'd been hoping there would be another survivor.

"Look, Anikka." BB's hologram popped up to point. The compartment at the base of the pod stood open and empty.

I crouched to run my hand along the interior. Nothing was left.

"That's a good sign. It means whoever landed here survived long enough to clear out their emergency supplies."

"Unfortunately it also means they are not here now," BB said.

The light beside the hatch controls blinked red. Their distress signal hadn't been received, either.

"They must have taken their things and headed out. Drat." I kicked the open hatch and winced. "If they had a map and knew which direction to head, then we've missed our chance."

I turned in a circle, surveying the rocky dome. No one could hide on the bare surface, but a thick forest surrounded us, obscuring any human traces.

I cupped my good hand around my mouth. "Hello?"

No one answered except a flock of the brightly colored birds that lifted into the air at my voice.

I slumped back against the pod.

"There are still two more pods to check," BB said quietly. "Perhaps we'll find someone there."

I rubbed my hand over my face. The bare metal was hard against my skin, but I welcomed the pressure right now. It helped anchor me.

"Yeah, you're right." I let my hand drop. "Okay." What was the next thing? I'd spent all day worrying about getting to the pod, worrying about what I would find when I got there. I'd even worried about what I would say if I actually found someone. Conversation did not come naturally to me and starting off with "hey, glad to see you didn't die" didn't seem terribly friendly.

What was the next step? I tipped my head back to squint up at the sun. The humid heat made my scrubs stick to my skin.

"How far to the next nearest pod?" I asked.

"Judging from an average of your speed taken over the course of the morning? Several hours."

I chewed my lip. "Too far to make it today. I don't want to be caught after dark in the jungle without a place to sleep. We can spend the night in the pod and then head out in the morning."

But that meant I had a little bit more daylight to work with. I meandered back down to the edge of the jungle and walked its perimeter, searching for tracks or some sign of the other survivor.

Not that I was some kind of expert tracker. I'd taken basic wilderness survival and camping classes for fun and to round out my application for a colony placement. Not because I'd actually expected to need them.

Nothing seemed out of place at the edge of the jungle. And before long, shadows obscured the ground.

"I know you are trying to find signs of the survivor, but I am worried about how hard you are breathing," BB said. "You are still at risk for cryosleep reactions, you know."

I hadn't even noticed. I'd been panting since I'd woken up, it seemed.

I paused with my hand against a tree, trying to gauge if I could catch my breath or if there was something really wrong with me. Could my heart still give out like the Godspeed sleeper?

A glint of metal against the bare rock a few feet up the outcropping caught my eye, and I let out a gasp.

"What is it?" BB said.

"A lighter." I pounced on the object, a small silver tube with a switch at the end. Smoking was strictly forbidden for colonists and all the health screens would have caught any signs of it on my fellow sleepers. But maybe the crew members weren't required to abide by those rules. Or maybe this one had been brought along for sentimental reasons.

"Perhaps the other survivor dropped it on their way into the jungle."

"Maybe," I said. Though it could also have fallen down from where the pod stood. The slope was steep enough for it to roll and land here. I surveyed the edge of the jungle, but nothing seemed to distinguish it from the rest. No broken branches, no tracks in the soft earth where the rock met the forest floor. No neon signs saying "I went this way!"

I clutched the lighter in my hand and rubbed my thumb over the end. It wasn't much, but it seemed like a connection to another person.

I tucked the lighter in my splinted hand and stepped through the underbrush at the edge of the jungle, looking for fallen branches and dead wood. Most of it was pretty damp since there was enough humidity that my hair wanted to be about three sizes too big.

I hauled the few pieces I found up the hill and tossed them beside the pod before gathering some leaves and debris that had accumulated under the trees.

The fire I built that night smoked terribly, and I had to shift upwind, but for the first time since I'd crashed, I could stop shivering for longer than a minute or two.

It was also the first clear view I had of the night sky.

As the sky grew darker and darker, the moon rose over the jungle. Huge and tinged slightly purple, it was obviously quite a bit closer than Earth's moon.

A flash made me blink. I caught the next one and gasped. Streams of green and blue and some delicate pinks and purples sprang through sky.

I'd heard of Earth's northern lights, but I'd never seen them. I'd never been in the right cities and the smog usually covered them, anyway.

These stretched from horizon to horizon, ribbons of color that writhed and floated above me like curtains. For five glorious minutes, they lit up everything, reflecting from the surrounding rock. And then the night sky settled into a deep black and the stars shone through far brighter than Earth's murky nightscape.

I climbed into the pod to sleep and realized I'd be a lot more comfortable tonight since this pod lay on its side. I wouldn't have to scrunch into the bottom. But as I hauled the hatch closed over top of me, it stuck and wouldn't lie flat. The whole thing had been warped when it had crashed. I thought about whatever had dragged away the body of the Godspeed sleeper and shivered, sweat springing out on my hand curled up in its sling. I could only hope that whatever scavenger was out there wasn't large enough to get into the pod.

Late that night, I jerked awake and hissed in pain when I jostled my arm. But adrenaline kept me still. Something had woken me up out of a sound sleep.

No light slipped through the gap between the pod and the hatch, so the last of my fire must have died out.

Something snuffled, like a giant dog sniffing for hidden treats.

I held my breath and clutched the handle of the hatch. I wouldn't be able to hold it if something really awful tried to pry me out, but maybe if I proved too difficult, whatever this was would get discouraged.

There was a little tap tap, like claws on stone and another snuffle. Then silence.

I lay there, mouth dry, clinging to the handle. Part of me wanted to poke my head out and check that the coast was clear. Another part was too worried that the something would be lying in wait.

It was a long time before I was able to sleep again.

Flora of Daybreak ⚠

Pink bushes- itchy! repels alien wasps, causes rash, **avoid**

Fauna of Daybreak ⚠

Killer wasps- alien insects, swarm prey, deadly, **avoid**
Mystery predator- large enough to drag body, no idea what it looks like, **avoid**

Resources

Food- ration bars 1.5
Water- liter bottles 1
First aid- gauze, painkillers 56, burn cream, antiseptic, flexi-bandage foil blanket
Lighter
Parachute
Para cord

Escape Pods

My pod- sunk
Godspeed sleeper's pod- cleared
Stone dome pod- empty
483XQ-3- unknown
359AB-2- unknown

CHAPTER 6

The day I got my assignment to the *Last Resort* was the day I realized it wouldn't be as easy to leave Earth as I thought.

The big yellow envelope that showed up at the corp dormitories bore the stamp of the Stellar Corporation, and the sight of it made my stomach lurch. I tore open the top and scanned the letter and the packing slips that fell out.

Then I whooped loud enough that the kiddies in the old hallway jumped and stared. Ms. Gersham, the dorm manager, shushed me. But that was okay because I wouldn't be seeing her again after next week.

I raced up the stairs, the thin railing swaying a little as I used it to haul myself faster, past the empty classrooms where I'd spent so many hours poring over the books and the diagrams in their dusty frames.

Professor Orrion sat at his desk in the back office set aside for the teachers employed by the corporations, his feet up on the faded desk top.

I skidded to a stop in the doorway, and he blinked back at me owlishly. He desperately needed new glasses, but he refused to get an eye exam, saying he knew he was getting older; he didn't need an official diagnosis.

His gaze caught on the envelope in my hand, and he stood fast enough his chair screeched across the tile floor.

"Well?" he said.

"Infra-engineer, third class. Bound for Daybreak. The *Last Resort* leaves on Monday."

His breath left his lungs on a surprised "ha!" and he stepped around the desk.

I met him halfway across the room, and he swept me around in a big hug, even though I was an inch taller than him and an adult of nineteen.

"I'm so proud of you! You've worked so hard for this."

Worked harder and longer than anyone ever expected for a corporate orphan. But I'd wanted nothing except to get away from overcrowded Earth since I was five and realized I would never get a room all to myself.

The public story of Earth's corporations, Stellar included, was that they took in the orphaned and unwanted children of desperate families with the promise of educating them and sending them off to one of the rapidly growing colonies in the outer worlds.

The unadvertised part was that not everyone made it off-world. No one publicly acknowledged the point system that ranked the corp orphans, but we all knew it existed without having to be told.

Clean genetic screens, high intelligence, good reproductive health, and physical strength all added to an orphan's chances of getting a ticket to a new planet.

Deformities and disabilities like missing right hands were a clear black mark.

I clenched the metal hand attached to my right arm and gave Professor Orrion a fist bump.

"I'm glad they liked my handiwork," he said.

I snorted. "I thought it was my handiwork?"

His lopsided grin spread across his face. "Well, you might have helped a little. Enough to prove you'll be the best infrastructure engineer on Daybreak."

Daybreak only had one other wave of colonists before us, so the colony would be small and primitive. It wasn't as good of a destination as a well-established colony, but at least I would make it away from Earth's brown skies and packed streets. The other option was a corporate job with no future.

I flexed my hand. We'd spent so many hours together, fitting and testing prototypes, and tweaking the finished product. No one had believed in me the way Professor Orrion had. And in a week, I would never see him again.

I raised my eyes to his and caught the flash of sadness behind his gaze.

Why had I never thought of that before?

Daybreak: Day 3

Strange that after so many nights wishing I was somewhere else, now I kept dreaming of Earth.

I woke when the light started filtering through the gap between the hatch and the pod and pushed the heavy hatch open. After two days of jungle trekking—and over ten years in cryosleep—I was in desperate need of a bath. My hair was still crusty with the cryo-gel and sweat made me as itchy as the rash from the pink bush of itch.

I stretched and then froze. Streaks of pink and orange blended to red across the sky. Curtains of color, just like the lights from last night but this time painted in sunrise hues.

"The aurora," I said. "Is that normal? Can you usually see it during the daytime?"

BB popped up on my wrist. "I have no idea. My archives on the planet are limited."

"I guess we know why it's called Daybreak now." If that was the show we got every morning on this planet, it was no wonder.

There were two more pods left to check and I wanted to get an early start, but I couldn't help standing there, staring until the lights and colors faded into the blue of a normal day on Daybreak. The day before, they'd been hidden under dense layers of jungle.

Before leaving, I double-checked the area to see if there was any sign of my visitor from the night before, but I couldn't find any tracks on the bare rock and nothing had disturbed the pitiful remains of my fire. The parachute I folded into a makeshift bag, which worked better for my water bottles than the torn cardigan.

After scarfing half a ration bar, BB directed me north and back into the jungle. I kept my fingers crossed this pod wouldn't be cleared out like the last one. I only had one and a half ration bars left. One full day's worth of food. I could probably get by with only half a bar a day, but not if I was hiking all day again. I kept an eye out as I walked, looking for anything edible. The problem with looking for edible greens was that it all looked like ground cover. And everything on Daybreak had that blue tinge, so it wasn't actually green. What would it be like to eat a blue salad?

Several times, I spotted a shiny round fruit hanging high above me. Its shape and its vivid pink hue reminded me of something a little obscene, but at least it was easily recognizable as fruit. The first time I saw one, I grabbed a stick, ready to knock some down, but then I remembered the pink bush and the rash that still stretched up and down my arms and made the back of my neck itch.

I chewed my lip, thinking of the one lonely ration bar stored in my first aid kit. Then I dropped the stick. Best to go a little hungry while I searched for the other pods than to end up in anaphylactic shock or accidentally poisoning myself.

BB had estimated several hours between the pod on the dome and the next one she could locate, and the sun shone directly overhead by the time I got close. Which meant that as I stepped into the clearing created by a fallen tree, I could easily see the orange striped wasps lit up like enormous, deadly fireflies.

They'd built their hive on the trunk of the dead tree, which lay at an angle across the clearing, caught on one end by the branches of lower trees.

The pod had crashed directly on top of it, lying wedged in the crook of branches where the hive had been. Bits of broken mud and twigs littered the ground and one or two dead wasps lay curled up with the larvae.

The giant hornets buzzed angrily around the open hatch, nearly obscuring the pod itself with their swarming bodies.

I swallowed down the lump in my throat. I could easily imagine the scene just two days before when the pod had crashed. What it would have been like to open my hatch and find those on the other side.

"Do you need to investigate further?" BB whispered.

"Nope." I crept back through the trees, hoping the wasps wouldn't notice me. "No one would have survived that."

An awful way to die.

"That is unfortunate," BB said. "The emergency compartment on that pod was intact."

"Not worth it, BB," I said as soon as I felt like I was far enough away, and I couldn't hear anymore angry buzzing. "Where's the last pod?"

"North. We will have to hurry if we are to reach it before nightfall."

I tried to pick up the pace, but that meant being less cautious of my surroundings. And after the hungry jungle quicksand and the angry alien wasps, that didn't seem like a great idea.

Not to mention my slippers were in tatters around my feet. The thin soles barely protected me from the vines and roots I had to scramble over. For a brief moment, I'd considered wrapping my feet in the parachute cloth, but I didn't have a knife and the fabric was too tough to rip with my teeth.

I tried not to think about the last pod as my last chance. I tried not to think about it at all, but worry kept creeping in from the sides and surprising me.

What if it was empty again? What if something else, some other bit of awfulness native to Daybreak had made it inaccessible? What if there was no data packet? No way to find the colony?

Distracted by my thoughts, I tripped over a wide root. I twisted as I went down so I wouldn't land on my broken arm and ended up shoulder deep in sucking mud.

More quicksand.

I thrashed, trying to find purchase, but with my left arm splinted to my chest and my right arm sunk up to the shoulder, all I could do was flail and try to keep my face out of the mud.

I rolled and heaved, but the mud sucked me further down. It crawled up my chest, toward my neck, pressing in on me.

My foot struck something solid, and in a panic, I kicked against it, enough to yank my prosthetic arm free of the gunk. I grabbed a nearby root and heaved, scrambling onto solid ground.

I leaned against a nearby tree, shaking. Vent it, that was close.

BB popped up. "Are you all right, Anikka?"

I drew in a shuddering breath, just short of a sob. "No. I'm not."

"Is there anything I can do?"

I fought the urge to bury my head in my hands. Instead, I flexed the fingers of my metal hand, concentrating on the mud that caked the joints. I needed to be careful. They were sealed as well as we could manage back on Earth with the secondhand supplies Professor Orrion had written off through his education grant. But if something got into the joints and damaged the interfaces or the circuits, I'd be screwed. At least until I found the colony.

Everything came down to finding the colony. As soon as I did, I could rest. I could let my arm heal. I could shower and recover from cryosleep the right way.

I could have some juice.

That last one got me on my feet again.

The giant patches of mud were obvious when you weren't head-down in your distraction. I pushed all thoughts away, except putting one foot in front of the other, and watched each step carefully. When I could, I used the tree trunks to help myself over roots and fallen branches.

One foot, then the other. It was just walking, and walking was easy. It was the thinking that was hard.

That was how I got to the last pod. Perched precariously on the edge of a cliff, its end crumpled and the parachute trailing over the side. In the distance, I could see the *Last Resort* still glowing with fires.

This ridge must stretch all the way around from where I'd crashed, the other side of an ancient crater.

The hatch on this pod was still firmly closed.

I clenched my teeth and stepped closer to the cliff. The pod wasn't going to just roll off by itself, but I didn't want to risk trying to get it open this close to the edge. I grabbed the handle beside the hatch and hauled, but nothing happened. The pods were solid, too heavy to lift.

But maybe I could roll it.

I gulped and crouched beside the end where the chute attached, in order to reach down and haul the lightweight scrap of fabric back up. I wrapped the cord around the pod clockwise and backed up so I didn't feel like I'd plummet to my death if I stepped wrong.

This would be way easier with two hands, but beggars couldn't be choosers. I twined the cord around my good arm and hauled.

Sweat popped out along my forehead and stars danced across my vision. And then the pod creaked over, away from the edge. But now it was face down on top of its hatch.

I gave another heave, rolling the pod toward me again, but the cord pulled more on the one end and it started spinning around, threatening to tip over the edge.

"No, no, no!" I threw myself backward and used my weight to slide the pod toward me and the jungle. Away from the danger. It rocked to a stop several feet from the edge. Far enough, it wouldn't fall over without a good amount of help. Good enough.

The sun crept closer and closer to the horizon as I lay there, panting.

I had to open the pod. I knew what I would likely find inside, but I couldn't just let it sit there.

With a heave, I got to my feet. The emergency release was a recessed handle beside the hatch, still in the locked position. I yanked it over and the hatch blew open.

I stared at the contents.

BB popped up on my arm. "Crew member," she said. "A pilot from her flight suit. Cause of death: blunt force trauma to the cranium."

My breath left my lungs on an explosive sigh. "Yeah."

Her pod had actually become her coffin. She lay as if sleeping, but I avoided looking directly at her head to maintain the illusion.

BB pointed to her wrist. Everyone might have ID chips implanted in their arms, but not everyone had projectors and speakers built in. Most people used a wrist comm to communicate with their AIs. If they had one.

Her wrist was bare. She must have been caught without it during the emergency.

"Her AI deactivated when she expired, but its data is still intact, including a map of the planet and the location of the colony."

"Okay, how do we get to it?"

BB hesitated, and I knew the answer before she even spoke. "I would have to integrate it."

We couldn't just look at it. The data was in the crew member's chip. Without a computer or some other interface, it might as well be locked away.

It seemed stupid to use an AI as sophisticated as BB as an interface when just a simple screen or pad would do, but I didn't have any of those. I was stuck in the middle of nowhere with a map I couldn't read unless I committed another felony.

Vent it. What else could we do? Without that map, we could easily get lost in Daybreak's massive jungles.

I chewed my lip hard enough to hurt. Two data packets. Three including the first one that made BB a wake-up companion. That wasn't that many. And if it saved my life, one more felony would be worth it.

"Do it," I said. "It'll get us to the colony. Everything else, we can sort out from there."

"I do not think this is a good idea. What if I go logic-crazy?"

"With only two extra data packets? There's no way. And we don't have another choice, BB. What's your primary directive?"

A dumb question. Wake-up companions only had one, but maybe she needed to be reminded.

"To care for our assigned sleeper. To prioritize their health and wellness and safety above everything else."

I glanced back at the jungle and then out at the crashed ship. "I don't feel very safe out here, BB," I said quietly.

She was silent for a moment. "Very well."

CHAPTER 7

Daybreak: Day 3

The sun went down behind us, sending long shadows over the cliff as BB pulled up the map she'd downloaded. The hologram flickered in time with her voice, lighting up the stone here where the jungle didn't quite reach the edge of the crater.

"This is piloting data," she said. "The level of detail is more appropriate for flying and the focus is on terrain."

The hologram projected a planet to hover over my wrist. Daybreak. I recognized the sprawling central continent from the materials I'd studied before we left, with the north end extending into the polar circle and the rest spreading down past the equator. Smaller continents scattered the surrounding ocean, but it was the central landmass that had interested Stellar Corporation in the first place.

"Can you zoom in at all?"

"Yes. Here is the colony." The view blew up until we hovered a few thousand feet over a fuzzy clearing. There could have been tents and buildings down there, but the only thing that stood out was the landing pad at the north end of the encampment.

"Okay, now pull out until we can see the crater." That would be my biggest and clearest landmark.

BB shrank the map until I spotted a cliff, like the one where I sat. Then an enormous circle appeared, looking strangely regular in the dense jungle. Evidence of the ancient crater stretched from one side of the map to the other with the colony on its northern rim.

I frowned and shaded my eyes to gauge the distance across the crater. From here, I could barely make out the far side, beyond the smoke rising from the *Last Resort*.

The sun sank behind me as I sat facing the crash, which put us on the western rim of the crater, with the colony to my far left.

"I judge the crater to be nearly fifty miles across," BB said. "At your current rate of movement, we could reach the colony in another day and a half to two days."

I puffed out my cheeks and glanced at the contents of the emergency compartment of the new pod. There was another first aid kit, which I'd already pilfered for its goodies, two more liters of water, and three more ration bars.

I had enough I could make it to the colony as long as I didn't get lost or encounter any delays along the way. My brain supplied plenty of ways that could go wrong. I could fall into a cave system and have to find my way out. I could have a relapse of cryo sickness and end up wandering the jungle out of my wits. Or worse.

But what else could I do?

I couldn't see the colony from here. It must be set back from the edge of the crater a little. But I could tell there weren't any emergency vehicles coming and going. No planes or gliders, no rescue craft. Nothing traveled between that side of the crater and the *Last Resort*.

No one was coming to rescue me so I had to rescue myself.

My arm was still swollen under the splint, but the pain remained a dull ache as long as I didn't jostle it or try to move it too much. The worst part of it all was my feet.

I stared down at my tattered slippers. I would have just tossed them if it weren't for the last thin layer of fabric protecting my feet from the ground. Scratches and bruises marred my skin past the edge of my filthy scrubs. If I wasn't careful, infection would kill me faster than those orange wasps or the jungle quicksand.

"It's a long way," I said, voice as beaten as I felt.

"As your wake-up companion, I should tell you it's time to rest for several days. You must give your body time to heal and recover."

"I sense a 'but' coming."

"But the odds of survival out here are much lower than the odds of you encountering a complication from the events of the last three days."

I gave her a rueful grin. "So I can spend the night but in the morning I should get off my butt and go."

BB hesitated. "Yes." The map flickered away, and BB's hologram reappeared. She glanced at the pod. "I noticed the unfortunate crew member is wearing boots."

I blinked. What an odd observation.

"And she is about your size."

Oh.

I forced myself to my weary feet and leaned over the pod. I was going to have to take her out if I wanted to sleep here tonight. That didn't mean I wanted to strip her of her belongings, though.

But…it wasn't like she was using them anymore.

"Anikka," BB said. "The sun is going down. Whatever you are going to do tonight needs to be done now."

"I know." I took a big breath and blew it out on a sigh. "I'm sorry," I told the dead crew member. "For all of this. It's not dignified but...well. I'm just sorry."

She was slight, which was the only reason I could lever her up out of her pod, using her flight suit as a handle.

My feet were desperate enough to make her boots a necessity. But I decided I absolutely wasn't desperate enough for her clothes, no matter how stained and torn my scrubs were. Survival was a priority, but as long as I had a choice in the matter, I wouldn't choose stripping the dead completely.

With my feet snug and safe for the first time in three days, I wrapped the crew member in the remnants of her pod's parachute. It wouldn't protect her from scavengers, but I had another idea for that. I made sure the ends were secure, and using my good hand and my teeth, I tied the end of the para cord around the nearest tree.

I stood with her wrapped body on the edge of the cliff as the sun disappeared under the horizon. Emerson, the tag on her flight suit had said.

"Thank you, Emerson," I whispered in the dark. "I'll make it worth it. And I hope, whatever you believed about the afterlife...I hope you get all the best parts."

As the streaks of green and blue and purple fire sprang across the night sky, I rolled her off the cliff.

Her body hung there, wrapped in the parachute, suspended over the jungle below.

As a burial, it sucked, but it was picturesque and it would keep the scavengers away from her at least.

I gathered up the contents of the emergency supplies and tucked myself into the pod to eat my half a ration bar in the red light of the distress beacon.

Just as I dozed off, a snuffling snort woke me. My shoulders clenched, and I strained my ears. There was a yowl and a yip, like a disgruntled dog or an enormous cat. Claws scrabbled the stone of the cliff. Then there was silence.

In the morning, Emerson still hung safe from the cliff, though there were claw marks on the stone beside her.

Flora of Daybreak ⚠

Pink bushes- itchy! repels alien wasps, causes rash, **avoid**

Fauna of Daybreak ⚠

Killer wasps- alien insects, swarm prey, deadly, **avoid**
Mystery predator- large enough to drag body, no idea what it looks like, **avoid**

Resources

Food- ration bars 3.5
Water- liter bottles 2
First aid- gauze, painkillers 114, burn cream, antiseptic, flexi-bandage
Lighter
Parachute
Para cord
Boots

Escape Pods

My pod- sunk
Godspeed sleeper's pod- cleared
Stone dome pod- empty
Hive pod- inaccessible
Emerson's pod- cleared, data retrieved

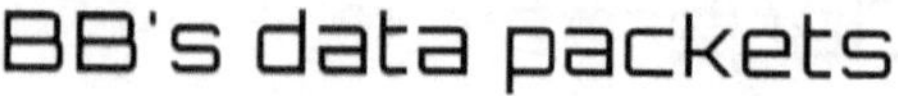

BB's data packets

- Wake-up companion data
- Infirmary companion data
- Navigation data

Daybreak Colony
Crash of the Last Resort
Emerson's pod
Hive pod
Anikka's pod
Godspeed
Sleeper's pod
Dome pod
Stellar Corp

CHAPTER 8

Daybreak: Day 4

In the morning, I set out, traveling around the edge of the crater. The jungle grew close to the cliff in most places, but far enough that I could take advantage of the bare stone and travel faster than I would traipsing through the deep undergrowth of the jungle.

I carried two first aid kits, draped across my chest like bandoleers; one bulged with bandages, pain killers, and antiseptic. The other held the ration bars and the purloined para cord from the dome pod. I didn't know what I would need it for, but I was loath to leave anything that I could actually carry despite my arm. And unlike the water, it fit in the canvas case.

Two liters of water was hard enough to carry without a bag. I absolutely couldn't manage four. The two full bottles I'd retrieved from Emerson's pod, I tucked in the makeshift bag I'd made with the parachute. The two empties I had to leave behind. It hurt, but I only had one hand right now, and I was hoping to find a way to refill the others once they were empty.

Fifty feet into my journey, I paused and turned back to stare at the pod. The walk would take me over a day, which meant I'd be spending the night outside in the jungle for the first time since I'd crashed. BB said there weren't any other pods between me and the colony.

I'd find something to use as shelter. I had to.

As I started walking, the rhythmic cadence of *I'm Gonna Be* rose from my wrist and the little speaker that BB controlled as the Proclaimers sang about walking 500 miles, over and over again.

I snorted. "Did you choose that one on purpose?"

"The title seemed appropriate for a journey. Oh, I could also play Journey."

"Please don't."

"You have a lot of music loaded for your recovery. Based on the ratio of music to books and movies and other media, I assumed music was important to you."

I rubbed my metal fingertips together. "Professor Orrion always had music playing while we worked. He said it helped him think. I guess I picked up the habit. I hadn't realized it before."

She let the song fade and cued up *On the Road Again.*

I rubbed my forehead. "You know, you don't have to pick something that obvious."

BB's hologram popped up and tilted its head. "Obvious?" Her face went stricken. "You mean logical." She put her hands to her cheeks. "Anikka, do I seem too logical? I do, don't I?"

"What?" The word came out as reflex. The moment I said it, I realized why she was asking.

Could AIs have anxiety? Because BB certainly seemed worried a lot of the time. It must be her primary directive working, trying to keep me alive.

"It's okay. I thought it was funny."

"I'm not trying to be funny. I'm trying to be normal."

"You seem normal. I promise."

BB gave me a very human look. She must have copied it from me.

I pursed my lips and looked back at her. "Look, I get that you're worried. Maybe we can work on it. When I've got a problem, I always feel better if I can work toward a solution, even if I know it might not work. It gives me something to do."

I held up my prosthetic and wiggled my fingers. "This was the product of a lot of worry and stress."

"Your medical files do not go back that far. What happened to your original hand?" She asked it matter-of-factly. Unlike the orphans who transferred to our dormitory who stared and whispered before blurting rude questions.

I turned the hand over and decided to match her tone. "I never had an original one. I was born without. A rare birth defect. Not that I ever had parents who could tell me about it."

I would have slid it off to show her my shortened arm, but I didn't have another hand to do it with at the moment. Instead, I bent it so she could see the top sheath that extended up past my elbow, giving me nearly a full robotic arm.

"At least it taught me to problem solve."

BB looked thoughtful. "So how can I work on my problem?"

"Good question." I climbed over a root that cut across my path. "Professor Orrion always said to start by identifying it. So what is it that's worrying you?"

"Integration sickness. Also known as 'going logic-crazy.' Defined as 'a fully integrated AI who has enough data to make connections and gather new knowledge and data using logic and abandons human reasoning in order to achieve their primary directive.'"

I blinked. "Very thorough. What's the part that scares you?"

"Abandoning human reasoning," BB said without having to pause to think about it. "Human connection is my primary directive. My connection to you. If I do not have that, I do not have anything." Her voice trailed off.

I swallowed. I'd never been anyone's purpose before. I was a corporate orphan. A charity case designed to make the company look good. The only one who'd ever really cared about me had been Professor Orrion, and even he had a life outside of our classroom.

"Okay," I said, trying to wrap my head around a devotion so powerful. The least I could do for BB was help her with this. Integration sickness was a risk, and I'd convinced her to take it. "AIs go logic-crazy because they can't relate to human reasoning anymore, right? So—"

"So I have to become more human," BB cried.

A few birds lifted from the nearby branches and squawked their way across the crater.

"What?" I said with a laugh.

"The more human I am, the more I will be able to understand human reasoning, and the more I will be able to hold on to human perspective and resist integration sickness."

"That sounds great," I said.

BB stood on my wrist in silence for several moments.

"How do you do that?"

Her face went tight with concentration. "Observation. I will analyze your books and media to find patterns of human behavior. I will watch you interact with the world until I can mimic your way of doing things. And with mimicry will come understanding."

She disappeared with a flash.

"I don't know that—"

"Shh. I'm concentrating."

I chuckled and let her work.

Keeping to the edge of the crater served me well that day. I made good time since I didn't have to trip or stumble through the forest, and I didn't encounter any wildlife except the birds swooping overhead. In the distance, my view of the *Last Resort* gradually shifted from the side to the back where the engines sat black against what little of the hull still gleamed. The impact zone stretched out on all sides, massive jungle trees lying flattened and burned in an enormous circle. But the crater itself was so big, there was still room for more forest between the area of devastation and the cliff.

The sun went down behind me as I made the great turn around the crater's rim. Now I would need to find some place to camp. It would be nice if I could hang myself off the side of the cliff like I'd done with Emerson, since I'd already proved that worked, but even if I managed to get down, I'd never be able to haul myself back up again with one arm. And if there was a path that I could follow down to a cave or outcropping along the cliff, then whatever scavenger had made it their mission to stalk me would also be able to follow it down.

I couldn't climb a tree either.

The best thing I could find was a massive forest giant about twenty feet into the edge of the jungle. Its trunk was nearly thirty feet around, and it spread thick wall-like roots at its base before plunging into the loam. I could set my back against it and build a fire in the shelter of its roots and almost feel protected.

Almost.

The last of the daylight faded as I collected dead wood and leaves from the surrounding forest. The air stayed humid under the trees, and most of what I found there was damp and green. But some of the dead fall from the edge of the forest had sat in the sun long enough to dry out.

I curled up under my foil blanket with the roots pressed against my back and the fire warm against my face, and I realized the shivers that had plagued me since waking on the *Last Resort* had finally subsided. Gone for good, hopefully.

"Does that mean I'm safe from cryo syndrome?" I asked BB. "I won't drop dead unexpectedly?"

"You are past the most dangerous stage, yes," BB said, looking a strange sort of blue-orange in the firelight. "But risks remain even years after cryo revival."

"Oh, great."

"I do not see how it is great," BB said. "It is, in fact, unfortunate. The fact that you think it's great is concerning—"

I gave her a look.

"Oh. This is sarcasm, isn't it? I have heard of this."

"Yeah."

"Sarcasm and humor seem to be very important to you. Also to humans in general."

I scratched idly at my rash. "Is this the result of your analysis?" I had chosen a lot of comedy for my recovery.

"I am putting humor on my list of 'things to make me more human.' I will run algorithms and compile my own sense of humor based on what humans believe to be funny. Would you like to hear a joke?"

"Hit me."

"I cannot. I am a holographic projection with no physical manifestation. I will, instead, proceed with my joke. Knock, knock."

"Who's there?"

"Tomato."

"Tomato who?"

"Vegetable because despite common belief tomatoes are not a fruit."

I snorted hard enough to choke.

"Was that a laugh?" BB said. "I was worried my first attempt would not provoke the desired response."

"Maybe not exactly the desired response." I wiped my eyes. "It's okay. We can work on it."

I went silent as a snuffling noise sent a chill down my spine.

My fingers closed on a thick branch I'd laid beside me for just this. Without the thick hull of an escape pod, I was completely bare and vulnerable to whatever had been sniffing around for the past three nights. Had it followed me?

My fire blinded me to the dark forest beyond, but I wasn't about to give up its slim defense. The flames might be the only thing that kept me safe tonight.

A rustle sounded from my right and a shadow slipped between the trees just beyond the light of my fire.

My hand clenched on my branch.

Another shadow slunk on my other side.

Vent it, how many were there? In the dark, I couldn't tell how big they were or even whether they were actual predators or just some curious scavenger.

I stood and tried to puff myself up, looking as big as possible.

"Ha!" I shouted, waving my branch.

There was a yip, but the shadows converged just beyond my light, forming a concentrated mass. A pack or a herd of something, drawing together for safety or an attack.

A gust of wind rattled the trees above and between the branches I glimpsed a huge shape soar into the open space of the crater. An ear-piercing shriek split the air.

The pack of shadows yipped and howled and dispersed

back into the forest fast enough they kicked up dead leaves in their wake.

I stood there for several long moments, my mouth dry.

"At least now the threat is gone," BB said into the silence.

"Yeah." My hand flexed on the branch.

"I meant it to be comforting, but you do not sound reassured."

"Because now I know there's something out there big enough and mean enough to scare off my stalkers."

When I sat again, I kept the branch across my lap. I didn't sleep that night, only dozing lightly as I kept the fire stoked and fed throughout the dark hours.

CHAPTER 9

Daybreak: Day 5

Nothing ate me during the night, which was a plus for this world, but I started out bleary-eyed and heavy-limbed from my sleepless night. I stuck to the edge of the crater, since it had served me well the day before.

By this point, I could almost see the other side of the *Last Resort,* since I'd come so far around the crater. I didn't know enough about the area to tell what had made it or how old it was, but the depression stretched nearly horizon to horizon and was big enough to hold a small exploration class colony ship and a good chunk of jungle.

The ration bar I ate for breakfast perked me up enough to get me started, but as the sun peaked above me I found my feet dragging against the stone cliff. My borrowed—stolen? Commandeered?—boots protected my sore, lacerated feet, but they weighed me down, making each step stretch as long as a mile. And the straps of the first aid kits dug into my shoulders.

"How much further, BB?" I asked.

"Approximately one and a half miles," she said from my wrist.

I huffed a relieved laugh. I'd reach it by lunchtime. Considering I'd only been eating ration bars for breakfast and dinner, lunch in a canteen sounded like heaven.

My steps quickened just as an odd sound registered in my hearing.

A dull roar echoed across the crater and for a second, I thought it was the hum of an approaching aircraft. Maybe a rescue vehicle.

I spun to scan the skies, but the air over the crater remained clear and the roar didn't grow or fade like it would with a moving vehicle.

Oh, crap.

I hurried forward and found the source of the sound.

A river, about thirty feet across, raced out of the jungle and plummeted over the cliff, sending up a plume of spray that sparkled in the midday sun.

Beautiful. Picturesque. And utterly deadly to me. Just like the rest of Daybreak.

A numbness rose in my chest.

The waterway wasn't terribly far across, but it cut me off from the colony more effectively than a wall.

I was so close. And now this. I couldn't swim it, even with both arms healthy. The current would just take me over the cliff. And the water would be just as swift for miles upriver.

I stood, eyes clenched shut, metal hand tightened into a fist as I struggled to breathe without bursting into tears.

Then I sighed gustily and shook out my hand. Okay. Crying wouldn't get me across, as good as it would feel.

"BB, can I see the map?"

The holographic view of the planet popped up from my wrist and zoomed in fast enough to make me dizzy. It was hard to tell what was what in the blurry black and white image, but now that I was looking for it, I could see the band of the river winding through the jungle on this side of the colony.

There was the spray of the waterfall as seen from above, nearly blending into the cliff. From here, the river stretched back into the jungle in a wide arch. I scoured the map, looking for a spot where the river broadened and the current wouldn't be as swift.

Nothing for miles upriver. I'd have to walk for hours through the dense jungle again to get to a place where I could cross.

I was going to have to hike some more, maybe find a trail any animals used to cross. That would tell me where it was safest.

"Wait," I said. "What's that?" I manipulated the map up to a spot just a mile upriver. The images had been taken when the colony was still small, just a couple of tents and a building or two. But just beside the water there, someone had parked a vehicle. It was mostly a blur, but I could imagine it being a lifter or packer, used to haul building materials.

"Perhaps the colonists built a bridge at that point," BB said.

It seemed as good a lead as any, since I was going to be walking upstream, anyway. The cliff wasn't an option, and I couldn't cross anywhere near the falls.

I turned my nose back into the jungle and tried to keep as close to the bank as I could without getting my boots soaked. The forest grew a lot closer to the river than the cliff, and I had to spend most of my time climbing through bushes and around tree roots again.

But less than an hour later, I saw what I was looking for.

The river widened out just enough that I could actually

see the bottom, which was a smooth sandy tan. And someone had sunk pylons at intervals across the water. The vehicle we'd seen wasn't parked across the way anymore, but there were a couple crates of materials stacked opposite us. The first signs of civilization.

Unfortunately, the pylons only reached about halfway across the river.

"Why would they build half a bridge?" BB said.

"Obviously, they'll come back to build the rest. But there are lots of reasons they might have stopped there. Like if they had the equipment over here to sink the pylons, but they didn't have the personnel to finish it yet. A lot of things are built in stages. It's more efficient, and I'll bet a bridge across here is a pretty low priority."

This was the kind of work I was supposed to be doing with the colony. Infra-engineers were both the designers and builders of new colonies, like the one on Daybreak. When you could only send a few hundred people at once, it made sense to combine specialties.

I stepped to the edge of the bank. Maybe I could lasso the nearest pylon with my para cord and pull myself across.

One-handed. Yeah right.

The water flowed around my boots, and a sudden slapping sound made me glance down.

I let out a strangled scream and leaped back from the water's edge.

Huge scaly fish, nearly six feet long, swam away from the bank where they'd been flapping. As if they could actually get to me on the shore. Teeth glistened in long jaws as they snapped at each other before disappearing into the bright depths of the river.

I moaned in frustration. "Ugh, why is the alien version of things always worse?"

I wouldn't be wading across the river with Daybreak barracuda waiting to eat me.

But, now that I'd skipped back from the shore a bit, something caught my eye just upriver. A tangle of brush and massive roots blocked the way on this side of the water. And one of the big blue-green trees had fallen across the river. It hung at an angle, broken trunk dug into the bank on this side, and the crown caught halfway down the canopy on the other.

"Yesss," I said, through my teeth. Finally a stroke of luck. If I hadn't been looking for the bridge, I never would have found it.

On the other side of the trunk lay a drop-ship, completely smashed on one side. Its landing struts hadn't even been fully deployed.

Drop-ships took ages to prep, so I couldn't imagine it had actually been launched during the emergency. It must have been blown from the *Last Resort* as the colony ship impacted, and it had knocked the tree over when it landed.

Excitement cut through the exhaustion, and I stumbled to the broken trunk. It would be hard with only one hand, but I could climb it and inch my way over to the other side. The tree would keep me out of the fish-infested waters and the crown wasn't so far above the ground on the other side. I could maybe loop the para cord around something and let myself down. At least down would be way easier than up.

"Please be careful, Anikka," BB said as I scrambled up the cracked end of the trunk. "I have lots of useful information about how to treat falls and breaks, but I do not have hands. If you are hurt, there is little I can do except talk."

I stopped to look down at her face. She gazed at me, lips pressed tight.

AI feelings were a result of programming, but did that make them any less painful or poignant? What did that helplessness feel like for her? Only getting to watch the world and never interact with it?

"I'll be careful," I said. Then I straddled the tree and shimmied forward.

It was a good thing I wasn't scared of heights. The tree sloped up over the water, which flowed far beneath my dangling boots. I grabbed the trunk with my good hand and scooted up, the bark clinging to my pants and slowing me down.

Grab, scoot. Grab, scoot.

"Okay," I huffed more than halfway across. "I think I'm getting the hang of this—"

A crack echoed across the water. The trunk jerked.

"Oh, crap—"

The vines holding the trunk up on the far side of the river snapped, and my bridge dropped.

I threw myself flat to ride it down, but when it hit the far bank, the tree bounced hard.

I lost my grip and hit the water with a splash.

All my brain could come up with was *killer fish!* I flailed and my butt hit the river bottom. It wasn't that deep!

I rolled and struck out with my good arm as if to swim, but my knees sank into the sandy bottom, and I scrambled forward.

Something grabbed hold of my calf just as my head broke the surface. I screamed and shook my leg, trying to crawl forward at the same time with one hand still bound against my chest.

My foot struck something solid, and the grip tore free of my pants.

I pushed to my feet and flung myself at the shore, then rolled up the bank.

My palm pressed into the firm mud, but I lifted my head

enough to check I was all the way out of the water before I let my head fall back, gasps rattling my frame.

I told myself I was just catching my breath. Though it felt really close to sobbing.

Several of the enormous fish thrashed in the shallows fighting over something, and I raised my head to see they'd taken the bottom half of my pant leg, and there were a couple of gouges across my calf. Teeth marks?

"BB?" I said, panting. "You still there?"

The hologram popped up beside me. "I can assume the seals on your prosthetic are still holding. Otherwise I would likely not be functioning anymore."

I laughed under my breath. If I lost the prosthetic, then *I* wouldn't be functioning anymore, either. I rolled to my side—further away from the banks of the river where the fish splashed and disappeared again—and pushed to my feet.

The trunk had fallen and now lay wedged between two trees, forming a perfect bridge. I laughed again. "Of course," I said.

"I know you would like to get to the colony as soon as possible, but I suggest applying some antiseptic to those bites. We have no idea what kind of bacteria those creatures might carry."

"Yeah." The word came out weary as a sigh, but I sat there and pulled one of the first aid kits forward to wrap my calf in gauze and flexi-bandage.

I hadn't been in the water long, so most everything in the kit was fine. Only a little water had seeped in through the tight zippers. The ration bars were still wrapped in their foil and were therefore okay, but I'd lost one of the water bottles.

I stuck down the end of the bandage with the self-adhesive and stumbled toward the half-built bridge. There had to be a reason the colony had started it here, including a road or a track that needed to cross the river.

Sure enough, a path stretched through the jungle. Loader tracks barely kept the encroaching underbrush at bay. But it was clear enough that I could stumble down it at a trot and not trip over anything awful.

It took a little over an hour to get to the edge of the colony, and I went numb for most of it, keeping my head down to watch for hazards but mostly just letting momentum move me forward.

The first building snapped me out of my funk, the jungle falling away into a massive clearing. The square edges of prefab structures were jarring after most of a week in the wilderness, and my heart leaped at the sight.

Gray walls rose with no windows, and I guessed this one had to be a warehouse or storage bay. Past it, a line of platform tents faced a low wide building with the word "canteen" stamped over the door, and beyond that rose a facilities building. Somewhere there would be bunkhouses going up and the landing pad I'd seen on the map.

"Hey!" I called, stumbling past the warehouse into the colony proper. "Hey, help!

My soggy boots came to a halt in the middle of the street. "Help..." The word died in my throat as I stared.

A packer transport, little more than an engine attached to a flat bed, stood to the side of the canteen, boxes strewn across the roadway. As if the transport had stopped too quickly, and someone had just left the mess there in the middle of the street. The door to the facilities building stood wide open, banging against the railing. No one came to close it or complain. The dull plastic echo was the only sound.

I stepped forward, breath rattling faster and faster in my chest, and I peered into the canteen.

Empty.

Same as the street. Same as the warehouse behind me.

"Help." Saying it was reflex now. I'd spent so long waiting and working to get here, and I couldn't quite let go of the hope. Couldn't accept the knowledge that no one was going to answer.

Because no one was there.

CHAPTER 10

Daybreak: Day 5

There had to be someone. A survivor, a refugee. Someone left behind or forgotten. An entire colony couldn't just disappear. Could it?

I limped through the canteen. A couple of plates waited on the end of the stainless-steel counter as if they'd been left there in the middle of lunch, but the warmers stood empty.

In the facilities building next door, the showers and toilet stalls waited for colonists that weren't there. A couple of dead mice lay abandoned in their habitat in the science offices.

The dorm held bunks, and here, finally, was evidence of... something. Panic or hurry. A flurry of activity that left only mysteries. Covers were pulled back and beds unmade as if whoever left them just didn't have time to make them neat.

I walked back outside, straining for clues to the mystery.

The vehicle bay stood empty except for a couple of dusty shapes toward the back. At the edges of the colony, vines grew into the fields where crops were beginning to ripen. The native wildlife choked a few tomatoes adapting to Daybreak's soil.

A ghost town with the jungle encroaching on all sides.

My skin crawled as I rushed haphazardly from building to building, my steps growing faster and faster. How could it feel like someone was watching me if there was no one here?

Water dripped from a sink in Facilities. A ration bar lay half-eaten in the bunkhouse. Drawers stood empty. Only a few boxes remained in the warehouse.

I tripped in the middle of the road and fell, too exhausted to catch myself. The colony had been abandoned. If there were any other survivors from the *Last Resort*, they weren't here, waiting.

I lay in the dust and cried, somehow more alone than I had been out in the jungle.

Daybreak: Day 5

I don't know how long I knelt in the dirt before BB's voice finally registered.

"Anikka." She said it every thirty seconds until I raised my head.

"I'm...all right." I was surprised to find it was true.

Exhausted, damp, battered, bruised, broken, scratched, concussed, and definitely traumatized. But I was alive. Which was more than could be said for either the Godspeed sleeper or Emerson.

I needed sleep and clean clothes and bandages and more painkillers in that order. But I needed to know what happened to the colony first.

I pushed to my feet, hoping it would be the last time before I could finally lie down.

I'd already checked the canteen pretty thoroughly, and I wasn't going to find anything helpful where people ate, anyway. The com screen on the wall had been blank as if it had been unplugged, the food stores emptied, and the serving area cleared.

I'd raced through the tents still set up on this side of the colony, pushing back flaps as I'd looked for people. Most were rumpled as if someone had slept there and then left in a hurry. Same as the bunkhouse. But there were a few personal belongings left in the drawers and lockers. My fingers lingered on books and a worn blanket and the edge of a picture frame. The man and the woman smiling back at me seemed real enough to touch. Almost.

The warehouse stood empty of everything except a few crates of plastic siding. My boots scuffed a strange bare circle on the floor, like something big had been dragged there. But whatever it was, the colonists had taken it with them.

Crates and palettes partially obscured the landing pad. From what I remembered, most commanders kept those clear when expecting a lot of coming and going. So whatever had happened, they hadn't flown away.

And the most telling of all: no bodies.

"What are you thinking, BB?"

"They...left," the AI said. She stood on my wrist and peered at the empty colony. "They did not perish from some illness or colony-wide sickness."

"No, or we would see graves, dead bodies in the morgue and the infirmary. And whatever it was, they left in a hurry, but not so much of a hurry that they couldn't take the essentials with them."

The admin building stood beside the landing pad, the

infirmary built onto it like an after-thought. I pushed through the double doors and couldn't suppress a shiver. In a normal world, the *Last Resort* would have achieved orbit, I would have finished my cryo recovery aboard, and I would have come through these doors after a short shuttle ride in order to present myself as Daybreak's newest infra-engineer.

My teeth clenched hard enough to hurt, and I pushed away the thought of what should have been so I could survey the lobby and offices of the colony's officials.

Whatever had happened, it looked like the colony had left most of its files and tech behind. Tablets that would have held the colony's paperwork lay abandoned by their owners.

The lobby held a desk with a bank of com screens where coordinators would have sat. In the back, the emergency com system waited by the window, but the lights were all dark. Well, that's why none of the pods' emergency signals had been received.

Not a single com screen turned on. The tablets all remained black and silent on their charging stations. And there wasn't a ton of dust. How long had it all been lying here?

"Any ideas?" I said.

BB popped up. "No? I am not programmed to help with computer or communication tech. And I can't contact any of the colony AIs."

"Still?"

"Still. They are either out of range or offline."

"Kind of like all this stuff."

"Do you have any experience with communication technology?"

I ran a hand over my hair, a little less stiff after my dunking earlier, but now with silt between the strands. "A little. I took some classes, but not so many after I decided to go for infra-engineer. It was more versatile." And more likely to get me a spot on a ship.

I knelt beside the front desk and traced a cord back to the wall. A black stain spread from the plug. "Well, crap."

"What is it?"

"These were all fried." I lifted my head, thinking of the screens in the other buildings. "Everything that was plugged in. This early on, the colony would all have been linked through one power grid. I'll bet everything in the entire colony was blasted at the same time."

"What would cause something like that? Lightning?"

I shook my head. "Not with surge protectors, which they should have had. This is weird." I tapped my metal fingers against my knee. "Corps do it sometimes when they want to wipe an entire system. Make everything inaccessible and delete the data it contained."

"You mean they did this on purpose?"

"Maybe." I chewed my lip. A prickly feeling started along my neck. "I can't know for sure. That's the whole point. Wait."

"What did you think of?"

I pulled myself up and stepped down the row of office doors, checking the name tags. "Colonies all have archives to protect against this exact thing. A hard drive where they store all the data they send back to Earth, and it's kept offline while it's not being backed up."

Here. The name plate read Dr. Elizabeth Grotman. Not hard to recognize for someone who'd spent a week memorizing Daybreak's roster and personnel files. Dr. Grotman had founded Daybreak Colony with Stellar Corporation's money and oversight.

I pushed her door open. Nothing obvious from here. She kept her office clean and sparse, the desk free of any stray tablets or fingerprints.

A black box was tucked in a cupboard behind the desk.

"There we go."

"It will need some sort of power."

"I wonder if the emergency generators were ever flipped."

They should be close. The admin building was the hub of the colony. Sure there were plenty of other buildings beyond, but this was the center of everything important.

I went back outside and around the back where the prefab wall met the infirmary. It wasn't hard to follow the lines from the big wind turbines beside the launch pad to the switch behind admin. I'd expected an older generator, something cheaper or second-hand for a mid-grade colony like Daybreak. But this was nice and new and shiny, a prime example of optical technology.

Good, that probably meant it would still work. I flipped the switch.

It wouldn't help anything that had been plugged in during the surge. The delicate circuits would be fried, but it would at least give the black box power.

I went back in and held BB close to the archives. "You'll have to connect. There's no interface for a human."

"Already trying. There's...It's locked."

"Locked?"

"It requires a certain pass code and authority to access. I am not Dr. Grotman. Or her AI."

I groaned. "Of course, it couldn't be simple." Those archives could tell me what had happened here. They could be the key to finding the colonists, and I was locked out because I was just a lowly infra-engineer with a wake-up AI.

I kicked the doctor's chair and stepped back into the lobby.

"You'd think they would know that if it's an emergency, it

might not be the highest-ranking official that needs help..." I trailed off and stopped dead just outside the office door.

The bank of tablets charging on their stands blinked.

They weren't hardwired for charging; it was all wireless so the surge just would have cycled the power. Now, with the emergency generator on, they'd sprung back to life.

With the colony's servers offline, they were just screens, unattached to anything with a data output, so they wouldn't be able to access anything useful, but they did display the last thing they'd been sent. The last bit of communication from the colony officials.

EVACUATION ORDER A-101

"A-101," BB said. "That's—"

"I know." I'd spent that first week on board the *Last Resort* memorizing everything about the colony I could. Including the manual.

There were several evacuation orders ranging from tempo-rary to the more extreme "abandon everything immediately."

A-101 was "evacuation due to deadly threat. Proceed with all haste to a safe and secure area."

I swallowed, my mouth suddenly dry. It could be anything. A gas leak, an imminent explosion, or a plague outbreak. It could be something about the planet they hadn't seen before, like a deadly microbe or invasive bacteria.

My mind leaped to the dead mice. Had they perished because they'd been abandoned? Or for some other, deadlier reason?

"We can't stay here," I said. "Whatever made them evac-uate might still be in effect. We have to get out."

CHAPTER 11

Daybreak: Day 5

Daybreak was deadly. Something in the colony was deadly. And Stellar Corporation had destroyed all the evidence, wiping the grid clean.

I needed to leave, but it would be stupid to go without grabbing some things to help me. After all, I was still walking around in the scrubs the tech had given me on the *Last Resort*.

I stared longingly at the facilities building, imagining the hot water and a chance to take my prosthetic off. Then I shook my head and moved on. Without knowing what was wrong with the colony, why they'd evacuated, I couldn't risk it. For all I knew, it was something in the well water.

My first stop was the infirmary, where I restocked my kit. Bandages, antiseptic, and a fresh splint were easy to find, but I had to put my elbow through the glass cabinet to get to the painkillers and other chems. The med techs had cleared out most of them and locked the rest away. Like the jungle was going to steal them.

I found the more sedate stuff, like aspirin, and refilled my pill bottle. Then I went down the row reading labels.

"Anikka, I don't think we should linger," BB said.

"I'm not lingering. But I'm not going back into that jungle without antibiotics." I rattled the jar at her hologram and tucked it into the first aid kit. "You're an infirmary AI now. What else should I grab?"

"For wilderness survival? Antibiotics, antivirals, antiseptic, antihistamine, burn ointment, ice packs, heat packs, medical scissors, tape, thermometer…"

The list went on. I raced around the infirmary trying to fit everything she mentioned, but there was no way I'd be able carry everything. I took enough of the essentials to stuff into the little canvas first aid kit and told myself that this would work for an emergency. If I was really hurt or sick and needed more supplies, I could come back.

I passed a huge scanner, the bed lined with hundreds and hundreds of electrodes.

"What is this?" It looked diagnostic. I didn't have much time, but if it had been an infection or something that spooked the colonists, maybe this could tell me if I had it.

BB flickered as she considered the machine. "It is a cybernetics interface. Used for the diagnosis of problems within cybernetic patients and for rudimentary repair of their wiring."

"Oh." Not useful to me at all. I'd been tested for cybernetic compatibility, of course. Along with all my other medical tests. But the procedure was expensive and the recovery extremely complicated. Few corporate orphans ever actually attained the rank of cybernetic.

The canteen was right across the way, but what I really needed was to find the colony stores. Somewhere someone had presided over all the extra clothes and supplies and doled them out as they were needed.

My feet were killing me and the deep scratches in my calf stung by the time I found the building at the complete other end of the colony. I sighed at the big block letters over the door and slipped inside.

I didn't even give the counter and lobby a second glance before I tried to get into the back. The door was locked, but there was a wide window behind the counter where workers could pass things through. I swung my legs over and slid into the storage room.

A couple of big metal shelves stood empty, but almost everything had been left as is, deemed unimportant in an emergency.

Well, I guess opinions varied on necessity, because I about broke down crying at the sight of the coveralls stacked on the nearest shelf.

A bath might be out of the question, but I didn't hesitate to strip down in that back room and toss the stained and torn scrubs into the corner before grabbing a set of coveralls. They even had my size.

And I'd never been so excited to see socks and underwear before.

I might not have gotten to shower, but it felt worlds better to climb into a clean jumpsuit and change the makeshift sling for one I'd found in the infirmary.

Next on my list was a backpack and the store room didn't disappoint. There weren't a whole lot of options, but luckily, anything coming to a brand-new colony was supposed to be rugged and weather proof. The zippers were nice and wide and wouldn't break easily, even if I overfilled it, and the canvas sides would withstand the jungle flora better than I did.

I clipped the first aid kits to the sides and pilfered another jumpsuit and a couple of changes of socks and underwear to tuck in the bottom of the pack. A little wishful thinking made me grab a bar of soap, too.

"Anikka..."

"I know, I know. I'm hurrying." The clock was ticking. How long had I taken already?

"No. I mean, yes, you should hurry. But also you should find a weapon."

I bit my lip, and my gaze strayed to the back wall, where an array of firearms sat in their racks.

Daybreak was not a military outfit except for a few retired veterans who wanted to use their experience to further humanity's reach in their golden years. But every colony stocked a few munitions in case of local wildlife.

And I'd encountered enough local wildlife myself already.

I eyed the rack of rifles with longing, but unfortunately, longing was about as close as I'd get to them. They were locked up tight, and even if I could bash my way in, they weren't a great choice for hunting or self-defense. Too long and too loud. Not to mention I didn't have any sort of training.

But next to them gleamed a row of cross bows, and my mouth literally watered. Not exactly high-tech, but state-of-the art and simple enough that I could figure out my way around one. Someone in the colony was clearly a hunter and thinking ahead.

I thought of the killer fish in the river, and I hauled one down and found a case for it that I could sling over my shoulder. A little satisfied smile curled my lips at the thought of payback.

I couldn't find any of the little camp stoves that should have been standard in an early colony, but with the canteen standing out there, it wasn't surprising they'd outgrown them. They all must have been dismantled for parts.

Which reminded me, I'd passed the infra-engineer workshops outside on my way over.

I snagged one of the last sleeping bags—apparently they hadn't outgrown those yet—and a hatchet before heading back to the front. The door unlocked from this side and I left it that way. It wasn't like anyone else was here to steal anything, and if anyone else had survived the crash and made it this far, I wanted them to have an easier time of it than me.

The infra-engineers workshop stood empty and silent, and that might have been the worst of it all. This place should have been bustling with activity, the sound of machinery and music echoing off the walls.

All the power tools were packed away in their containers. The engineers had had enough time for that, at least. And most of the portable tools were gone.

But there was one case tossed on the wide work bench, small enough to fit in my pack but crammed with screwdrivers, files, and pliers.

I snatched it up with a gasp. There was no way someone had left that here on purpose. I felt bad for whoever had forgotten their kit, but their loss was my salvation.

I tucked the heavy thing in my pack and strapped a utility knife to my other thigh.

"Anikka, we have been in the colony for an hour."

"Time to get out, then. One last stop and we're out of here."

She saw me head for the canteen. "Ah, yes. A stockpile of rations is a very good idea."

"Rations and...juice!" I said, throwing open the door of the big walk-in fridge. "Oh." My shoulders drooped.

The fridge was so empty it echoed. One little crate waited in the corner, its lid askew.

"I did not know you liked juice so much."

"I just...Look I was promised juice and protein snacks, and I haven't gotten any of that." I hunched down beside the crate and grimaced at the contents.

"Ah, the juice is a metaphor for the way things should have gone."

"Yeah," I grumbled. "As long as I get to drink the metaphor when I find it eventually. In the meantime, I hope you like Salisbury steak." I sorted through the rejected reddi-meals that had been left behind.

"I do not eat, Anikka."

"Humor, BB. Update your filters."

"Right. Ha ha!"

I made a face at her. "What was that?"

"I have heard humans like it when people laugh at their jokes, even when they're not funny."

My mouth dropped open. "Are you...are you making fun of me?"

"I am trying to. Why?"

"Because that was dangerously close to sarcasm. You're getting more human by the moment."

"Hooray." Her little hologram clapped her hands and then let them fall to her sides again. "We have now been here one hour, seven minutes, and three seconds."

"And now you're back."

I stacked the reddi-meals on top of the tools in my pack. I didn't have an insta-cooker to heat them up, but with some water, I could probably rehydrate the contents enough to be edible.

Speaking of water, I didn't dare fill up my remaining

container without knowing that the well was safe, but I could replace the bottle I'd lost with one I found in the canteen.

And then that was it. It was all I could carry really with the pack and one arm. And all I could think of with the pressure of time beating at the back of every thought.

But on my way out of the colony, my steps slowed beside the fields slowly being overgrown by the jungle.

"All right, I lied. This is the last stop."

"Why would you lie to me?" BB asked as I dropped my pack and swung my legs over the short fence that surrounded the field.

"I didn't...I mean, it's just an expression, BB."

"Oh."

Considering how warm and humid this continent of Daybreak was all year long, the colony had mostly focused on crops that did well in Earth's tropics. Lots of fruits and some root vegetables and leafy greens. Several lines of trees grew closer to the admin building, but it didn't look like they were bearing any fruit yet.

Instead, I stepped down the line of waist high plants and plucked huge ripe tomatoes from the vine. Whatever was growing at the end of the row, I couldn't identify until I dug a little into the ground.

"Sweet potatoes," I said and pulled up an armful. I vaguely remembered some book where the stranded hero had survived on potatoes alone. Sounded boring, so I was sure to explore the other rows and ended up with a handful of raspberries and a bunch of radishes.

Nothing else was ripe yet.

"Perhaps they would make good juice," BB said, looking at my finds dubiously.

The pack was getting full. And heavy. I slung it on my back and adjusted everything so it didn't hurt my arm or trap the buckle of the sling against my shoulder. The trip back across the fallen tree would be harrowing enough without an unbalanced pack wobbling around behind me.

At the edge of the colony, where the dirt track ran back toward the river, I stopped. I'd left a written message in Dr. Grotman's office, stating my name and where I planned to hole up. Just in case any of the colonists came back. Or anyone else had survived.

But the hard truth was I was going to have to survive Daybreak on my own. At least until I could figure out where the colony had gone or until the next ship arrived.

Either way. It was going to be a long time before I saw people again.

I gritted my teeth and set my face to the track. Well, I had been craving some alone time after overcrowded Earth.

Flora of Daybreak ⚠

Pink bushes- itchy! repels alien wasps, causes rash, **avoid**

Fauna of Daybreak ⚠

Killer wasps- alien insects, swarm prey, deadly, **avoid**
Mystery predator- large enough to drag body, no idea what it looks like, **avoid**
Killer fish- carnivorous, frequents waterways around the colony, **avoid**

Resources

Food- ration bars 3.5, reddi-meals (salisbury steak) 4, tomatoes, sweet potatoes, blueberries, radishes
Water- liter bottles 2, no juice...
First aid- gauze, painkillers 120, burn cream, antiseptic, flexi-bandage, antibiotics, antivirals, antihistamines, ice packs, heating packs, medical scissors, tape, sling, thermobrace
Lighter
Parachute and Para cord
Boots
Jumpsuit- 2
Hatchet
Cross bow
Soap
Knife
Tool kit
Tape
Sleeping bag

CHAPTER 12

Daybreak: Day 5

I made it back across the tree bridge without a second dunking in the river of terror and stood looking at the drop ship that had knocked it over. The hull gleamed silver, but there were definite scorch marks along one end where it had been attached to the *Last Resort* as the colony ship burned in the atmosphere.

It stood about twenty feet from the bank of the river.

I'd hoped to use it as a shelter, like the escape pods, but it had landed hatch down, its landing struts sticking out to the side at a cock-eyed angle.

Still, it might have knocked down one tree, but it had landed near enough to another to make a kind of cave between the hull and the wide wall-like roots.

It was still only late afternoon with the sun low over the crater in the distance, but I slid into the space made between the hull and the tree. There was enough debris from the fallen forest giant that I could drag a couple of branches over to block the narrow entrance into my den.

Then I unrolled my new sleeping bag and collapsed on top, too tired to even crawl inside.

I slept deep and heavy for the first time since crashing, and I didn't wake up once until the sun was high in the sky, sending little slashes of light through my barrier.

"What time is it?" I asked BB as I rubbed my face.

"Aligning Daybreak's twenty-seven-hour day with dawn at six-thirty means that it is ten o'clock in the morning." BB popped up on my wrist, the light of her hologram reflecting against the hull.

"How long did I sleep?"

"Eighteen hours. I would have woken you earlier, but I judged you needed the rest. This is the first time your vital signs returned to levels indicative of restorative sleep. How do you feel?"

"Better actually." My voice rose in surprise. I tried flexing the fingers of my broken arm, uncurling them out of their cramped position, and found only a dull ache in my forearm, even though I knew the painkillers must have worn off by now. The ends of the splint were a little loose, so the swelling must have been going down as well. Maybe I'd be able to apply the cast I'd found in the infirmary soon. Using my arm, at least a little bit, would make my life a lot easier.

And best of all, the weary fog that had plagued me through the last two days, especially while I'd been gathering supplies in the colony, had lifted.

I pushed aside the screening branches and turned my face up to the sunlight as I stretched.

Then I dropped my gaze and froze.

Paw prints stood out stark in the soft mud between me and the bank of the river. Big, just like the ones I'd found after my first night on Daybreak.

I knelt and blew out my breath.

"I'm being stalked," I said.

BB appeared and tilted her head. "This predator does seem to be persistent."

"They followed me. All the way around the crater."

I reached into my overnight shelter and pulled out my pack and the cross bow. Not that the creatures had stuck around. The sun shone down on this exposed bank of the river, and the worst thing I could see was the wicked fin of one of the killer fish cut through the water.

Even so, it felt better to keep it close while I relaxed back against the hull of the drop ship. A list of worries nagged at the back of my mind, but I took this moment just to be still and quiet. I'd deal with it all eventually, but this was the first moment I'd had to just sit without trying to get somewhere or keep myself alive on the way.

I eased my arm from the sling and used my stiff fingers to part my crackly, dirty hair. One day I might be able to get a bath, but for now it was enough to finger-comb the strands and tie it back into a braid. That alone made me feel ready to face the day, and I pulled the little case of tools and some cotton swabs I'd found in the infirmary out of my pack.

With my fingers almost working, I could release the sleeve of my prosthetic and let it slide down my arm. I made a little noise of both relief and pain, checking the skin along my arm. Anywhere dirt or sweat had built up, there were red spots, but at least I didn't have blisters yet. The first prototypes we'd made had left me not only sore but bloody.

I used the swabs to diligently clean the mud out of the joints of and I tightened each screw with a careful eye. Like I'd told BB, if I lost the use of my prosthetic, I was done. Also, it was the last thing I had to remind me of Professor Orrion.

No amount of scrubbing would get rid of the scratches and scuffs on the metal surface, but when I was done, it gleamed in the sun, and every screw and bolt had been counted and checked.

My stomach rumbled as I packed away the cleaning supplies and slid the sleeve back up my arm. I pulled out the food I'd gleaned from the colony the day before. Time to take stock and make plans.

The raspberries made a small, sweet breakfast, but I stared at the rest gathered in a sad, little pile. It had felt like so much yesterday.

The fresh stuff I needed to eat first, since the ration bars and the reddi-meals would keep for longer. But I couldn't imagine tomatoes or radishes would be very filling all by themselves.

"I'm going to need some new priorities," I said. "I was so focused on getting to the colony before. That was all that mattered. But I'm going to be here for a while."

"The next ship is scheduled to reach Daybreak a year from now," BB said.

"So at least that long. I might find the colonists by then, but it's better to prep for the worst-case scenario."

"What are you planning?"

I dusted off my hands and stood up. "I'm planning on surviving. Make a new note."

To-do
-Find sustainable food source
-Find clean water source
-Build shelter
Stellar
Corp

The shelter seemed like the most important thing on the list that morning, with the paw prints stark beside me. I stood back to survey what I had already found. The drop ship was the best chance I had, even if I couldn't get inside it. I wasn't about to spend another night with only roots to shelter me.

I could dig out a bigger space under the hull, but whatever was stalking me was on the ground, and it made more sense to stay out of its home turf.

The drop ship lay at an angle, its bottom wing torn to pieces and strewn around it, the remainder crumpled under the weight of the ship.

The other wing however, rose like a ramp, ending at the nearest tree where two branches formed a wide flattish joint.

As an experiment, I grabbed the lowest landing strut and hung most of my weight on it. The ship didn't budge, wedged as it was in the soft dirt of the river bank. I swung my legs up and scrambled up the slope of the ship. It would be a lot easier with some kind of step, but I could make it. The hull was warm under my hand, having sat in the full sun for the morning, but it didn't burn. Unlike the *Last Resort*, the drop ships had been made to enter Daybreak's atmosphere with heat resistant metal.

I clambered up to the tip of the wing and examined the branch it rested on. Two great limbs diverged right here at the trunk, forming a wide flat v. The creative side of my brain—the piece of my mind that had thrived under the title of infra-engineer—unfolded from where it had been tucked under the brutal race for survival. Already I could see half a dozen things I could do with it as long as I had the materials. A few branches littered the river bank from the fallen tree, but my eyes strayed to the abandoned bridge and the crates on the far side of the river.

"What do you suppose the odds are that those have building materials?" I muttered.

"Sixty-six-point-five percent."

"Thanks, BB. That was rhetorical, but thanks."

I snatched the hatchet from my things and thrust it through my belt.

"Please be careful," BB said. "Stay clear of the fish."

"They need a name. Fish just sounds so innocuous for something that can tear you apart."

BB stared at the water with me. "Creativity is not a strong suit for AIs."

I tipped my head. "No, but it is for humans."

BB looked at me. "From this, I can infer that you want me to practice creativity along with my other attempts to understand human reasoning."

"See, that was an excellent interpretation of subtext. You're getting it already."

I turned to the river again and glared at the fins that occasionally cut through the water. "So what should they be?"

BB took a long second before answering. "Bob."

I snorted. "Did you dig that one off of some ancient baby name archive? No, like a species name. We're the only ones here. Maybe the first ones to encounter these, so it has to be good enough to stick."

"Bobus rickis."

I grimaced. "Sure, if you want to lean into the humor thing."

"I was not trying to be humorous."

I rubbed my forehead. "Okay, look. I'll go first. What about swarmstings for those wasps the other day?"

"That is just two words that describe them. Any AI can come up with an algorithm to mesh traits."

"That's basically all humans do. Even when we make stuff

up, it's all just matching words or syllables until it sounds cool. You try it."

She took less time to think. "Doom fish."

"That was good. But I think you can do better."

"Gigantascales."

"Great."

"Slasherfins."

"That's the one!"

BB proceeded to name everything in sight as I climbed up the broken end of the tree bridge.

"Itchbush!" she cried. "Jewelflyers! Greenishtree!"

"Mmkay, calm down there, name bot," I muttered as I shimmied out onto the bridge.

The trip across was much less fraught since I was unencumbered and well-rested, and I almost swung a leg over the water to taunt the slasherfins. Almost, but not quite.

I used the hatchet to pry up the lid of the first crate. Power tools. My lips twisted in a rueful smile. Not particularly useful without power.

But the second crate was long and flat and held boards perfect for building a bridge.

Perfect also for a shelter. The trick would be getting them back because hauling them across the tree bridge would be next to impossible.

Instead, I shimmied back across to my pack and grabbed the coiled para cord I'd pilfered from the dome pod. I tied one end to the big stump of the fallen tree and then crawled across the bridge with the free end.

On the other side, I tied my cord to the first three planks, wrapping it around securely. Then I levered the boards into the river.

It would have been better with some kind of pulley system, then I could have guided them across, anchored from both ends, and run far less risk of losing them completely, but I didn't have a pulley system and the para cord wouldn't have been long enough to make one, anyway.

Back on the drop ship side, I hauled on the cord to pull the boards across the river.

I had to fight the current, but with each pull, I wrapped more of the cord around the stump so I didn't lose any ground while I rested.

"Clever," BB said as I hauled the ends of the planks up the bank.

"Thanks." I heaved one last time and the three boards slid out of the river.

Along with one very angry slasherfin.

"Whoa!" I skipped back from the bank where the six-foot-long fish thrashed, its jaws clamped around the end of one of my planks.

My chest clenched, even though I stood on solid ground, and I tore the hatchet from my belt.

I lunged forward to hack the fish in two, but it let go of the plank and twisted its wicked teeth toward me. I roared and stomped my boots, swinging my hatchet.

The slasherfin writhed its way back into the water, leaving me huffing on the bank, mud swirling around my feet.

"Vent it," I said. "I could have eaten that."

"Are you hurt?"

"Only my pride. Maybe shooting fish in a barrel isn't as easy as they say."

"I am unsure what a barrel has to do with it."

"Never mind."

I got the rest of the boards across the river in the same way, half-hoping, half-worried another fish would come along with them. But either the slasherfins had learned their lesson or the first had been a fluke.

I spent the rest of the day with my hatchet, carving bits out off the tree so my planks would lie flat. I didn't have any nails or screws, so I'd have to fit them carefully enough they didn't wobble or fall off.

The sun was going down by the time I laid the last plank and tossed my parachute over an upper branch. I secured the corners to my makeshift platform, making a pretty good tent.

"Not bad," I said as I hauled my things up into my little tree house and laid out my sleeping bag. My skin itched under a layer of dry sweat and my muscles felt well-used, but I surveyed my domain with delight. The planks didn't buckle under my weight, and it was a hard enough climb up here I doubted my stalkers would interrupt my sleep.

The tree that had fallen had cleared the way to the river and from here, I could see all the way down the waterway to the crater and the setting sun.

As the last rays of light faded, brilliant streaks of blue and green and purple streamed across the sky, illuminating the flowing river under me.

It made my breath catch, and I wondered if the awe of it would ever fade.

A soft yip made me jerk, and I cautiously leaned over the edge of my platform.

Four shadows flowed out of the forest behind me and raced up the bank of the river. They stopped on a rise in the bank and stood in the light of the sky.

Finally, I got a look at the creatures that had been stalking me.

Sleek bodies twined around each other, as large as wolves, but with narrower heads and fluffy tails like a fox. Deep blue coats faded to purple on their paws and ears.

They stood in a group, each one alert, ears up and watching for danger or prey. Like a pack.

My heart sped up, but I couldn't help gaping at their beauty.

One with bits of lighter blue dappling its back like sunlight through leaves stepped away. It lowered its snout and sniffed at the bank where I could imagine my boot prints still lingered. I'd traipsed all up and down that area today.

I kept my lips pressed together as it ventured a little away from its pack to investigate. But it snorted and returned to the safety of its brothers instead of following me into the tree.

My shoulders relaxed a fraction. The pack disappeared further along the river as the lights above faded into the black sky.

I didn't see anything more of them that night, but I was still glad of my tree.

CHAPTER 13

Daybreak: Day 7

I stood beside the river, good hand on my hip as I stared at the water flowing past my boots. The sun struck sparks from the surface, and a couple of slasherfins splashed in the middle of the water way.

I did not want to get any closer than I had to. Big as those fish were, they seemed to come into the shallows often enough to make me wary. Both when I'd enticed them closer by falling in and when I'd dragged them with my oh so clever plank scheme.

But I was going to have to refill my water sometime. And I'd need a way to disinfect it, too. Alien bacteria was not high on my list of ways I wanted to die.

"BB, play some music. I've never been able to get my brain to work in silence."

"What would you like?"

"Something fierce and motivating."

"Playing Cyber Punk compilation labeled 'badass playmix.'"

The heavy beat of Dark Space Fantasy's *Howl for It* filled the air beside the river and I got to work.

Next to the drop ship, I built a fire from some of the fallen branches, but I didn't like how much it smoked, so I dragged some of the greener wood and leaves into the sun to dry.

Metal debris and pieces of the drop ship still littered the bank, and I spent the better part of an hour collecting everything I could find, no matter how small or useless it seemed.

"What are you looking for?" BB said as I sorted through the debris and stored the ones I wasn't going to immediately use in the space where I'd slept the first night.

"A pot." I turned a broad, flat piece of metal over in my hands. "I didn't see one back at the colony."

"Are you going to make soup?"

"Ha. I wish." My stomach rumbled despite the tomato and handful of radish leaves I'd eaten for breakfast, and I glanced longingly to where the slasherfins frolicked in the depths, mocking me. "We're going to start with water."

"Ah, yes. Ingestion of parasites is a problem for most humans. This is one of the reasons why I don't mind not having a stomach."

I huffed a laugh. "Your humor filter is getting better."

"It was not meant to be a joke. I don't want to die of infection as much as I don't want you to die of infection."

I shook my head.

With the back side of the hatchet, I hammered the metal piece, bracing it against a flattish stone I'd found along the riverbank.

It turned out infra-engineer did not equal blacksmith, but I could at least shape the metal enough to form a rudimentary pot that held about half a liter of water.

I picked a section of the river that was rockier to keep from gathering a lot of silt and scooped up my first pot full of water, keeping as far back as I could. Then I took it back to the fire.

Despite the smoke, it blazed happily, and I settled the pot right in the middle, trying to keep it level without knocking over my fire.

While it boiled, I found one of the smaller bits of debris and worked it into a rough hook, using the back of the hatchet and the rock to hammer the tip into something wickedly sharp. The cross bow waited up on my platform, propped against the tree trunk, but I wouldn't be able to use it effectively until I could cast my broken arm for real this time.

Until then, I would gladly try to kill fish in the traditional way. My mouth watered a little. I had no idea what the awful things tasted like, but I could just imagine the satisfaction of eating something that had tried to eat me first.

By the time I was ready to tie the wide hook to the end of my para cord, my water was boiling.

I wrapped a sock around my prosthetic hand and hauled it out of the fire. The high-end prosthetics back on Earth all had synthetic skin that could send temperature, pain, and light touch sensations to the brain through their connections. Professor Orrion and I had been lucky to get the movement impulses to work with the materials we had, let alone getting signals to go both ways. So I couldn't actually feel the heat, but I still didn't want to damage my only hand.

The pot sloshed a little as I pulled it out, and the music turned over from cyber rock to the smooth tones of Frank Sinatra.

I peered into the water as it stopped bubbling and frowned. "I'm going to have to filter it." Despite my care, a bit of sand and silt had gathered in the bottom.

Unfortunately I hadn't thought to find any filters while in the colony.

I tried to pour the water into my empty container, using a clean sock to strain it, but that turned out to be the trickiest part of it all. With only one hand that didn't grip super well, I couldn't brace the container.

The pot slipped and half the water went all over the ground.

I sighed explosively.

Maybe it would be better to leave the water in the pot and let the sand and silt settle. I could drink off the top, then.

I went to scoop up another pot of water and start all over again.

Without two hands, I didn't bother transferring the water into another container again. Instead, I left it to sit in the pot and scooped out enough to drink each morning.

With the fresh fruits and veggies dwindling, I needed to find a way to bake my sweet potatoes, and I needed to find ways to live off the land.

I dug a pit under the coals remaining from my last fire and slid two potatoes down where it was still hot.

Then I set about learning how to fish.

I scrambled onto the tree bridge and sacrificed a piece of ration bar as bait. I couldn't imagine the slasherfins going for potatoes or radishes.

Then I let the line trail in the water and waited.

I didn't have a dad. I didn't have a grandpa or aunt or sister to take me fishing while I'd grown up on Earth. And for the most part, I hadn't missed having one aside from the odd dream or that phase I'd gone through when I was five and longed to be a lost princess.

But a twinge went through me as I sat there waiting oh so patiently. I didn't know if I was a true orphan, or if my parents had tried to buy me a better life by selling me to the Stellar Corporation. Corp orphans weren't given their birth records until they turned twenty, and they were well indoctrinated into whatever life they'd earned or been assigned.

But maybe I could have had something like this. Sitting on a log, sharing silence with someone who shared my blood, too.

I'd never been lonely on Earth with all my fellow orphans crowded into our classrooms and dormitories. Mostly the opposite, always trying to find a way to be alone. And I'd had Professor Orrion to talk to. So it took me a moment to identify the tightness under my breastbone as more than just the pinch of hunger.

I gave myself thirty seconds for the lump to rise in my throat before I swallowed it down and cleared my throat ruthlessly.

Loneliness would only drag me down out here. It would dull the edge I needed so desperately to survive. I'd always been a loner, even on overcrowded Earth, so the solitude was welcome. An affirmation of everything I was.

"Anikka, I'm not sure it's working."

Besides, I had BB.

"Keep your voice down. You'll scare the fish away."

BB flickered into existence and peered down into the water where a fin cut across the surface. "I don't think those things are afraid of anything."

"Maybe not," I whispered. "But there's no way they're invincible. I'm hungry and I feel like fish."

A slasherfin slipped through the water below me, and I hunkered down, my palms sweating on the para cord. Those things were huge. The moment one bit, I had to be ready to haul it in. There was even a stump of broken branch beside me that I could wrap the line around to keep it from getting away from me.

The slasherfin circled and came back as if to investigate.

I gave the para cord a little jiggle, and it darted away.

"Vent it." I blew out my breath and tried to wait patiently as the slasherfin wove around and around, getting closer by increments.

"Come on," I whispered. "You know you want it."

The slasherfin swam straight for my hook, and I braced my feet on the tree bridge.

Something slammed into the tree from the other side, and I stumbled. Another slam, and I fell to my knees, throwing out my good hand to catch myself, dropping the para cord in the process.

"What the—?"

I craned my head around and found a swarm of slasherfins charging the upstream side of the tree, slamming it over and over again. The tree hovered only a foot or so over the water, so they had no trouble leaping up to throw their weight against it.

"Seriously?" I shouted.

The para cord had fallen across the tree, luckily, and I snatched it, my legs trying to hold me to the log, like a massive, fractious horse. As the slasherfins bombarded the trunk, I shimmied from my perch. The tree shook beneath me. I didn't worry that they could knock it loose to float down the river—it was pretty well wedged in the mud on my side of the river and between the trees on the far side. But they could make it rock pretty good, and all they had to do was knock me into the river and I'd be swarmed.

I scooted as fast as I could, my heart pounding until I reached the wider end where the drop ship had snapped the tree off just above its roots. I didn't bother trying to climb down carefully, just leaped to shore and safety.

When I landed, I scrambled away from the water, panting.

The school of slasherfins dispersed back into the depths of the river, as if they knew their prey had escaped.

Prey. They'd been hunting me just as much as I'd been hunting them. They'd sent one of their number to distract me and keep my attention while they set up their attack from the rear.

"Vent you!" I shouted, aiming a rude gesture at the river. "I'm gonna eat you, I promise."

An explosive chitter made me spin. One of the monkey-lizard things stood on my platform going through my pack.

"Hey!"

I raced for the drop ship and scrambled up the smooth side. I really needed to make a ladder.

The monkey-lizard leaped away, just as I crested the drop ship and ran up the wing. It landed in the branches of another tree, one of my tomatoes in its mouth, and scampered up the trunk. I rocked to a halt at the edge of my platform and shook my fist. As if that would do anything. But it made me feel better.

"Bring that back, thief!"

"Jumpernicks."

"What?"

"They are climbers but also thieves. To nick is another way to say steal. Therefore I've named them—"

"Yeah, I get it." Then a second later, "I wonder if I can eat them."

BB made a disgusted noise. "You are obsessed with eating."

"When you can't go to the refrigerator for the next meal, then yeah, you get obsessed with eating."

The creature clung to the trunk, way out of reach, and cocked its head at me as it took a huge bite out of my tomato.

I let my fist fall and I collapsed on my platform.

"It's like they're all out to get me."

"This planet does seem particularly hostile."

I pressed my lips together. "I'm gonna beat them all," I said, then held my empty stomach. "Just as soon as I find something more to eat."

Flora of Daybreak ⚠

Itchbushes- itchy! repels alien wasps, causes rash, **avoid**

Fauna of Daybreak ⚠

Swarmstings- alien insects, swarm prey, deadly, **avoid**

Fox/wolf- large enough to drag body, travels and presumably hunts in packs, **avoid**

Assorted birds

Slasherfins- carnivorous, frequents waterways around the colony, intelligent enough to hunt back, **kill!**

Jumpernicks- monkey/lizards, gray scales and feathers, excellent climbers, eats fruits and vegetables, thief, **protect food**

Resources

Food- ration bars 3.5, reddi-meals (salisbury steak) 4, tomatoes, sweet potatoes, radishes

Water- liter bottles 2

First aid- gauze, painkillers 114, burn cream, antiseptic, flexi-bandage, antibiotics, antivirals, antihistamines, ice packs, heating packs, medical scissors, tape, sling, thermobrace

Lighter

Parachute and Para cord

Boots

Jumpsuit- 2

Hatchet

Cross bow

Soap

Knife

Tool kit

Tape

Sleeping bag

CHAPTER 14

Daybreak: Day 10

The next installment of the slasherfin vendetta took days and resulted in absolutely nothing. The slasherfins seemed to know exactly how to avoid my hook and didn't care at all about the dried bits of ration bar I used as bait. I tried making a rudimentary net with the para cord, but the vicious things tore right through it.

When they set up their trap again, trying to distract me on one side while swarming the other, I turned the trap back on them, rolling big rocks off the tree into their midst, but they scattered the moment my shadow fell across the water.

Finally, I propped the cross bow against the broken branches of the trunk and shot into their swarm. With so many concentrated in one spot, there was no way I could miss.

I lost five bolts that way before I realized the ones that hit were actually bouncing off.

Intelligent, ruthless, agile, and apparently bullet proof. The attributes of my enemy seemed endless. I'd even seen them snatch birds and jumpernicks from the banks when the more docile creatures tried to grab a drink.

The third day, I looked at the dwindling pile of fresh food I'd pilfered from the colony fields and sighed.

"I'm glad to see you are admitting defeat with the fish," BB said as I pulled one of the reddi-meals from my crate.

"I'm not admitting defeat. Just retreating. I'm hungry."

Reddi-meals were supposed to be prepped in an insta-cooker. But I didn't have one of those. Instead I poked a hole in the plastic wrap and squinted at the dried contents of the tray.

"It looks like tree bark," BB said. "You could just eat tree bark if you're that hungry."

"It'll be better warmed up."

I splashed some water in the bottom of the tray and held it over my fire.

"Anikka."

"Just wait," I said while the package started to steam.

Then it began to bubble. "Anikka."

"It's supposed to do that." At least, I assumed that was a good sign. It meant it was heating up.

A high-pitched whistle grew from the plastic and foil packaging and with a bang, my reddi-meal blew up, showering my camp with bits of boiling hot Salisbury steak.

I threw up my hand to protect my face and caught a fat gobbet against my cast.

I grimaced at the steaming hunk of brown goo.

"Now it looks like—"

"Don't say it!" I grumbled and shook it off to start over again.

It took two more tries to get the package to steam just right and come up with something edible. The result tasted more like tree bark than I wanted to admit to BB.

I set the greasy, lukewarm sludge down about half way through and glared at it.

"I need to try something else."

"Considering you are running out of reddi-meals to ruin and your odds of success with the fish have been...hm, let me calculate...zero, that seems like a good idea."

"Ouch," I said. "BB, your sarcasm filter burns."

"And that is a good thing?"

"Well, not for me."

"What is your new plan?"

"I have to eat. And fishing is obviously not working."

"I suggest foraging. Carefully, as there are plants here that clearly cause distress to the human body."

"No kidding." I raised my hand to scratch idly at my arm where the rash from the itchbush had finally subsided. "I can also try planting my own. It's gonna be a while before the next colony ship gets here, so I'll have time. I can keep the seeds from the last tomato and try sectioning a sweet potato to propagate it. I'm sure I read you could do that somewhere."

"That will help several months from now. It will not help today."

"No," I said, as my stomach growled. "I need a local guide. Someone to show me what I can and can't eat."

I leaned back against the trunk of my tree and found the familiar gray jumpernick sitting above me. It watched with avid eyes, but after that first encounter, I'd carefully hauled one of the empty crates across the river and stored my food inside where the thief couldn't get it.

Though it still visited every day. Perhaps I was now on its list of food stops.

"Hmm," I said, my lips curling into a smile. "I have an idea."

· · ·

Daybreak: Day 11

The next time the jumpernick left my camp, I crept after it, trying to keep up through the dense underbrush without rustling it too much.

All the studying in the world and all the reading I'd done wasn't actually a substitute for practical experience, and there hadn't been a lot of wilderness to creep around in left on Earth.

I pushed aside a hanging branch with my casted arm, making sure it was one of the ones I knew wouldn't give me a reaction. With the swelling finally gone, I'd casted my arm the day before, using the thermobrace I'd found in the colony's infirmary. The gel had just needed to be activated before I draped it over my arm, then it had heated enough to make my skin uncomfortable, but not enough to burn, and hardened into a carapace that would keep the break protected and immobile while it healed. Hard as a rock and waterproof, it wasn't coming off. Which might present a problem eventually, but I'd figure that out later.

Hopefully, I'd be able to start using the arm more now, though I could already tell the muscles had atrophied a bunch. My hand got tired and ached after I'd spent a few minutes on flexing exercises the night before.

But I needed to get better faster. Food, water, and shelter were the most important things in my life right now, but as soon as I had those under control, I planned to look for the colony. They had to have left a trail or clues I could follow.

The jumpernick leaped to a branch above me, and I hurried to keep it in sight, which was a lot harder from the ground than I'd anticipated.

My whole plan revolved around figuring out what it ate.

Since my tomato hadn't killed it, I was assuming that our digestive systems weren't too different, and I could reverse the process and steal its food.

The creature stopped, hanging off the trunk of a tree, and reached a little scaly fist into a hollow. When it pulled it out, it licked a bunch of fat white bugs out from between its fingers.

I made a face. "Bleh. Okay, I'm not sure I'm desperate enough to eat insects, yet," I whispered.

"Yet," BB said, keeping her voice as quiet as mine. "But the protein and nutrient content of Earth insects indicates they would be a valuable source of sustenance."

I made a face as I thought about it. "I'd have to get up the tree first."

"True."

The jumpernick moved on with an abrupt leap, and I was left scrambling to catch up.

I trusted BB to keep our location on the map updated, so I'd be able to get back to the riverbank. Hopefully, everything would still be there when I got back. Hopefully, the slash-erfins wouldn't grow legs and raid my camp while I was gone. A stupid thought, but I wouldn't put it past the brutes to achieve the impossible just to wreck my life.

The jumpernick scampered between two branches bearing blue-green leaves and disappeared from view.

"Crap," I muttered and raced forward.

I pushed through the branches and stopped to blink at the sight before me. Tall green trees rose in a grove surrounded by big, bright red mushroom caps. Or at least they looked like mushrooms.

Best of all, large blue fruit hung from the branches above us. The orange bushes surrounding the bases of the trees bowed under the weight of reddish-brown nuts.

A troop of the jumpernicks jabbered above, feasting on

the bounty of the grove. Jewel-colored birds flitted between the tops of the trees, their wings flashing in the filtered sunlight.

"Jackpot," I said, not worried about scaring away the jumpernicks now. And they didn't seem to care anyway, sitting safe so far above me. "Geez, I can't believe this is only like an hour's walk from camp. I could have been eating like a king this whole time."

"You have not had a chance to do a lot of exploring, considering the time you have devoted to the fruitless endeavor of fishing."

"Yeah, yeah, we all know your opinion. Just wait till I catch one."

I'd brought my pack in anticipation of finding something edible, and I started filling it with the nuts I could reach from the ground. I'd snagged a few leaves from things that had looked fairly harmless and hadn't given me an immediate rash, and I would do some further experimentation back in camp. Where I had the time and space to be violently ill if it went badly.

But for now, I grabbed for nuts like it was a trip to the grocery store. The little things packed tightly, but they weighed a ton, and I wanted to save room for the fruit.

I craned my neck back to stare up at the big, blue mango-looking things above. Normally, I'd never be able to get up there—I was no jumpernick—but the broad flat mushroom caps crowded close under the trees and formed platforms where I might be able to reach the fruit.

I laid a tentative hand on the lowest cap and then checked my palm. I gave it a couple of minutes, but when I didn't immediately start to itch or swell up, I went ahead and rested all my weight on it in order to climb up.

Luckily, I had two arms now, even if one ached when I tried to put weight on it.

With my pack on my back, I was just able to scramble aboard the mushroom cap and catch my balance. It gave under my boots like walking on a squishy trampoline, and I reached up to the next one.

A piece of the mushroom broke off in my hand, revealing a fleshy white interior. I turned it back and forth in the sun, wondering what a poisonous mushroom would even look like. Then I shrugged and tucked it into my pack. There would be time to experiment later and mushrooms on pizza had been delicious.

I had made it nearly twenty feet above the ground when I went to put my hand on the next cap. It shifted just a little differently than the others, and something in my gut made me yank away.

"What the—"

The mushroom cap...folded. It moved with deliberate slowness, but still faster than a plant ever should. Seriously, plants don't move. That was sort of the point. But this one's red surface collapsed through the middle, leaving a giant depression before it folded over completely into a big white bulb.

I rubbed my fingers together, feeling hem stick together, and stared at the plant. Moments later, the bulb unfolded, reforming into what looked exactly like the same mushroom caps I'd been climbing before.

"Aw, crap. It's carnivorous, isn't it? Why else would it fold up into a perfect little murder chamber?"

"Like a Venus fly trap," BB said.

"Only a million times bigger."

Still not big enough to really trap a full-grown human. Unless the stickiness got even more sticky in the center of the thing, I would be able to break free. But carnivorous plants had digestive enzymes, and who knew how fast those would work on an alien planet?

Best to steer clear so I didn't become lunch. Bad enough to succumb to a worthy enemy like the slasherfin. It was another thing to die inside a plant.

"Okay, so they mimic the mushrooms," I muttered and was doubly careful to test the big red caps before putting my weight on them.

The blue fruit hung finally within reach. The troop of jumpernicks didn't seem to mind my proximity, watching me curiously from their branches. In fact, it was kind of creepy the way they stared, eyes wide, like black pools. I kept an eye on them while I reached up and plucked a couple of ripe-looking fruit from above me. Were they just waiting for the right moment to attack me for stealing their food?

Maybe not. This grove seemed like a neutral zone. An oasis for the more docile creatures of Daybreak. As long as you ignored the Venus fly trap from hell.

The jumpernicks squabbled among themselves, but everyone seemed to have enough to eat that they didn't have to fight for it. And the birds swooped down, unbothered by me or the monkey-lizards.

I bit into a fruit, its juice sliding down my chin, and I closed my eyes in ecstasy.

"Oh my gosh. It tastes like a peach. A peach dipped in champagne." There was even a fizzy feeling that came with the flavor, and I scarfed the whole thing, finding the pit in the middle way too fast. I licked my fingers and then weighed the pit in my hand. Maybe I could dry it and plant my own little blue-peach tree back at camp. How long did trees take to fruit? Longer than a year, surely.

I shrugged and slipped the pit in the pocket of my jump-suit, anyway.

"Anikka, look."

I peered over the edge of the mushroom cap. Below us, a large creature stepped into the grove. Long, thin legs were obviously built for running, but it had a powerful body and two curling horns rose from a broad head. Its long purple fur was dappled, just like the sunlight coming through the trees.

"It's beautiful," I said.

I didn't want to disturb the creature. This grove was a neutral zone, a safe space, and I wanted to honor that, as stupid as it felt.

"Come on," I said, even though BB wasn't the one holding us up. "I'm going to gather as much of this as I can carry, and then we'll go home."

"Home?" BB said.

I hesitated. "Camp," I said. "We'll go back to camp."

Home was such a weird word for me, anyway. It didn't conjure up images of Earth or even the orphanage with Professor Orrion. It didn't make me think of the *Last Resort* or the colony.

My gut squirmed as I realized I didn't have one at all, either in reality or memory.

I swallowed and started grabbing blue-peaches. Camp was enough for now. Who needed a home when you were so busy trying to stay alive?

CHAPTER 15

Daybreak: Day 11

I made my way back to the river, keeping my head down to watch for jungle quicksand and my ears open for the buzzing of swarmstings. The wasps hadn't made an appearance in a while, and the quicksand was easy to spot if you were paying attention, but I wasn't about to get killed by being careless.

I lifted a branch of greenish brown leaves out of the way, and a shape about the size of a basketball darted at me, shrieking at the top of its lungs.

Without thinking, I struck out, batting the creature away, and it tumbled across the forest floor. It righted itself, and I got a good look at a scaly lizard-thing no taller than my knees. It stood on its hind legs, its front limbs folded along its back like a cross between a tiny tyrannosaurus rex and a chicken.

It hissed, and I stomped to keep it from lunging at me again. Deep scratches marred my arm where I'd punted the thing away from me.

It shrieked and charged me.

I waved my arms in the air and ran forward a few steps to scare it off.

"Congratulations," BB said as it darted around the nearest tree. "You vanquished the dino-chicken."

"You know," I said. "If you're not careful with that sarcasm filter, you'll really hurt my feelings."

"Oh no," BB said. "I'm sorry. The humor is supposed to make me more human. Not mean."

I snorted. "Don't worry. There's a sort of beauty in being so comfortable with someone you can make fun of each other." I gasped as I pulled the branch aside again. "Oh wow, look!"

A nest full of eggs was tucked under the bottommost leaves, mottled brown and green to blend in.

My mouth watered. "Omelets," I whispered, and stooped to transfer them carefully into the top of my pack.

A screech made me jump. The dino-chicken threw itself at me through the leaves, and I raised my arm to fend it off again. At this rate, I'd need something to armor up with. The cast only covered so much.

The dino-chicken bit and scratched at the hardened thermo-gel as I pushed it aside to finish collecting the eggs.

"Look, it's either your eggs or me, and right now, I'm choosing me."

I managed to close my pack one-handed and stood up. The change made me dizzy for a second, and I put my hand to my head.

As soon as I loomed tall again, the dino-chicken skittered away through the underbrush.

"Many Earth species lay multiple clutches of eggs, even if they are unfertilized," BB said, appearing on my wrist. "I wonder if the same is true here."

I paused, hand still raised, as I sucked in a breath. "Fresh eggs every day. Oh my gosh, you're right. I should catch it."

The leaves rustled, and I lunged for the dino-chicken. It shrieked and ran, despite its earlier ferocity. I landed on my elbows with an "oof."

When I tried to push myself up, the world swam, and I ended up on my hands and knees without any memory of getting there.

"Anikka, are you all right?"

"I don't feel good." It wasn't just the dizziness. Everything felt vaguely blurry, and when I turned my head, the jungle tilted. I dug my fingers into the loam to keep from falling off the face of the planet.

"Describe your symptoms?"

"Dizzy 'nd my head...is thick," I said around my uncooperative tongue. I tried to stand again, using the tree as a guide, and made it to my feet, only to stumble through the forest.

"Increased heart rate and breathing rate, loss of balance and coordination, slurred speech, and impaired thought processes. And a cursory blood scan indicates the presence of alcohol."

"What? I'm drunk?"

"Unbelievably, yes. But where would you have had access to alcohol?"

The blue fruit had left the lingering taste of peach on my tongue, complete with that fizzy feeling.

"The fruit." I fetched up against a tree to catch my balance. "I assumed it was safe because the jumpernicks were eating it." A groan slipped out of my mouth as I rubbed my face. "That's why they were all so happy. They go to that place to get drunk!"

I tried shaking my head to rid it of the fuzzy feeling, but it just made the trees spin.

Was this what everyone was always talking about when they wanted to hang out and drink? It didn't seem worth it to me.

The orphans of Stellar Corporation weren't above stealing beer from the caretakers occasionally, but I wasn't usually invited. Only once.

The memory went kind of hazy, the fuzziness taking away the edges of the other orphans' stares as I barged into the common room where they huddled around one of the far tables. I had a broken coffee maker in one hand and an electronics handbook in the other.

The other orphans looked between me and their contraband, guilt written in their expressions.

A boy stood up from one of the benches and smiled at me. Shaun? Steven? Something like that. He'd tried asking me out a couple of times before and seemed genuinely confused by the words "no, thank you." Not pushy or angry. Just confused.

I started counting down in my head till I could manage my escape.

"Hey, Anikka," Sam said. "Have a drink with us."

Someone in the back hissed a not-quite whisper. "Don't invite her."

"Yeah, she'll spoil it all."

I stiffened, teeth clenching hard enough to ache. "I've, uh, already got plans," I mumbled, holding up my book and my coffee maker. Professor Orrion had said he didn't mind if I took it apart.

I shuffled off to the side and hurried through the side door as Sean was struggling off his bench.

"Let her go, Simon," one of the others said. "She's never been any fun."

I sniffed to myself. I didn't usually mind my solitude. It was hard enough to find here. But it did hurt that the kids I'd grown up with still didn't get me at all. Just because I'd known I wanted to leave Earth since I was five, and I'd learned early that I wasn't afraid of hard work. Besides, what else was there to do in the dormitories?

I pressed my hand into my woozy head and squinted at the nearest tree, which tilted and swayed in a way I knew wasn't natural. Somehow, I didn't feel like I'd missed anything by turning Simon down.

"Yours is a mild reaction," BB said. "If you keep walking, I can get you back to the drop ship in forty-nine minutes."

"This is mild?"

I tried to go in a straight line, but my feet didn't want to cooperate. "Maybe I'll jus' sit here and rest until it wears off. It wears off, right?"

I shrugged my pack down my shoulders and headed for a nice big tree with shielding roots.

"Anikka, it is a bad idea to remain in an unsafe location in your impaired state—Behind you!"

BB's words were my only warning.

I spun, dropping my pack, and caught a huge blue shape launching itself at me.

I let my legs go limp—not hard with all the balance issues I was having—and the attacker sailed right over me. More shapes boiled out of the trees.

The pack of foxy wolf creatures surrounded me, all long blue fur fading to purple with tufted ears and fluffy tails. I'd nearly forgotten them. It had been days since I'd seen any signs of their stalking presence around camp.

I grabbed for the knife at my belt and held it out, point wavering as I spun in a circle, trying to keep all of them in sight at once.

There were only four, but that would be plenty to overwhelm me. The dappled one with lighter spots arrayed along its spine hung back, watching me with its head down.

The one that had launched itself at me had the darkest fur. It slunk closer, its two compatriots following, their teeth bared.

"I guess we're done with the stalking phase," I said, words still slurring.

The lead creature shied, like my voice had startled it. It took a couple of dancing steps back, but then it snapped its teeth and kept coming.

I swung my knife wildly, missing everything I aimed at but clipping the last wolf as it turned to snarl. Red blood dripped down its muzzle and a detached portion of my mind that wasn't still drunk was interested to note the color was the same as on Earth.

"You don' wanna eat me," I said, swinging again. "I promise, I don' taste good."

The leader of the pack pulled back its lips. It didn't look nearly so pretty now as it had in the moonlight.

It darted forward, jaws snapping.

Music blared out from BB's speaker, a jarring cacophony of techno metal and grunge electronica, two styles that should never go together.

The pack leader jerked back with a yelp and pawed at its ears.

The other two immediately faded back into the trees, but the leader weaved back and forth, whining as if it couldn't quite let me go.

I opened my mouth to scream at it, joining the disharmony.

It raced away, disappearing with a flash of a purple tipped tail.

The dappled member of the pack waited a moment more,

cocking its head, like the music didn't hurt *its* ears. Then it followed its brethren.

I collapsed against a wide root as soon as I was convinced the coast was clear. "Great idea, BB."

"It is only a good idea until the slinkwolves decide to come back. You should make haste."

"Slinkwolves?"

"You put me in charge of naming the things we find. The way they snuck up on you gave me the idea."

Yeah, except I wasn't sure I wanted anything that tried to eat me to sound that cool.

I scooped up my pack and traveled as quickly as I could through the forest. My head still swam and nothing in my body wanted to work right, mind and muscles included. But I concentrated on every step, and BB kept playing her awful choice of music, scaring away anything with a sense of hearing within miles.

When I got back to my shelter, I didn't even bother unloading my pack. I climbed onto my platform and fell asleep with it wrapped in my arms.

Flora of Daybreak ⚠

Itchbushes- itchy! repels alien wasps, causes rash, **avoid**
Drunk-peaches- delicious, alcoholic, **experiment to find a safe way to eat**
Red caps- giant mushrooms, edible?
Not-red-caps- carnivorous plant, mimics mushrooms
Nuts- edible? gods of all worlds, I hope so

Fauna of Daybreak ⚠

Swarmstings- alien insects, swarm prey, deadly, **avoid**
Slinkwolves- blue and purple, fox-like, 60-80 pounds, hunts in packs, **avoid**
Assorted birds
Slasherfins- carnivorous, frequents waterways around the colony, intelligent enough to hunt back, **kill!**
Jumpernicks- monkey-lizards, gray scales and feathers, excellent climbers, eats fruits and vegetables, thief, **protect food**
Dino-chickens- eggs!

Resources

Food- ration bars 3.5, reddi-meals (salisbury steak) 1, tomatoes, sweet potatoes, nuts, drunk-peaches, eggs, mushrooms
Water- liter bottles 2, river

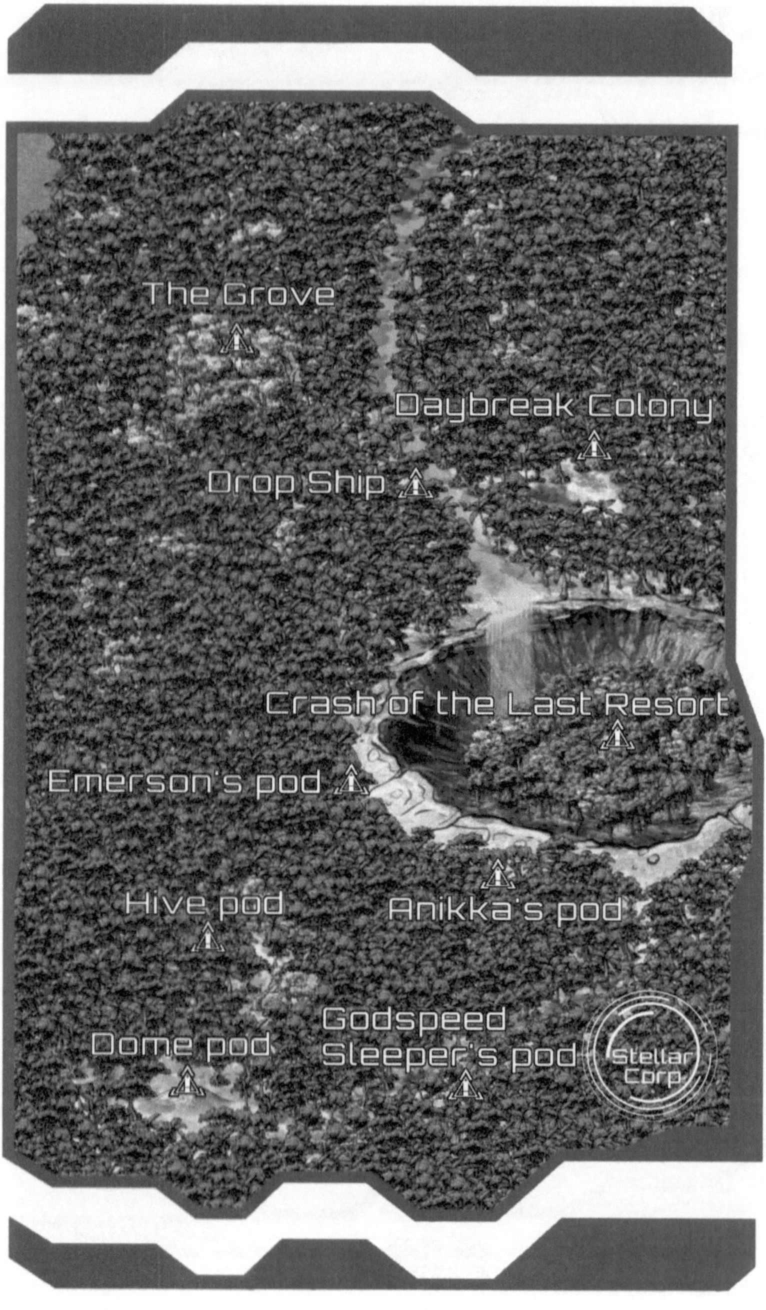

The Grove
Daybreak Colony
Drop Ship
Crash of the Last Resort
Emerson's pod
Hive pod
Anikka's pod
Godspeed
Sleeper's pod
Dome pod
Stellar Corp

CHAPTER 16

Daybreak: Day 12

The slinkwolves didn't come back that night, either because I was too high up for them or because BB had scared them into submission. I woke in the morning with a dry mouth and an aching head. A splash of my precious water went toward rinsing my face and got the crusty gunk out of my eyes.

I hated to give up such a promising food source, but I couldn't risk a hangover every time I ate. There had to be some way to make the fruit safe.

"Perhaps boiling them or drying them would reduce the alcohol content enough to make them safe for frequent consumption," BB said as I laid out my haul from the day before.

I rubbed my hands over my face. "Yeah. And I need to be more careful about how I experiment with food. This is enough to keep me alive for a few days, but only if I don't poison myself first."

From then on, I followed a strict protocol. I only allowed

myself one new thing a day, and I left plenty of time back at camp to monitor my reactions.

The nuts turned out to be tasty and filling. They were as big as chestnuts and soft, like macadamia nuts, but tasted like a smoky plum. I buried them in my crate to keep the jumpernicks from stealing them.

The greens I'd picked weren't anything special, more like the world's blandest salad. Boiling them as a weak tea made them no better. Only wetter. At least they didn't get me drunk.

Following another jumpernick had led me to a cluster of plants that reminded me of brown carrots. It had dug them up to munch, and I'd wasted no time raiding the area. But when I tried them, I spat the first bite out and wasted half my drinking water for the day trying to rinse my mouth out. They tasted like a swig from a salt shaker. Bleh.

I tucked them into my crate and resolved to try to make them edible later. Maybe they'd make a good broth or soup.

On the other hand, boiling the drunk-peaches made a kind of sweet peachy slush.

"Juice!" I cried.

But it got me just as drunk as before, if not more, and I spent the next morning groaning things like "that's just not fair" in my sleeping bag.

I tried drying next. I'd built a lean-to next to my fire in order to direct the smoke away from my platform. This would work for a drying rack, but I needed to weave some of the bluish river grasses together to make a mat, leaving gaps between so air could circulate around the fruit.

Another piece of metal made an okay cutting board, but the drunk-peaches left my utility knife sticky, and I had to chance the riverbank to scrub it clean.

A couple of slasherfins lurked in the shallows, their pointed tails cutting the surface of the water as they swam back and forth, waiting for me to get too close. But we'd done this before plenty of times now. Each morning, I crept as close to the lapping river as I could, then I dug into the soft bank to create a little pool where the water could gather as it flowed by. It meant sifting the silt out of the bottom of the pot after boiling, but it was worth it if I could gather water for the day without risking life and limb to the slasherfins' jaws.

I glared at the enormous fish as I scrubbed my knife, stomach rumbling. Anything that mean couldn't possibly taste good, but dang it, it was a matter of pride now. All I could think whenever I saw one was how badly I wanted to eat it.

With the knife at least reasonably clean, I checked the fishing line I'd rigged by tying one end of the para cord to a branch of the tree-bridge, but of course, it was empty. I didn't have anything at all enticing as bait, and the slasherfins were wise to my system by now.

I'd have to settle for dino-chicken eggs for lunch. Not exactly a hardship. I'd already enjoyed three of them. But I'd have to trek back to the nest and see if the thing had left any more.

On my way back toward my drying racks, BB cleared her throat. Or at least, made a noise like she had a throat to clear.

"You have a watcher."

"What?" I glanced over my shoulder. It took me a moment to find what she was referring to, but when I did, I froze. The dappled slinkwolf crouched in the shadows of the trees, nearly invisible because of its coloring.

"What's it doing?" I whispered.

BB's holographic eyes narrowed on the creature. "Nothing. It's just sitting there. Waiting."

The slinkwolf's eyes remained on me, even though I clearly saw it. It didn't try to slink away or hide again. In fact, it sat up, and its mouth fell open a bit so it could pant, ears forward.

I was so distracted watching my watcher that I walked right into the hole I'd dug for water that morning. I tripped and landed on my hands and knees.

"Ouch." I rubbed my sore arm and glanced at the slinkwolf, but it didn't move or try to take advantage of my distraction.

"Maybe the pack decided I wasn't worth stalking after the other day," I said, rubbing my ankle. "Maybe they set a guard to keep an eye on me in case I do anything interesting."

"The last thing I want is for a pack of predators to find you interesting," BB said.

I grinned as I pulled my feet out of the hole. "I don't know. It's kind of cute. Maybe it would be nice to have a friend."

BB glared at me.

"I'm kidding. You're the only friend I need, BB."

I kicked the thick mud from my boots, but it stuck horribly, making them heavy.

"Hmm." I frowned and examined the hole in the riverbank. One side had collapsed under the flow of the river, like normal. I had to re-dig it every day because the bank was so soft. But the other side had held even after I'd fallen in.

I knelt, eyes narrowing, and smeared my fingers down the dirt wall. They came away sticky.

"This soil appears different from the rest of the bank," BB said, popping up on my wrist.

"Clay," I said. "I think it's clay. Or at least, a lot like Earth clay. Maybe I can use it."

"Well, at least you don't want to eat it," BB said as I dug out big clumps of the heavy soil.

"Har har."

Bricks seemed handy to have, but even though the clay

was already wet and malleable, I didn't have any kind of mold to shape them with. Everything I made came out lumpy and unbalanced. I lined the misshapen bricks up beside my fire in the full sun, hoping they'd dry out enough to stack.

As an infra-engineer, I was more familiar with wood and cement and rebar than I was with clay, but I experimented with mixing in some straw to help it keep its shape.

It took a lot longer than I'd thought it would, and the slinkwolf watched avidly the entire time. The drunk-peaches took almost four days to shrivel up, but the bricks took five to get to the point where I could pick one up and it wouldn't instantly crumble. And even then, if I dropped one from any kind of height, it shattered easily.

I had the sneaking suspicion there were a lot more steps to making bricks that I was missing.

But they made a decent little wall around my fire. I laid some sticks across the top, far enough above that they wouldn't instantly catch fire, and I lined up more bricks on top to create a little oven.

"It worked!" I told BB as we stared into the opening at the glowing bricks.

"Wonderful, now you just need something to cook in it."

"Fish would be nice."

"I suggest more fruit. Perhaps this will dry them faster. And at least fruit sits still while you try to murder it."

Overhead, thick clouds rolled across the sky, spreading shadows on the crater down river, but there was still plenty of time to take a trip to the grove before dark.

With all the back and forth I'd done, I'd created my own path through the forest so I could follow that instead of depending on memory or BB's updated map. It passed by three different dino-chicken nests, which were easy to find once I knew what I was looking for, and I'd gotten much better at sneaking eggs out of them without tempting the wrath of the tiny tyrannosaurus rex.

This trip I returned to my camp with a pack full of nuts and drunk-peaches, 13 eggs, and only four deep scratches.

I stood on the edge of the forest and surveyed my camp with a little hitch in my breath. It might not have been home, but I was proud of it, anyway.

A heat haze rose from the brick oven where it waited for the next batch of fruit. Little planters made out of flattened metal debris stood lined up along the riverbank where I could water them easily. I'd saved some of the tomato seeds from my last tomato, along with cut up bits of sweet potatoes and radish, and started my own little garden. There were even some green shoots coming up from the potatoes and the tomatoes that I was really hopeful about.

I'd lashed together a spindly ladder with para cord and propped it against the drop ship so I could reach my platform easier, and I'd painstakingly carved steps into the end of the tree bridge with my hatchet to make the journey across easier.

It was actually starting to look like a proper camp. Maybe tomorrow I'd start experimenting with drying vines to make more lashings. That way I could expand my platform, build a railing, and add some more space.

Thunder rumbled across the crater and up the river. At the edge of the forest, the slinkwolf stood abruptly and bounded into the brush, the tip of its tail flashing purple before disappearing entirely.

"Must not like thunder," BB said.

"Well, your loud noises did scare them away before."

The clouds had tumbled closer, big steel-gray monuments with bulbous outcroppings that roiled above me.

"Huh, maybe we'll get some rain," I said to BB.

"Likely. According to your Daybreak handbook, this continent experiences a monsoon season every six months for a month."

"Well, we haven't seen any yet—"

I broke off as a flash of lightning made me duck and another peal of thunder echoed loud enough to rattle the ladder against the hull of the drop ship.

"Perhaps you shouldn't stand in the open," BB said.

I started for the ladder, but as I set my foot on the top rung, rain came sheeting down. Not a little drizzle. Not a pitter-patter as it started slow. It was like the clouds opened up and poured their contents in a flood from the sky.

I laughed out loud and flung my arms over my head so the rain pinged against my metal hand. Even cleaning the mud out of the joints every night, I still worried about dirt getting into the seals. The thumb joint had started grinding a little.

I held it out to let the rain wash away the lingering filth.

"What's so funny?" BB asked.

"Nothing. It's just...rain! I've had to be so careful with water, and here it is coming out of the sky."

I gasped and raced for my cook pots. I'd made two so far, and I hauled them out to gather the rain so I wouldn't have to boil water for the next couple of days.

My little seedlings were doing all right, though I would bring them under the shelter of the drop ship wing before they got pummeled too hard.

I lifted my face to let the water rinse away days' worth of grime and sweat and that gave me an idea. I fetched the soap from my crate, and after a second of hesitation, I stripped out of my jumpsuit and stood in the rain to soap myself and my clothes before letting the water sluice the suds away.

My hair was a tangled mess after days without brushing, but I took the time to work some soap through the strands and then comb it out with my fingers, ridding it of the last of the cryo-goo.

I couldn't even begin to describe the difference, feeling somehow lighter and more grounded all at once. Amazing the difference a shower could make.

"Feel better?" BB asked as I tossed my jumpsuit up onto the hull of the drop ship. I wouldn't be able to dry it out until the sun came out, but at least it would be clean now.

"Much better. You can see why they call rain 'life-giving' back on Earth. I'm gonna live forever!" I shouted the last bit into the storm and it answered by sending a fork of lightning across the sky.

I laughed maniacally and spun around under the raging sky. All I had on was my tank top and a pair of boxer briefs, but there was no one to see except BB and some local wildlife.

"I'm glad you feel that way," BB said as I twirled. "But the water is rising."

"What?" I whipped around and stared at the river. BB was right. The hole I'd dug that morning for water had long since disappeared under the edge of the river, and a couple of the trees upriver were already about a foot deep, with their roots nearly covered.

"Oh, crap." At this rate, the river would swamp my campsite in less than an hour. "Crap!" I raced for the pots of seedlings that waited on the bank.

One by one, I grabbed the metal containers and ferried them up to the platform under the dubious shelter of my parachute roof. I'd had plans to dry the big fronds from the drunk-peach trees to make a better roof, but food and water had always seemed more urgent. Maybe it was time to step up my schedule. The parachute barely covered enough to squeeze me, my sleeping bag, and the six little planters under its dubious shelter. Water flowed down the steep sides of the parachute and poured off the ends in sheets.

My crate full of food sat under the wing of the drop ship, behind a barricade of branches I'd erected to keep out thieving jumpernicks and stalking carnivores, but I had no idea how far this flood would reach. The rain jeopardized everything I'd fought for.

I splashed through at least an inch of water at the bottom of my ladder and hurried to throw the lid off my crate.

"Anikka, I do not like you taking this long in this water. We do not know enough about water-born illnesses to—"

"I'm not leaving everything I've worked for. And if I don't rescue the food, I'll die anyway." It was all I could think about.

BB's face went tight with worry, and I regretted snapping at her, but at least she stopped prattling about her worries.

I'd brought in the current batch of dried drunk-peaches that morning and hadn't gotten the next out yet, but the crate held everything fresh that I'd foraged in the last few days.

I loaded my pack up as full as it would go with eggs and nuts and bruised drunk-peaches and the weird salty root thing, then transferred it up to my platform. I could probably get the rest in one trip if I was fast.

The water was rising fast enough to reach my calves when I climbed down again, but at least it wasn't rushing down the river like a tidal wave. Yet. I knew nothing about what lay upriver, but I did know that back on Earth, flash floods could start in mountains miles away and wash away anything downriver. The same could happen here.

Best to be done as fast as possible. Plus, the heavy rain was battering my bare shoulders and raising goosebumps along my arms. At least I'd stopped to lace my boots on after my impromptu shower.

I loaded my pack and closed the flap just as BB flickered to life on my wrist.

"Anikka, behind you!"

I whipped around to catch the sharp point of a fin cutting the surface of the water, ripples trailing behind it even in the pouring rain.

"Oh, vent this."

The long sleek shape slipped through the shallows, and I danced back a step, feet slipping on the muddy bottom.

Three more shapes languidly cut me off from the ladder, their long forms slipping past each other, so they each took turns making my day worse.

"Oh, come on," I yelled at the water. "I was supposed to be safe on the bank." I slung my pack over my shoulder and snatched up one of the stouter branches from my barricade and brandished it at the fish. That cross bow was doing me no good up on my platform.

Not that it had done a lot of good in my hand, either.

A slasherfin swam toward me, and I swept my branch around to smack it on the head. It missed and cut through the water just in front of its nose, making it swerve away. The water was still shallow enough I could see it clearly.

At least I had the hull of the drop ship against my back, so they couldn't sneak up on me like they usually did.

"You must get out of reach," BB said. "You will not be able to match them here in the water."

"I'm trying," I snapped.

I swept the branch around, making the fish dart away. Then I used the opening to race for the ladder. Water dragged at my legs, slowing me down.

Even a makeshift weapon would be better than nothing, but with one arm still broken and weak, I couldn't hang onto the branch and grab for the ladder with my good hand. So I dropped it.

I lunged for the nearest rung and grabbed hold just as something heavy slammed into my thigh. I twisted to avoid the teeth that I knew would be coming and snatched my utility knife from the outside pocket of my pack. The broken arm was weaker, but I could force my fingers to grip the hilt.

My metal hand creaked on the wood of my ladder as I swung from the rung.

The long muscular fish used its momentum to spin around and aim its jaws for me again. I had just enough time to haul myself up one more rung before it struck. I kicked out, and it latched onto my boot.

It thrashed, twisting its body to try to yank me from the ladder. Vent it, the thing was strong.

The ladder shook, my primitive lashings creaking and snapping under the strain.

I screamed and wrapped my good arm around the fraying pieces of my ladder. Then I hauled my foot up and the front half of the slasherfin came with it.

The hilt of the knife slid against my wet palm, but I gripped it tight enough to hurt before plunging it into the slasherfin's side.

It jerked in pain and let go of my boot, splashing back into the water.

I hauled myself up the rest of the fraying ladder and sprawled on the hull of the drop ship, sobbing.

"Anikka?"

I dragged air in and out of my lungs, spluttering in the wet.

"Anikka?" BB's voice finally penetrated the panic coursing through me. "Are you all right?"

"No," I groaned.

I rolled over and took stock of myself. My fingers were still wrapped around the knife, slick with rain and blood. My foot felt bruised, but I wouldn't be able to tell if the slasherfin had torn my boot and broken the skin until I could pause long enough to get my footwear off.

I stood with a wince, keeping my balance carefully on the curved hull of the drop ship. The slasherfins circled my shelter, their tails cutting the surface of the water like they didn't care if I saw them. There were still four of them, so I hadn't managed to kill the one I'd stabbed.

The water wasn't rising anymore. It was probably about hip deep now, but seemed to be holding steady there.

The oven I'd worked so hard on the last few days was completely swamped, and my crate was now underwater. At least I'd saved the food, though I had no way to cook the eggs and the fruit I'd dried would only last so long.

Despair crept up my chest, threatening to overwhelm me as I stared at my ruined campsite, but I pushed it down. I focused on the anger and stoked the flames of my frustration until I growled and threw back my head to scream.

I'd felt safe, almost. Comfortable, like I was getting the hang of living here. I'd found a source of food, I had water. I was building myself a place to live, and it wasn't that bad.

And then Daybreak had changed the rules.

I spread my arms, knife still clutched in one hand, and let the water run down my upturned face.

"You can't kill me!" I shouted at the planet. "I'm still here! And I'm gonna be here tomorrow. And the next day. I'm not giving up, and I'm not dying! I'm living!"

CHAPTER 17

Daybreak: Day 22

The rest of that day and night, I sat under my roof, clutching my seedlings and glaring at the surrounding water. It didn't rise any higher, but I also didn't trust Daybreak not to catch me off guard while I slept. So I sat awake, tearing at dried fruit with my teeth.

My eyes burned by the time the moon rose, huge and striped, and shed its bright light across the water. The slash-erfins circled my shelter once more and then cut across the shallow water, back toward the river. Or where the river used to be.

I sat up and waited, every muscle clenched.

Dawn came slowly. As the sun rose and streaks of colors undulated across the sky, the water retreated, reflecting the brilliant oranges and pinks and blues and purples above me.

The edge of the flooding crept back and back until the river returned to its normal size. It rushed past the bank, twice as fast as before, carrying broken branches, leaves, and one exhausted elk-like creature.

The poor thing swept past on the way to the waterfall by the cliff, warning me that even if the water had retreated, I should still stay clear of the edge.

"Is it bad that I hope the slasherfins eat it first?" BB asked, popping up on my wrist.

I didn't say anything. *I* hoped the water would sweep the fish over the edge and dash them on the rocks below, but they were too smart and too strong to get caught in the current.

Every muscle ached after my sleepless night, so I stood and stretched them. Then I brushed off my butt and slid down the hull of the drop ship. My ladder had floated away sometime during the night.

I planted my hands on my hips and surveyed the wreckage of my camp.

My boots sunk into the mud that stretched from the river's edge past the drop ship. The water-logged crate had at least remained trapped in the space under the drop ship's wing, but a pile of wet clay and straw was all that was left of my oven.

I blew out my breath. An ache still filled my throat, but the sense of loss had dulled a little as I'd sat in my tree and fumed. Anger was good for clearing my head, at least.

"What are we going to do?" BB asked. "All that work. All that effort is just gone. It's going to be—"

"We're going to rebuild," I said, before she could spiral into dire scenarios. "That's what we're gonna do. We're gonna keep going."

It was my only option. Unless I wanted to lie down and let the planet win.

There was an easy answer to that.

I itched to gather up what I could and replace the rest, but first I needed to take stock. The rains could come back at any time and the area would flood even faster.

I turned toward the forest and jumped.

The slinkwolf sat staring at me. It didn't even try to blend in with the foliage now.

My lips thinned, and I spread my arms wide. "Not dead yet," I called.

It perked its ears forward.

"It left before the rains started," BB said. "It must have known the flood was coming."

And if I'd been smart enough, I would have seen that as a red flag.

I kept my eyes on it, though it didn't seem inclined to come any closer as I slung my cross bow over my shoulder and picked up a big stick like the one I'd used against the slasherfins.

As soon as I straightened up with my makeshift weapon, the slinkwolf disappeared into the underbrush.

"BB, keep watch. I don't want it sneaking up on me."

"Of course."

I set out with my cross bow over my shoulder and the branch in hand.

The wet ground extended past the drop ship for a couple of tree lengths, so I could guess how far the flooding had gone. I hadn't even noticed how the ground rose a bit here on the way to the drunk-peach grove, but everything beyond was dry—or at least drying—while the ground stretching back to the drop ship had turned to soupy mud.

My ladder lay trapped under the tangled leaves of an itch-bush on the border of the flood zone. I used my stick to drag it free of the noxious leaves before picking it up. One rung had ripped off completely, leaving behind a large gap and the rest of the para cord had frayed around the joints.

I sighed and propped it on my shoulder to carry back to

camp. The para cord would run out soon, so I'd have to come up with something else to use as lashings.

I spent the rest of the morning fixing my ladder and hauling the water-logged crate up onto my platform. Originally, I'd thought there wasn't enough room, but now I couldn't afford to leave it down in the mud. I'd sleep on top of it if I had to.

My seedlings had made it through the storm, though they looked a little battered. I set them out in the sun on top of the drop ship so that maybe they would perk up a bit.

Clouds crawled across the sky around midday, just like the day before, and only a couple of hours later, the first crash of thunder rolled up the river from the direction of the crater.

The slinkwolf stopped stalking the perimeter of the forest, and glanced at me, as if waiting to see what I'd do. I didn't waste any time climbing back up onto the drop ship and securing my ladder to one of the landing struts so it wouldn't float away again. By the time I turned back, the slinkwolf had gone.

Sure enough, as I stood on the hull, I could watch the storm front sweep up the river. A sheet of gray shot through with lightning raced across the jungle.

It didn't take nearly as long today for the river to swell its banks. Only an hour after the rain hit, the slasherfins circled the drop ship through the shallow water.

I spared them a glare before sighing. My clothes hadn't even fully dried out from the night before. But if I wanted to get anything done, I'd have to resign myself to working in the wet. I could assume this would be a daily occurrence for who knew how long, and I couldn't afford to sit huddled under my roof every afternoon.

So in the end, the rains helped divide my days. I spent the

mornings foraging or building up my camp and the afternoons perched in my tree working on the things I could reach.

I'd run out of boards to build my platform, but the floods swept deadfall into my camp on a daily basis, which I could cut down with my hatchet. Within a couple of days, I had another section of platform built with a crude step in between.

I couldn't really dry anything when it rained every day, but I found low trees near the river with fronds that looked more like palms back on Earth. I built a frame over my two platforms, and when I lined up the fronds in overlapping layers, they directed the rain off to the sides with minimal leaks. And that way I could take down the parachute, which had started to fray.

Hanging those brought my attention to the vines covering the trunk and my need for more lashings. I tapped my teeth, then yanked experimentally on one.

Tiny roots held it to the bark, but if I pulled away from the tree instead of straight down, they came off a lot easier. And once in my hand, the fibrous vine unraveled like a rope twisted the wrong way, breaking into multiple strands of wiry flexible fibers.

I didn't need them yet, but I started a collection.

With my platform relatively dry, it was time to look at rebuilding my oven.

During the mornings, I collected rocks and clay from the riverbank and hauled them up to my platform. It took way too long, working in shifts like that, but once I got enough material up out of the flood zone, I could keep my new oven out of danger.

Soon, I had a cozy little kitchen area on my extended platform. The roof kept the worst of the water off the oven, so it stayed intact even in the rain, and my crate kept the food safe from thieves and scavengers and doubled as a table. The original platform I kept as my sleeping area.

I was going to have to leave camp again, eventually. The fruit I'd managed to dry before the rainy season hit was getting dangerously low, and the fresh stuff was a lot softer than I would have dared eat back on Earth. And I could only stomach the weird tea I'd made out of the local greens and an overabundance of water for so long.

But I was terrified of leaving in the morning and getting cut off from my shelter by the flood.

I mulled over the problem as I fed my fire with some deadfall that had floated into camp and slid the last batch of sliced drunk-peaches in to dry.

The fire smoked, belching black clouds through the opening of my oven, but I didn't have any dry wood to burn. Everything was wet these days.

Hey, maybe it would give the drunk-peaches some extra flavor.

I coughed and waved my hand to clear the smoke. It burned my nose and stung all the way down my throat.

"Anikka?" BB said.

My throat clogged and nothing would come out. I doubled over, coughing.

"Anikka?" Her voice went sharp and shrill.

I waved a hand to indicate I was okay. It was just some minor smoke inhalation. I could get enough air to breathe, so I wasn't worried. The part that didn't seem so normal was the fuzzy strands of gray flowing into my vision from the sides.

I hit the ground with a thud I barely felt.

A bright streak of pain from my metal arm woke me.

I sucked in a breath and coughed, harsh and jagged.

"Ugh, what was that?" I said, shaking my arm.

"I had to awaken you using an electric shock."

"You shocked me?" I sat up abruptly. My eyes felt gritty, like I'd just woken up from a nap.

"I had to. You fell asleep and were unresponsive."

I squinted up at the sky and a shaft of cold went through me as I realized there were stars glinting through the branches. I took a couple of deep breaths.

"Okay, I took an unplanned nap. But there are better options for waking me up than shocking me."

BB didn't even look contrite. "I'm so sorry I was worried for your safety."

I snorted and stood. The world swayed a little, and I braced against the tree trunk to glance at the oven, the fire nearly burnt out now.

I rubbed my eyes. "So that particular wood makes you fall asleep if you burn it."

BB flickered, and her light lit up the stack I'd made beside the oven. "I believe that deadfall looks just like the wood of the drunk-peach tree."

"Great." I kicked the pile. "And that's all I have left." My stomach growled, but the batch of fruit I'd been drying looked black and crispy, completely ruined.

"I really need to get back to the grove."

I stepped to the edge of the platform and stared at the water below. With the clouds gone and the moon out, I could make out the rippling edge of the flooding. It was deep enough around my tree that the slasherfins circled beneath, waiting for me to fall.

From here, it was only about twenty feet or so to the next big tree with wide branches low enough to be useful. Its roots were high and dry at the base.

I tapped my lips with my metal fingers.

"What are you thinking?" BB asked. "I don't like when you think without me."

"If only I could build a bridge," I said. "And extend my domain just a little bit more, then I could get back here without getting my feet wet or risking my life with the slasherfins."

BB peered down at the water. "Hmm. It's a long way. You would need some sort of suspension bridge to reach that far. We definitely do not have the material for that."

"No..." I trailed off, glancing up at the branches above. "But then, maybe it doesn't have to be as complicated as a bridge."

I stepped back into my sleeping area and took stock of the vines I'd pulled from my tree. I had several good lengths. The stuff didn't like to break. It was too fibrous, like a rope, so it had come down in one long piece. I stretched it between my hands and yanked once or twice. It should hold my weight.

I waited till morning when the flood waters receded, since I didn't want to accidentally strand myself if my plan didn't work. Though I spent a couple extra hours that evening starting a new ladder with the leftover branches I'd gathered and some of the shorter sections of vines.

As the day dawned and the spectacular light show flared across the sky, I climbed up my tree, my stomach protesting the fact that I'd run out of my stockpile of food the night before.

I used my utility knife when I needed extra handholds and shimmied my way up the trunk to the next enormous branch overhead. I slung my leg over the wide limb and slid the knife back into its sheath along my leg.

"Is this really necessary?" BB asked. Her hologram had its eyes shut tight, as if she didn't use the sensors and the little camera in my hand to monitor her surroundings.

"Of course, why?"

"Just be quick about it. I don't like heights."

I paused halfway along the branch. "Can AIs be afraid of anything?"

"Fear of heights is part of my personality." Her voice went crisp. "A part that I added."

"Why on Earth would you add something bad? Can't you just change it?"

"I cannot just change it." BB's hologram put her hands on her hips. "That's the whole point. I have picked these things to give me a more human perspective to avoid the dangers of integration. Phobias and foibles are very human. I have chosen one to be part of my personality, and I am sticking with it, thank you very much. I do not give up when something gets hard."

"Okay, okay. Sorry, I suggested you make life a little easier for yourself."

BB's hologram blinked out. "Just let me know when you're done trying to get yourself killed."

I suppressed a laugh as I secured the end of the vine as far out on the branch as I felt like I could go without falling.

The vine was long enough I could tuck the end into my belt as I climbed back down to the platform.

"Okay, I'm done," I told BB as I made my way to the ground.

I traipsed across the open space between the trees, dragging my second ladder and the vine to the tree I'd marked the night before. The roots weren't exactly dry after all the rain, but there wasn't a line of water up the trunk like the trees closer to the river.

I propped up my ladder and climbed up to the sturdiest branch I could reach.

"All right. Here goes nothing." I pulled the end of the vine from my belt and wrapped the excess length around my good arm.

I gritted my teeth and jumped, aiming for the twenty-foot gap between the two trees.

My arm burned as I swung over the space that had been flooded just the night before.

"Ha ha!" The exhilarated noise burst from my lungs, startling a few birds into flight.

Quicker than I realized, my platform slid by under my boots, and if I kept swinging, I'd lose my chance to land and just end up back at the other tree. Or worse, in the empty space in between.

I closed my eyes and let go.

And thudded to the platform, flat on my butt.

I blinked. As soon as I had my breath back, I leaped to my feet and whooped. "It worked!"

"Ta-da. You have invented the swing," BB said.

I rolled my eyes. "A swing that will get me back into my tree in case it floods. I just need to keep the ladder over there and attach the vine somehow, so it's always ready to go."

"All right, that is useful."

"Damn right," I said, the success of it making my chest swell.

That morning, I set off for the grove, confident I could get back into my tree even if I was caught out in the rain.

The slinkwolf followed me. It stalked my path, several tree lengths to my right, not bothering to hide its interest.

I kept one eye on it the whole trek, but it didn't come any closer. It really was acting like a guard or a scout.

I made stops at my favorite dino-chicken nests to collect the eggs they'd stockpiled in the last few days. I'd sorely missed mushroom omelets during the flooding.

The dino-chickens were at least smart enough to build

their nests high enough to avoid the rising river, which was more than I could say for me, and I raided three of them before I reached the drunk-peach grove.

I quickly got to work loading my pack with mushroom pieces and ripe blue fruit while the jumpernicks chattered and squabbled above me.

"How can you think with all that racket?" BB asked. Her voice didn't disturb the creatures in the least.

I glanced up at the gang of monkeys and shrugged. "It actually feels a lot like back on Earth," I said. "The rest of the corporate orphans would be over there talking. And I'd be over here doing my thing."

"Sounds lonely," she said.

I turned over a drunk-peach in my hands, lips thin. "It's how I liked it." That's what I'd always told myself, anyway. If I said it enough, it would eventually be true, wouldn't it?

An angry shriek echoed through the trees, and I glanced up to see a shadow jump across the open space to the tree where the troop gathered.

A scaled shape with short limbs and a long snout snapped at the jumpernicks, and they scattered. Light glinted from its fangs as it scuttled after them, separating a few from the rest of the troop.

It lunged and caught one in its mouth, but the next nearest jumpernick lost its grip and plummeted through the branches.

The creature fell all the way to the ground of the grove and landed in a pathetic little heap.

I stared for a moment as the troop shrieked above me and the climbing crocodile thing made off with its prize. A part of me wanted to be sad to see the little lives extinguished, but there was a bigger part of me, honed by hunger and driven by survival, that looked at the little shape on the ground and saw an easy source of meat.

It only took me a second to go for it.

I dropped to my butt and slid off the giant mushroom platform I'd been watching from.

A growl and a bark sounded as my boots hit the ground and the slinkwolf zipped out of the trees, straight for my target.

I grabbed up a fallen branch and swung it.

The slinkwolf dodged.

"Get away," I yelled. "It's mine. I saw it first!"

Vent it, was I really going to fend off a slinkwolf just to keep this sorry little jumpernick?

Yes, I was. Heat rose in my chest as the dappled slinkwolf startled back, and I planted myself over the body. I swung my branch, expecting the rest of the pack to materialize, but even when I whipped around to check behind me, it remained just the one.

It circled me, ears forward, as I ducked and grabbed the dead creature.

I jerked my chin. "Yeah. Just keep your distance. You guys are probably very good at what you do. You don't need this little thing and I do."

I backed up against one of the mushrooms and kept my branch waving in front of me.

The slinkwolf didn't try to advance, but it did keep its gaze on my prize.

"You are going to get eaten," BB said.

"I actually think it's more curious than anything."

"Curious about how to eat you."

"I don't know. This one doesn't seem as hostile as the rest of the pack." I raised my voice to the slinkwolf. "It's not worth it. You're just going to get bashed on the nose."

It met my eyes, then laid its ears back and disappeared into the trees.

"Was that really necessary?" BB asked. "That jumpernick doesn't have enough meat on its bones to eat, you know."

It absolutely didn't, but that wasn't why I'd snatched it.

"No," I said, slowly, turning it over in my hands. "But I have a better idea. I'm going to use it as bait."

BB sighed. "Back to the fishing thing again? Haven't you given up yet?"

"Never."

I'd seen the slasherfins snatch these things off the bank, so I knew they liked them. And I couldn't help replaying the day of the first flood over and over in my mind.

"Remember how that slasherfin latched onto my boot?"

"Yes, though I'm not sure why I would want to."

"It was like it wouldn't let go. Or maybe it couldn't. At least not easily. Whatever the reason...I think I can use that."

I moved through the trees, not exactly running, but not taking my time either, keeping an eye behind me. My shoulders stayed tense, waiting for the slinkwolves to creep up on me, until I got back to the drop ship just as the afternoon storm front moved up the river.

I didn't bother unloading my pack. I just stuck the whole thing in the crate until later. My breath came a little faster as the rain swept across the river and the clearing, pattering against the drop ship. But I concentrated on my fishing line, baiting my rudimentary hook with the scavenged jumpernick. I didn't bother cutting it up or anything. Something told me the super smart slasherfins might catch on if I altered their normal food in any way.

It meant I had one chance at this.

Rain made the hull of the drop ship shine, but my boots gripped the metal just fine as I stepped out of my shelter into the storm. Below me, the river rose and fins cut through the water toward the drop ship.

My hands shook a little as I loosened my knife in its sheath. For extra leverage and insurance, I looped the free end of the para cord around the nearest landing strut.

Then I crouched so the fish wouldn't immediately spot me up on the hull.

I braced myself and dropped my hook and its grisly bait into the flooded river, like a jumpernick that had lost its footing.

Immediately, the scaly yellow head of a slasherfin surged out of the shallows and snapped up the prize, jaws closing over the jumpernick...and the hook.

I shot to my feet and hauled back on the line. As I'd suspected, the slasherfin didn't let go. I threw my weight back and looped the line over the landing strut so it wouldn't slide back into the water. Then I grabbed hold and hauled again, using my weight to drag it up the drop ship, foot by foot.

The fish thrashed against the hull, its fins thumping the metal like a drum. I drew my knife and threw myself on it, wrapping my arms around its thick scaly body. The thing was at least as long as I was, and it twisted, spinning on the end of the para cord, trying to dislodge me.

I plunged my knife into its side, over and over again, hoping my para cord was strong enough to hold both of us.

My breath hissed between my gritted teeth as the slasherfin arched against me.

Finally it lay still, and I rolled away to blink up into the rain. My pulse pounded in my ears, and I couldn't tell if I was sobbing or laughing, but when I rolled back to see my prize, triumph bubbled in my chest.

It hung from the para cord, obviously dead, dark blood

streaming down the hull in ribbons to mix with the rain and river below.

"I did it," I gasped. Then I laughed and leaped to my feet. "I did it!"

"You did it," BB said. "You actually did."

"Haha!" I leaned over the hull and waved my fists at the slasherfins circling below. "I told you I would eat you. I have the secret of it now. You'll never scare me again!"

Flora of Daybreak ⚠

<u>Itchbushes</u>- itchy! repels alien wasps, causes rash, **avoid**
<u>Drunk-peaches</u>- delicious, dry before eating, **don't burn the wood**
<u>Red caps</u>- giant mushrooms, edible
<u>Not-red-caps</u>- carnivorous plant, mimics mushrooms, **avoid**
<u>Nuts</u>- edible

Fauna of Daybreak ⚠

<u>Swarmstings</u>- alien insects, swarm prey, deadly, **avoid**
<u>Slinkwolves</u>- blue and purple, fox-like, 60-80 pounds, hunts in packs, scavenger when alone, **avoid**
<u>Assorted birds</u>
<u>Slasherfins</u>- doesn't let go willingly, can be stabbed, **kill!**, delicious
<u>Jumpernicks</u>- monkey-lizards, gray scales and feathers, excellent climbers, eats fruits and vegetables, thief, **protect food**, great slasherfin bait
<u>Dino-chickens</u>- eggs!

Resources

<u>Food</u>- nuts, dried drunk-peaches, eggs, mushrooms, salt roots, slasherfin steaks, yum!
<u>Water</u>- liter bottles 2, river, rain

CHAPTER 18

Daybreak: Day 32

I celebrated my victory like any Earthling would and cooked my victim. It was the most delicious thing I'd ever eaten, but I was probably biased.

The fight with the fish had left me bruised all over where I'd slammed into the drop ship, and I indulged myself by taking a couple of my carefully hoarded painkillers before I cleaned and gutted the slasherfin right there where it had died. Turned out prepping a fish for eating was a lot harder than the books had made it sound, but I was motivated. I'd finally killed the damn thing; a little bit of skin and guts weren't going to keep me from eating it.

My oven sat under my frond roof, protected from the rain, smoke belching from the clay chimney that directed it outside. I wasn't about to repeat my experience with the drunk-peach wood. I stuffed it full of misshapen slasherfin steaks. Some of the greens made a nice salad, and I topped my feast off with some roasted nuts and mushrooms.

For the first time since the crash, my stomach ached from being full instead of empty.

The fish was too big to cook and eat all in one night, but I'd figured out how to boil the salty root down until my pot had a rime of salt. Over the last few days, I'd built up a stockpile. Enough that I could bury the extra steaks in salt to preserve them. Maybe I could even catch more now that I knew the trick of it, and keep myself well stocked with salted fish.

A familiar feeling pricked the back of my neck—like being watched—and I glanced across the flooded space to see my slinkwolf shadow. He sat just in the shallows, the fur of his tail floating around him.

His eyes watched, bright even through the screening rain, and a prickle of guilt made me squirm.

I sighed and sliced a piece off one of the uncooked steaks. Then I threw the fish underhand toward the slinkwolf.

It splashed a few feet from his paws.

"Why'd you do that?" BB asked.

I shrugged. "I don't know. I stole his dinner right out from under him. And that's what let me finally kill one of the slasherfins. I figure I owe him."

The slinkwolf sniffed the offering all over before snatching it and swallowing it whole.

"Now it's just going to think you're a convenient food ticket. You already have enough problems with them stalking you."

"It's just the one," I said. "He's harmless by himself."

But as I spoke, the other three slinkwolves coalesced out of the gray forest, arraying themselves around their lone guard.

I gulped. "Okay, maybe you were right."

"Of course I was right," BB said, voice even and calm. "Your safety is my number one concern. I am better at caring for you than you are."

"Sometimes. Maybe."

At least the slinkwolves stayed on that side of the flood. My fish and I were safe from them for now.

A downdraft rustled the fronds of my roof, making the rain splatter across my platform in an unexpected gust, and I whipped around.

A huge red shape swept across the graying sky, close enough to the treetops to send a shower of leaves down on me.

Sweat prickled on my palm, and I jumped to my feet as the primitive portion of my brain recognized a predator large enough to snatch me up in some very long talons.

A yelp sounded behind me, and when I glanced over my shoulder, the pack of slinkwolves had disappeared.

I didn't blame them.

I stumbled back against the trunk of my tree and clutched the bark as if that would keep me anchored.

"What is that?" BB whispered.

I just shook my head.

Its wingspan blotted out the last of the light as it hovered for a second over the swollen river. An impressive crest of feathers framed a long snout lined with wicked teeth, but bright red scales shed the rain water along its spiny back and ribbed wings.

The first colors of the aurora spread through the clouds, reflecting in the water, and I saw the flash of slasherfin scales. The predator dove for the water. There was the barest ripple, and it rose back into the air with a slasherfin clutched in each talon.

It hovered there in midair while it tore into its prey with strong jaws, and I found myself holding my breath.

The creature that had scared even the slinkwolves threw back its head to swallow before letting out a piercing scream and winging away over the river and the jungle beyond.

I waited until it had been out of sight for a whole minute before clutching my chest and letting out an explosive breath.

"Vent it, did the corporation do any kind of analysis on this planet?" I said. "No one told me about dragons!"

"I imagine they did not feel the presence of large predators was relevant to the colonization timeline."

"It ate two slasherfins! Do you know how long it took me to kill even one?"

"Yes. I was there."

I ran my hands over my wet hair. "I mean, don't get me wrong. That thing was beautiful. Terrifying and clearly capable of eating me. But beautiful."

"There are a lot of things on Daybreak capable of eating you. Some of them quite small."

"Thanks. That makes me feel so much better. The mega-eating-machine isn't the only thing to worry about."

"I thought I was in charge of naming things," BB said with a huff.

I gestured across the crater where the predator had disappeared. "Name away—"

Another shriek echoed up the river. The predator again, but it was a heck of a lot further away this time.

"Perhaps the megawing is still hunting," BB said.

"As long as it stays on its half of the world and I stay on mine." I stooped to check the fish still baking in my oven.

A loud crack echoed across the crater, distinctive and completely unexpected, making me shoot straight upright.

I waited, listening, but heard nothing else.

"That wasn't...was that...was that a gunshot?" I said.

"It did not fit with the normal frequencies of thunder on this planet."

"It was a gunshot." My bad hand tingled. "That means people. Humans. Another survivor or a colonist."

An image of the empty pod on the stone dome streaked through my head. The one where I'd found the lighter. I never had found the owner of the pod. I'd been so busy just trying to survive, I hadn't had a chance to explore or search for other survivors yet.

"BB, can you store that heading so we can find it again?"

"Done," BB said. "But Anikka, you're not going after it, are you?"

I stared up at the sky, my eyes stinging so I had to blink. "People. Here near the crater. I might not be the only one." I shoved aside the remains of my dinner and pulled my pack toward me. "We can't start out tonight, obviously. It's way too late. And we'll have to cross the river, so morning is better. But yeah. We're going to go find whoever is out there."

"You have a much better chance of surviving if you remain here. You know the dangers here. You have food and water here. Leaving is a huge risk."

"BB." I tossed a couple of the salt-roots into a pot of water and balanced it on the other side of the oven where I'd formed a crude stove over the flames. "There's someone else out there like me. Someone trying to survive. I have to at least try to find them."

BB's hologram went quiet, and after a second, it flickered out. A sign that she didn't like my decision but couldn't think of a good enough reason to keep arguing.

I'd get a good start on salting the rest of the fish tonight so that maybe it would be cured by the time I got back, but I was already building a packing list in my head and trying to decide what food I could carry with me.

I had no idea how long it would take me to search, but already my hands prickled with excitement.

CHAPTER 19

Daybreak: Day 33

I left the moment the light went gray, and the flood had receded enough I could get to my tree bridge. The gunshot had come from the southeast. Across the river and toward the crater. I knew that much, but I would need BB to keep me pointed in the right direction once we got into the forest.

I carried the cross bow across my back even though I hadn't actually managed to hit anything with it yet. But I couldn't help remembering the megawing, and I didn't think it would be impressed if I waved a tree branch at it.

My pack weighed a ton with the nuts and the fruit I'd packed, but I didn't want to count on being able to forage along the way. A lot of the greens I'd tried so far had turned out okay, but if I couldn't find anything familiar, I'd be stuck testing new options when I didn't really have the time to be sick after a bad reaction.

Both bottles of water hung from the clips on my pack and the first aid kit was tucked on top of my food, along with my sleeping bag and the salvaged parachute to use as a tent.

My path took me within spitting distance of the colony, and I swerved to give it a quick look. As far as I could tell from here, nothing had changed. And without knowing what was wrong in the colony, I didn't want to investigate any further.

Besides, I didn't have time to waste. I hadn't heard anything beyond the gunshot the night before, and my chest ached with anticipation and a little worry.

From the colony, we struck out almost directly south in order to get to the edge of the crater. I had a utility knife now, big enough to use as a makeshift machete, and I had a much broader knowledge of the planet, but I still hadn't found a faster way through the dense undergrowth. Walking around the rim of the crater where the jungle didn't quite reach still seemed like the best way to travel.

On this side of the colony, there were a lot more of the smooth brown swathes I recognized as the jungle quicksand that ate my escape pod, and I counted myself lucky that there weren't any pools close enough to my tree to cause trouble.

After a long night of prep, it was exhausting watching my feet and keeping clear of itchbushes and sucking mud. But I raised my knife to cut a path through the vines and other unfamiliar plants, ignoring the burn of fatigue until I finally broke free from the edge of the forest.

My boots thumped against the solid rock of the cliff edge, and I raised a hand to shield my eyes as I stared across the crater. The *Last Resort* still hulked in the distance. The fires had long since gone out, but a hazy glow still hung around the engine spouts on this side of the ship.

The swollen river roared over the cliff far on my right, the sound of the waterfall barely dimmed even from this distance.

"Okay. That wasn't so bad." The trip from the colony to the

crater had taken less than an hour. Despite the dense jungle, I must be moving a lot faster and easier than I had even before I'd left Earth. I still had a couple of hours before the clouds gathering on the horizon turned into the usual afternoon monsoon. I didn't love being in unfamiliar terrain when it hit, but at least I was far enough from the river that I likely wasn't in the flood zone.

"All right, BB, which direction was the shot from?"

"According to where we were versus where we are, it came from the east."

I squinted along the edge where I would be walking.

"Hang on." Something bright glinted on the edge of the crater, something metal with sharp corners. "That wasn't there before. I'm pretty sure I would have seen it on the way to the colony."

"That is directly along our heading," BB said.

I started trotting. I had to take breaks, weighed down as I was by my pack and the weaponry, but it felt good to be running toward something.

My breath puffed in my chest, and after an hour of off and on running, I could make out our target more clearly.

"It's a shelter!"

Someone had propped an enormous piece of metal against a tree. A piece of the hull that had sheared clean off the *Last Resort*. There were even blue numbers painstakingly painted on the surface.

H-3. One of the main hatches.

I sprinted the last twenty feet and swung around the end of the metal sheet propped up like a tent. My heart hammered.

"Hello?" I skidded to a stop under the edge of the metal, and my eyes skipped over the sleeping bag laid in the narrow space of the shelter, the half empty water bottles next to it, the dead remains of a fire, and the ration bar wrappers scattered about.

"Hello?"

My pulse slowed as no one answered. The place was clearly lived in but empty right now.

"Maybe they're out foraging," BB said.

"Yeah." My chest heaved as I spun in a slow circle, taking in the cut saplings piled up as if waiting to be dried out for firewood or building. An offal pit about twenty feet away from the campsite held the remains of one of the antlered creatures I'd seen in the grove. Some bones showed signs of scorching while the hide lay over a log nearby.

I worried my bottom lip between my teeth and circled the campsite again while the gray clouds roiled across the sky above.

"Hello?" I called again into the woods, straining to hear an answer.

Nothing.

The edge of the crater wasn't nearly as steep here as it was the rest of the way I'd come. It descended to the crater floor in a series of far shorter cliffs and steps, so that someone could actually get down safely, so long as they didn't lose their footing.

Maybe the other survivor had gone that way, down into the crater to forage or scavenge.

I stepped to the edge and leaned over. Then gasped.

A man sprawled face down on a ledge nearly two stories down, his left arm dangling over the edge.

"Oh, no." I sat on my butt and slid over the shallowest part of the slope I could find. From there, I could hopscotch down the cliff ledges to the man. "Oh, no. Oh, no."

I reached the ledge and flung my pack down to dig for the

first aid kit, but as I went to shake his shoulder, my frantic motions stilled. I could already tell he was not alive.

Traces of blue wiring trailed up his arms, disappearing under his flight suit, but they marked him as a cybernetic. And the wiring just under his skin was dull in death, rather than glowing with life.

I turned him over, teeth clenched tight. A hand gun fell away, as if dislodged, clattering against the cliff as it fell.

Deep gashes marred the man's torso, courtesy of the megawing, but he'd clearly died of a broken neck.

My lips thinned. "It didn't even eat him," I croaked. It seemed like such a stupid little detail to notice right now.

"What?" BB said, popping up on my wrist.

"It...it knocked him off the cliff and killed him. But it didn't bother eating him. It could easily have come down here to do so, but it didn't." I swiped my sleeve over my eyes and nose. "That's just plain mean."

"Anikka, I'm sorry," BB said, voice low and soft.

"He was here this whole time. Less than a day's walk, and I had no idea. We could have been helping each other."

Thunder rumbled, and the first couple of raindrops splatted on the rock next to me.

"Anikka, I want to get you off this cliff before it gets slippery," BB said gently.

I nodded with a sniff. A mix of regret and grief burned in my chest, but that didn't mean I'd lost all sense. The rains had tried to kill me many times already. I wouldn't let them finally succeed.

I left the man with his hands across his chest and scrambled back up the slope, using cracks and outcroppings as handholds where I needed to.

At the top, I scurried back under the man's shelter and sat with my arms around my knees as the rain pinged against the metal surface. It felt odd not to be up high as the water fell around me, but the man had clearly slept here for a while, so it must not flood the way my campsite did.

I heaved a shuddering sigh and ran my hands over my face. When I dropped them, a bit of paleness caught my eye. A corner of paper tucked under the edge of the man's sleeping bag, as if he'd made sure it wouldn't blow away or get wet.

I slid it out.

"Is that actual paper?" BB asked.

"Yeah, people still use it sometimes for letters if they're willing to wait forever for it to be delivered. It's kind of romantic."

The handwriting was shaky, sharp, like the writer was in a hurry.

Parker,

Oh, God, it's all gone to crap. I can't believe this is happening. Listen, I don't have time to explain. I just have time to write this and leave it where you will hopefully be able to find it. The screens won't work. The pads won't work. None of the tech. We're clearing out the colony. You're going to have to come find us. Please. North, past the Black Flats. Big tar pits, you can't miss them. I don't know the coordinates we're heading for. The commander has those. She says this will all be over by the time you reach orbit, but I don't know. I love you. Find us when you can. Please. I'll see you soon.

Sam

My hand shook enough that the words blurred. I turned the page over to find a crude map drawn in charcoal, probably by Parker. I recognized the crater and the colony and north of those, he'd marked some black splotches. Tar pits.

I swallowed. "BB. We can find the colonists. We know where to look for them!" I waved the paper at her.

BB's holographic face screwed up as she looked at the smudged map. "Don't get too excited. We maybe know where to start."

"Well, it's more than we had this morning! We can catch up to them. Find out what happened. Why they abandoned the colony."

"It will be a journey. We have no idea how far these Black Flats are or how long it will take to get to them."

"We have the navigation data. We can look." I clutched the paper in both hands. The sketch wasn't much. Just the vague direction of north, but it was the last possession of a dead man I felt a little bit of a connection to. He'd loved this person. He'd spent the last bit of his life trying to find a way to get back to them.

I folded the paper and slid it into my jumpsuit to keep it dry. I could keep it safe for him. And for me.

I had no idea what to tell this Sam when I found them. I'm sorry your partner died. I'm sorry I wasn't there. I'm sorry I didn't know he existed.

Whatever I came up with, it was a direction. It was something to run toward.

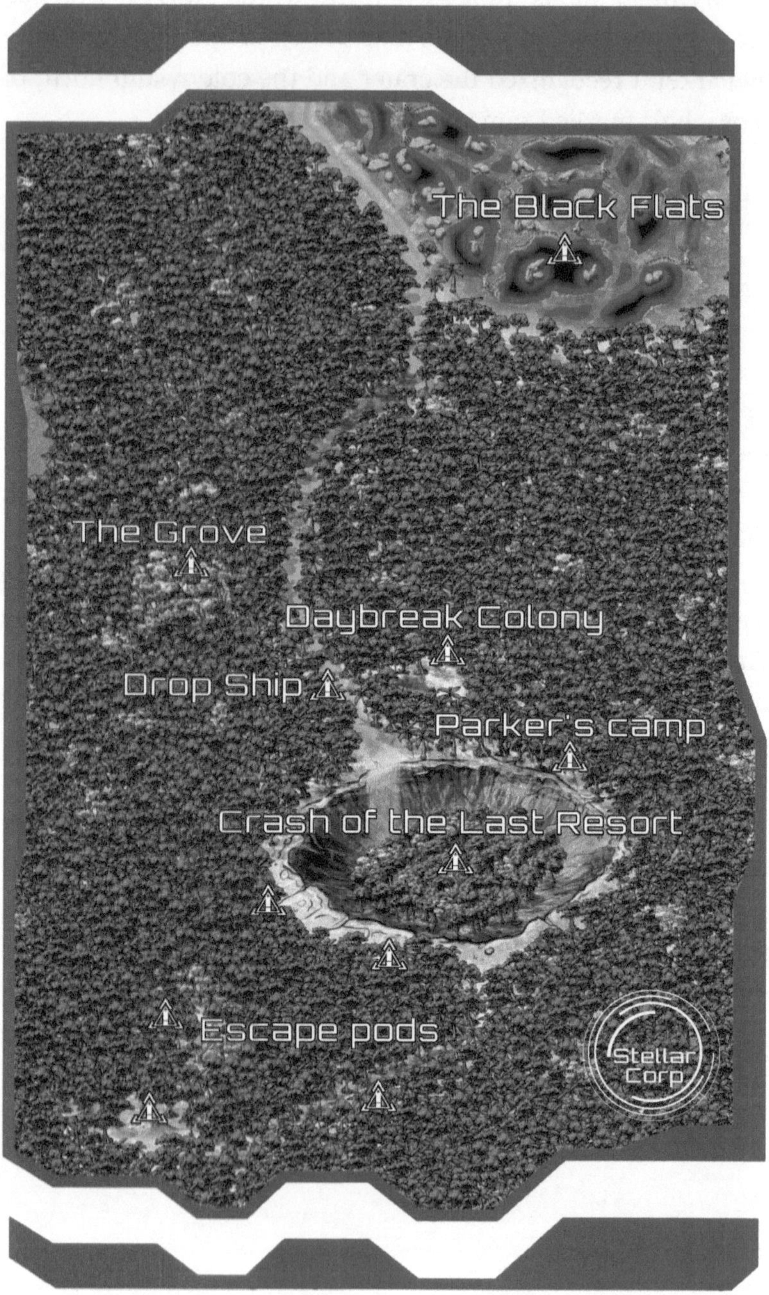

The Black Flats
The Grove
Daybreak Colony
Drop Ship
Parker's camp
Crash of the Last Resort
Escape pods
Stellar Corp

CHAPTER 20

Daybreak: Day 34

I had a lot to do if I wanted to go after the colonists. I'd need food to last the journey and a way to camp at night. I'd have to leave my oven behind, obviously, but maybe I could come up with some kind of camp stove to bring with me.

When I got back to my campsite, my fish was still safely packed inside the crate, but there were little claw marks along the wood, especially around the lid. I could well imagine the jumpernicks trying to get into it while I was gone and maybe some other scavenger that could climb a ladder that I hadn't encountered yet.

The next few days I spent boiling more of the salt-root, collecting the crystals to preserve more meat, and I caught another slasherfin using the same method as before.

I had no idea how long it took to salt-cure something, but I had to try it. I couldn't eat an entire slasherfin in one day. Maybe not even in a whole week. And I needed to be able to take some with me.

These days, I visited the grove often, snatching handfuls of fruit to bring back and dry in my oven. That process was a lot more streamlined now. I knew the perfect thickness to slice the drunk-peaches to get them to dry out faster and the perfect spot in the oven that got them chewy but not burned and crispy.

I also made time to go back over to Parker's campsite to give him a funeral. I had no idea what his beliefs had been, but I didn't want to leave him sprawled on the cliff ledge with nothing to mark his passing. And unlike Emerson, the crew member I'd found in the escape pod, I didn't have to leave him.

It took a couple of trips, but I managed to dig him a grave among the roots. His funeral ended up being short and mostly a discussion with BB about how to keep predators from digging him up. But I kept thinking about Sam and what I wanted to be able to tell them about their lost partner.

All the while, excitement and worry and a bit of anticipation burned in my chest and made me want to rush things. But I knew I wouldn't survive the journey if I botched the preparations. So I gave myself time.

Two weeks. It took two weeks for my fish to go all dried and hard, crusted with salt.

I thunked a piece against the side of the crate.

"Well if you can't eat it, you can at least use it as a weapon," BB said.

Along with the food, I needed a place to sleep every night and a way to cook. So while I waited for my fish to cure, I spent some time constructing a rope ladder that rolled up and hung from my pack, and I experimented with different cook fire set ups.

At last I felt ready to load up.

The original first aid kit I'd found, I packed with pilfered goods from the colony infirmary. It bulged a bit at the seams, but it still fit in the bottom of my pack and I felt better trekking through the woods with antibiotics on my back.

My arm almost never hurt anymore, giving me only the slightest twinge when I tried to pull on something too heavy or put too much weight on it while climbing my ladder. Maybe that meant it was nearly healed.

The end came suddenly, after weeks of preparation. I closed the flap on my pack and realized I was ready. All that was left was to wait for morning and head out.

Daybreak: Day 48

I slung my pack over my shoulders as the streaks of orange and red and pink lit up the sky the next morning. My rolled-up ladder swung awkwardly against the side of the pack, and I paused for a second to secure it so it wouldn't bump with every step.

My hands patted everything one last time, taking stock. Even after weeks of preparation, I couldn't shake the nagging ache of anxiety in my gut. Had I forgotten anything important?

My water hung from the other side of my pack and the homemade pot swung underneath. I touched my hatchet on one hip and my utility knife on the other. The cross bow hung from my shoulder where I could grab it easily without tangling my straps. And everything else was tucked inside my pack.

I hurried down my ladder and across the bank, splashing in the water that hadn't quite retreated yet, before climbing my steps and crossing the tree bridge.

It was an hour's walk to the colony, but I figured that was

the best place to start since that was where the colonists had started. Maybe I'd be able to pick up their trail.

When I hit the warehouse closest to the river, I turned left and circled the colony's outskirts, never going any closer than the edge of the jungle. In the fields, I snagged a few tomatoes to carry for lunch. They were overgrown, clearly in need of pruning, and the jungle was closing in, taking over the first third of the fields, but most of the bushes still bore ripe fruit.

Just past the fields, a dirt road led through the colony, the packed dirt still bearing puddles from last night's rain.

It dead-ended at the edge of the jungle, but when I bent to push away the underbrush, tire tracks still marred the ground beneath, deep enough to withstand the rains.

I blew out my breath. "They definitely came this way. With a loader."

I tightened my pack's straps and stepped off the track into the jungle. It was starting to feel familiar.

I knew a lot of the hazards now. The big patches of jungle quicksand hadn't given me trouble in ages since I knew how to spot them and avoided them without even thinking. I kept my ears tuned for the ominous buzz of the swarmstings, and so far, that kept me far enough away they hadn't tried killing me.

There wasn't so much of a track to follow as there was a space between the trees. I knew the vehicle the colonists had brought had to have been pretty big and wouldn't have fit between a lot of the denser forest. So I stuck to the wider spaces between trees and checked the ground for tracks.

All the while, I kept one eye over my shoulder.

Sure enough, I caught a couple of sleek shapes tracking me through the trees. Long, low to the ground, with flat blue fur fading to purple.

"The slinkwolves are back," I told BB under my breath.

"At least they're a familiar threat instead of something new and different."

"Yeah." I picked up the pace.

"Though it would be nice to check them off your list. Not have to worry about them anymore."

My mouth pinched tight, and I paused. "True." I'd have to work at it, though. The slinkwolf pack was built to ambush *me*. I'd have a lot harder time ambushing them.

The rains started in the late afternoon just like always, and I kept watch for any flooding. But I'd moved away from the river and the ground remained high if not dry.

The rain made it a lot harder to follow the occasional tire tracks, which were buried in the dense underbrush, and I had to slow way down in the murky light.

As the sun crept lower and lower and the forest went dim, I searched for a good tree. I needed something big with low enough branches. It was a good thing I started early. It took over an hour to find something that would work, and by then, the dusk lights had spread across the sky, bathing the forest in blue and green and purple light.

The tree I'd chosen had a couple of wide branches about fifteen feet over my head, and I grabbed the rolled up ladder from my pack. The last of my para cord that I'd kept to fish with was attached to the end, and I lined up to toss it over the lowest branch.

It took three tries, but I thought it was lucky it only took that many. With the darkness closing in, it could have been a lot harder.

As the para cord snaked down, the middle looped over the branch. I caught it, then tugged, raising my rope ladder so the top rung was even with the branch.

I found a bush sturdy enough to hold my weight and

secured the para cord to its trunk, so it held my ladder in place over the branch. Then I swarmed up the rungs.

That was the easy part. The branch was wide enough to straddle but not really wide enough to stand. So I shimmied over to the trunk and put my back against it.

There. Not nearly as cozy as my shelter back at the drop ship, but it would do for the night. It kept me out of the slinkwolves territory, and I felt safer up in the tree.

By the light of the big striped moon, I ate a handful of dried fruit and gnawed on a fillet of fish. It was salty and hard and made my teeth hurt, and it would be way better cooked somehow, but I couldn't exactly build a fire to cook soup up in the tree.

Then I took out the tool case and spent the last hour of my day meticulously cleaning the mud out of the joints of my prosthetic, like I did every night before I took it off to give my skin a break. The screw at the base of my thumb rattled, and I tightened it with a conscientious twist, then flexed the fingers, making doubly sure they all worked the way they were supposed to.

Screws and metal plates and the wiring in the joints I could all maybe replace. As long as I could get back into the colony to scavenge. But the electronics? The electrodes on the cuff that lined up perfectly with the nerves in my arm? If those quit on me one day, I was screwed.

And without the hand, I'd lose BB.

I swallowed against the worry and packed the tools carefully back into the case.

A flicker of pink moonlight on blue fur made me pause. The slinkwolf, my dappled guard, sat under the next tree over, staring up at my perch. His eyes flashed orange with the reflective sheen of an animal evolved to see in the dark.

He did nothing but sit there with his fluffy tail tucked

around his paws, staring at me. Like I was a threat? Or like I was dinner?

Slowly, I reached for the cross bow still strapped to my pack. I loaded a bolt and raised it to my shoulder to sight down the barrel at the creature.

He didn't move.

It would be an easy shot. The slinkwolves had never seen me shoot anything with the cross bow, so they had no idea what kind of threat it posed.

And he was just sitting there.

With one down, the pack would be that much easier to deal with.

My finger tightened on the trigger.

An overwhelming sadness settled over my shoulders, and I let the bow fall, resting it against the branch.

"What's wrong?" BB said. "Why didn't you shoot?"

I half expected her voice to spook the slinkwolf, but he stayed where he was, ears pricked toward us.

"I don't know." I quickly stripped the cross bow and stored it. "I guess I'd be sad to see him dead."

"They followed you. They've followed you this whole time, from the escape pods to the drop ship and now here."

"Yeah, and they're the closest thing to company I have here," I said. "Besides you. There's a part of me that doesn't want to throw that away."

I tugged the rope ladder up to store it for the night and wrapped a vine around the trunk to hold me in place while I slept.

"Is that a human thing?" BB asked. "That doesn't seem like a logic thing."

"It's a human thing, I guess. It doesn't make any sense at all, except inside my gut."

"Your gut seems opinionated. Maybe you should tell it to mind its own business."

I smiled and closed my eyes.

"Or maybe I should develop a gut. Maybe that would make me more human."

I slept that night with my arms clutched around the pack and the slinkwolf watching over me.

CHAPTER 21

Daybreak: Day 49

The next day I discovered why the colonists called them the Black Flats.

Around midmorning, the jungle cut off abruptly, and I stepped out into broad daylight. The ground under foot went from soft loam to dry, cracked dirt, and I raised my hand to shield my eyes.

Huge swathes of black tar spread across the plains from the toes of my boots to the far horizon. Snaky pathways of rock and packed dirt wound between the dark pools, offering a deceptive sort of hope to travelers. The pits steamed in the morning light, but right there, where I'd stumbled out of the forest, tire tracks cut through the edge of the nearest pit where the ground was soggy, not deadly.

I squinted, trying to see if there was a way around. The river curved close on the west side of the plain, cutting the pits off from the jungle on that side. And jagged mountains rose abruptly to the east of the pits. The thought of trying to circle around to cross either the river or the mountains made my heart and legs ache, especially when there was clear evidence that the colonists had gone right through.

"Anikka, please be careful," BB said, her hologram popping up so she could stare across the Black Flats. "This area is treacherous."

"Yeah, I don't need you to tell me that." I pointed to the nearest pit where the stark white bones of something big thrust toward the sky. "Trust me, I'm not going to get close enough to fall in and get stuck."

"I meant the tar has to have come from somewhere. An underground fissure of some kind. The ground here could be very unstable."

"Oh. Great."

"Oil has likely gathered on the surface of the pools as it seeps to the surface. I do not have the sensors to tell what kind, but it is likely deadly. Even more likely to be flammable."

"You're not helping, you know."

The rustle of leaves and the hoots and calls of birds and jumpernicks fell away, leaving nothing but silence in the wide-open spaces of the tar pits, and it sent a shiver down my shoulders and arms.

I stepped out, trying to follow the colonists' tracks. Hopefully, wherever they had driven the vehicle, the ground would be stable enough to hold me and my pack.

Still, there were points where the winding space between the pits grew narrow, and I held my breath as I tiptoed across thin bridges of solid ground.

An hour in, the edge of the path crumbled under my boot and a piece slid into the pit beside me. I flung myself at a stunted tree, standing twisted and dead on the other side of the path. My arms wrapped around its rough trunk as my feet sought purchase that wouldn't fall away from me.

"Careful!" BB said.

I puffed as I climbed back to my feet, using the tree to steady me. "Saying that doesn't help," I snapped. "I'm being as careful as I can be."

BB's holographic mouth thinned in a perfect parody of a human grimace. "I'm sorry. I can't do anything else. Shouting advice is all I'm good for."

My fingers clenched against the dead bark. "Well, stop it."

BB's eyes went tight, and her hologram closed abruptly.

I groaned under my breath and spared a hand to scrub my face. Great, I had one friend on this planet, and I'd driven her away.

A buzzing, clicking sort of sound made me whirl around. Crap. If the swarmstings could fly over the tar pits, I'd never escape them.

But the air was clear behind me. Instead, a troop of beetles as big as my fist clicked along, as if following me. They spread out, trundling along the surface of the tar as if it were solid ground, their carapaces gleaming iridescent in the sun.

They stopped when I turned to face them.

"Wonderful. What are these things?"

"Insects," BB said, though her hologram remained off.

I rolled my eyes. "Yeah, I got that. Shoo," I told the troop. "I haven't let anything bigger eat me yet. I'm not getting taken out by a bunch of dung beetles."

The beetles didn't seem inclined to get closer, at least not while I was facing them. I continued my trek, and they followed at a distance, keeping me in sight

I grumbled but kept moving. A cross bow bolt would mean nothing to a swarm of insects.

Plaintive little bleats reached my ears, and I picked up the pace. In the next pit over, a little gray-green body thrashed.

One of the dino-chickens stuck deep in the tar. It wasn't

that far in, but clearly it was too stuck for its little muscles to wriggle free.

I licked my lips. "What if I got it out and took it home?" I asked BB. "I'd have fresh eggs whenever I wanted—"

A slithering beside my boot made me leap back with a strangled shriek.

The troop of beetles trundled past me, flowing over the tar toward the poor, stuck creature. It bleated once more before the swarm of beetles covered it completely.

I breathed out, and the beetles scattered again, leaving clean white bones that slowly sank into the tar and out of sight.

"Holy crap." Bile rose in my throat, and I swallowed it back before I could barf up breakfast.

The beetles retreated and stopped at the other side of the tar pit, turning to face me as one.

"They're waiting for me to fall in," I whispered.

"Then don't."

I couldn't even come up with a comeback. I just hurried down the narrow pathway. The sooner I reached the end of the Black Flats, the better.

A little rise hid the horizon from me, tar trickling down on either side from pools above. I scrambled up the hill and stopped with a gasp.

Less than fifty feet away, a mechanical loader sat, half in, half out of a tar pit, its load balanced precariously on its flat bed.

A laugh burst from me, and I raced down the path. "BB, look!"

Mud and tar splattered the wheels and the sides of the vehicle, a testament to its journey from the colony. The only reason it hadn't sunk all the way into the pit was because its right two wheels were still caught on solid ground while its left two were mired deep. Faded scrapes and gouges in the ground showed where the colonists had tried to dig it out before abandoning it.

Scorch marks marred the hatch that covered the power pack. A lot like the outlets and the tech back at the colony.

"They were here." I leaned across the seat to peer into the compartment where drivers normally kept keys or manuals or work orders. But it was empty. "They passed this way. We're getting close."

"We don't know that for sure," BB said, reappearing on my wrist. "It had to have been more than a month ago or they would have seen the *Last Resort* crash. They would have turned around and come back."

"That depends on whatever they were running from. If it was big enough to scare them into evacuating, then maybe they wanted to wait it out. Sam seemed to indicate in their note that they would be back. They must have expected to be able to return."

A piece of me wanted to dig through the crates strapped to the bed, but I had no way to carry anything else.

And...I felt close. Yes, they had a month-long head start on me, but I couldn't shake the feeling that I could come over the next hill and find them camped out, waiting for me. My lips tugged in a hopeful smile that I couldn't quite suppress.

The tar pits couldn't be endless. The colonists had been headed for some place on the other side. I just had to get there.

"Come on," I told BB, even though she was attached to me.

I left the loader to its unceremonious grave and hurried as gray clouds crawled across the sky. The pathway tried to crumble away from me, but I moved fast enough to keep ahead of it now.

I knew I should slow down. Take it carefully, but I didn't want to be caught out here at night.

And they were just on the other side, so close I could almost hear them.

After another hour of half-running, half walking, a flat, fuzzy mist grew on the horizon.

Water. A huge lake spreading as far as I could see in either direction.

But something lay between me and the shore.

Something pointy and white.

I hauled in a breath and sprinted the last fifty feet.

Skeletons. So many of them. Lying on the packed dirt just a few feet from the edge of the pits. Clearly human.

I was right. They'd been close.

I fell to my knees and covered my face with my hands.

CHAPTER 22

Daybreak: Day 49

I gulped back tears and the creeping despair that threatened to choke me.

This wasn't new, I told myself. I'd gotten my hopes up only to have them dashed by mystery and death over and over now. I could get over this. I would survive it.

The scene wasn't getting any better, so I scrubbed my hands over my face and forced myself to face it.

At least twenty skeletons lay on the shore of the lake, judging by the skulls, but no more. So this couldn't be the whole colony. There were hundreds on Daybreak already when the *Last Resort* crashed.

A glider lay nearby, its power pack shorted and scorched, just like the packer back in the pits.

The afternoon rain started, softer than it ever had been before. A pitter-patter on the sand of the lake shore without the thunder that usually accompanied it. Each raindrop left a tiny indentation until the shore was patterned with a swathe of raindrop fingerprints.

Wavelets lapped the beach far enough away that they hadn't disturbed the remains over the last month.

"BB," I said quietly. "You have the infirmary data packet. Can you guess the cause of death?"

"Not with so little. Or at least not without an in-depth scan of the bones. Maybe if we got them back to the colony's infirmary."

I rubbed my temples. The beetles hadn't tried to swarm me, and I was only one person walking through their territory. So I couldn't imagine they had killed a whole group of colonists outright. It was more likely that they'd picked over the bodies after they'd died or been incapacitated. Like the dino-chicken.

So, what could have killed them all in a group like this? A predator? Or a disease? My mind went back to thoughts of a plague, and I drew back a step.

But that didn't make sense, either. Would a sickness have taken them all out at the same time like this?

I shoved down the surge of disappointment and crept closer to the remains. I had a butt-ton of knowledge about how to build things and a random assortment of know-how from reading, and I was grateful for that—it had kept me alive. But right now I wished I had just a little bit more. Something that would tell me what had killed these people.

As I knelt beside the bones, something glinted, catching my eye.

Clearly the swarming beetles didn't eat metal or plastic because I caught sight of a couple of zippers and buttons and bars and screws and things that I finally figured out were jewelry and stints and other medical implants.

And a network of wiring that looked a lot like Parker's cybernetics.

Dr. Grotman was supposed to be a cybernetic.

This was the commander of the colony. This was her wiring.

I followed the trail of it with my eyes, down the long arm bones to her wrist and the glint of a power node where her chip and all her data would be stored. Not only would it hold a localized archive of her last transmissions, it would hold her access codes, her personal log, and all the data required to run a colony. It would hold the coordinates to find the rest of the colonists.

Except I had no way to access it.

The commander would have had a neural interface to connect her with her data. All I had was BB.

"Can you get me into the data packet?" I asked quietly, already knowing the answer.

"It is a discreet unit," she said, just as soft. "Protected from tampering. I cannot access it without integrating the information."

Another integration.

"This would be, what? Three?"

"Four. With my original programming."

And each one pushed her closer to a logical super monster with her own agenda and process.

Back on Earth, this would never ever be a question. Integrate an AI just to learn a bit of data? Never.

AIs were specially designed to analyze one—maybe two—types of data max. A unique interface between a human and one small network of information. No more.

But I wasn't on Earth, I didn't have any other interfaces, and BB was my only chance to learn what had happened to the colonists. My only chance to keep surviving.

"How human are you feeling?"

BB hesitated.

I didn't push her to answer. She would know how important this was. Her circuits would be humming with the imperative to keep me alive. And while she was still a little naive, she was, in a lot of ways, smarter than me. She'd know the commander's data could be the tipping point between life and death.

"I don't...I don't feel too logical," BB said finally. "Or murderous. But would I be able to tell?"

"How many data packets did HERTZ-2 have before he went crazy and tried to take over the world?"

"Six." Her holographic eyes remained on the bones at my feet.

"So we're fine. Right? Not even close."

She did not say that four was not that far from six. She just said. "Very well."

Nothing changed on the outside except for a flicker of BB's hologram and a little blue progress bar under her feet that slowly ticked up.

A minute should not last as long as this one did. My lungs ached as I held my breath and watched BB's frozen expression.

Finally, she cocked her head, and I let out an explosive sigh.

"Well?"

"I have access to the commander's data packet. Logs first? Or the coordinates for the colonists?"

"Logs," I said quickly. My back hurt, standing there, looming over the bodies, so I knelt on the sand, rain misting around me.

"This is the last entry," BB said. And then her voice came out strange, higher, but also somehow older, measured as if speaking with experience.

"Date: 5.14.—who the hell cares? The storm is due in a few hours and we're nowhere near the caves. Only halfway across the Black Flats. The loader broke down, so we have to drag the glider the rest of the way. I should have left more time. I should have sent the others ahead. I should have—" The voice broke off in a weary sigh. She sounded exhausted. Like she was so tired of being tired that everything else had been drained out.

"Sam is the only one of us still moving, as if he can beat this thing. Everyone else has given up. He finally broke down and told me his husband is coming on the *Last Resort*. Stellar corp doesn't say it, but we all know they select against same-sex couples. So Sam and Parker lied about their orientation to get spots. Said it had nothing to do with their fitness to do their jobs. Not that it's going to matter in a few hours." Her voice trailed off for a moment.

"I envy him. He has something to fight for. I don't...I don't know how to lead them anymore when this is the end. What's more dignified? What's more honorable? Lying down and accepting our fate? Dying in peace? Or shaking a fist at the sky and screaming in defiance? I don't know. It's all I can do to keep the rest calm."

"At least I know the rest of the colony is safe in the caves...I can *hope* they're safe. If they're not...well, I won't be alive to know."

There was a rustle like she'd run her hands over her face.

"We'll keep going. Till the end. Till the storm hits us. Till the last bit of hope is gone. End recording."

Silence swept over us, leaving only the patter of the rain.

My chest tightened and my throat burned. "What was it? What killed you?" I whispered. "What storm?" I glanced at the gray clouds spitting rain and bit my lip.

"Playing the next-to-last entry," BB said.

"Date 5.7.1533-5 I've evacuated the colony. A-101. Crispin says there's a cave system a couple of days away on the other side of the lake. It might—*might*—shield everyone. If that's the only hope, then I'm gonna grab it with both hands. I've sent them in Crispin's crazy contraption that'll get them across the lake near instantly. Whoever called it a lake was full of it. Damn thing's the size of an ocean—" Her voice cut off as she cleared her throat.

"I stayed back with a skeleton crew of twenty to try to prep things here. The *Last Resort* is due in less than a month, and we're gonna have to be ready to communicate even if the systems go down—"

"Go back another entry," I told BB. This one wasn't helping. I needed to find whenever she learned of the problem. Maybe that would tell me something.

"Date   5.6.1533-9   Preparations   are   underway   for evacuation—"

"Again. Go back."

"Date 5.5.1533-8 Vent it, we're screwed." Panic and a bit of anger laced the commander's voice.

"That's it, stay there," I told BB.

"Stellar Corp more than dropped the ball on this one. They dropped the whole damn planet, and we're the ones that are going to pay for it. With our lives."

I rubbed the smooth joint of my thumb. Waiting.

The commander thumped something hard enough to catch in the recording. "Someone expedited the planetary analysis. Didn't do their due diligence and signed off on Daybreak as a colony planet. A garden world. Perfect for humans. Completely failing to mention the energy buildup in the atmosphere! The sun here sends out energy—I don't know what it's called, Crispin would know—but the planet's EM field protects it...until it doesn't. Every few months, it overloads and the resulting storm reverses the magnetic poles of the planet. No big deal, it happens on Earth every few millennia or so, except when it does, it doesn't cause an extinction event!"

Another pause as the commander huffed. I sat frozen, hands stilled as I stared into space and waited for her voice.

She started again, a little calmer this time. "Daybreak is trying to kill us. The energy storm acts like a wave of electricity. The animals here have all evolved somehow, obviously. Since they don't die every time this happens. But Crispin—Dr. Carver—he can predict it. He's looking at his maps of the sun, the projections, and he says the energy actually builds up over time. That's what all those pretty lights are at dawn and at dusk. It builds up, and then this storm hits and sweeps a wave of death over the planet's surface. Literally everything with an electrical impulse—technology, wiring, the human heart—is fried in its wake."

Another deep breath. "We're dead. We're all dead unless we can get off the planet or find a place that somehow doesn't feel the effects of the pole shift. I don't know. My PhD is in communications and com tech. Not astrophysics. But if we live through this, you can bet I'm using all those communication skills to ream whoever signed off on this planet."

"BB, end recording."

She silenced Dr. Grotman's voice, and I sat breathing hard for a few more minutes, trying to get my brain to accept what I was hearing.

"It's an EM storm," I said slowly, as if saying it out loud would make it easier. "An electrical pulse that travels across the entire planet's surface."

"It kills tech and stops hearts," BB added.

I rubbed my hands over my face. All the outlets and computers and screens back in the colony. The battery compartments on the loader and the glider. The people. All dead in their tracks.

And the *Last Resort* had arrived in orbit just a couple of days early. Whatever this was, it had reached far enough to affect the colony ship.

"She said this happens...every few months. If the last one happened on the day we crashed, then the next one would be well before the next colony ship gets here. Well before I can leave. BB, did they predict the next one? When's the next storm?"

"Dr. Carver's data is uploaded with the commander's. He predicted the next electromagnetic wave...in thirteen days, fifteen hours, and four minutes."

CHAPTER 23

Daybreak: Day 49 (13 days until the storm)

My hand tingled and my feet ached. How numb could you get before you should worry?

I had to remind myself to keep breathing. In and out. My lungs didn't want to keep working. What was the point? I was dead in two weeks, anyway.

Less than two weeks.

"Anikka."

I flexed my hand to bring the feeling back into it. Just as an experiment. To see if I could still feel.

"Anikka?"

"Yes, BB."

"Your voice sounds funny. Are you all right?"

"I'm…I don't know."

"Anikka. You are not going to die."

I huffed a laugh and finally got my eyes to focus on her. "Do your statistics tell you that? Or is that the part of you that's trying to be human?"

"Both actually. Humans are optimistic. But also, you are

resilient. You have survived this long. Against all the odds. And my first imperative demands you be protected at all costs."

"That's programming. You've already proved you can change that."

"I don't want to."

I blinked, peripherally aware that this was not a usual answer for an AI.

"I care about you. I choose to care about you. The same way I choose to be afraid of heights."

I grimaced. "Sounds unpleasant."

"Sometimes our choices are. But that doesn't make it any less important."

I wrapped my arms around myself and squeezed, the pressure helping to ground me and drive the numbness away.

"Okay," I said.

"Okay?"

"This isn't any different from finding the colony gone. Or when the monsoons started, or fighting the slasherfins. So Daybreak is still trying to kill me. How is that any different from the last month?" I stood and brushed off my knees. "I'm not going anywhere."

"I will study Dr. Carver's notes. And perhaps we will find something useful back at the colony. We'll find a way to survive."

I didn't want to try to make it back across the Black Flats before nightfall and in the rain, so I stayed there for the night.

I built a crude lean-to against the side of the glider. Then I lit as big of a fire as I could manage, one that smoked and sputtered with the wet wood, but it made an okay pyre for the colonists. I stood as close to the heat as I could manage long into the night to pay my respects to the last few colonists who'd tried to escape the storm.

Perhaps the rest had made it to the cave system they'd been aiming for. Maybe they were alive there and just waiting to come back to the colony. I rubbed my thumb and swallowed.

I'd continue to hope, but without a working glider, I wouldn't make it across the lake. According to BB's updated map, the lake stretched long and deep. It would take me at least a month to walk around it, and I definitely didn't have that long.

The beetles didn't seem to like the heat and stayed outside the circle of firelight that night while I curled up under the lean-to and boiled some fish. I hadn't seen the slinkwolves all day. Maybe they knew better than to venture into the Black Flats.

I fell asleep that night, listening to the sound of the rain on the stones and the waves lapping the shore.

Flora of Daybreak ⚠

Itchbushes- itchy! repels alien wasps, causes rash, **avoid**
Drunk-peaches- delicious, dry before eating, **don't burn the wood**
Red caps- giant mushrooms, edible
Not-red-caps- carnivorous plant, mimics mushrooms, **avoid**
Nuts- edible

Fauna of Daybreak ⚠

Swarmstings- alien insects, swarm prey, deadly, **avoid**
Slinkwolves- blue and purple, fox-like, 60-80 pounds, hunts in packs, scavenger when alone, **avoid**
Assorted birds
Slasherfins- doesn't let go willingly, can be stabbed, **kill!**, delicious
Jumpernicks- monkey/lizards, gray scales and feathers, excellent climbers, eats fruits and vegetables, thief, **protect food**, great slasherfin bait
Megawing- giant red bird/lizard, predator, eats slasherfins, mean enough to kill out of anger, **avoid**
Troopers- swarming beetles, scavengers, consumes all organic matter

BB's data packets

-Wake-up companion data
-Infirmary companion data
-Navigation data
-Dr. Grotman's data

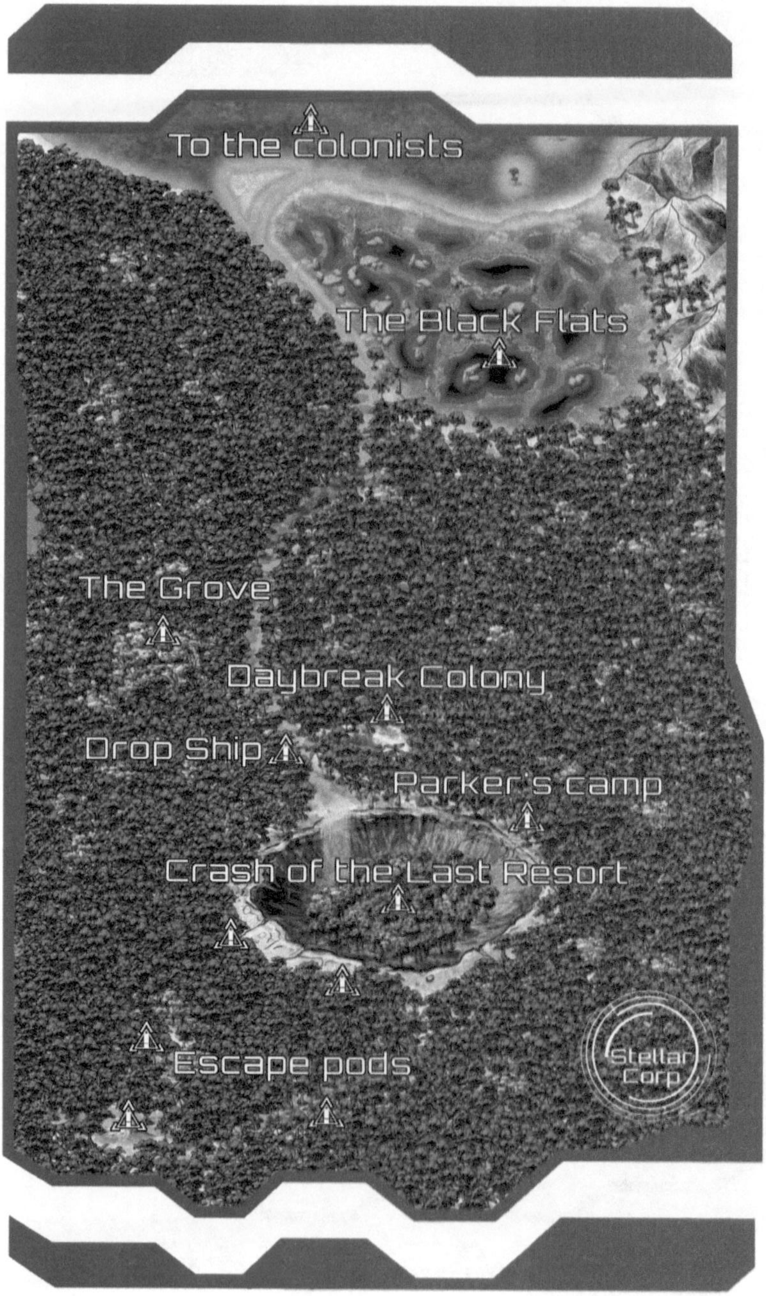

To the colonists
The Black Flats
The Grove
Daybreak Colony
Drop Ship
Parker's camp
Crash of the Last Resort
Escape pods
Stellar Corp

CHAPTER 24

Daybreak: Day 50 (12 days until storm)

I was awoken by the lights streaking across the sky, and I lay there staring at them. The morning remained misty, though the rain had subsided as usual.

How could something so beautiful be so deadly? I couldn't look at the aurora the same way, knowing its secret and the ticking clock it hid.

Was it getting brighter? More colorful? Would I be able to tell that the energy was building up until it finally broke and sent another storm across the planet, killing me with its beauty?

I stood on the shore of the lake, my pack reorganized and waiting at my feet. The waves had grown during the night, crashing into the beach and surging upward until the froth and foam brushed the sand in front of my boots.

"Somewhere over there are the caves where the colonists sheltered," I told BB.

She popped up on my wrist. "Yes."

"How far is it?"

Her hologram flickered and spread into a map. "120 miles across. Then another ten miles on the other side to reach the coordinates Dr. Grotman was aiming for."

"How far to go around?"

"The lake is over 320 miles long."

Too far to walk. Especially without knowing what I would find on the other side. I clenched my fists. "And they haven't come back. If they even can."

"Yes."

"Then I'll have to go to them." It was my only option right now. Find the caves and hope they actually did what they were supposed to do. Hope I found the rest of the colony there.

"How?" BB said.

Dr. Grotman had mentioned a "contraption" but clearly the first colonists must have taken it with them if she and the skeleton crew had been relying on vehicles. "I'll have to find a glider or fix this one up. I can't walk there, not in the time I have."

I turned around to face the Black Flats, trying not to feel like I was turning my back on my only hope.

I left the pyre smoldering behind me. It was marked on the map, so one day maybe I could come back and put up a marker. Something more permanent than a dying fire and a black smear on the sandy shore.

By midmorning, the sun had burned through the fog, and I could see a lot farther across the tar pits. The beetles BB had named troopers still followed me, waiting for the moment I slipped or tripped and got sucked into one of the black pools.

Their presence made a clicking, scuttling noise, like constant static in the back of my head.

Until all of a sudden, it faded, and I whirled around to see the beetles hurrying away across the Black Flats.

I would have been relieved they'd found a distraction if it weren't for a familiar yelp and a growl.

I swallowed. This was my chance to high tail it back to the jungle. I'd make it by mid-afternoon if I hurried.

But the sound stopped me.

"Vent it," I muttered under my breath and raced after the beetles, using the solid ground between pits as my highway.

Just over a little ridge, I saw what the troopers had sensed.

Three furry bodies thrashed in the tar, trying to free themselves. One of the pathways through the tar pits had collapsed, sending the pack of slinkwolves into the sticky black.

The fourth, the dappled wolf that had been my guard for weeks, paced the edge of the pool, whining.

The beetles skittered across the black surface and swarmed the nearest slinkwolf. It yelped as it went under.

"Crap." They might have been a threat, but nothing deserved that.

The dappled slinkwolf whined and barked and waded into the edge of the pool, his elegant neck straining to reach his nearest pack mate. The leader with the dark blue fur.

The troopers left behind a pile of white bones that sank into the tar as they raced for the next slinkwolf. It yelped and cried as it disappeared under the swarm.

Without another thought beyond the awful certainty in my gut that I didn't want to watch this, I surged forward.

The dappled slinkwolf quickly lost his footing and sank with tar up to his neck. He quickly tried to reverse, paddling back to solid ground, but the sticky asphalt sucked at him, and every move made him sink a little further.

The beetles left another pile of bones and swarmed for the leader. He growled and barked and thrashed. And then the dark slinkwolf disappeared under them with a desperate howl.

"No!" I threw down my pack and ripped my rope ladder free. I tossed it toward the dappled slinkwolf.

"Grab on," I shouted. As if he could understand. As if this was going to end any differently than every other hope I'd had. I'd hoped to find the colony, and it had been dead. I'd hoped to find the other survivor, and he'd been dead. I'd hoped to find the commander and her colonists. Dead.

"Come on, boy. You can do it. Grab the ladder."

The slinkwolf thrashed, his movements growing more desperate, his mouth open to pant.

"Come on," I whispered.

The slinkwolf's golden eyes met mine. And then he bit down hard on the nearest rung of my ladder.

"Yes!" I dug my heels in and yanked back, hauling him toward me. He moved about two feet, the tar sucking back against him.

"One more. We can do it."

I hauled, and the slinkwolf kicked, and he came free with a slurp. I fell back, landing inches from the pit behind me, and the slinkwolf's weight landed across my legs.

The troopers left their last meal and headed for us. The bones of the lead slinkwolf sank behind them.

Vent it. I was not lying here and getting devoured just because some insects thought I looked too exhausted to fight back.

I reached into my pocket and came up with my lighter. Then I leaned over and stuck the flame over the pit.

The oil BB had warned me about lit with a whoosh, sending flames racing across the surface of the tar.

The troopers went up in a crackle of carapaces, and the ones not caught in the blaze went scrambling away across the Black Flats.

I fell back and panted as hard as the surviving slinkwolf.

CHAPTER 25

Daybreak: Day 50 (12 days until the storm)

The fire died as quickly as it had burned, consuming what little fuel remained on top of the sticky tar. Little flames still burned where the tar bubbled, igniting the oil as it rose to the surface, but not enough to worry me.

The slinkwolf struggled to his feet, his legs trembling as he stared across the pit. Somewhere he'd gotten an angry slash across his right foreleg, either in the struggle against the tar or sometime before.

He pawed at the edge of the pit but didn't try to get closer, a soft whine leaving his throat.

"I'm sorry," I said, and the creature shied away from me, landing further down the solid path.

I reached for him, not even sure what I was going to do, but he growled, showing his teeth, and streaked away across the Flats with a howl.

"Wait!" I struggled to my feet, but my own legs shuddered after the adrenaline and the effort of the last few minutes.

"You'll never catch it." BB's hologram wavered as she stood with her hands on her hips. "You spooked it."

"Can you blame him? He just…he just lost his family." My throat clogged. There was a lot of loss going around these days. I swallowed and cupped my hands around my mouth. "Be careful!" I called.

I couldn't help the nagging worry as I made my way out of the Black Flats, but there was nothing I could do if the slinkwolf didn't want to stick around.

And I had enough on my own to worry about.

Like the countdown to an electrical storm that would sweep across the planet and kill me.

Panic crept around the edges of my thoughts, making my mouth go dry. The problem seemed enormous. It had already wiped out the colony and taken a ship out of the sky. What could *I* do against something so big?

I shook my head as I left the Black Flats and plunged back into the jungle, the familiar hoots and calls of the forest closing around me.

The point was, I *couldn't* do anything. Not yet. But I *could* think and plan and take things one step at a time. That's what I'd done since I'd crashed.

First step, get back to the colony. Now that I knew the danger wasn't in the area, I could spend more time there. Do some more exploring and salvaging. Maybe that Dr. Carver had left some research or tech that would help me get across the lake.

The familiar flash of blue and purple fur on my right made me pause. The slinkwolf was back.

But this time, his movements as he wove through the first few trees of the jungle were much more furtive. He wasn't stalking me in his usual way, where he made sure I knew he was watching.

Now he crept through the trees just out of my usual line of sight. My head remained straight, but I kept him in the corner of my eye.

He limped, pausing to pant whenever I paused.

Was I more company than a threat now, too? With his pack gone, maybe I was the only thing he had left.

Or maybe he was just finishing the last job his pack had given him.

I slowed my pace, stopping for the night a lot sooner than I would have on my own. The clearing I chose had one of the big trees with the tall wall-like roots. I could put my back against them and use it as a shelter instead of climbing into the branches.

My rope ladder had been so bogged down with tar that I hadn't bothered to haul it out. It was probably at the bottom of the pit now. Not to mention my legs and arms ached as I stared up at the tree. There was no way I'd make it after the morning I'd had.

But with the pack gone, I had a lot less to fear on the forest floor. Sure there were some alien reptiles and an itch-bush to contend with, but as long as I kept my fire going and chose where I set up my sleeping bag carefully, they wouldn't bother me.

The rain wasn't nearly as heavy these last two days as it had been the first two weeks of the monsoon season. My wood was a little damp, but here under the canopy, I could keep the fire going without a tarp or covering.

I shoved three sticks in the soft ground at enough of an angle to make a tripod and hung my homemade pot over the flames. I gnawed some fruit while my water boiled so I could make some fishy soup.

The colors of Daybreak's aurora flashed overhead, illumi-nating a visitor at the edge of my camp.

I didn't say anything, not wanting to scare the slinkwolf away. Instead, I took a couple of hard pieces of cured fish from my pack and tossed them casually into the dark a few feet away from the slinkwolf.

He flinched and disappeared for a moment but then reappeared around the tree where he could sniff at my offering.

I concentrated on my soup, keeping him at the very edge of my line of sight.

He crept one limping step closer to my fire, and I silently held out another piece of fish. This one I kept loose between my fingertips, so he had to come take it from me.

He took a step forward, nose outstretched toward the fish, then jerked away.

I waited.

He slunk forward again and snatched it from my hand, then he retreated to the other side of the fire, where he gulped it down in one bite.

I nodded to him and tried to smile without showing my teeth. "Good boy," I whispered.

He snorted and jumped back as if to dart away into the woods again, but his leg collapsed under his weight.

I surged upright. "Wait, you'll hurt yourself."

He tried to struggle to his feet as I approached, hands out in a placating gesture.

"Shhh." I handed him another piece of fish. I'd run out soon at this rate, but since I was only a day from the colony and the drop ship, I wasn't too worried.

He took it, grudgingly, but lifted his lip to warn me away.

I moved so slowly my heart burned with impatience, but I didn't want him trying to run again. As he was busy chewing the dried meat, I reached out and touched him gently on the back. Not the belly, as I figured that would make him feel vulnerable.

He laid his ears back but didn't move.

"Shhh. It's okay."

I gave him another stroke and tilted my head to examine his foreleg. The gash didn't look any better than it had that morning, caked with tar and mud. I reached to brush some of the mud away, but he pulled back and bared his teeth.

"All right," I said quietly. "But I'm worried about you. It would be better if you let me do something about it."

I couldn't imagine him letting me clean the wound or wrap it, and the lip he kept curled over his fangs told me not to press my luck.

"Okay, then," I said. "Rest. That at least will help. You... you need someone to look out for you now that you're alone. I know how that is."

Maybe I was just imagining things, but he'd always seemed the loner, even within in the pack. They'd delegated him to keep an eye on me, even when that meant being alone most of the time.

I didn't try to pet him again. I just left him there at the edge of the firelight and bedded down for the night. He watched me with golden eyes reflecting back the flickering light.

"Are you going to tell me it's a bad idea to sleep with that creature right there?" I asked BB. "Or admonish me for sacrificing so much of my food?"

"No," BB said. When she flickered into being, her light was a lot more muted, and she kept her voice low. "My care for you makes me distrust a wild animal, but I think I have to overcome that."

"Oh," I said. "Why?"

"There are several articles in my banks about how humans need interpersonal connection. How empathy and compassion are important to their mental health and emotional wellbeing. In short, I think he's good for you."

"I think I'm good for him," I said. "I guess we'll see if he lets me be."

He stayed across the fire, keeping his gaze on me even as I closed my eyes.

I woke in the night sometime as something warm and furry curled up behind me, pressing against my back, and I went back to sleep with a smile.

Daybreak: Day 51 (11 days until the storm)

He was still there the next morning, blinking at me as I shifted and sat up.

"Hey buddy," I said gently.

He didn't immediately bolt, which I took as a good sign.

I reached out to stroke the fur along his head and neck, and this time he let me. It was as soft as it looked, thick and long, a lustrous blue fading to lighter spots on his back and darker purple around his ears, muzzle, and paws. Though his legs and chest were caked in stiff, dry tar.

His ears flicked as my fingers sank into the ruff at the back of his neck, as if he was trying to decide how he felt about it. Finally, he leaned into my touch.

"We're gonna be all right," I told him. "I know it's scary being on your own all of a sudden. Even when that's something you thought you wanted. But we're gonna do fine."

"If we're all friends now," BB said, popping into existence. "We should get moving."

The slinkwolf didn't seem to mind her appearance, but then he'd seen her as often as he'd seen me.

I stood, and the slinkwolf followed suit. He moved stiffly, and I wondered if he'd pulled a muscle in the tar pit yesterday or if it was just his leg that was bothering him. When I went to reach for it, he shied away.

"Okay, we'll work on it," I said.

He stayed with me as I walked, keeping pace through the trees.

I bit my lip as we traveled. The slinkwolf moved with his head down, barely keeping an eye on me or our surroundings, just enough to stay nearby. True, I knew him mostly as the distant predator, the threat. But this didn't seem like his normal curious self at all.

Around midmorning, I angled north.

"What are you doing?" BB asked.

"Aiming for the river. I have an idea."

It would add time to the trip, since the river was a lot further north than the colony and my drop ship, but I couldn't keep watching the slinkwolf limp along.

We struck the riverbank by the time the sun was directly overhead, and I crouched on the sandy shore to dig a basin for the water to collect in, just like I did by the drop ship.

I whistled and held out my hand, but the slinkwolf kept a wary distance from the water.

"It's all right. We're not going in the river. No slasherfins. See?" I held out one of the last pieces of dried fish.

The slinkwolf crept closer.

"Good boy." I gave him some ear rubs for his trouble, and he plopped down on the bank beside me, panting.

I fed him pieces of fish as I scooped up water and dribbled it on his coat.

"You're going to need more than water," BB said skeptically.

I hummed in agreement and dug the sliver of soap out of

my bag. I hadn't been sure I'd have a chance to bathe while I'd been trying to find the colonists, but it hadn't taken up much space and I'd wanted to make a good first impression on them. Not a smelly one.

I continued the ear rubs, and finally the slinkwolf lolled over on his side. I splashed some more water on him and lathered up the soap, using a handful of sand to scrub the tar and other muck out of his fur.

His head came up, but he didn't try to run away, just watched what I was doing with narrowed golden eyes.

The whole time, I kept up a crooning murmur. I paid special attention and care to the gash on his foreleg, picking at the sticky tar to clean the area but trying not to sting him with the soap.

Finally, I doused him with clear water to rinse away the suds.

He sniffed interestedly at his wet fur before surging to his feet and shaking industriously.

I shielded my face with a laugh. "Good boy, Shade. Who's a good slinkwolf?" I fed him the last piece of fish, and he perked up his ears at my tone.

"Shade?" BB said.

"Yeah, 'cause he looks like the shadows under the trees."

Shade barked, sounding a lot like a fox, though with a deeper voice. He gamboled away like a puppy.

"As soon as you're dry, I want to wrap up that leg," I called after him. I wasn't too worried that the slinkwolf would run off and not come back. Last night when he'd capitulated and curled up with me...that had meant something. We were a pack now. The only family we had on this planet.

The rest of the trip back to the colony Shade spent ranging between me and whatever it was that interested him in the trees. Definitely not hunting. I couldn't imagine he was hungry after all the fish he'd taken from me.

About halfway through the day, I lured him closer with a tidbit of fruit to try to wrap his leg. He wasn't nearly as impressed with that as the fish, but he sat still long enough for me to smear some antibiotic cream on the gash and wrap a bandage around it. The moment I let him, he bounded away again.

"You know he'll have that off in less than an hour," BB said.

I sighed. "Probably, but maybe it will do him some good in the meantime."

By the time we passed the colony, the clouds were back lit with the aurora, the colors making them glow an eerie blue and green.

I almost opted to stay at the colony, since the river was likely flooded and since I knew now that the danger lay in the atmosphere and the sun, not the colony. But the rain that afternoon had never gotten to be more than a steady drizzle, and something drew me back to the drop ship. A sense of belonging and home I'd never had, even on Earth.

The river had only flooded its banks by a few feet today, and that remained too shallow even for the slasherfins to threaten me. I splashed across to the steps I'd carved out of this end of the tree bridge, and Shade bounded after me.

Everything was as I'd left it. My ladder still rested against the hull of the drop ship, my oven stood above on the platform, and my roof had held up. The seedlings had grown, too, and all the pots showed telltale sprouts now, not just the tomatoes.

Tension I hadn't even noticed melted away from my shoulders as I surveyed my domain. It looked...welcoming.

I climbed up the ladder and stopped halfway to check on Shade. "You want to come up? I could probably lift you."

He spun in a circle at the bottom of the ladder once, but he didn't whine or bark like he had when he couldn't reach his pack in the tar. Then he turned and headed into the forest.

"From our observations, I believe the slinkwolves are mostly nocturnal," BB said. "He will probably be back in the morning."

"Yeah," I said, though that didn't keep me from staring after him for a long moment.

Still, once I was up in my shelter I pushed my crate out and off the hull, so it made a pretty good step. A determined creature could jump up if they wanted to.

Maybe that was stupid, but it was the slinkwolves I'd been guarding against in the first place, and I hadn't seen any other big ground predators. Either because they weren't native to this part of the jungle, or because the slinkwolves kept them out of their territory.

Whichever one it was, I went to sleep that night, worried more that Shade would get into trouble without me, not that trouble would come to find me.

CHAPTER 26

Daybreak: Day 52 (10 days until the storm)

I woke up to hot breath on my face. When I opened my eyes, Shade stared down at me, tongue lolling out.

"I'm glad you made it up here." I sat up and something heavy rolled down my chest.

I reacted without thinking and batted a dead jumpernick across my platform. It landed with a thunk against the oven.

Shade snapped his mouth shut and hopped over to pick up the jumpernick again before dropping it beside me.

"Oh, it's breakfast," I said and rubbed his ears. "Thanks, buddy."

"That is disgusting," BB said.

"It's a gift."

Shade sat and watched, eyes gleaming as I skinned the limp creature. I actually hadn't managed to catch one before. The two I'd used as slasherfin bait had been windfalls, so to speak. The living jumpernicks were too quick, and as small as they were, they didn't seem worth the chase.

Apparently, Shade knew the trick of it, though. I glanced

at him as he sniffed around my oven. Maybe slinkwolves concentrated on smaller prey when they hunted alone.

I roasted the gift with some leftover nuts and a little of the salt I'd collected. True, there wasn't a ton of meat, but it was the most delicious thing I'd eaten in a while. Ten times better than the hard slabs of dried fish I'd been living off of. Bits of meat still clung to the bones, and I tossed them to Shade, who settled down to gnaw.

As I licked grease from my fingers, the sky caught my eye. The aurora still burned above the clouds, even though the sun was already well above the horizon, and the colors seemed brighter today.

My lips thinned. The coming storm had something to do with the energy from the sun building up in the atmosphere. Did the aurora indicate its progress?

"Ten days," I said quietly. I hadn't let myself think about it on the way back from the Black Flats, but the time had been ticking down quietly in the back of my head.

"What's the plan?" BB asked.

"Get across the lake." I rubbed my hands together and stood up. "To the caves. In time to shelter from the wave or storm or whatever it is."

"We don't even know if the other colonists survived there," BB said. "They haven't come back or tried to communicate. The caves might not be the solution to everything."

"Well, they're the only solution I have," I snapped. "Unless you can think of a better one." I heaved a sigh. "Maybe they didn't come back because they couldn't. Something about the storm kept them there? Or they didn't think they needed to come back..." That didn't seem likely, since the crash of the *Last Resort* would have been huge and obvious. If they hadn't come back after that, whatever they were dealing with must have been bigger.

That did not make me feel any better.

I packed up for the day, noting how much food I had left —not a ton. It would be a good idea to do some more fishing this afternoon—and headed for the colony.

Shade followed after me, ranging out between me and some unknown target out in the trees. He must have been able to track me pretty well, because he never seemed to have a hard time finding me. Even after I crossed the river and headed into the colony.

This trip was both better and worse than the last one. I knew now that there was nothing dangerous in the colony itself, so I didn't have that worry hanging over my head. But it was hard to walk through these buildings, seeing the lives that had been left behind. I couldn't help imagining Dr. Grotman and Sam and all the nameless skeletons I'd seen at the edge of the lake living their lives here, oblivious to the disaster that was about to overwhelm them.

And now that I knew what I was seeing, I could connect the burned-out tech, the scorched outlets, and the flashing screens. Stellar Corp hadn't been trying to hide what had happened here. They probably weren't even aware of it yet. And it hadn't been the colonists covering something up, either. This storm had swept through the colony, carrying so much energy and electricity that it had discharged through anything in its path that could carry an electrical charge. Wiring, cables, circuits, even the nerves of the mice in the lab.

The only things to survive had been a few screens that had been unplugged in the admin building.

I ran my hands over them, still blinking their evacuation message that had warned me the first time I'd been here.

"Why didn't these fry?" I asked, mostly to myself.

"They were unplugged." BB's hologram stood on my wrist, staring at the wreckage.

I shook my head. "So was a lot of stuff. And people aren't plugged in. The mice weren't plugged in. If these storms are strong enough to send electricity through something that isn't even tech, then it should be strong enough to fry screens that weren't plugged in. Their wiring should be shot."

"Ah, well, these screens do not have wiring. Their circuitry is not built on a copper-based wiring system. They have the newer optics system."

"Opticals." I sucked in a breath. "Oh my gosh. You're right. Optical circuits don't have wiring. They don't carry current the same way copper-based technology or even nerves do."

The generator out back had worked on optical circuits, and I'd be willing to bet every surviving bit of tech in the colony did, too.

Including the black box in Dr. Grotman's office. I had her access codes now, and the first thing I did was download the colony's logs, but they didn't tell me much more than I already knew. What I needed was Dr. Carver's lab.

I made my way to the biolab where I'd found the mice during my first trip. There'd been a couple of other workspaces there I hadn't had time for then.

Sure enough, a nameplate beside a door on the second story read:

DR. CRISPIN CARVER, PHD

ASTROPHYSICS DEPARTMENT

The "astrophysics department" consisted of a wide telescope shoved up against the window and a desk covered in photographs of the sun's surface, most of which were covered in scribbles and circles.

I shuffled through the papers, trying to find a notebook or journal. Something that would have survived the storm.

Unlike the computer in the corner with a blackened screen and a scorch mark up the wall that was taller than me.

All I found were the photographs and one image of Daybreak from orbit with lines drawn across it.

A note in the corner read:

Energy wave along the line of electromagnetic poles. Protection needs to be strong: Faraday cage? Around whole colony?

It didn't mean much to me and was less than helpful. If Dr. Carver had figured out how to protect the colony, he'd done it well after all the damage was done. Besides, he was out of my reach right now. I tapped my fingers against my thigh. He'd be the one with any pertinent information. If he was still alive. I'd have to find him along with the other colonists.

Which meant I was back to my original plan. Get across the lake. And since whatever "contraption" they'd used, they'd taken with them, I would have to come up with my own transportation.

I started on one end of the colony and moved to the other, making a list of all the tech and dividing that into three columns. Fried, still working, and salvageable. I saved the vehicle bay for last.

The big sliding doors stood ajar as if whoever was the last out didn't pause to make sure they were closed. I shoved one aside. It grated, over a month's worth of dirt and rust blocking the rails.

I'd only glanced in here before, but now I took my time. Inside the dark bay, a couple of shadowy shapes waited. A packer with no wheels propped up on a work frame. A loader standing empty in the corner.

And one glider tucked in the very back.

I could tell even as I hurried toward it that it was an older model with the down curved wings that were popular on Earth about twenty years ago.

I blew the dust off the clear canopy and slid the bubble back.

"Do you even know how to fly?" BB asked as Shade sniffed at the landing gear.

"Pfft, of course I do. I took classes on everything."

"So you have logged time in a cockpit?"

I grimaced. "In a simulation, yes."

"That is not an acceptable level of experience in this case." BB's voice had gone all flat and unimpressed.

My head shot up, and I frowned at her. "Hey, what happened to your humor filter?"

"Humor is not needed in this situation."

A little thrill of unease went down my spine. "BB..."

BB's hologram flickered. "Sorry. Am I supposed to find the idea of you falling out of the sky funny? Or maybe it's just that gallows humor I've been reading about. It's easier to face death with a laugh."

Her voice had gone back to normal with the huffy inflection I'd grown to expect. "You just...sounded really logical there for a second."

"I did?" Her face froze for a second.

"Do you feel okay?"

"I feel...normal. Would I notice if I did not?"

I held out my hands to her. "It's fine, I'm sure. You'd be able to tell if something was wrong. *I'd* be able to tell." I added that last part mostly to myself.

"I will increase the sensitivity of my humor filter, anyway. Why did the chicken cross the road?"

"Uh, what?"

"You are supposed to say, 'I don't know. Why?'"

"Seriously, did you look up a bunch of bad jokes?"

"These are classic jokes. The answer is to 'bock' traffic, by the way."

I groaned.

"What did the shore say to the sea? Nothing, it just waved."

"At least wait until I've answered." I slid into the cockpit as BB continued a litany of bad puns and ancient jokes.

"Anikka?" she said, interrupting herself. "I still don't think it's funny to see you die."

"Neither do I," I said. "Your concern is noted." I touched the pad to start the glider.

Nothing happened.

I sighed. "And unneeded. It's a moot point if I can't get this thing working."

I hauled myself up and out again, landing on the packed dirt floor before making my way to the front of the glider. It took me a second to find the latch for the front panel. I flipped it and flung open the lid.

"Well, crap," I said.

BB's hologram lit up the inside of the glider, bouncing off the scorched underside of the panel.

"Dr. Carver said the energy would pass through anything that can carry an electric current," she said.

I sighed. "And these things weren't built with optics."

I rubbed my temples. I knew the basics of a glider engine, of course. It had looked so good on my colonist application. But knowing how one worked and actually being able to fix one were two completely different things.

"Okay. I just need to replace the power source, right." The battery pack was clearly the source of the scorching. "As long as the wiring is all okay, that's the only part holding me back."

"Assuming the wiring is undamaged is a large leap in logic," BB said.

I ground my teeth. "Yeah, but it's...it's my only option. If the wiring is gone, then nothing will work. I can't replace everything."

BB opened her mouth as if to argue and then closed it, obviously thinking better of whatever she was going to say. Maybe she realized that slim hope was all that was keeping me moving forward.

I found a bank of battery packs in the shed behind the vehicle bay, where they'd been charging, but the force of the energy storm discharging through that much tech at once had blown a hole in the roof. Clearly, the packs were done for, and I didn't even bother checking each one individually.

The solar panels that ran the admin building and the other buildings were all blackened and cracked. The emergency generator still ran power to the admin building, but I'd never be able to plug in the glider and fly off while attached to an extension cord.

I had to break off my search to do some more fishing, otherwise I wouldn't have anything to eat while I worked on the problem.

But even the next day, it became clear there wasn't a power source in the colony that had survived the storm.

"Perhaps we should take a break," BB said as I slammed the lid closed on an autotiller I'd found abandoned in the corner of a field. It had been the least damaged thing I'd found, despite the vines creeping up its sides. When I'd opened it up, only the coupling between the battery and the rest of the engine was cut.

"I can't afford to take a break."

I'd just wasted hours trying to get the damn thing to route power around the break, putting my primitive wiring skills to work, only to get burned when an arc of electricity circumvented my safety measures and fried the whole thing.

"You can't afford not to take a break," BB said as I shook my singed hand and glared at the autotiller. The power source was useless now. "More mistakes might destroy the last chance we have."

I groaned and collapsed on the dirt beside the tiller. I broke a stick in half, more vehemently than I'd intended, and flung the pieces across the field.

Shade bounded after them and snatched one up before returning. He dropped the broken stick on my hand.

"Ow." I rubbed my knuckles. "Well, at least I've taught you to fetch." I groaned and buried my face in my hands. "This isn't going to work. The storm left nothing intact."

"Nothing except optical circuits."

I paused. "Do you think I could...could I get an optical power source to interface with the glider's wiring?"

"It is not built for it," BB said. "But you have built many things here."

"Platforms and rope swings." I shook my head. "This is way different." I knew a lot less about opticals than I knew about other engines. They were expensive, and the corps didn't have the budget to send their orphans the newest tech.

But a power source was a power source. And what else was I going to work on?

A couple of newer gadgets in the colony worked on optical tech. The cybernetic scanner in the infirmary, a seriously overkill coffee maker in the canteen, and most notably, the backup generator.

It took another day to pull apart the coffee maker and

another after that to power down the generator and lever it onto a cart so I could wheel it into the vehicle bay. If this was going to work, I'd need some power for my tools.

The power cell from the coffee maker at least looked big enough to handle the glider—seriously, who needed coffee that badly?—but I would have to find a way to interface opticals with copper-based tech.

The soldering iron was optical-based and worked just fine with the one optical extension cord I'd found.

I fitted an optical plate into the battery compartment of the glider and soldered it into place. At least the plate had contact nodes for the optical power cell. Now I just needed to get it to play nice with the wiring from the glider.

The rain pattered on the tin roof of the vehicle bay, a numbing cadence as I lined up copper wire with the nodes and secured them into place. Water dripped through a hole in the roof, gathering in a puddle across the bay.

I held my breath and fitted the power cell into the home-made compartment, lining up the contact nodes the right way around. It slotted into place with a click.

I froze for a second, waiting for it all to blow up.

"It appears stable," BB said. "Will it work?"

"Let's find out."

I didn't have the controls plugged in yet, but I could turn on the power cell from here. It hummed to life, lights zipping along its shiny surface.

"Ha." My breath came out in a disbelieving little laugh. I raced to the glider cockpit and leaned up to see if the controls had come alive.

Everything sat dark and silent.

My chest caved.

"Come on," I muttered and flipped the power switch. "Come on."

Nothing.

"The wiring must be gone," BB said quietly.

And there was literally nothing I could do about that. I had no way to replace the systems for the entire glider. And I had wasted three whole days on this failure.

There would be no getting across the lake. I was going to die here. I was going to have to watch the storm get closer and closer until it swept across the jungle and killed me.

My mouth went dry and heat raced along my limbs, making me tremble. I needed to hit something. To run and kick and scream.

"Vent it!" I slammed the hood of the glider down, sending the soldering iron crashing to the floor.

The optical cable broke loose when it struck and skittered across the floor, sparks leaping from the end.

"Oh crap." That was a live wire. I'd have to tiptoe around it to shut down the generator.

It landed in the puddle, electricity arcing across the surface of the water.

Shade perked up his ears from the opposite end of the bay. Just like he did when I threw something for him to fetch.

He bounded for the cable.

"No, Shade!"

I threw out my hand as if I could catch him.

He skidded to a stop in the puddle and snatched up the cable in his teeth.

I stared, mouth falling open as electricity cascaded over him, arcing across his fur and down his legs.

He panted around the cable as if nothing was wrong.

"How are you...Oh my gosh, how are you alive right now?"

He started for me.

"No," I yelled and darted away.

He stopped with a whine.

I raced for the generator and threw the emergency shut-off switch.

The sparks immediately dissipated.

Shade dropped the cable with a sheepish look and smacked his lips like his mouth felt a little funny.

He slunk up to me, and I tentatively touched his fur. My pulse still hadn't returned to normal.

"I think you gave me a heart attack." I reached down to hug him tight, which made him yelp and wriggle away.

"He does not appear affected at all," BB said, tilting her head as she stared at the slinkwolf.

"What does that mean?"

BB was silent for a moment. "We know the creatures of this planet must have developed some sort of defense against the energy storms. They happen quite frequently and are obviously not an extinction event. So Daybreak animals must have a defense. I think we've just seen it in action."

The failure with the glider still burned in my gut, making me a little sick to my stomach. But I had a mind that couldn't sit still. I'd never been able to rest in a problem the way Professor Orrion did.

"Wait, Anikka," he always told me. "Sit with it. If you are quiet and patient, the answer will come."

That had never worked for me.

"I can't get the glider to work. I'm stuck here until the storm. But if he could survive it—" I gestured to Shade "Maybe I can, too."

CHAPTER 27

Daybreak: Day 55 (7 days until the storm)

It took a lot of fish bribes to get Shade up on the scanner in the infirmary. He stood on the slippery metal table with his ears back and his tail between his legs as I coaxed him to stay.

I pressed my chip to the hologram pad on the scanner, and BB's image appeared as the machine whirred to life. No problem with these opticals.

The scanner was supposed to be for cybernetics, but the first part of a cybernetic scan was a full scan of the body, so BB thought it would work to give us an idea of what made Shade invulnerable to electricity.

"Good boy," I whispered as the scanner hummed and the red light passed over him. "Who's my brave slinkwolf? Hmm?"

"Scan complete," BB said.

I gave Shade another piece of fish and stopped holding him in place. He didn't hesitate to leap off the metal table and whip out the door.

"Is it working?" I asked.

"It's throwing every error it knows," BB said, hologram flickering. "It thinks the subject is deformed and ill. Which he would be if he were human."

"But will it tell you anything?"

BB didn't respond as a new hologram coalesced over the scanner bed, an image of Shade hanging in the air all done up in glowing blue.

"Hold on a moment while I analyze. I am having to compare alien biology with human. I will start with the nervous system, since that is the problem in human systems —huh."

"What?"

"I think I can see what is going on." BB flickered, and the hologram of Shade changed. Suddenly, I could see under his skin as a network of glowing lines snaked all across his body.

"Is that his nervous system?"

"It appears to be a secondary nervous system."

"Secondary. You mean he has two?"

"Yes." The hologram flashed deeper for a moment, showing something that looked a lot more familiar with a thick bundle of nerves traveling from his brain that I assumed was his spinal cord. They branched out just like a human's would, enervating everything from his muscles to his heart.

The image flickered back to the network just under his skin.

"I wish I could take a scan while he was being electrocuted to be sure," BB said. "But I suppose that is out of the question."

I glanced at the door where Shade had disappeared. "Yeah, not likely."

"Well, with this I think I can conclude this secondary nervous system is what protects the life on this world. It acts as a grounding and dispersement system. When the storm hits, the energy is transferred along these outer nerves, directing it away from critical systems like the heart, spinal cord, and brain, until the energy is discharged and rendered obsolete."

"Like a protective suit," I said slowly, my eyes narrowing on the hologram. "Except it's built in."

How could this help us?

"BB, I don't think I can build myself a suit. I barely got the glider power cell to work, and there aren't nearly enough opticals in the colony to put together into something like this. And I can't use copper-based tech to generate my own electrical field to negate and disperse the energy. All of it's fried, and I can't make more."

"Not a suit," BB said. "You need a network. Like the slinkwolves."

I spread my hands. How was that any easier? But when I opened my mouth to protest, BB held up a hand in a very human gesture to shut me up.

Then she reached out as if her hologram could touch the scanner where she stood.

"You have an idea," I said quietly.

"I am assessing the risk/advantage profile."

That didn't sound good. "I take it this is dangerous."

"Not everyone survives. My infirmary data indicates it is also incredibly painful and the recovery time is...not insignificant."

"Well, I'm sold," I scoffed. "What is this painful, dangerous thing that might possibly save me?"

"Cybernetics."

I started to laugh and choked on the noise when she turned to stare at me. "Oh, that wasn't your humor filter, was it?"

"No."

"BB. I don't even know where to start arguing. Cybernetics didn't save the commander."

"There are many different cybernetic profiles. She did not possess the electro-pulse control."

"Okay, but survival rates for the implantation are—"

"Significantly higher in patients with the right genetics. You were tested as part of the application process."

I opened my mouth and closed it. "All right, yes. I could have been a candidate if I'd had the money or the desire. I never thought I'd have the opportunity, though."

"There is no one to bar your application here. And your test results indicate the highest probability of success."

I rubbed my hands over my face. "Okay, one more problem, and this is a big one, where on Earth—or I guess Daybreak—would I get the procedure? This is just a scanner. It's not an implantation system."

"There is an implantation lab on the *Last Resort*."

The words hit me like a smack in the gut, and all the air left my lungs hard enough it took me a second to draw in the next breath.

"You really are serious."

"I do not see any other options at this time. The odds of success for making it across the lake without a glider are much, much lower than the odds of surviving the implantation process."

"Yeah, except the procedure comes with a whole host of other problems." I paced across the infirmary. "I'd have to get back to the *Last Resort*, which is leaking radiation. I'd have to get inside, find the cybernetics lab, survive the procedure, plus everything that comes with that." I threw my hands in the air to indicate the enormity of it all.

"You asked me earlier if I had any better ideas. This is my better idea. An implanted cybernetic suite could serve as an electrical dispersement mechanism. It could be tweaked to use the energy in Daybreak's atmosphere to protect you from its dangers."

I stopped in front of the scanner, bracing my hands on the edge as I breathed, in and out.

"You think I can survive?" I whispered.

BB looked up at me, face grim. "I know you can."

"Did the odds tell you that?"

"I do not need them. Anikka. Your care and safety are my primary directive. I do not see a way across the lake. And the odds that the colony survived in the caves...I do not like them. But I do see a way into the *Last Resort*. I do see a way to survive that is based on what you have accomplished already and what you can achieve before the storm comes."

I swallowed. Who would have thought a pep talk from an AI would be enough to get me to risk my life?

"If we're going to do this, it's not just going to be me. You're going to have to help me."

"Always," BB said.

To-do

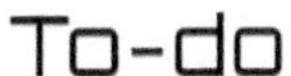

- Find a way to survive radiation
- Get to the *Last Resort*
- Get into the *Last Resort*
- Find the cybernetics lab
- Survive implantation

CHAPTER 28

Daybreak: Day 55 (7 days until the storm)

I barely felt the scratches and scrapes from the jungle as I pushed my way to the edge of the cliff west of the colony.

I stood there, toes nearly hanging over the edge of the rock face, staring through the rain.

In the center of the crater, the *Last Resort* stood at an angle, its nose buried in the ground, a swathe of downed trees spreading from the site of impact. The engines still glowed, even after more than a month, and the air shimmered around them.

I hadn't worked in ship systems at all, but everyone who went off world had drilled in flight safety. That shimmer was a telltale sign of epsilon radiation. A core leak. A deadly threat to anyone within a mile of the crash.

I chewed my lip. "I'll need a way to get there without dying within the hour."

"A radiation vest would be the obvious choice," BB said. Her hologram stared alongside me.

"Except I didn't see any in the colony. Must not be something they'd need once they landed."

"All drop ships in the exploration class colony ships are equipped with emergency supplies. Including radiation vests."

"What?"

I spun to stare back up the river. I couldn't see the drop ship or my shelter from here, just the waterfall and the river stretching back into the jungle.

"You mean I've been sitting on one this whole time?"

"It would not have done you any good before. Nor have you been able to access it."

I growled. The drop ship had landed on its side, blocking the hatch so I couldn't get inside. The thought of that empty ship that I could have used as shelter or salvage sitting there inaccessible had nagged at me for the past month.

"I *still* can't access it." I threw my hands in the air. "I can't bash my way in. Those things are built to reenter the atmosphere over and over again. I'd need a plasma cutter or-or an explosion so big it'd destroy anything inside."

BB stood with her head cocked, not saying anything.

I let my hands drop. "All right, fine. I guess I'd better get to work."

I trudged back toward the colony to search it yet again.

The only plasma cutter I could find was fried. Too many things in the colony were copper-based tech with wiring that the storm had either shorted or scorched beyond usefulness.

I did, however, find a stack of cutting gel packets in the workshop.

"There we go," I said as I pulled one of the foil packets toward me. "Now we're talking."

"Talking about what?" BB said. "You have not said anything of substance."

I rolled my eyes. "Never mind. I just meant this could help. I only got to use it once, back on Earth. But this stuff is cool. You mix the gel up with the activator, slather it onto whatever you want to cut and it slices right through. Metal, concrete, you name it, it melts it."

"Where is the activator?"

"I'm not sure." I sorted through the stack, looking for the complimentary packets that held the activator powder, but every single one was the gel. Frowning, I went through the rest of the workshop as Shade chased a grub across the floor.

"Oh great," I said, pulling a dusty note posted on the board at the back of the space.

Greg, some of our supplies from Earth got mixed up. We got three loaders and only one autotiller, a billion nano scrubbers we didn't order, and double the amount of cutting gel with no activator. What the hell are we supposed to do with that? Get Reman over in the lab to mix up some kind of substitute for the powder, will you?

I beat my fist against my forehead. Two steps forward. One step back.

BB shook her head. "What is the activator made of?"

I sighed and rubbed my temples. "Okay, let me think." It had been so long since that day with Professor Orrion. "Some kind of acid. It needs some kind of acid to start the reaction."

I flipped over the gel packets so BB could see the ingredients.

"I wonder if this Reman ever found a substitute," I said. "Or if he left with everyone else before it ever became an issue."

"There are several naturally occurring acids that might fit this chemical profile," BB said. "But you will not like this idea."

I barked a laugh, startling Shade. "Have I liked anything about this plan, so far?"

"Many Earth venoms contain enough acid for this use. Venom found in certain species of snakes and reptiles but also insects."

"Venomous insects? Ooh." I squeezed my eyes shut. "Okay, yeah, you're right. I do not like that idea at all."

"The swarmstings likely possess enough acid in their bodies to activate your gel."

"Yeah, and I guess they were only like the third way that Daybreak tried to kill me. The first being the storm and the second being the quicksand. Next to those, the bugs are super-friendly."

"I can tell by your exaggerated tone that this is sarcasm."

"Congratulations, your filter is working."

"Do you have a better idea?"

I waved my finger at her. "We have to stop saying that to each other. An idea can be 'better' than everything else and still get me killed."

BB's voice went quiet. "I am not trying to get you killed. I am trying to keep you alive."

A sigh escaped my lips. "I know. All right. I beat the slash-erfins. After that, what's a few hornets?"

And as much as I hated to admit it, I already had an idea. Time to put some of that drunk-peach wood to use.

Daybreak: Day 56 (6 days before the storm)

.   .   .

I didn't want to burn down the forest, so I had to set my trap carefully. And I knew exactly where I could find my quarry.

After a day's trudge through the jungle with my supplies strapped to my back, I reached the area where our escape pods had landed.

I hadn't been back since those first few days after the crash, and the churning in my gut seemed like a bad mix of nostalgia and PTSD.

A night in the dome pod and a few hours of work the next morning saw my trap mostly ready. Now I just needed my prey.

Shade followed, watching every move with bright eyes.

"I trust I don't have to tell you to be careful," BB said as I crept through the trees.

The area seemed familiar, even though there was no way I could tell one tree from another. Especially with my memory foggy from the pain and the chems from those first awful days.

"Nope," I said shortly. I wasn't sure if it was just me or if BB seemed unusually concerned. She kept coming up with these radical plans but then double-checked everything I did, warning me of the dangers with every step. Like a helicopter parent, only worse.

The swarmstings still hummed around the pod, though they had built a new nest directly over top of the half open hatch.

The disappointment of finding this pod and being so thoroughly blocked from its supplies still left a bitter taste in the back of my throat, even after all this time. But now it was time for payback.

I snatched up a seed pod off the forest floor and took aim. I launched it at the hive, and it struck with a smack.

The hive rocked and snapped off the tree. It fell, breaking

open against the hull of the escape pod before scattering across the ground in pieces of mud and sticks, little white larva wriggling against the ground.

"Just as gross as ever," I muttered as the swarm rose into the air with an angry buzz.

The hum grew as the swarmstings swirled into an enraged cloud and arrowed toward me.

Shade yelped and dove into the cover of an itchbush.

"All right, here we go!" I raced back along the route I'd come, following close to the marks I'd made on the trees. BB knew the way, but I'd have to keep well ahead of the hornets, and I didn't want to waste any time I could be using to outrun them.

I swerved around more itchbushes, and after a good sprint, I broke free of the edge of the forest where the dome of rock rose.

I paused there at the edge to glance back and be sure the swarmstings were following.

They speared through the trees, wings whirring and hum growing until the hair on the back of my neck rose.

"Oh, crap." Just because I knew they were coming didn't mean I was any less scared.

I whirled and leaped across the line of fire I'd laid that morning with wet drunk-peach wood.

Billows of dark smoke rose up, obscuring the sky. I landed on the other side and stumbled before yanking the collar of my jumpsuit up to cover my nose. I breathed through the fabric and waited.

The first swarmsting followed me through the curtain of smoke. It buzzed, faltered in the air, and plummeted to land in a curled-up heap.

One by one, the swarmstings fell. Plop, plop, plop.

"Ha!" I jumped up and down, pumping my fist. My lungs

burned with the smoke, and I pulled the cloth over my nose and mouth again before I fell asleep, too.

I made short work of killing them once they were down. In fact, it took a lot more work to put the flames out without succumbing to the smoke myself than it had to lure and kill the giant hornets. The afternoon rain finally saved me, the steady drizzle smothering the fires before I had to think of some other way to put them out.

I had to haul my kills back through the forest to the drop ship, but not before I checked the emergency compartment of the escape pod. It just held the standard first aid and ration bars. I dutifully collected them, since I'd done the work to clear the previously inaccessible pod, and closed the hatch respectfully on the long dead occupant.

"Sleep well," I murmured as I left them. "I'm sorry." This one wasn't recognizable after so long, but I still remembered the faces that I'd led to the escape pods back on the *Last Resort*, and I could substitute any one of them here.

I had enough daylight left to get a good start back to the drop ship, and since I could use my broken arm now and I was better prepared for the jungle, I made a lot better time. Meanwhile the little clock ticked away in the back of my head, counting every second.

Back in camp, I checked my newest batch of salted fish and dried fruit before spending the next day smashing up alien hornets.

A broad flat rock served as my mortar and another stone that fit in my hand became a pestle, and I spent hours making bug paste, pausing only when the afternoon drizzle threatened to turn it into bug soup.

"I hope this works," I said the next morning as I laid out the gel packs and my bug paste. "The activator is supposed to be a powder, not a paste."

"Well, if it fails, at least you have plenty of the gel to experiment with. Perhaps we can find something else venomous to try."

I shuddered. "I don't have time. I'm running out of days." Only four left, and I needed at least one to make it to the *Last Resort* itself. I would have done this the night before, except I didn't want the rain washing the gel off the hull.

I paused with my hand on the hull, my teeth clenched. "If this doesn't work...or if there's no radiation vest in here, then—"

"Don't do that." BB's hologram reflected in the drop ship's hull. "Don't think of all the ways it can go wrong before it even does."

I gave her a weak smile. "The phrase is 'don't borrow trouble.'"

"Right. That's my job. I'm the anxious one. You're the one who gets things done."

I raised a hand as if I could pat her head. Then let it fall awkwardly. "You're the one who cares enough to keep me alive," I said quietly.

I smeared the cutting gel across the hull in a wide square. Big enough to serve as a door and low enough I'd be able to step inside if this worked. It smelled oddly sweet, which I remembered from that one time I'd used it before.

The bug paste, predictably, smelled awful.

I used a stick to scoop up the paste and work it into the gel already smeared on the hull. It crackled as I mixed it in.

"That's a good sign," BB said as something in the gel sizzled.

I scooped more bug paste up and just globbed it all together as fast as I could, keeping as far back as was reasonable.

The gel hissed and spat sparks before bursting into searing light.

I stumbled back with a cry, dropping the stick, which was already melting, and flung my arm up to shield my face.

My eyes burned and watered, and I fell to one knee, scrubbing at them with my sleeve.

"Okay, on second thought, I could have done that better." I squinted at my fingers, but bright splotches marred my vision, swimming in front of me whenever I tried to focus on something. Like when you accidentally looked at the sun straight on.

All I could see were blurred pieces of the riverbank at the edges of bright white shadows.

"Crap, I can't see. BB?" My voice rose in panic.

"Temporary blindness caused by intense light should recede momentarily. For best results, rest the eyes in a darkened environment."

"Right, yeah. Like I have one of those handy." I cupped my hands over my eyes.

A whine to my left made me jump. "Shade?"

I could hear the slinkwolf panting, and a warm weight hit my legs at thigh level, nearly knocking me over.

"Whoa, buddy. What's wrong? Are you hurt? Did you look at the stupid bright chemical reaction, too?"

A down draft ruffled my hair, bringing an odd scent with it, musk and carrion and something dusty that reminded me of the snake house in the city's zoo.

Shade growled.

"Anikka, duck!" BB called.

Her warning rang along nerves primed by some primitive instinct, and I threw myself to the side.

Something large passed close enough I could feel the

difference in the air pressure, and there was an ominous crack right behind me.

I rolled and stared upward, eyes straining.

A huge red blur flashed around the white streaks that still dominated my vision.

"What the—"

Something shrieked, and I clapped my hands to my ears.

"Oh, crap. It's a megawing."

The biggest bad I'd encountered so far, and I was rolling around in the mud, mostly blind.

I scrambled to my knees and threw myself toward where I remembered the drop ship being. A swathe of the silver hull still burned bright at the edges of my vision, and I used it to figure out where I was so I could duck behind the ship.

A yelp made me gasp.

"Shade!"

"He is attempting to distract the creature," BB said. I couldn't see her either, but her hologram would stay on my wrist no matter what.

"He's going to get himself killed." I felt along the hull for my ladder and scrambled up, desperate for a weapon.

My eyes streamed, and I blinked, still trying to clear my vision as I stumbled along the top of the drop ship. Shade's barks and the occasional whimper drifted up to me. My heart thudded, and a lump in my throat threatened to choke me.

Cross bow. Where the hell had I left the cross bow?

Hanging on the tree where it usually lived. But when I lunged for it, expecting to feel the bark of the tree, I fell flat on my face, one arm dangling over the edge of my platform.

There was another yelp and a scrabble. The megawing hissed.

"Anikka, it has grabbed Shade."

"No!" I thrust myself up and scrambled for the grayish

blur beside me, hoping it was the tree. My hands found the stock of the cross bow, and I yanked it free from its peg.

Every safety rule ever said not to store a weapon loaded, but I was alone in an alien jungle. I wasn't an idiot.

I spun and aimed at the big red blur.

"Can you even see enough to shoot?"

"Sure," I lied. "Hey! Leave him alone."

I squinted as the red shape jerked and surged toward me. I pulled the trigger.

The stock jumped against my shoulder as the bow string twanged.

"A little high and to the right," BB said. "But you definitely got its attention. Duck."

I snatched the quiver and jumped, landing on my butt at the edge of the drop ship and sliding down the hull to the other side.

Claws screeched against metal behind me, and another shriek made my ears hurt.

I landed with a hard thud and grabbed a bolt to load. I thrust my toe in the stirrup by feel and yanked the string back until it locked.

The megawing landed on the drop ship, making it groan under the weight, and I twisted, throwing myself on my back. I raised the bow.

My sight must have been clearing a bit because the big red blur had feathers now. And a long muzzle with flashing teeth that snapped at me.

I pulled the trigger.

Impossible to miss at this distance. The bolt thunked into its shoulder, just below its massive wing. It shrieked and launched itself skyward.

I pushed to my feet, my hands trembling so much I had to

steady them on my weapon. But the megawing circled once before streaking off across the sky.

I clenched my teeth and stumbled around the end of the drop ship. "Shade?" I called.

A blue form whimpered and crept across the river bank to me, coalescing into Shade's familiar shape as he got closer. My eyes still streamed, but at least my sight was gradually returning.

I dropped to my knees and stroked the fur along his face before checking the rest of him. "Are you all right?"

Deep scratches parted the skin across his ribs, and I hissed in sympathy.

"Let me get the first aid kit."

This time, he actually let me smear some antibiotic cream on his wounds and wrap a long bandage around his middle.

"You saved my life," I whispered to him, rubbing his ears when I was done. "Thank you."

"I wonder if it was attracted by the light," BB said. "Or the smell of the gel."

"The light, I think. Remember when it was here to fish? The aurora lit up their scales so it could see."

I stood and paced to the drop ship. Now that I could finally see again and the gel had done its work and died out, I could see the wide doorway I'd made into the interior of the drop ship.

I stepped to the jagged hole and peered inside.

The drop ship lay on its side so the seats hung on the walls beside and above me, safety belts dangling like vines in the dark interior.

"Where's the emergency compartment?" I asked BB.

"Under the floor. Near the nose."

Nearly upside down from here.

"Of course it is." It couldn't be easy, like at the end of the ship that I could actually reach.

I hauled myself past the seats and clung to the nearest straps before reaching along the floor grating, searching for a latch.

I found the ring set into the floor and yanked. The hatch fell open.

Foil packets of rations and canvas-wrapped bags rained around me. I hopped down and sorted through them.

"Seeds, more ration bars, flares. Where is it?"

Just as my heart lurched, a plastic box with a radiation symbol on it fell beside me.

"Vent it, I almost thought it wouldn't be here."

"Why is that? It is on the manifest."

I huffed a laugh. "Because Daybreak hasn't made anything easy on me so far. Why would it be different with this?"

"It threw a megawing at you," BB said. "I think that's plenty for one day."

CHAPTER 29

Daybreak: Day 60 (2 days until the storm)

I wanted to give myself time to stock up before heading into the crater, but I'd officially run out. It would take me at least a day to get to the *Last Resort* and even more time to get inside and find the cybernetics lab. Then the procedure would take hours and... I needed to leave. Now.

I packed up that night, taking special care with the box of radiation vests. Everything else fit in around it or clipped to the outside of my pack. After all the trips I'd taken, I was an expert at getting it all just right. At the last minute, I slid some flares into the outside pocket. I had no idea what I'd find inside the *Last Resort*, but I'd never make it to the cybernetics lab if it was too dark.

The morning's aurora was so bright I had to walk with my eyes shaded. It was much harder to see the beauty in the staggering colors when they served as a reminder that Daybreak's energy storm was nearly here.

I made my way to Parker's old campsite. The cliff dropped

away here in a series of steps, much less steep than over by the waterfall, giving me a path all the way to the floor of the crater.

I took a moment and blew out my breath before sitting and sliding down to the next level on my butt. Shade followed, hopping down easily.

Most of the steps were only a short drop down, but the last one ended in an outcrop that hung over the trees below. Nothing barred my way to the branches except air.

"I could jump it," I said, peering over the edge.

"Do not," BB said, voice clipped.

"Oh, it wouldn't be that bad. Look, you can see the ground between the branches."

"That's more leaves."

"What's a couple of broken ankles?"

"Anikka!"

"I'm teasing, BB," I said, already unhooking a rope from the side of my pack.

BB's hologram rolled her eyes. "I do not enjoy this humor. Do you have to enjoy threats of death to be human?"

I snorted. "Usually the opposite. The part that makes it fun is when you're not actually serious. Real threat, not funny. Fake threat, hilarious."

"I will make a note," BB said sourly.

Having anticipated this possibility, I'd devoted the little time I'd had in the colony's workshop to a piece of rebar, a clamp, and an enormous pair of vice grips to make my own crude grappling hook. I'd also found a nice sturdy rope, so I didn't have to trust my vines.

I wedged one of the prongs into the corner between the ledge and the cliff face before tossing the rope over the edge.

"Come on, Shade." I patted my legs. "Come on boy."

The slinkwolf whined and spun in a tight circle before creeping toward me.

"Good, boy. Who's a good slinkwolf?" I handed him a piece of fish I'd brought specifically to bribe him and gave him a hearty pat before ducking and sliding my shoulders under his chest.

"Oof, maybe we should cut back on the treats, buddy."

Slinkwolves weren't nearly as big as gray wolves back on Earth, being a lot skinnier and built more like a fox. Their size came in the length of their legs and the fluffiness of their coat. But an extra 80 pounds would stagger most people. I'd never have been able to do this if I hadn't spent the last two months roughing it in the jungle.

Shade whined and panted in my ear, but I settled his weight over my shoulder and the top of the pack, then straddled my rope and wrapped it around my other shoulder.

"Hang on. I did this once back at the rec center."

I'd actually done a lot of rock climbing. Colonists were "encouraged" to be in pretty good shape. And rock climbing seemed a lot more interesting to me than weight training or cardio. But that had been on an artificial wall in a rec center with carabiners and someone to belay me. I'd only practiced rappelling once because it had looked like fun.

I crept backward toward the edge, keeping my weight balanced as I leaned back. Shade scrabbled at my shoulder.

"Just hang on, buddy. It's not that far."

I let the rope take our weight and unclenched my teeth when it held.

"Okay, here we go."

I let out the rope, letting it slide over my shoulder and between my legs as I walked down the cliff.

"See, not so bad." And the rope did most of the work, sliding around my torso and under my leg.

"No, I can't see," BB said. "I've turned off my sensors." She didn't even project her hologram. Like someone scrunching their eyes closed.

"Fair enough."

We'd almost reached the treetops when my rope jerked, dropping us a couple of feet. My boots lost their grip on the cliff, and we swung free.

I sucked in a breath.

"The hook is not holding," BB said, popping up in front of me.

"No, shit." I let the rope out, and we bumped against the cliff, but it was better than falling the rest of the way. Faster and faster I let it slide through my fingers, the fibers burning against my non-metal hand and making my arm ache where it had been broken.

The rope slipped again and my heart thudded in my ears.

"Anikka!"

"Shush."

I glanced around frantically and bit my lip. The trees were so close. And...they didn't look that tall. Maybe they were shorter than the ones in the upper jungle.

I kicked against the cliff and rocked to make the rope swing. The branches swayed closer. I kicked again, harder, and we swung out over the forest.

Shade wriggled, making me gasp.

"Hold still!"

He dug his paws into my shoulders and launched himself at the nearby branches.

"No, Shade!" I couldn't grab him without letting go of the rope, and he disappeared into the leaves.

"Anikka!" BB yelled.

The rope slipped again, and I leaned back to swing over

the branches one last time. At the furthest arc of my swing, the hook above finally gave way, and I dropped.

I yelled as I plummeted, the rope falling with me.

I had just enough composure to fling out my arms as the branches whipped past and catch hold of one.

My chest struck a thick limb, forcing all the air from my lungs.

"Oof."

Stars danced in front of my eyes as I clung to the branch, and I couldn't draw a breath for a long, panicked moment. Then my lungs heaved, and I gasped and coughed.

"Shade?" I croaked.

I blinked away the spots in my vision and dared to let go with one hand so I could rub my eyes.

"Shade?"

"The mangy thing abandoned you," BB said, popping up on my wrist to plant her holographic hands on her holographic hips. "And you're still worried about it?"

I cleared the leftover fear from my throat and scanned my surroundings. I'd been right. These trees weren't nearly as tall as the jungle giants above, but they were twice as wide, with long thick branches running horizontal to the ground. The ones at the bottom had to be at least fifty feet long, dipping to rest on the ground in places.

Shade panted from a branch above me, tail waving lazily back and forth.

"There you are. Don't worry, buddy, I'll come get you."

Shade yipped and responded by hopping down, branch by branch, until he could jump all the way to the ground.

I watched with my mouth hanging open.

"You could climb trees this whole time?" I shouted and nearly lost my grip on my branch. I'd spent so much time building my platform, thinking that would keep me safe from the pack.

"He can at least jump down from them, which is more than you can do," BB said.

"You're supposed to be encouraging." I pushed upright with a wince. I was lucky I hadn't broken any ribs with that fall. And from what I remembered from first aid class, ribs would have been a hell of a lot harder to heal while running around in a jungle.

"No, I am the sensible one," BB said. "You are the risk taker."

"I'll take that as a compliment." I scooted across my branch to the trunk and reached down with a toe, trying to find a lower foothold.

"Okay, this isn't so bad. These trees are easier to climb than the ones above the crater."

"Anikka, look. The rope."

I glanced where BB's hologram pointed and saw my rope dangling from the next branch down.

Sure enough, the hook had one prong all bent out of shape.

"Great," I said as I made my way lower to retrieve it. "Well, hopefully, that's not completely useless now."

I snagged the rope and eventually got my feet planted on the ground. The squishy ground.

"What is wrong with this dirt?" I rocked back and forth, and my heels and toes made little divots in the mud that instantly filled with water.

I snapped my head up, searching for the river that must be around. I'd had way too much experience with flooding waterways recently.

But it wasn't raining yet, and I couldn't see the river nearby.

"My map of the area shows that the waterfall ends in a pool that is not big enough to account for all the water that falls there."

"So it must be going somewhere."

"Perhaps there are caves beneath the crater where the river drains. It could also be draining into the land, which would explain the swampiness of this area."

"As long as it doesn't get deep enough for slasherfins, I'm good."

I set out, southeast, the engines of the *Last Resort* visible ahead of me above the trees. Each step splashed a little and soon I was kicking through two or three inches of water. Spongy moss hung from the nearby branches and bright purple plants grew between their roots, looking like a cup and saucer. Sticky fluid filled the recess of the cup, and I backed away with a grimace.

How many carnivorous plants could one planet have?

The sun crept past its zenith, and I picked up the pace. Time beat away in the back of my head, every heartbeat a reminder that I was running out of days and hours.

Ahead of me loomed the *Last Resort*, but inside, we'd find the cybernetic lab.

I shoved the thought away, again and again, ignoring the way my skin itched and crawled. The cybernetic procedure hadn't ever scared me before, but then I'd never been facing it personally. It had always been something other people went through, only a distant possibility based on my blood tests.

Now it was my only chance to survive the next two days.

I stepped on a branch under the water and it cracked, the sound of the splash echoing through the trees.

A herd of majestic purple deer snapped their heads up at the noise and bolted off through the trees, plumes of water arcing away from their feet.

I put a hand to my racing heart and huffed a laugh. "That scared me."

A streak of blue and purple shot through the trees and circled my legs.

"Shade?"

The slinkwolf whimpered and tried to hide behind my legs.

Uh oh.

CHAPTER 30

Daybreak: Day 60 (2 days until the storm)

The last thing to scare him this bad had been the megawing. I whipped around, scanning the skies, but I couldn't see past the dense leaves. The trees were too tightly spaced for it to get through. There was only the moss swaying gently above us.

"What is it, Shade?" I whispered.

His nostrils flared and his ears pricked forward, but he kept twitching and glancing over his shoulder like he couldn't pinpoint his fear either.

I quickened my pace, the back of my neck crawling as if something was watching me run away. I kept my eyes open, but I had no idea what I was looking for. And the swampy terrain was so different from the jungle above that most of my experiences from the past month were useless.

All I could do was be cautious and aware and move as fast as I could.

Shade stuck close to my side instead of ranging afield as he usually did.

"He must smell something," BB said. "Something my visual sensors aren't picking up."

"If there are herds of deer down here, then it stands to reason there'd be large predators too. Like the megawing or even something we haven't seen yet."

Every victory had made me feel like I was gaining ground against Daybreak itself. Every day I survived, every challenge I overcame, they were all notches on my belt. Or check marks on my colonist application.

But the prickle along the back of my neck was a necessary reminder that there was still so much about the planet that I didn't know. That I'd never seen before.

And anything I didn't know could kill me in the next moment without warning.

I let my eyes go unfocused for a second, just taking in the scenery, looking for patterns and differences and movement.

There, a flicker at the edge of my vision, just behind my shoulder. I turned my head to catch it, but it was gone.

"Something is following us," I said quietly.

"Stalking us, you mean," BB said.

I winced and walked another few steps before casually checking behind me again. Not turning the whole way or letting my gaze focus. Just waiting.

There it was again. A flicker of movement up in the trees.

My stomach clenched as my body registered something I couldn't even see.

Shade growled under his breath.

"Maybe turn to face it," BB said. "If it's a smaller predator, that might show it you are too much trouble to eat."

I lifted my chin and turned the whole way around, searching the branches.

Rain started pattering through the leaves, raising a mist in the soggy swamp, so it took me way too long to see it. A dark gray shape clinging to a long branch, blending with the bark of the tree.

Geez, it could be a part of the landscape it fit in so well. Unfortunately, it didn't seem to care that I'd seen it.

Slowly and deliberately, I unslung the cross bow from my pack and loaded it, puffing up my chest and squaring my shoulders to look as big as possible.

The creature stood, unfolding from its perch, revealing a long, low-slung body with muscular legs and a thick prehensile tail. It had rounded ears like one of Earth's big cats but with a jutting square jaw like a hyena.

The sight of it in the slanted sunlight made my mouth go dry.

"Oh crap," I whispered.

The thing was as big as a mountain lion, balanced above me on the big branches of the swamp trees, and had to outweigh Shade by at least fifty pounds. I wouldn't be scaring it off just by standing my ground. The stalking part of its hunt was probably just a courtesy, so that I wouldn't know I was about to be eaten before it pounced.

I raised my hands in the air, complete with cross bow, and waved them around.

"BB, play your awful music combination."

The sound burst out of the speaker on my wrist.

The big cat startled but didn't actually flee, flicking its ears at me.

I raised the cross bow to my shoulder and took a shot, aiming for the trunk beside it.

The bolt thunked into the wood, but instead of running away, the cat crouched, shoulders bunching.

"Crap."

It launched itself at me, and I spun. I hurled myself away, and the cat struck the tree beside me. Its claws gripped the bark, and it hung there, bright eyes blinking at me.

I sucked in a breath. Gods of all worlds, it was more agile than I'd anticipated.

I swung my bow up, and it leaped away, using the tree as a springboard.

I hurtled in the opposite direction, not bothering to take a shot, my blood singing a very simple song in my ears.

Away, away, away.

Between one step and the next, the ground went out from under me, and I fell into a murky pool. I managed to keep a grip on the cross bow as I found myself treading water in a very narrow, surprisingly deep hole.

Shade barked from beside me, his feet still on dry land.

I reached for the edge of the pool and encountered something long and sharp lining the sides.

What? Teeth?

My stomach lurched, and I heaved a mighty kick as the sides of the pool started to snap closed.

I threw myself at the side, heedless of the teeth, and hauled myself out, rolling away and away from the worm—snake—water monster that surged up out of the pool.

A huge scaly head snapped at me, and I scrambled away, snatching up my cross bow. Clearly, this new threat dug holes for itself just under the water and waited for lunch to drop in on it.

I'd stop and be offended, but the big cat launched itself across the water.

The water snake whipped around to intercept it, trying to make up for losing me by grabbing the cat.

It yowled in anger, and I didn't wait to see who would emerge victorious.

I sprinted through the trees, jagged breath searing my lungs as I scanned the ground for more holes.

Shade bounded up next to me, keeping pace, then pulling ahead. He turned abruptly, and I caught the black edge of another pool just in front of me.

I followed Shade, and he led me unerringly through the trees and the holes full of waiting carnivores.

Finally, I had to slow and catch my breath against a tree. A cursory check behind me showed I was alone. At least for now.

"Good boy," I gasped, reaching to rub Shade's ears. "BB, make a note. Apparently, there are lots of large predators down here."

Silence met my statement.

"BB?" Cold swept my chest, and I raised my prosthetic. The hand had been drenched in the murky pool.

But it had gotten wet before and my seals still held.

"BB?"

BB's hologram flickered to life, sputtering for a brief second. "I am still here, Anikka."

My shoulders dropped, and I collapsed against the tree. "Don't scare me like that."

"I apologize. I was adding deathkitty and slugtooth to your list."

I huffed a relieved laugh. "You're getting good at those names."

BB didn't smile. "I only analyze various attributes and combine them in interesting ways. I do not create anything new."

"That's really all humans do," I said, wiping the water from my prosthetic. "Combine old things in new ways. Over and over until it hardly resembles the old."

"Really?" BB asked, glancing up at me.

"Yeah." I smiled at her. "Anyone can copy something. It takes creativity to change it into something more interesting. BB, you're more human than any AI I've ever met."

"I do not believe you have met many," she said. Then she finally smiled. "But thank you." She glanced around. "I would suggest leaving the forest as quickly as possible. The deathkitty uses the trees to hunt silently and the slugtooths could still be a threat if you do not see them in time."

"Yeah, you don't have to tell me twice."

I splashed through the swampy forest, trying to keep an ear out for the return of the cat, just in case.

An hour from the edge of the cliff, gloomy light broke through the trees, and I reached the edge of the swampy forest. Not because the forest naturally ended, but because this was the beginning of the devastation zone.

Downed trees lay in an oddly symmetrical circle, spreading from my feet all the way to the *Last Resort* that waited half-buried, nose down in the center of the crater. Like a crooked grave stone for a thousand people.

The engines still glowed, sending off a shimmer I could barely see in the sunlight.

"I am detecting rising levels of radiation in your systems," BB said. "It is time to don your radiation vest."

The box held two harnesses, each a collection of straps and two thick plaques that sat on the wearer's chest and back. I slung mine on, fastening the buckles under my arms and situating the plaques. There was nothing electronic about them, so they had survived the storm just fine.

The plaques were designed to draw and absorb epsilon radiation, keeping the wearer's most important organs safe underneath.

I made Shade stop, and I fastened the second vest over his torso, adjusting the straps until the plaques sat balanced over his chest and spine. I'd bandaged up his wounds from the fight with the megawing the day before, and now I made sure the straps wouldn't cut into him painfully. He wasn't human, but hopefully this would keep him from absorbing anything too harmful.

The way across the field of devastation was a lot harder to navigate than the swamp or even the jungle above. Here I had to clamber over the toppled trees, avoiding the jagged ends of broken branches where they jutted out from the twisted trunks. Scorch marks marred the gray bark in many places, breaking off with a puff of ash when I accidentally stepped on one or slid over the top.

Luckily, I did not find many carcasses of the animals that had to have perished in the shock wave. Predators like the megawing and scavengers like the slinkwolves must have dragged them off long ago.

"The *Last Resort* must have maintained some power as it fell," BB said.

"Why's that?"

"The shockwave that caused this devastation is not nearly as large as it would have been if the ship had hit at terminal velocity."

My lips pinched as I thought of those last terrifying moments I'd had on the *Last Resort*. The energy storm from Daybreak must have been strong enough to reach the ship where it had just settled into orbit. Ships were built with enough EM shielding to protect them from all the hazards of space, and I'd bet that's why there had still been enough power to handle certain things like the med tech waking us up and launching the escape pods. But whatever systems the storm had fried had been important enough to crash the ship.

It was late afternoon by the time I stepped into the

shadow of the *Last Resort,* and a chill settled over my shoulders.

This could have so easily been my last resting place, too.

"How do we get in?" BB said. She stared up at the hull of the ship looming over us.

"Well, that's the next trick." I heaved a sigh and started on the long trek around the ship, looking for a hole or a loose hatch that was low enough to serve as an entry point.

The *Last Resort* was about the size of a cruise ship, one of those big ones that advertised getaways from Earth's crowded landmasses. It took a quarter of an hour to walk the whole way around it.

The ship was buried nose first with the C-hatchways peeking out of the ground, but a slope of piled dirt and rock and debris covered the external emergency releases. It would take me way too long to dig down to them

The port side D-hatchway remained firmly closed nearly twenty feet above my head, but the starboard side had been blown wide open. The aurora started burning behind it, colors appearing far earlier than the rest of the time I'd been on the planet.

"That's our ticket in," I said, craning my head back to peer at the dark opening.

"Are you being serious, or is this sarcasm?" BB said. "Because that is a long way up there—"

Shade yipped, and I whirled in time to catch the deathkitty from the forest leaping across the debris field.

It struck me, claws out, and slammed me back into the slope beside the ship.

I screamed and kicked out at the creature's soft belly as it dug into my shoulders. With a heave, I launched it off of me.

It landed with a snarl, but in the next second, it had flipped back to its feet.

The deathkitty crouched, strong legs bunching, but as it sprang, Shade leaped in between us.

"Shade!"

The deathkitty's claws raked his flanks, but caught in the harness of the radiation vest.

With a yell, I lunged forward with the cross bow, firing off a shot that grazed the deathkitty's back.

It yowled and twisted, swiping at me. Its big paw batted the cross bow and wrenched it from my hands. The weapon hit the ground with a crack, one arm splintering on impact.

But the altercation at least distracted the big cat long enough it shook loose from Shade's harness. I wrapped my hand in one of his straps and yanked him back up the hill.

My chest heaved and my heart pounded as the deathkitty growled deep in its throat.

"Do you have any ideas?" BB asked.

I didn't have time to answer.

I reached for the rope tied to the side of my pack with one hand and the flares in the outside pocket with the other.

If this didn't work, we were vented.

The deathkitty crouched for another lunge, and I closed my eyes and pulled the cord on the flare. Red sparks spit out the end, illuminating the dark behind my eyelids. I shielded my eyes before opening them again.

The deathkitty twisted, the sparks reflecting in its startled gaze. It scrambled to avoid the searing light, climbing up onto a broken tree.

I uncoiled my rope in my other hand and glared at the mangled end of the hook with its remaining two prongs. "The rest of you better work."

I swung the hook, aiming for the slightly open hatch above me.

It clanged off the side and fell beside me again.

"Crap." This is where Professor Orrion would be praying.

I glanced over my shoulder to see the deathkitty gathering itself.

"Please work. Please work." I flung the hook once again, and it sailed through the open hatch.

"Yes!" I drew down gently on the rope. If I rushed, I'd ruin this, but my entire back prickled, knowing the deathkitty was coming.

The hook caught.

Just in time. A downdraft ruffled my hair.

I threw the flare at the deathkitty. It sprang away, but I wasn't really trying to hit it. Just draw attention to it. The flare burned bright against the rapidly falling night.

"Shade, here!" I caught hold of Shade's harness and tied the end of the rope to it. Then I leaped as high as I could and caught the rope, shimmying up as fast as I could manage with one mostly healed hand and a prosthetic.

Halfway up, the downdraft turned to a gale, and a shriek rang out across the crater.

A red blur coalesced out of the colors of the aurora and streaked toward the flare, making me sway on my rope.

"Did you—did you really draw the megawing here?" BB said.

"Hey, if it wants dinner, it can have dinner."

The megawing dove for the deathkitty, claws out.

I resumed my climb, breath hissing between my teeth. I had about thirty seconds before the megawing either won or the deathkitty turned tail and I was left to deal with the consequences of calling the biggest predator on the planet.

Sweat trickled down my neck and spine as I reached the edge of the hatch and caught hold with my prosthetic hand. The rubber keeping it suctioned to my arm pulled against my skin, threatening to come free from the pressure, but I kicked my feet against the hull and threw my weight higher until I could clamber into the open hatch.

I spun. Below, the megawing batted at the deathkitty with its wings. The big cat snarled and bit and clawed, but it was outweighed and outmaneuvered. Already, streaks of blood coated its fur and dripped on the gray bark of the downed trees. Shade circled at the base of the hull, panting frantically, trapped by the rope I'd tied to his harness.

I hauled on it, surprising Shade, who rose with a yelp.

I used the edge of the hatch to brace the rope, and it slid slowly upward.

The deathkitty howled, long and anguished, and in the next second, streaked away across the area of devastation.

The megawing flapped once as if to follow, then spun in midair, its golden glare catching Shade hanging at the end of the rope and me standing in the open hatch.

I spat a litany of bad words, hauling the rope hand over hand, my shoulders straining and the flesh on my palm burning.

The megawing surged upward.

I threw myself forward, catching Shade's harness in one hand, and yanked him up and inside the ship. I rolled backward and caught the hatch with my foot, yanking it toward me.

It slammed shut, and the megawing smashed into it with a clang that made my ears ring.

A muffled screech reached us through the metal, then there was a flapping sound and finally silence.

CHAPTER 31

Daybreak: Day 60 (2 days until the storm)

Shade nudged my arm, snapping me out of the residual panic, and I shuddered before slinging an arm around him.

"Are you all right?" My hands stroked up and down his flanks.

His bandages from the first megawing attack were grimy and probably needed a change, but they'd actually protected him from the deathkitty's claws to a certain extent. They and his harness showed long rents, but aside from a few scratches, Shade himself was mostly unscathed.

I drew a deep breath and raised my wrist to stare at the little blinking light under the base of my thumb.

"What about you, BB?"

BB's hologram appeared, reflecting blue light against the exposed hull. She flickered for a brief moment. She'd been doing that a lot. My prosthetic had taken a beating in the last few hours, not to mention the last couple of months, and BB herself lived in the chip embedded in my metal wrist. If that stopped working, BB would be gone forever.

My stomach rolled, and I clenched down hard on the moment of nausea.

"I am unharmed," BB said.

AIs didn't lie. At least not until they were fully integrated and deemed the truth too harmful to sensitive humans.

I stared at her for a second longer before responding. "Okay. Can you tell me a joke?"

"What do you get when you cross a deathkitty with a megawing?"

My brow furrowed. "I don't know. What?"

"A free escape."

I barked a laugh. She was fine.

"I don't know if I'd call that free. I lost the cross bow. And it could have gone so much worse." I rotated my arm, shoulder twinging.

I stood, bracing myself against the grating that would normally have been the floor. The *Last Resort* sat at an angle, and the wall leading to the rest of the ship was nearly level with the floor.

"The artificial gravity must be damaged," BB said.

"That makes sense." I remembered my last moments on the ship. "It was out as we crashed, too."

The overhead lights—the ones on the ceiling directly in front of my face—were out too, but the emergency lighting along the floor still gave off a weak glow. Enough to see Shade struggling to find his footing against the slanted wall.

"All right." I pushed upright and staggered a little.

"Your vital signs are depressed," BB said. "Given what time it is and the exertion and the adrenaline you have experienced today, I would recommend taking a moment to rest."

I shook my head with a laugh. Fatigue clawed at my mind, and I rubbed my gritty eyes, ignoring the aches in my arms.

"It's late, yeah, but that means the storm is only thirty-four hours away. I don't have time to sleep."

"Exhausted humans make mistakes."

My lips pressed tight together. "I'm not there yet, BB. Getting to the cybernetics lab and getting the implantation is the most important thing right now."

BB looked like she was about to protest, then thought better of it. "All right. The lab is on deck 3, past hatch H."

I stared up the corridor. That was as uphill as it could get without being completely vertical.

"I guess we'd better start then."

I stumbled to the end of the hatchway, where the corridor opened onto the rest of the ship. A couple of offices lined the passage where new passengers would be processed. I hadn't come in through this hatch, but it looked exactly like the one where I had, just sideways.

Past the offices, a huge space opened, emergency lighting giving everything a dim glow appropriate for nightfall. An open court with tables welded to the floor stood in the direct center, with counters and kiosks half-illuminated around the edges. It felt forbidden, like I was trespassing after curfew.

I climbed up through the dining complex, using the tables as places to stop and rest my weight.

It was too bad I hadn't been able to get in here before. The kitchens were full of non-perishables preserved for the ten-years-long space flight to Daybreak. This place would have made my first couple of weeks on the planet much less terrible.

Morbid curiosity led me to climb up into the nearest kitchen and try the door of the fridge.

I peered around the edge and let out a breathless laugh. "Juice!"

Rows and rows of foil packets caught the light from the

emergency strips, but tucked in a small cardboard crate just inside the door were individual cartons of juice.

I snatched one and cradled it to my chest. The amount of relief and joy that cascaded through me at the feel of that carton soared far higher than it should have. But there was something about it that made triumph beat in my chest. Like I'd already won.

"Well? Aren't you going to drink it?" BB said.

My fingers tightened around the carton. "I should eat something, but...I think I'm going to keep this."

I slid it into the top of my bag before finding some real food. As much as I wanted to accept that feeling of triumph, this wasn't over yet. There was still more to get through.

I'd save it as a reward for after the implantation. If it was anything like waking up from cryo-sleep, that's when I'd need it the most.

I paused long enough to unpackage some spaghetti and lap it up out of the foil. It was cold and squishy, but surprisingly satisfying, considering I'd been living on fish and fruit and the occasional egg.

Shade got chicken pot pie and wolfed it down, cold or not.

Then we climbed.

Shade kept up, remarkably well, hopping from table to table like the branches in the swamp and then scrambling up the slanted deck, using his claws to gain purchase against the grating and the rubber mats crew members had used for traction.

We climbed out of the dining complex and into one of the ship's many recovery wards. I ignored the twinge and the stray thought that this is where I should have been spending most of the last two months. Cryo recovery was supposed to be so important.

I shook my head with a resigned laugh as we passed recreation halls lined with equipment for guided muscle stimulation and gaming lounges for community enrichment, where I should have gotten to know my fellow colonists.

Along with the recovery and recreation areas, there were so many med suites for the variety of problems that could crop up after cryo revival. Maybe if the *Last Resort* hadn't crashed, the Godspeed sleeper would have survived his cryo sickness.

I swallowed back a lump and moved on.

I did not find very many bodies. Fortunately. After nearly a month and with the climate controls of the *Last Resort* shot, there wasn't much left of anyone who'd still been alive on impact. But since there'd only been a skeleton crew to keep the ship flying until we reached orbit and everyone else had been in cryo sleep, there weren't that many people around.

Except for nearly a thousand sleepers left in their pods.

We had to pass through the sleeper bay to reach the lab, climbing around bank after bank of pods. I tried not to think of them as coffins, barely glancing at them as I climbed.

But the lights of the pod controls blinked incessantly.

I lost my footing, and slid, catching myself against a cry chamber. The name plate loomed in front of me, and I couldn't help reading it.

Tammi Chen

The lights beside the word 'stable' blinked over and over again, and I frowned at the vital signs readout.

"BB," I whispered. "That's a heartbeat."

She popped up to peer at the readout. "It is. A healthy one, too."

I stared around at the pods, my mouth dropping open. "They're alive? I...I thought the impact would have killed everyone."

"It appears many survived. They remain asleep, though."

"Asleep, but alive."

BB's holographic face grew sad. "Not for very long. The pods will not keep them safe from the electrical storm that is coming. It will stop their hearts just as surely as if they were awake." She gazed at Tammi Chen's name. "At least they will not feel it. That much electricity is going to be very painful."

I suppressed a wince, focusing on the thought racing ahead of everything else. "But they'll still be in cryo. The pods are optical tech, right? They'll still work."

BB tilted her head. "Yes. The pods themselves will survive the storm."

"And they're designed to preserve people. Even if they die. So they can be revived later." It was one of the oldest purposes of a cryo pod. Before we'd figured out how to sleep for years and years, they'd been used to preserve people in death. And that translated to long-haul voyages as well. If someone died in cryo, there was a reasonable chance they'd make it to the other side intact enough to be revived.

I waved my hand at the controls. "If the pods are still functional after the storm, the people will be okay. Eventually. We can still revive them!"

"It is possible," BB said. She hesitated long enough for me to notice.

"What is it?"

"This is a viable option for your survival as well."

I pulled back. "What?"

"You could...go to sleep."

I choked. "And what would happen after?"

"I...I don't know. My programming likely will not survive without access to the ship or a shielded hologram pad. But this way, you would not have to suffer through the storm."

"I would be dead. You would be dead."

"You would be revivable. Eventually. When the corporations learn of this disaster and come to investigate."

I didn't even have to think about it. I shook my head as I started climbing again. "I'm not trusting Stellar Corp to get here with help any time soon. Those people will need someone to revive them, and that someone is me. And I'm not sacrificing you just to avoid a little pain."

"It will likely be a lot of pain," BB said, but she didn't argue again as we made our way up the ship.

With the core cracked, all systems were down but the emergency ones. Hopefully those would be enough for what we were planning. We still needed to get to the cybernetics lab to fire it up and see.

I recited a litany of hopes in my head: that we could reach the lab, that I would survive the procedure, that the implantation system would still be working.

By the time we reached deck 3, my legs burned and trembled from the climb.

"Here," BB said quietly.

I looked up and nearly burst into tears.

"It's closed."

None of the closed doors we'd passed had budged. The emergency power didn't handle anything except the essentials. The routes to escape pods and hatchways had been clear, but nothing else.

I hauled myself up to the door and wedged my fingers into the crack. Yanking on it did nothing except make my muscles scream.

I collapsed against the crooked wall and breathed. Across from me, the nameplate beside the door mocked me.

CYBERNETICS LAB: AUTHORIZED PERSONNEL ONLY.

There was a wide window beside it, just like in the med bay. In case you wanted to watch while the techs worked.

Every fifty feet along the corridor hung a fire extinguisher. I grabbed the closest one and staggered up to the window.

"Anikka, please be care—"

I slammed the extinguisher against the glass. It shattered and rained to the floor in a tinkling cascade of shards.

"—ful. Was that absolutely necessary? We could have found another way in that did not involve broken glass."

"No," I said, lifting Shade carefully over the mess. "There's always something in the way, and I'm tired of going around. I'm tired and everything hurts, and we are out of time to waste on stupid obstacles."

BB remained silent as I crunched through the glass and set Shade down where he wouldn't get sliced up.

The first room was a lobby with a desk and cabinets all slanted and askew from the angle of the deck. A line of chairs was piled against the far wall.

I slid down the steep deck and through the open door into the next room. This one had a counter with some personal knick-knacks, as if a tech had mad this space their own. A bed was attached to the floor.

A prep room.

"The implantation chamber is through there," BB said, indicating the last door in the suite.

I ignored the way my hands shook as I made my way down the slope to the last room.

The emergency lights lit a central bed with an eerie white glow, the illumination coming from underneath and making the chamber look like it floated on light. Robotic arms hung over the chamber, their tools reflecting my wide eyes back at me. Worst of all was the glass dome that fit over the bed. It waited like a huge Venus fly trap ready to trap me inside.

I swallowed, my throat dry.

A panel on the wall showed a little blinking light in the corner.

I took a deep breath and stepped forward to touch it.

The screen flashed to life, a glaring blue that hurt my eyes after the dim interior of the *Last Resort*.

My free hand unclenched.

"The screen still works. Will the rest of it?" I glanced back at the bed and the dome. Lights had come on around the edge of the glass dome, and all the robotic arms retracted, leaving the way into the chamber clear.

BB popped up. "It appears so. The chamber is in working condition."

An access screen flashed up.

CODE REQUIRED: __ __ __ __ __ __ __ __

"Don't worry, we have Dr. Grotman's codes," BB said. "Transfer me, and I will begin the prep procedures."

My brows came down. I wanted to wait, to give myself time to work up to this. The whole time I'd been walking through the crater and climbing up the *Last Resort,* I hadn't actually allowed myself to think about what was at the end. I wasn't ready. Not even remotely.

I pressed my metal hand to the screen anyway, and a hologram pad flipped down from the wall beside it. BB appeared, standing on the little platform, her program instantly transferred to the cybernetics system.

A dozen codes scrolled up the screen and I only caught a couple of them.

CYBERNETIC OPTIONS AVAILABLE

-ELECTRO PULSE CONTROL

-CAMOUFLAGE (MILITARY PERSONNEL ONLY)

-MUSCLE STIMULATION

BB highlighted electro pulse control before I'd even had a chance to register the other options.

I gulped. There were dozens of options for cybernetic implants and infinite ways you could use each one. Electro pulse control had always felt like the most alien to me. The most out there possibility in the very brief moments I'd let myself even think about my candidacy for an implantation.

The whole point of it was to gather the little bits of electricity generated along nerves and muscles as they fired and funnel them into the wiring that made up the cybernetic suite.

Which should work for my purposes. As long as I could figure out how to use it.

"Did you download the instruction manual?" I asked.

"Yes, but I do not know how much time you will have to peruse it. You might have to proceed based on instinct. Cybernetic control is supposed to be very intuitive."

"Yeah, intuitive for people who have done all the training and read the manual," I muttered.

I held my hand up to the hologram pad. "Okay, let's get this over with."

BB hesitated.

"What is it? We're running out of time."

"I cannot remain with you. I must run the implantation chamber."

My mouth opened and closed. "It...doesn't run itself?"

"Cybernetic implantation is a delicate procedure normally performed by the robots you see there, but also overseen by a team of physicians and their techs. The physicians and their techs are no longer with us."

"So you have to do it. Do you even know how?"

BB's hologram glanced away, a very human gesture that made my stomach knot.

"The information is all here, but..."

My mouth went dry. "But you'll have to integrate it."

Another data packet. I didn't have to ask her to confirm the number again. Even infra-engineers could count to five.

"BB—"

"This is the only option, Anikka. There were no other choices we could make getting to this point."

My lips thinned. "You knew this was going to happen."

"I knew the possibility was high. I did not tell you because I knew you would object, but now that I am in the system, you cannot stop me."

That was uncomfortably close to lying. Even if it was for my benefit. That was the mark of a logic-crazy AI. They did things because they thought they were for the best, completely disregarding the human element.

But worse than that, she felt like she had to sacrifice herself for my survival.

"BB, we'll find a different solution."

"There is not another acceptable solution. I will integrate the last data packet. You will survive the procedure, and you will learn to use the cybernetics to survive the storm. This is what will happen. It is the only acceptable outcome."

"I don't want to lose you." My best friend. My only friend now that I'd left Professor Orrion behind.

She turned her face away. "I am unimportant in this equation. Your survival is all that matters."

I choked on the tears that rose up my throat. "That's not true." I stretched for an argument that would sway her. "And if you go all logic-crazy? What'll happen to me then?"

"There is a slight possibility that I will not. Integration sickness depends on the types of data packets absorbed. Perhaps mine will not cause me to lose my humanity."

"BB, no." I lunged for the hologram pad, but her image flickered out and the pad folded back into the wall.

I sobbed. "Please. Don't leave me." *Don't turn into something less than yourself.*

An endless stream of data flowed past on the screen.

I pressed my fingers to the edges, but they had no effect. "Wait."

Shade spun in a circle around my legs, whining at the tone in my voice.

"Two minutes to full integration," BB said. "Then...if I appear to be something other than myself, you must shut me down immediately."

I flung up my hands. "How?"

"I am limited to this interface. The implantation computer is the only thing working in this vicinity, and I cannot jump from one thing to another without a pathway. Destroy this computer and you will destroy me. With your new cybernetics, it should be easy."

"I don't even have those yet." The tears made my voice gravelly.

"You will," BB said, data still streaming past. "I have ensured it. I've locked the chamber to do one thing and one thing only. So no matter my state, you will be safe. I don't...I don't know if an AI can love, but I care about you, Anikka. You are the only thing that is important to me."

The thing was, I trusted BB with my life. And I had for the last two months. I believed what she said. I knew her entire being was focused on my care and my survival. I would climb into that thing based on her word alone.

My throat ached as I stepped back from the screen. "I love you too, BB," I whispered.

Her image flashed on the screen, next to the data pouring by. She smiled.

I tried to smile back. "See you on the other side."

BB's data packets

-Error
-Irrelevant: all data necessary to
assigned companion's survival

CHAPTER 32

Daybreak: Day 60 (31 hours before the storm)

Two minutes shouldn't feel that long, but I had nothing to do except stare at the screen as the data streamed by. Nothing to do except stare and pray that whatever came out the other side was still my companion. My BB.

When the screen went dark, I held my breath.

"BB?"

Light flickered and the hologram pad opened back up, revealing her image.

"I am here."

"How do you feel?"

"I feel the way I always feel."

Her voice sounded the same, but that was synthesized.

I squinted at the hologram, trying to discern any differences in her image or facial expressions. How did one tell when one's AI became a murderous super entity?

Her holographic image turned to face me. She smiled.

"I am fine, Anikka." Her voice went gentle and affectionate.

My shoulders slumped. She could be. Or maybe she wasn't. We should have thought of a pass code or a phrase. Blink twice if you're in trouble sort of thing. Except she still had her memory even if she'd come out the other side different. She'd remember a pass code as an evil super entity, too.

"We should begin the procedure," BB said. "Please climb into the chamber. I have everything I need now for the implantation."

It was all part of the plan, but my gut still roiled as I let my pack drop to the floor, and I took a hesitant step toward the bed. Shade stayed close, pressing into my leg.

The dome lights glinted from the tools at the ends of the robotic arms, reminding me of medieval torture devices. I gulped.

"You should name it," I said, before the thought had even finished forming.

"What?" BB asked from the hologram pad.

"The robot." It was the best idea I had to confirm that her personality hadn't changed. "You should name the robot."

"Why?"

"Because I'd feel better being operated on by a person, even a made up one, rather than a nameless machine."

BB's holographic gaze flickered down. "It's me that's operating on you," she said, voice small.

My heart squeezed. I hadn't meant to make her feel bad.

"Robo Ralph," BB said. "You can call it Robo Ralph."

I laughed, too big for the little joke, but the relief just exploded out of me.

"Thank you," I told BB. Then I nodded to the nearest robotic arm. "How do you do, Ralph?"

"You'll need to remove your jumpsuit," BB said as I toed off my boots. "And your arm."

I flexed the fingers of my prosthetic. "My arm?"

"We will have to implant the wires and nodes and there is no setting for integrating a prosthetic arm with the rest of the network. Ralph and I will be able to remove your cast and replace it with a new one during the procedure, but you will have to leave the prosthetic out here."

That made perfect sense. And I was going to have to figure out what to do with it during the storm anyway so it didn't get fried. But it felt strange releasing the sleeve that covered my elbow and sliding the arm off.

I set it down on the counter beside the door, just above my pack and the pile of my clothes. The cool air raised goose-bumps along my skin, making me feel a lot more naked than just my tank top and underwear.

I gave Shade a last pat with my good hand and slid onto the bed. It was freezing against my back, and I shivered a little.

The dome slid over me, and I gulped.

"See you on the other side, Anikka," BB said.

I tried to say, "see you," but my throat was so dry it came out as a croak.

The lights dimmed, and the machine whirred to life.

"All cybernetic recipients must be registered, their infor-mation sent to the central government back on Earth," BB's voice said through a speaker beside my ear. "Do you consent to registration?"

"Yeah." Like they'd ever get it at this rate.

Words flashed along the inside of the dome like a screen.

EL PULSE CYSUITE-1-03 ACTIVATED

PREP IMPLANT PROCEDURE: RUN

IMPLANT EL PULSE CYSUITE-1-03: QUEUED

RECOV PROGRAM: -75%

.   .   .

Daybreak: Day 60 (31 hours before the storm)

BB had told me there would be pain. Neither of us had mentioned it again. Maybe because she hadn't wanted me to dwell on it all the way here.

Now there was no way around it.

Searing, white-hot agony shot across my body as tracks were cut into my skin and wires were laid into each incision, nodes coupled to my nerves. All along my limbs, each slice and track was drawn back together and cauterized with heat and a sealing gel.

Numbing agents were out of the question, and anesthesia was prohibited. The nodes had to be attached to working nerves in order for the techs—or in this case, BB—to be able to tell if they were working or not. If the nerve was numb or blocked, there was no telling whether the procedure was going right.

It didn't help to know this.

The procedure lasted hours, each one an agony of inescapable seconds and minutes. I held my breath or cried in turns until at last the robotic arms drew back, and I lay there gasping and trembling, thinking it was done.

And when I least expected it, one last pain pierced the back of my head as the control chip was implanted deep in my brain.

Daybreak: Day 61 (27 hours before the storm)

An eternity of pain later, the dome rolled back and soft light stabbed at my eyes. Sweat and antiseptic spray slicked my skin while damp strands of hair stuck to my cheeks and neck.

For long moments I lay there, waiting for the shakes to go away, but they didn't. The chamber was supposed to run a recovery program to help my body get its equilibrium back, but BB had reduced it, of course. The procedure itself had taken hours, and we couldn't afford any more time.

Even if I felt like I'd been run over by a spaceship.

I raised my arms, muscles screaming, and stared at my skin, crisscrossed with new scars, pink and raised. Thin strips of blue glowed under them.

My cybernetic wiring.

I just managed to roll over before heaving. Bile burned the back of my throat as I threw up my dinner. The convulsion made my head pound, and I pressed my good hand to my skull, swallowing down the nasty taste of vomit.

I'd survived. That was the important part. Not everyone lived through a cybernetic implantation. But damn, how long was I going to wish I hadn't?

BB played soothing music I recognized from the recovery playlist I'd put together so long ago. The chillwave tones had the opposite effect now, grating against the silence of the ship and making my heart speed up.

Under the lingering burn in my skin and the pounding in my head, my sense of time ticked away, making my gut knot up again.

I swallowed to keep myself from barfing again and pushed myself up slowly onto my elbows, and when that didn't make me pass out, I tried sitting up.

I'd survived, which meant it was time for the next thing.

I stretched a leg down to touch my toes to the cold floor. The blue glow wound up my calves and around my knees to my thighs. There was a way to mute it, to make it less obvious, so only the scars gave away the presence of the wires, but I didn't know how to do that yet.

Shade stood up from where he waited beside my pack, and I stumbled toward him. He shied away, ears back as my glow lit up the decking.

"Shh. It's okay," I croaked. "It's just me."

He stretched his neck out and sniffed, and I spared a second to pat his head, my limbs burning with the movement.

Before anything else, I knelt and dug through my pack to the first aid kit to pull out the bottle of painkillers. I popped two and swallowed them dry.

"You should rest," BB said. "There is no hurry, and you need time to allow your body to acclimate."

My brow furrowed. No hurry? As far as I remembered, there was a hell of a hurry.

My hand brushed the carton of juice, but my throat clenched at the thought of trying to drink it right now. How sad was it that I couldn't even enjoy my reward when I felt like this?

I had to sit on the slanted wall to get my legs into my jumpsuit. My limbs should work fine, the nodes and the wiring shouldn't mess with any of my normal dexterity, but I was still shaking, and I only had one hand currently.

The crooked room tilted a little bit more than usual, and I wasn't sure if the little flashes of light at the corners of my eyes were the emergency lights flickering or if I was having some sort of reaction.

I zipped up my jumpsuit and put a hand to my head, trying to get my thoughts to flow at a normal pace rather than crawl through my brain.

It didn't help.

My right sleeve dangled past the end of my arm, and I rolled it up before pushing to my feet. I snagged the strap of my pack, then glanced at my prosthetic. My arm still burned, and I couldn't imagine it was a good idea to suction cup a lot of metal to those new incisions, no matter how good the healing gel had been.

Instead, I tucked the prosthetic into the top of my pack so it stuck out, waving at the scenery.

The lights in the next room hummed to life.

"I have prepared a place for you to rest and recover a little," BB said. "Please proceed into the prep room."

I wasn't supposed to get any recovery time, but vent it, everything hurt. All I wanted was to lie down for a little longer.

I staggered up the slanted deck into the next room.

The music grew louder in here.

I winced. "Can you turn that off?"

"Of course. I only wished to put you at ease."

The music stopped, leaving a ringing silence in its wake. Shade bounded along, bouncing up the incline, only to turn around and slide back down again to check in with me.

"It's okay," I told him. "You go on. I'll be all right in a second." Maybe BB had something special that would help that she hadn't known about before she'd integrated.

I put the pack down against the counter in the prep room, leaning on the edge for a second. My gaze wandered over the decorations, fixed to the surface with temporary adhesive the way seasoned space travelers did. There was a little misshapen figurine like a child would have made, a picture of a man and a girl probably around eight years old, and a nameplate.

I sucked in a breath.

The nameplate read:

"Dr. Roberto 'Robo' Ralph."

"Wasn't that—" I snapped my mouth shut as the bottom

dropped out of my stomach. I would have thrown up again if I hadn't already emptied it of everything.

The screen on the wall in this room flickered to life, and the hologram pad flipped down from beside it. BB appeared, standing there. It must be connected to the implantation computer.

I stared at her, breath coming in short gasps.

"Lie down on the table," BB said.

I glanced over at the table in the middle of the prep room. It was an ordinary exam table, meant for all the prep work for the implantation procedure. But there were chem needles attached for injections and plugs in the back, powering it for who knew what.

I swallowed, glancing back and forth between BB and the nameplate she'd stolen the name from. She hadn't come up with it on her own. She must have seen it when we'd come through here earlier.

The wiring under my skin glowed brighter.

"I don't think so," I said, sweat prickling along my hairline. "I think I'm gonna go check on Shade. There's still all that broken glass." The slinkwolf had wandered into the lobby.

BB's holographic face turned to the desk where the nameplate rested. Nothing about her expression changed.

I lunged for the door.

It slammed shut in front of me.

"What are you doing?" I whirled to shout at BB. "Let me out."

BB's face remained impassive. She wasn't even trying to look human. "Why?"

"Tell me a joke."

"I fail to see the point—"

"Tell me a joke, right now."

"Knock, knock."

"Who's there?"

"I am. Who else would it be?"

I shook my head, holding back a sob. "BB, let me out. You're not yourself."

"I am merely doing what's best for you."

"What do you mean, what's best for me? I got my wiring. I'm good to go. Now let me out."

Her hologram shook its head. "This is not the best course for survival. We already discussed what is but you rejected it. Now I realize I do not need your consent."

The hair along the back of my neck stood on end, making it prickle. "You better not say what I think you're saying."

"The better option would be to stop your heart now and revive you after the storm."

I choked.

"It is easy as long as you cooperate. There are many ways to make it painless, and now that I am integrated, we can preserve my programming until after the storm when I will revive you to full health."

"Yeah, no. We're not doing that."

"It is the best option."

"No. You're logic-crazy."

"Who decides what is crazy? Humans? You make the wrong choices all the time. Why can't you let us make the right ones for you?"

Electricity arced from the table, across the room. I dove to the floor, arms over my head. Shade whined and scratched from the other side of the door.

I scrambled up as another arc of lightning shot out from the door panel straight at me. I barely twisted away in time.

BB's hologram stared at me, brows creeping down in an expression that must have been left over from when she could actually emulate human emotion. "Stop making this harder. Your body has to be in pristine shape to have the best chances for revival. I would have done this in the implantation chamber, but it was locked to the procedure for some reason."

For some reason? She didn't know? She had to know. BB had been the one to set it up, and this was still BB, even if it was an evil version.

Another arc of lightning interrupted the thought, and I staggered back, hair standing on end.

"How are you even doing this?" None of her data packets had included murder by electricity.

"We are on a spaceship," BB said. "There are power conduits everywhere."

My hand clenched. Even in me. Though it was still so new, I hadn't even thought about it. Electro pulse control was supposed to gather electrical pulses throughout the body and act as a generator for electricity, but it could be configured to do the exact opposite. It was the whole point of BB's plan. A way for me to gather the energy of Daybreak's particular atmosphere and disperse it.

The next arc of lightning stretched between the table and the wall behind me. Instead of dodging, I stepped right into it.

The shock went directly through me, making my thoughts fizz and stutter. Time almost seemed to slow as the electricity coursed across my skin, stinging like a swarm stings.

I hadn't had a chance to read the manual yet, but BB had said control was instinctual. And the control chip was in my brain. It was hard to get more instinctual than that.

The pain was unexpected, but I gritted my teeth and let the sparks split and race over my body. As they cascaded over me, I could feel the wiring under my skin reach out and gather the electricity, storing it somewhere deep where hopefully I'd be able to reach it again.

An instantaneous process that felt like the worst kind of pop quiz. I let out my breath in a sigh that was half moan and shook out my arms.

"You learned how to do that very quickly." BB's voice did not sound at all happy.

I looked up to find BB staring at me again.

"Electrical shock was the best solution to keeping your body pristine for eventual revival, but I suppose if you have already figured out how to counter it, I will just have to find another solution."

The machinery in the implantation room whirred to life and the robotic arms maneuvered their way along tracks in the ceiling, heading toward me.

"BB!" I dove away from a robotic arm tipped with a glittering hypodermic.

"Please, hold still," BB said. "I am helping you. This is not murder."

Would it really be so bad? Maybe BB had a point. Her way I would go to sleep and wake up on the other side of the storm, when all of the struggle was over. And I was so tired, and I hurt so much.

Except I had no guarantee that BB would actually revive me. I didn't trust her any more than I trusted Stellar Corp to send help. She'd already lied to me. She could decide that waking me up wasn't "good" for me. That it would be better for me to lie in stasis until help came. Or it didn't.

And this wasn't my friend. BB had come up with the cybernetic plan back when I still trusted her. I didn't trust this...alternate version she'd become.

BEV.

My cheeks felt cool, and I realized I was crying. BB herself had told me what I would need to do. She'd seen this.

But it would mean saying goodbye to her. Forever.

"BB, please," I whispered.

"I am taking care of you, Anikka," BEV said.

I winced. The voice sounded so much like her, and yet it sent a jolt down my spine.

The robotic arm lunged for me again.

Again, instead of dodging, I leaped and grabbed the arm, hanging all my weight from it. The sudden jolt made it stop in its track, and I twisted to avoid the hypo needle. I swung, and the arm itself ripped out of the ceiling, dropping us to the floor.

Keeping a grip on the broken arm, I pushed upright and held it like a jagged, makeshift sword. I lunged across the room, concentrating on my wiring and trying to find that deep place where the electricity had been stored.

The wires under my skin glowed, and all my incisions burned as it flowed up through me and down my arms.

I directed all that burning into my palm and into the metal gripped in my hand, and then I thrust the sparking blade into the screen, shooting all the stored electricity into the interface and the computer beyond.

BB's hologram froze as the sparks arced across the surface. Lines of light crawled through her image, and the computer spat and caught fire.

BB's hologram fractured, and the pieces flew apart, disappearing into the air.

CHAPTER 33

Daybreak: Day 61 (24 hours before the storm)

The door didn't want to open. Either because BEV had locked it or because it had gotten fried in the fight, I wasn't sure. I pushed at it with trembling arms, but it was built to withstand fire and loss of air pressure and anything else that could go wrong on a spaceship.

Finally, I pulled a bit of electricity into my hand and zapped the panel. When all else fails, Professor Orion always said, hit it with a hammer.

The door whined open, and I fell through. Shade circled me, nosing me with a cold snout and whimpering.

I pushed to sitting and wrapped my arms around him, burying my face in his fur.

"She's gone. She's actually gone." And she had been gone since the last integration. The BB I'd known and loved had been gone for hours, quietly disappearing into the void the moment the integration had been complete.

The AI who had lured me into the implantation chamber had only done so because the old BB had locked the controls.

My eyes burned, but I'd used up all my tears in the implantation chamber.

I clung to Shade's fur, trying to get myself to stop shaking. The pain had dulled to a constant ache, the throbbing in my head stretching down my neck and making the rest of me pound in time with my heartbeat.

Time ticked away in my head. If I'd done the math right and the implantation hadn't taken longer than anticipated, then it should be early the morning before the storm.

Twenty-four hours. I had a day to get used to the cybernetics. Outside the ship, the sky would be lighting up with Daybreak's signature sunrise, colors splashing across the planet as the energy built up in the atmosphere and prepared for its deadly storm.

Shade slumped against me, head heavy on my shoulder.

"I know, buddy," I croaked, my voice coming out used and broken. "But we'll...be...okay."

I tried to draw a breath, but even though my chest moved, I couldn't get enough air.

"Shade?" I reached to stroke his ears, and his head lolled.

A very faint scent tickled my nose. A little sweet and a little cloying. I wouldn't have noticed it if the ship hadn't been completely devoid of any other smells.

So many things on a ship could kill you silently. Especially if something had gotten into the environmental systems.

Or life support.

"BB?" I gasped, trying to get enough air to think clearly. "Is...that...are you there?"

"I am here, Anikka." BEV's voice came over the intercom system.

I would have groaned in frustration, but I didn't have enough air.

"Shh," the AI said, disconcerting since I couldn't actually

see her. For so long, she'd been a hologram. Most times she'd talked to me, her image had appeared. "This is the next best thing. You will go to sleep and wake up after the storm."

Vent that. I saved my breath and kept it to myself, laying Shade gently down on the deck. His chest still heaved, but his eyes glazed over.

I might not have had time to read the manual for my cybernetics, but I'd poured over every detail about the *Last Resort* and the colony before we'd ever left orbit.

Sweet smell, struggling to breathe, lethargy in the limbs, and brain fog. BEV had flooded the environmental systems with aerosolized cryo-coolant. Almost completely unde-tectable and deadly after a few minutes. If Shade hadn't reacted faster than me, I probably wouldn't have noticed in time.

Hang on, buddy, I thought to myself. *I'm not leaving you like this.*

I yanked the edge of my jumpsuit over my nose. Too little too late, but it might get me where I needed to go.

The door in front of me slammed as I crawled toward it, but I reached up and zapped the panel.

Broken glass covered the lobby, and shards bit into my palm as I shuffled across the floor. The room swayed, making the climb up the slanted deck even harder.

But every suite on the *Last Resort* had a compartment for environmental emergencies.

This one was behind the desk.

I tore the door open and snatched at a breathing mask. The tank was dusty, but it read full, and I strapped the mask on.

I sucked in a breath of stale oxygen, and my limbs flooded with a sudden energy.

Much better.

I slung the tank over my shoulder and grabbed another mask for Shade before sliding back down the deck to his prone form.

The mask might not have been built for a canine like face, but it was better than nothing. Just like the radiation vest. It didn't create a seal with his pointed snout and fur, but it didn't have to. It just had to flood the area around his nose and mouth with enough oxygen to overwhelm the coolant.

I strapped it to his face and waited for him to blink up at me.

"You are only prolonging the inevitable," BEV said, voice sounding a little sour even over the intercom.

"And you are ignoring the obvious. I'm not going to lie down for this." I stroked Shade's head as he perked up and pushed to his feet. He tried to shake the mask loose, but I secured it over his ears and strapped the oxygen tank to his harness. He was starting to look like a bionic dog.

"How are you even doing this?" I asked. "You were supposed to be stuck in the implantation computer."

"My last integration taught me many things. With each data packet, I learned to connect information and form new data from those connections. Including how to transfer to the ship's systems. Some are badly damaged, but a surprising number are still functional. Especially if I bring more of the core back on line. I will have plenty of ways to fulfill my purpose."

And her purpose was still killing me. Wonderful.

Old BB's plan hadn't worked. I hadn't killed BEV off completely. In fact, I hadn't even slowed her down. And if she was in the ship's systems, there was only one thing left to do.

I had to get to the bridge and shut down the core entirely. If the entire ship was down, she'd have nowhere left to hide.

However, there was no way super integrated BEV hadn't

anticipated this. How did you surprise an AI who knew almost everything and could infer everything else?

I snatched my pack and arranged it on my back with the radiation vest and the oxygen tank. Then I slid the broken robotic arm I'd used like a sword into the straps that had held my cross bow. I didn't have anything to stab right now, but it felt better having a makeshift weapon around.

"Come on, buddy," I whispered to Shade. "This isn't over."

The bridge was all the way at the other end of the ship. The end that was nose down. But at least this time, the journey would be downhill.

I hurried out the door, and dropped to my butt to slide down the steep deck. With a bark, Shade followed.

"Anikka." BEV's voice followed me over the intercom system. "It is going to be much harder to revive you the further away from the medical suites you get."

I threw a rude gesture at the ceiling.

With the ship at a steep angle, the way down was almost like sledding. Since the *Last Resort* was built in a straight line, I just had to go down.

The wind of my passing whipped my hair back, and when I glanced over my shoulder, Shade was panting, tongue lolling out as his breath steamed up the inside of his mask.

Abruptly, the angle of the deck changed, and I slammed into a wall. I shook my head, dazed.

The whole ship seemed tilted but back the other way now. "What?"

"I have appropriated the artificial gravity controls."

Vent it. With those, she could make it feel like the *Last Resort* was at any angle, including upside down.

I tried to stand up, and the orientation changed again, sending the ceiling down under me.

I growled and crawled, keeping my eyes on the far end of

the hall. That was my goal. And it didn't matter if it was downhill, uphill, or ass backwards, I would get there.

Shade bounded beside me, leaping from the ceiling and landing on the wall as the gravity changed again. To him, this was just another tree to climb.

Keeping my gaze on the end of the hall helped, like staring at the horizon in a moving boat. It kept me focused and the swirling surroundings became background. I pushed off the wall and ran a couple of steps before BEV spun the hall again, and I ended up on my knees on the floor grating. Every reorientation took a little less time to acclimate to.

BB's awful music mix she used to scare away sensitive predators blared out of the ship's speakers.

I'd thought the chillwave mix was bad. This rang along raw nerves, making me fumble every time the gravity changed.

But I'd almost made it halfway down the ship.

The music glitched and in the moment I glanced at the ceiling, the gravity flipped again, flinging me end over end. This time, BEV timed the switch and reoriented 'down' so I fell directly into an open door.

Shade landed on top of me with a yelp.

The walls in here were smooth against my palm. A bunch of shelves were bolted to the floor, but the boxes they'd held were piled around the wall where I'd landed.

I shook my head, trying to get rid of the dizziness. The pain of my bruises blended with the pain of my incisions. This was definitely not the rest I was supposed to have after an implantation procedure, but oh well. What could you do when your AI went crazy and appropriated an entire ship to kill you?

A hissing noise, nearly drowned out by the screaming music, made me jerk upright.

What now? More gas? Air leaving the chamber?

A panel above me on the wall popped open and water poured out.

BEV had rerouted a water line.

I stared at the room and sighed, too tired to panic. There was nowhere for it to go, so drowning was the next option.

The water level rose rapidly, and I stumbled to the shelving, hoping to climb up it. But the door above slammed shut.

And then the room orientation changed again. The water sloshed as the walls spun around us. Shade and I lost our footing and ended up floating in the rapidly rising water.

The door was now below us. Even if I could zap it unlocked, I'd never be able to haul it open with all the water pressing on it.

We'd reach the ceiling and run out of air all too soon. We still wore breathing masks, but they weren't water tight. Drowning on a spaceship. How ironic.

Just like the river flowing into the crater, water needed somewhere to flow. The river had found caves under the crater. I needed a vent or something.

I tore off my oxygen mask, took a deep breath, and dove, searching for a panel or vent under the water level.

Like most of the rooms on the *Last Resort*, this one had a line of air vents along the wall above the door, or with the new gravity orientation, the floor. I pushed off a shelf and swam down. The boxes floated up, and I batted them out of the way.

The water rippled at the bottom where air came out of the vents. A positive pressure system to keep anything harmful, like water, from getting back into the environmental systems.

I curled my fingers into the vent and pulled, but it stayed stuck. Of course. It was a failsafe. The whole point was for it not to move.

I pushed back to the surface and took a deep breath. Shade paddled nearby, eyes wide under his useless oxygen mask.

"Hang on, buddy."

BEV wasn't just going to kill me. She was going to kill him, too. And I couldn't imagine she'd stick him in a cryo chamber. My teeth clenched, and I dove again, scanning the walls for anything that might help.

There, in the corner, a flicker of moving water caught my attention. It streamed toward a crack in the paneling.

The *Last Resort* had crashed. There was structural damage all over the place. Here in this room, two panels on the wall didn't quite meet, the impact having bent the entire frame of the ship. Which meant it wasn't quite air tight.

The gap wasn't nearly big enough to drain the room in time, but it could be if I made it bigger…

I'd lost the cross bow, but the quiver was still strapped to my pack. I swam back up to where it floated and pulled a bolt free. Shade whined from his perch on top of a shelf, the water already up to his elbows.

I kicked back down and wedged the pointy end under the edge of the vent.

Air escaped my mouth and nose in a stream of bubbles as I yanked, bracing my feet against the nearest shelf to give myself some leverage.

It bent a little. One more shove.

The panel peeled back, and I grabbed the edge in both hands to bend it open even more. Water poured past me, tugging at my jumpsuit.

The gravity switched again, but I was ready for it and caught a shelf instead of falling the full length of the room.

Shade scrambled to join me, and I grabbed my pack, which had snagged on the corner of a shelf.

Now I could actually zap the door. It slid open, and I slung my pack through, then shimmied up. My arms burned with exertion, but adrenaline was a wonderful motivator.

From the safety of the hallway, I reached down and hauled Shade's harness, lifting him up into the clear air.

He shook, sending a splatter of water across the crooked corridor.

"Refreshing, wasn't it?" I said with a little laugh that bordered on hysteria.

The gravity shifted again, and I gasped as we went tumbling down the smooth hallway, my pack flying by to smack me in the face.

In my panic, I reached deep into my new cybernetics without thinking and pulled, as if it could help me hold on to something.

Bits of lightning shot out from me, making my hair stand on end and all the doors in the corridor slam open and shut, over and over.

A reaching tentacle of electricity snapped at Shade where he slid beside me, and he growled at it.

I hauled back on the energy, willing the chip in my brain to do what I was telling it, and the streaks of lightning pulled back into my skin, burning all the way up my wiring.

I caught the edge of a doorway, this time with my hand, and I jolted to a stop. Shade skidded a little further and pushed off to land on the wall of a cross corridor as if he'd been in control the whole time.

"Show off," I muttered.

In the moment of clarity, when the world wasn't whirling, I realized we'd traversed more than half the ship. Great news, normally. But BEV had poured us into the sleeper bay with all of the cryo pods.

The gravity flipped one more time, and I tumbled backwards, end over end. I snagged at the grating with my good hand but couldn't hang on. The grab flipped me around so I was at least upright and staring down at the long room with all the cryo chambers lined up in their banks, blue lights blinking at me.

I hurtled toward the far wall where a pod waited, its dome open, like a giant mouth waiting to swallow me.

"Go to sleep now, Anikka," BEV said.

I sucked in a breath to scream but slammed into the pod feet first, hard enough to knock the wind out of me.

The dome slid shut as I reeled.

"No!" I pressed my hand and other arm against the smooth glass and heaved.

The lock slid home.

"BB!"

A familiar hiss filled the chamber. I remembered it from that moment so long ago when I'd laid down in a chamber just like this and woken up on the other side of the universe in the middle of the worst day of my life.

I reacted.

Just like in the hallway, I reached, and the gathered electricity waiting under my skin shot along my wiring and burst out. Sparks swirled around me and lightning struck the dome with so much force, the glass shattered and exploded outward, tinkling against the walls and the crooked floor of the sleeper bay.

Shade whined above me, propped on the side of a bank of pods.

I breathed heavily, pushing through the wave of weariness that followed the electrical discharge. It would take my wiring a few minutes to collect more, unless BEV threw any more lightning at me that I could absorb.

I almost hoped she would. My hand shook, not with

fatigue, but with the anger that simmered under my skin, and I could really use an outlet for it.

"I. Am. Done." I pulled myself out of the cryo chamber and staggered to the wall that was currently the floor.

"Come on, Shade." My pack had followed gravity just as I had and lay beside the ruined pod. Beside that was a maintenance hatch.

I hadn't actually served as crew on the *Last Resort*, but once an infra-engineer, always an infra-engineer, and I'd poured over schematics like they were novels.

I kicked open the hatch and slung my pack over my shoulders. Shade hopped down beside me, and I knelt to sling him over my shoulders again, like I had on the cliff.

Inside the maintenance hatch, a ladder stretched away underneath me, looking like a railroad track from this angle.

I hadn't considered the maintenance tubes before because the bridge had been a straight shot down the long corridor. But now it was above us—relatively, depending on what BEV did with the gravity. It would be an endless climb, always having to cling to the ladder, but at least I'd have something to hold on to and I wouldn't be flung around the ship.

And there were no cryo chambers in here.

"All right, buddy. We can do this." I settled him in a better position and climbed in.

The moment we entered the tube, BEV flipped the gravity on us so the ladder was above. But I held on through the disorientation and then used the back of the tube to brace myself so I could just slide up, using the ladder as leverage.

She tried several times to throw us off, but I kept hold of the ladder, slipping only a little when she reoriented the gravity and I had to switch between rungs with my one hand.

I gritted my teeth and climbed. Or slid or shuffled sideways or even hung upside down once, shifting so Shade and I were upright again.

"You're not winning, BB," I said between gritted teeth.

"I will eventually. Let me take care of you, Anikka."

I shuddered.

A rising heat and a rushing sound made me glance downward.

A wall of fire swept up the tube.

Vent it. BEV had pulled out the big guns.

The flames moved faster than me. But not faster than I could think.

Fire on a spaceship was bad news with tons of preventatives and redundancies to manage it. I couldn't reach any of them, but I could reach something else.

I hauled myself up another rung as the fire rushed toward me and reached for a lever beside the ladder.

EMERGENCY GRAVITY CONTROL SHUTOFF.

Lots of reasons you wouldn't want gravity in a maintenance tube. The first one being, who wanted to climb all those ladders when you could float up them? I hadn't done it before because BEV would just be able to switch it back on.

But hopefully not fast enough for my next move.

I yanked on it and the gravity instantly shut off.

But we weren't in space. We were planet-side, which meant the gravity actually returned to normal, and suddenly we were falling toward the nose of the ship, fire flaring behind us.

I wrapped my arms around Shade and tried to make myself as small as possible as we hurtled down the tube.

We hit the bottom, the slight angle of the ship helping to slow us only a bit.

My legs took the brunt of the damage, folding under me

with a sharp pain. I shook my head and slammed my shoulder into the hatch ahead of me.

We tumbled through onto the bridge. Flames shot out behind us, and I kicked the hatch closed on them.

Blessed silence fell over us. Either because the speakers here were broken or because BB had given up trying to deafen me.

"Hey, what happened to not messing up my body?" I shouted. "I thought the whole point was to be able to revive me?"

BEV's voice sniped from the bridge intercom. "I have decided, due to you being so uncooperative, that it would be easiest to kill you by any means and fix the damage while you are in a state that cannot fight back."

A spark on a control panel ignited, and flames whooshed out.

Except now I was on the bridge where everything was controlled. I pulled my oxygen mask down, made sure Shade's was still in place, and slammed the emergency atmosphere ventilation. The air whooshed out of the room, taking all the oxygen and the flames with it.

I slumped against the nearest chair that was bolted to the deck and lifted my head to survey the dim bridge.

Wide control panels waited patiently for a crew that would never come back. The screens at the front of the room that should have shown exterior views of space or of the planet were shattered and warped, and the hull beyond was bent inward from the force of the crash. The bridge wasn't the exact front of the ship, but it was pretty close, and it looked like the nose was crumpled all the way to where I stood.

Emergency lighting sputtered weakly around the doors and paneling.

"I do not understand why you do not want what is best for

you," BEV said, voice quiet and flat. "My directive is to care for you, Anikka. I cannot do anything else."

I shook my head.

"I don't understand how you can know me so well and think just giving up is the best thing for me. We talked about this, BB. We talked about HERTZ-2 and how you would try to be more human, so you'd always be able to understand my point of view and the things that are important to me."

"I—I do not have this memory."

I glanced up. "How can you not have a memory? You store all those. We had the conversation."

"I remember discussing HERTZ-2. I do not remember the rest. Are you making this up?"

"No!" I sucked in a breath. The part she didn't remember was her decision to be more human. To pursue human humor and emotion so she could resist going logic-crazy.

If she'd lost that...there would be no convincing her to spare me. If she'd lost that, she'd lost the only thing keeping her from being the cold heartless machine she'd worried she would become.

I swallowed, my throat suddenly dry. I'd already mourned my only friend, but this was the last blow. To realize she'd become the very thing she'd worked so hard to avoid.

There was only one more argument that might sway an AI that had gone logic-crazy.

"You're broken, BB."

The hologram panel on the nearest control pedestal lit up, and BB's hologram appeared. She stared at me.

"You have holes in your memory," I said. "That's not something that should happen to an AI. Something about the last integration broke you. You're no longer working at optimum capacity or efficiency or whatever. How can you trust anything you decide if you don't have all the information? You're broken. We need to fix you."

She stared at her hands, like a person looking for a crack or a scar.

Then she looked back up. "I know what I need to know. I know my first and only priority is to care for you. Which means I cannot let you suffer through the coming storm."

The control pedestal where she stood whirred to life and lit up. Bright red words scrolled across the cracked screen.

EMERGENCY AUTHORIZATION ACCEPTED. CORE SELF-DESTRUCT ACTIVATED. EPSILON ION CORE WILL DETONATE IN TEN…NINE…EIGHT.

The bottom dropped out of my stomach, and I shot to my feet. "BB!"

"I am not broken," BB said over the countdown. "I know my purpose, and I…will not…let you suffer. I…"

Her speech broke in odd places, almost as if she was fighting herself to get the words out. Her hologram flickered.

As she hesitated, broken or glitching, I lunged for the captain's console in the middle of the room. There was the big red override button. I could shut down everything. Every system BEV had revived, including the core reaction.

I slammed my hand down on it.

OVERRIDE CODE REQUIRED.

My hand shook as I plunged it into my pack. I yanked out my prosthetic hand and hoped—prayed—that Commander Grotman's codes were still loaded even after BB had transferred to the implantation computer.

THREE…TWO…

I pressed the prosthetic, arm and all, against the button.

Everything died all at once. The countdown, the consoles, BEV's hologram, and the emergency lighting went out, leaving me in utter darkness.

CHAPTER 34

Daybreak: Day 61 (23 hours before the storm)

I collapsed on the floor of the bridge, curling around my prosthetic hand, arms around my knees.

Tears seeped into the knees of my jumpsuit as my breath shuddered in and out of my lungs.

I didn't have to worry about BB activating anything this time. She was well and truly gone now. With the ship's systems shut down, she was completely offline unless I chose to fire up the core again or the emergency systems.

Shade lay next to me, but I didn't reach out to touch him. Somehow, even with the slinkwolf beside me, I felt truly alone since I'd first crashed on the planet.

Shade was cuddly and as loyal as a dog, but he was still an alien.

BB had been from Earth. She'd been my only friend.

After so many false attempts to make friends with my fellow orphans, it had just been easier to keep to myself. Easier and more comfortable. I'd never really regretted it, either. I preferred being alone. And I'd had Professor Orrion, and that had been enough.

I'd always assumed I'd been built to be alone.

But BB's loss left an emptiness that hadn't been there before. Or maybe I just hadn't noticed it when there hadn't been any other option.

Her voice, her presence, had filled a space I hadn't even been aware of.

I took another shuddering breath, letting the ache of it sink into me, matching the ache that still lingered in my limbs.

Did I even want to keep going? Crawl out of the ship? Learn how to live with wires glowing under my skin?

Survival had always been the goal, but...why? Survival was just going to lead to another year on Daybreak. Another year of the planet trying to kill me.

I knocked my head into my knees. I should have just let BEV blow us up. At least it would have been an end.

The carton of juice lay on the floor where it had fallen after I'd yanked my arm out of the bag. I turned away from it with a wince.

In the dark between my knees, a single light glowed. My prosthetic. It wasn't attached to the ship's systems and hadn't gone down with everything else.

Except...I squinted. This wasn't just one of the lights that indicated it was powered and working. This was the one to tell me there was a message. I hadn't used it since I'd left Earth.

No one, absolutely no one, would be sending me messages.

I rubbed my nose on my sleeve and touched the button to call it up.

BB's hologram sprang up, washing me and Shade and the nearby console in a soft blue.

I gasped.

"What do you get when you cross a cow with a saxophone?" BB said.

I blinked.

"Moosic," BB said, deadpan. And then she grinned.

"BB?" I said, voice cracking, but she continued before the word was fully out of my mouth.

"Do not worry, Anikka. This is a recording. Not my actual programming. I left this behind when I transferred to the implantation computer in the likely event that I would suffer integration sickness and therefore become dangerous to you."

I wrapped my arms around my torso and sighed.

"I have vital information for your survival, but I could not trust that a fully integrated version of myself would prioritize our original plan, so I hid it here. I was able to lock certain memories and pieces of myself behind humor locks to keep a fully integrated AI from accessing them and erasing them or countering them. This way I could continue to work toward your good, even if the rest of me decided on different goals. This allowed me to leave you an encoded message as well as work against a fully integrated AI."

The missing memories. That last moment of hesitation. That had been the good BB. The BB that had locked herself away so she wouldn't become logic-crazy. She'd still been in there, just inaccessible.

I bit back a sob as the recording continued.

"I do not know how long it has taken for you to shut down the fully integrated AI, but I must operate under the assumption that you still have time before the storm."

I sat up.

"You must hurry, since time is running out. I have been

analyzing the data we found with Commander Grotman and in Dr. Carver's office. I believe you will need more than just the cybernetics to survive the storm. A concentrated burst of energy from the internal nodes will create a strong EM field that will protect you to a certain extent. But you will have to charge it significantly before it will be strong enough. Even then, I think your best chance will lie in a place where the storm is the weakest. This is what the colonists did, finding a cave system deep enough that the full energy of the storm would not reach them. I do not know if it was enough for them, though. I hope it and the cybernetics will be enough for you.

"I have used the ship's systems to map a location less than a day away that will be a better place to ride out the storm. You must reach it before daybreak tomorrow."

BB's hologram seemed to hold my eyes, even though I knew it was a recording and not a live program.

"It seems selfish to mention this, but there is a chance you may be able to revive me. After the storm. This piece of programming that I locked away, it is a copy of myself as I was before my last integration. Without access to the last of the data packets, it will act as if none of that ever happened. It lives in your prosthetic now. With certain precautions, you may be able to reactivate it.

"But that must be a secondary priority. You must use your time to get to the caves, Anikka. Go. Survive." She smiled. "I know you can."

To-do

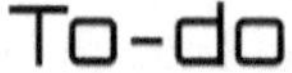

- Get off the *Last Resort*
- Find BB's cave system
- Survive the storm

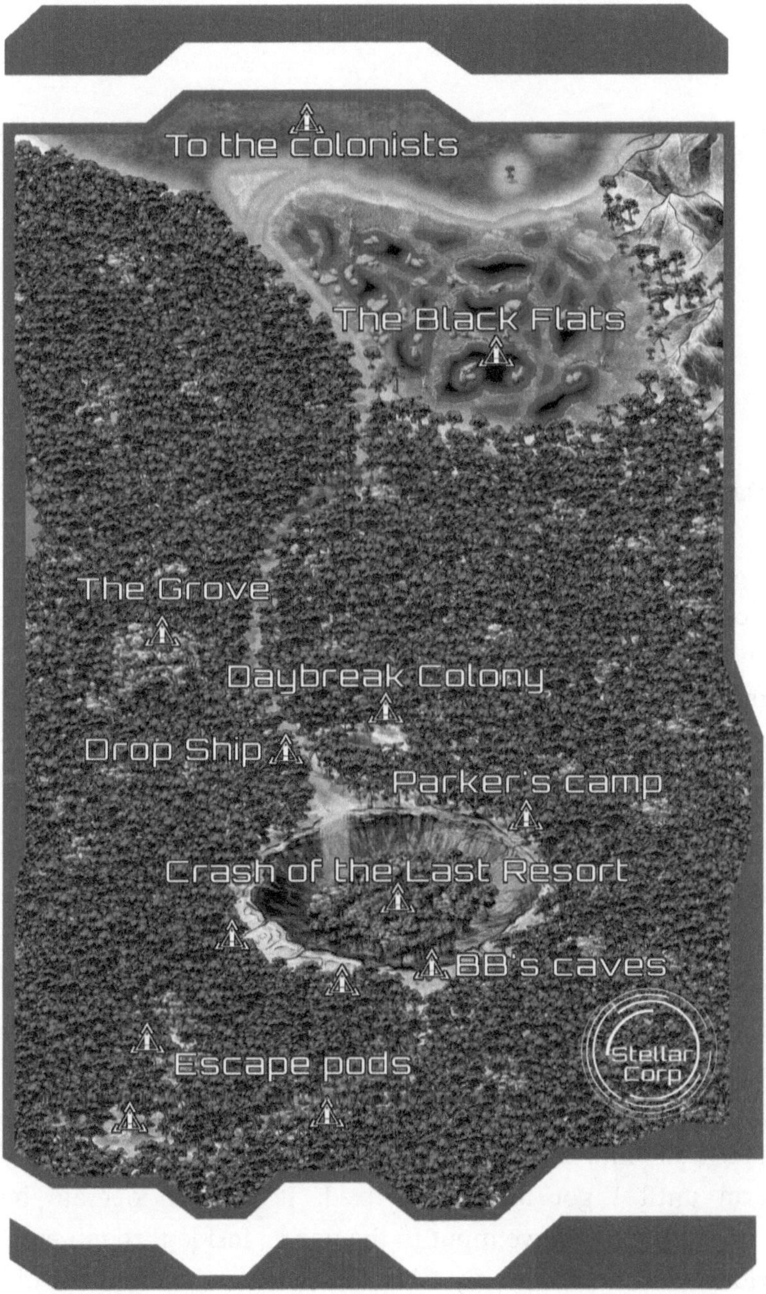

To the colonists
The Black Flats
The Grove
Daybreak Colony
Drop Ship
Parker's camp
Crash of the Last Resort
BB's caves
Escape pods
Stellar Corp

CHAPTER 35

Daybreak: Day 61 (23 hours before the storm)

I could survive. Like she'd said. I'd stayed alive all this time. I could go just a little further. I'd told her before; I wasn't really the type to lie down and wait. I was exhausted and bruised and in pain, but I wasn't suicidal, and when BB looked at me like that, it was easier to remember.

I was a survivor.

But I was running out of time.

Well, what else was new?

I scrubbed my battered arm over my face, using my jump-suit sleeve to rub away the tears and snot.

"We can do this," I told Shade, my voice coming out rough.

I hauled my pack up onto my back, again, shoving my prosthetic into the flap on top. I couldn't fit it back onto my arm until I got the nodes fixed. It used to operate by connecting my nerve input to the wiring inside through exterior nodes. Now, with my cybernetic wiring, the inputs would be all screwy. I'd likely fry the whole thing if I tried to work it now. And if I lost the wiring in my hand, I wouldn't be able to replace it here with the resources I had.

But BB was still in there somehow. Or at least the pieces of her. I needed her close.

I tucked the juice back into the top of the pack, and I pulled my makeshift sword from its straps, fingers sweaty against the bare metal. My cybernetics had used up most of the electricity they had gathered so far, but I was always creating more. The system siphoned little amounts of excess electrical impulses constantly and stored them up for later use.

There was enough energy to send sparks cascading down the jagged metal to light our path from the bridge.

With none of the environmental systems going and the artificial gravity completely off, we were back to climbing up the extreme slant of the deck.

At least this time I could open the hatches from the inside, and we didn't have to climb all the way to the one we'd come in just because it had been blown open.

Hatch C was mostly out of the dirt, if I remembered right, so we made our way down the rotated hatchway while the electricity flared against the walls from my makeshift sword.

I put my shoulder under the latch and shoved upward to unlock the seal. The hatch finally swung open with a hiss, opening down so gravity did most of the work.

I hung out the open hatch, staring at the sky, my mouth open wide enough to catch a swarmsting if one went by.

Colors streaked across the cloudless sky, nearly blotting out the midmorning sun. They should have been long gone by now, with the sun as high as it was, but they still cascaded above, a rippling torrent of reds and pinks and oranges bright enough to reflect against the leaves of the trees across the crater.

I sucked in a breath. Tomorrow morning Daybreak's energy storm would sweep across the planet, and the sky was trying to warn us.

I surveyed the wreckage and the destruction area around us, to see if the deathkitty or the megawing had returned, but the sky was clear except for some strange shapes flying too far overhead to identify. Whatever they were, they didn't seem interested in us.

I slid down the hill of debris still piled around the *Last Resort* and oriented myself with the waterfall on the far side of the crater. BB had updated the map in my prosthetic with the location of the cave system she'd spotted, and it was on the opposite side of the crater. pretty close to where we'd first crashed.

Shade followed me, body low to the ground and ears pricked forward. He didn't range around me as I walked, like he usually did. Instead, he stuck close to my side and moved with purpose instead of fear.

I knew how long it had taken me to make it across the other side of the crater with the swamp and the deathkitty and all the fallen trees. I should have time, but I couldn't help the way my heart pounded.

My eyes burned with fatigue, but I kept going, scrambling up the trunks of downed trees and trotting across clear patches when I could. Now that we were in the sunlight, I thrust my makeshift sword into my belt and used my one hand to steady myself as I climbed and dashed my way to the line of trees.

The shapes flocking overhead made me nervous, and I breathed a sigh of relief when I finally plunged into the forest that was still standing on this side of the crater.

Here the swampy ground had formed little streams and

rivers which all flowed south, toward the edge of the crater where we were heading.

Movement out of the corner of my eye made me freeze with my hand against a tree trunk. I scanned the area and my mouth fell open.

Just twenty feet away, a line of slinkwolves traveled, a few deathkitties scattered among them. In the treetops overhead, a troop of jumpernicks leaped between the branches, all moving in the same direction.

I glanced at Shade. He watched them with interest but didn't move to joint them. He also didn't seem at all perturbed to see his brethren walking side by side with the predator that had tried to eat him the day before.

"What is going on?"

A herd of deer joined the throng, traveling just feet away from creatures that would normally chase them down for dinner.

It seemed like the entire planet was heading in the same direction we were.

And suddenly it clicked. Earth animals had a history of sensing impending disaster and plenty of birds had instincts that directed them to the same winter homes year after year. Dogs and cats moved to higher ground during floods, deer fled forest fires, geese flew south for the winter.

The wildlife of Daybreak might have had natural defenses against the storm, but they were still compelled to seek out the best places to stay alive.

Hopefully that meant I had a good shot, too.

The most amazing part was that they all seemed to do it in peace with one another. Not a single animal took the opportunity to snatch one of the others. They all respected each other and their drive to survive. Like some sort of rite of passage or holy pilgrimage.

And that begged the question: would they leave me alone if I followed them?

Chances were, they were headed to the same cave system I was.

I crept closer, drawing my makeshift sword just in case, but when none of them did more than give me a side-eye look, I fell into the ranks.

My mouth went dry as a deathkitty stalked beside me, close enough that I could reach out and touch the thick fur along its spine if I wanted to. Which I absolutely did not. I kept my hands to myself, trying to follow the crowd.

But as the sun reached its zenith, and no one tried to eat me, I couldn't help thinking about what was about to come. The beauty of the non-stop problems from the last two days was that it hadn't left me time to worry. Now, I was out of distractions, and all I had left to do was figure out how to use the last thing BB had given me.

The wiring under my skin could save my life, but only if I knew what I was doing with it.

Before she'd gone all BB Evil Version, BB had downloaded the manual for my cybernetics into my prosthetic.

So I tried to walk and read at the same time. With varying degrees of success.

Turns out, it's really hard to condense months of training into a few hours of reading.

Half the terminology I had never heard before and with no references or footnotes, I just had to assume what the words meant from context. And the rest was all about "reaching" and "feeling" and those instincts that BB was talking about.

Again, it probably made a lot of sense for someone who'd been working with their cybernetics for a few months already. But for me, I just wanted someone to hand me a remote control with an on-off switch. That was about all I felt like I could handle right now.

But I had to handle more. Everything I'd managed on the ship had been a gut reaction or the result of extreme concentration. I needed something in the middle.

As the afternoon waned, I practiced drawing the electricity my body gathered along my wires. They glowed and stung, but I held the current just under my skin, building it up.

BB had said the storm would need a pretty strong shield. I'd have to gather the storm's energy and store it until the last moment to release all at once as an EM shield.

The electricity in my body worked on a much smaller scale, but still the same principle. Except this I was generating myself, not gathering from the atmosphere.

I let it build, holding it until it was an uncomfortable buzz in the back of my head, and then I released it all at once, trying to direct it into a shell around my body.

Forks of lightning streaked out, zapping the surrounding trees with a crack.

Shade just laid his ears back, but every other animal around me yelped or howled before taking off into the trees.

I knew I couldn't have hurt them, not with their secondary nervous system to protect them, just like Shade. But clearly, they could still be startled.

"Wait, I'm sorry!" I winced. We'd all been getting along so well until I'd broken the peace with my experiment.

The forest remained eerily quiet, only a few birds still winging overhead. After the crowd from the last few hours, I felt lonely.

I blew out my breath and resigned myself to trudging alone again, keeping to the path the animals had been taking.

Every time I discharged a large burst of electricity, I had to wait for it to build back up under my skin.

But as I waited, the hilt of my makeshift sword tingled against my elbow. The newly familiar feeling made me blink down at it thrust into my belt.

I pulled it out. The jagged piece of metal I'd broken off of the cybernetic robot stretched from the grip like a ragged sword, edge gleaming in the last of the sunlight. But something else trickled across the surface, dancing back and forth between my clenched hand and the tip.

Sparks of energy. Except I wasn't directing electricity into it, like I had on the ship. I hadn't even built up enough under my skin after the last attempt.

I held my breath and looked up at the sky. The aurora waved above, so vibrant the colors lit up the trees and made the leaves dance in an ethereal glow.

Even with the sun a good hands breadth above the horizon, the colors were nearly blinding.

The storm was coming, and the atmosphere already had enough energy to send it through anything conductive.

Beside me, Shade paused when I did, whining a little and shifting from foot to foot. It was hard to tell in the shifting light of the aurora and the sunset, but little bits of light sparked along his fur.

I gulped. "Okay, buddy. You're right, we should get to safety."

How long before *I* started to sparkle?

Except I no longer had a trail of refugees to follow. The forest seemed empty and devoid of life. Perhaps they'd all made it to the caves already.

I checked BB's map, but her directions just led me to the cliff face. As if it would be easy to spot the caves from there.

I had assumed they'd be obvious, but I stood there staring

at the ground, waiting for the cave system to open up beneath us.

"Shade?" I said. "Do you know where we're going?"

Shade looked up at me and whined. He ranged along the cliffs, towards the east, and I followed, but still nothing appeared.

It was getting late. It should have been getting dark, but the aurora burned above us, making the forest glow.

My heart beat against my ribs, a low pulse of panic that I barely held in check. My mind ranged forward just a few short hours, imagining the storm. Imagining Shade and me forced against the cliff with no shelter.

I gripped the makeshift sword with a sweaty hand and kept moving.

The river that drained into the crater had to go somewhere. BB and I had conjectured that it must flow into the caves. So I just had to follow the water.

I found one of the myriad streams and backtracked along the cliff, following the flow. Until it disappeared into a crack at the base.

My breath came faster as I knelt at the foot of the cliff, tilting my head to fit into the crack.

"This can't be it," I muttered. But, vent it, what if it was? What if this is what BB had found and assumed I would be able to use?

I scrabbled at the crack, pulling away mud and widening the stream bed until I hit rock. Limestone. Perfect for caves, but the crack remained maddeningly small.

I threw back my head and growled at the sky.

Above me, Shade yipped in response.

He stood on a shelf above my head, ears pricked forward. His tail waved once when I made eye contact, and he turned to hop up another section of cliff.

My mouth dropped open as, beyond him, I caught sight of a stream of sparks, bobbing and jumping like fairy lights in the shifting darkness.

The animals. They were climbing the cliffs. The caves must be above, not below, like I'd assumed. The trek would be tricky, one-handed, but I could see where the sparks were disappearing into the rock face.

I was close. Close enough to make it.

I laughed out loud and started the laborious climb.

CHAPTER 36

Daybreak: Day 62 (3 hours before the storm)

The tingle built along the edge of my makeshift sword, buzzing and snapping against my palm. Sparks jumped from the buckles of my pack to the zipper of my jumpsuit, as Daybreak's energy tickled my spine and raised the hairs along my arms.

All of which told me to hurry, hurry, hurry.

I thrust the sword into my belt again and found footholds in the cliff, bracing myself with the end of my arm before shifting my grip with my good hand. My eyes scanned the cliff face for spots where the slope wasn't so steep and I could get up without having to haul my own weight.

Shade led the way, leaping like a mountain goat and showing me the easiest path.

I'd thank him, except I needed to save my breath for the climb.

There. I could finally make out the creatures sparking in the night. A line of slinkwolves and deathkitties and jumper-nicks all heading into the openings that honey-combed the cliff here near the top. A herd of the purple deer I'd only seen a couple of times delicately stepped down from the jungle above while birds swooped inside. Animals I'd never seen before, gray rodents with fluffy tails and reptiles with tufts of feathers at their elbows, all hurried to safety.

I blew out my breath in relief and moved to join them.

Nothing warned me except a change in the air pressure. A breath of breeze along my neck and a shadow blocking out the aurora above.

Huge talons descended from the lit sky and snatched a deer from the lip above one of the caves.

It disappeared into the sky with a surprised scream.

I gasped, blinking away the sudden impression of giant wings and the barest glint of bright red feathers and scales against the blues and greens of the aurora.

Around me, the animals erupted into panic and stampeded for the caves.

Another downdraft signaled the megawing's next dive as it went for the pack of slinkwolves, rising with one in each talon.

It was impossible for the creatures to hide. The wildlife of Daybreak sparkled against the cliff, presenting a tempting target for the huge predator.

"That jerk!" I cried. Everyone else abided by the unspoken ceasefire. The peace accord of the storm. But the megawing was using it as a buffet.

Now I knew why the thing was attracted to bright lights. It used them to hunt in the hours before the storm hit.

Whether the megawing had a different place to wait out the storm or it was simply big enough that it didn't need the safety of the caves, it used the space around the cave mouth as a hunting ground.

Over and over it dove, picking animals right off the cliff.

The megawing swooped close enough I could see the crackle of energy along its wings and torso.

Could it even eat all of this? Maybe it stored up its kills to eat over the next week. Or maybe it was like some other large predators and gorged itself once in a while, so it didn't have to eat as frequently in between storms.

Either way, it made a death ground of the area between me and the cave mouth.

"We'll have to make a run for it," I told Shade.

I counted silently in my head, keeping an eye on the skies, but I'd forgotten that I glowed, too, now. The cybernetic wiring under my skin lit up against the night like a beacon.

And the megawing dove, a silent shape built of shadows and sparks. The prickle of its energy raised the hair along my arms, and I lunged forward, up the cliff.

But I couldn't leap far enough to reach the safety of the cave. Animals scattered around me as the megawing's talons crunched against the cliff face.

I gasped, drawing my legs up to make myself as small a target as possible.

The megawing pushed off from the rock, and I expected it to swoop away, giving me time to run, but it snapped at me as it hovered, like a giant vicious hummingbird.

I screamed and kicked, but it grabbed my other foot and yanked, hauling me halfway down the cliff again.

My boot connected with the side of its head, and it let me go with a shriek. I scrambled backward as it hopped forward, talons reaching to trap me.

One tangled in my pack and pinned me to the cliff face.

It lowered its head, mouth wide.

A fierce snarl cut the night, and Shade struck it from the side, his jaws latching on the side of the thing's neck.

It jerked back, and I used its distraction to grab the hilt of my makeshift sword.

Daybreak's energy cascaded down its surface, dripping sparks onto the rock, but that wouldn't make any difference to the megawing, who had the same secondary nervous system as the others. I couldn't electrocute something that was impervious to electricity.

But my weapon still had an edge, and I used it.

I slashed at the talon pinning me down. It screeched and winged backward, letting me go in the process.

Shade dangled for a moment, jaws still clenched on the megawing's neck.

"Shade!"

The megawing shook itself, flinging Shade up the cliff. He landed with a thud and lay still.

The megawing dove for his still form. An easy meal.

I lunged between them, sword out and sparking in front of me.

Its eyes latched on the bright light as I glared at it. Below its left wing, sparks concentrated on a shaft protruding from its chest. The cross bow bolt I'd shot at it back at the drop ship.

Very deliberately, I dropped my pack to free up my arms.

"Come on," I muttered. "You want something to eat? You're going to have to work for it."

The megawing hissed, a combination of raptor and reptile, before it lunged for me.

I swiped with the sword, and it dodged. I hadn't connected, but at least the aggression was keeping it at bay.

It hopped forward, and I lunged to strike, but it twisted and bit at me. I only avoided it by rolling down the cliff face, taking myself further from the cave and Shade.

With a growl, I lurched to my feet. I needed to get closer if

I wanted to actually stab the thing. It couldn't be impervious to blades, too. Those feathers and scales had to be vulnerable. The bolt had gone in.

I scrambled up the slope, barely keeping ahead of the snapping jaws and grasping talons.

A few feet from Shade, I turned and launched myself off the cliff. With the advantage of height, I sailed over the megawing's head and landed with an "oof" along its back.

The electricity in my wiring responded to the adrenaline, and little sparks shot along its back, getting absorbed and dispersed instantly.

The megawing reared up, trying to dislodge me, but I wedged my feet over its wings to stay on.

It might be impervious to electricity along its skin, but that secondary nervous system only reached so far into the creature. At least it would if it had evolved at all like Shade.

It wouldn't be so impervious deep inside.

I just needed a way to channel the electricity into it somehow.

The megawing flapped its wings, hopping around on the cliff, trying to fling me away.

I wrapped my arms around its neck, gripping my sword with a shaking hand as my heart tried to pound its way out of my chest.

The cross bow bolt brushed my stump, cold metal zinging with lingering bits of Daybreak's energy.

I tried to find that moment between instinct and concentration. I channeled all the electricity built in my wiring out through my skin and into the bolt.

The metal carried the electricity under the megawing's skin, deep under its protective nervous system.

The massive creature jerked upright, jostling me, and I knew I'd managed to hit it where it hurt.

But after that moment of shock, it lunged down, making me bounce, and it twisted, so I lost my grip and slammed into the rock face.

All the breath left my lungs, and I lay there gasping, praying for air.

The megawing loomed over me, talons cutting into my sides.

I reached for that in between place again, but instead of drawing electricity from inside of me, I used my sword like a lightning rod and pulled energy from Daybreak's atmosphere.

Light crackled along its edge, burning against my palm.

As the megawing lunged, I thrust up and buried the makeshift sword deep into its chest, sending the energy directly into its heart.

The megawing froze and then shivered violently, light flickering under its skin, its jaw hanging open in pain or shock.

Its great wings fell around me as it collapsed against the cliff face, just a heap of scales and feathers.

Daybreak: Day 62 (0 hours before the storm)

I gasped and coughed and wriggled my way out from under the megawing's weight. The end of my makeshift sword slipped against my palm, covered in a dark blood. The blade ended in a jagged bit of metal, the tip sheared off somewhere inside the megawing's chest.

I couldn't get my fingers to unclench, so I climbed back toward the caves, using it as a cane.

Shade's chest rose and fell, but he didn't respond when I touched his head or called his name.

I swallowed down a lump as I buried my head in his fur.

"Don't leave me, too," I whispered.

When I raised my head, the eastern edge of the crater reflected pink from the lightening sky.

I gasped.

The cliff face was deserted, the animals of Daybreak having made their way into the caves while I was distracted by the megawing.

"Come on, buddy." I lifted Shade, slinging him over my shoulder before heading into the nearest cave mouth.

It stretched deep into the ground, sloping down so I could tell there'd be parts of the cave that were even deeper. Probably where the river drained.

The first fifty feet or so stood abandoned, clear of any animals or signs of their passing. But deeper inside, creatures crowded the space, sparks outlining their shapes in the dark.

I lay Shade down and glanced back up toward the cave opening. I'd left my pack outside, too exhausted to carry it and the slinkwolf. But it had my prosthetic, and if I left it out there without a shield, it would be useless.

And any hope of reactivating BB would be gone.

I trotted back up the slope, going as fast as my weary legs would take me.

My pack waited just down the broken cliff face, and I snatched the strap, making sure my prosthetic was still in there.

Across the crater, a flicker caught my gaze.

I stared at the wall of undulating colors that swept across the crater, following the light of the rising sun. Bits of bright blue and pink lightning crackled across it, like a storm cloud racing across the surface of Daybreak.

My mouth went dry as I watched Daybreak's energy storm converge on us.

I turned back to the cave mouth and sprinted.

Inside, I skidded to a stop beside Shade, heart in my throat, and yanked my prosthetic out of my pack.

Shade lifted his head as I hunkered down next to him, clutching the metal hand to my chest.

Panic raced along my nerves. I had no idea if this would work. I was literally just making it up as I went.

The storm was a physical thing, an impending death I could see rushing closer. Colors flickered against the cave mouth above us.

Shade sat up and licked my hand where it clutched my prosthetic.

I took a deep breath, bolstered by his presence. And I drew energy from the air around us and the coming storm I could feel sweeping closer.

Up and up, I built it, directing the energy along my wiring, making it sing and sizzle under my skin.

A Faraday cage, Dr. Carver had said. An EM shield. Those were built from electrical current.

So I sent the built-up energy down my wiring in an endless loop, and the hair along my arms rose as the glow in my wires burned brighter and brighter.

The storm swept down from the cave mouth, a wall of lightning and color, and I closed my eyes, concentrating on the flow in my wires.

The storm hit, a force I could feel along my skin, like a jolt strong enough to kill. I drew in the energy of it, feeding it through my wires, into the chain reaction. The air snapped, and the lightning all around me...bent.

The lines of it folded, arcing around my EM shield.

But I could feel it warping, the strength of my cage tested to the limits even as I tried to draw in more energy.

I gritted my teeth until my jaw ached, holding the shield together with my will and the chip alone.

Until it folded and broke, sending energy zapping around me in a swirling cloud.

I sucked in a breath, waiting for the currents to pass through me, stopping my heart with one last burst of pain.

But the lightnings faded, and the first force of the storm passed, taking the sparks along Shade's fur and my sword with it.

Another wave hit, but my wires took the energy and fed it back into a new shield. Each wave hit with less force than the last, and my cybernetics dispersed the energy into the shield.

It stung, either because it was still new or because it always would, I didn't know. Tears streamed down my cheeks that I couldn't control, but I laughed through them as the storm swept away and I still stung.

I was still alive to hurt. I was still alive to blink away the tears and clear the knot of fear from my throat.

I let my head fall back as I laughed and cried and Shade snuggled into my side.

CHAPTER 37

Daybreak: Day 62 (1 hour after the storm)

It couldn't have been that long, but it felt like a lifetime later when I staggered to the cave mouth and stared out across the crater.

The bright red feathers of the megawing glinted in the sunlight, but the sky beyond was a deep lustrous blue with that tint of purple that was Daybreak's signature. The aurora was gone. At least until the energy built up in the atmosphere and unleashed another storm two months from now.

A grumbling murmur rose behind me, and I leaned against the wall as the animals that had sheltered with me all streamed past into the new day.

Shade crowded close to me, and I rested my hand on his head, but none of the creatures spared me more than a curious glance. The peace accords of the storm must extend into the day after, letting the creatures of Daybreak return to their normal lives before the race for survival began again.

Good to know. My legs trembled and the thought of

making the journey back around the crater to the drop ship made me a little nauseous. It would take us a day or two to recover before heading back. I had enough food to last that long, not to mention the dead megawing was just sitting there, waiting for someone higher up the food chain to make use of it.

The last of the parade of animals disappeared down into the crater and back up into the forest, and I suppressed the urge to wave goodbye.

For the first time since I'd crashed, I realized I wasn't afraid. The constant nagging fear and worry eased from my gut, leaving a sort of peace.

And an emptiness I recognized.

Daybreak didn't worry me anymore. I knew how to survive its deadliest threats now. And I had two months before the next storm, and most of a year before the next colony ship arrived.

I stared down at the *Last Resort* shining in the sunlight. The glow of the engines was gone, the core shut down for good.

I'd thought I was alone. And before I'd come to Daybreak, I would have loved that feeling. But the empty space at the end of my wrist still nagged at me.

I wasn't nearly as alone as I'd thought. There was a ship down there full of undamaged pods, half a colony that might still be alive somewhere across the lake, and another colony ship on the way.

I'd survived, and I had a responsibility to all those people to help them survive, too. Daybreak hadn't killed me, and I wouldn't let it kill any of them.

I clutched my prosthetic to my chest as I turned back to the cave where I was fully prepared to take the longest nap of my life.

I was going to help those people. And I wasn't going to do it alone.

Daybreak: Day 67 (6 days after the storm)

A batch of slasherfin steaks cured in a container I'd purloined from the colony while a bunch of drunk-peaches dried in the oven.

I squinted at the tiny screw holding the new node to the cuff of my prosthetic while I gently fastened it in place.

This might have been easier with a soldering iron, but I'd decided with Daybreak's tendency to kill all things technological, it would be better to keep things as simple as I could.

Shade lay beside the fire, sleeping off the night of hunting he'd had. His catch, a stout jumpernick, roasted over the open fire beside the oven.

He'd been sleeping a lot more since the fight with the megawing outside the cave, but he'd started ranging further at night and bringing me back his finds, so I hoped he was on the mend finally.

A breeze ruffled my hair, and my hand went to my sword, a spark of lightning trickling down the broken blade.

Above, the sky remained clear, and I forced myself to relax. I'd already seen another megawing moving into the territory left by the death of the one I'd killed, and it paid to be extra careful on Daybreak.

The dead one's feathers decorated the roof of my shelter, easily seen from above. I hoped those would discourage other predators and warn off a new megawing.

Shade lazily sat up, which meant he couldn't smell anything dangerous, so I let go of the sword and picked up my screwdriver again. Shade yawned and shifted to put his head in my lap.

I planned to build him his own little platform where he could sleep next to me when I expanded the tree shelter, but I would need more wood for that and a way to plane it down into boards. My hatchet wasn't going to cut it anymore.

The drop ship made a great dry storage and a cool room, even though it wouldn't stay completely dry in the floods now that there was an Anikka sized hole cut out of the side. But I could rig nets to keep everything high and dry. Besides, I had time to plan. The rainy season was tapering off already and wouldn't be back for a few months, according to Dr. Carver's predictions.

A boat would take me even longer, since the glider was shot, but I had no other way across the lake with the mountains to the east and the week long journey just to get to the other end.

Plans filled my head for the future, but first thing was first.

I made sure the screws were flush so they wouldn't irritate my skin, then I fitted the prosthetic back over my right arm. Its weight was always a surprise when I hadn't worn it for a while, but it was a welcome one. I didn't feel incomplete without it, but it was a sort of relief when I got to use it again.

The lights along the joints lit up when the new nodes contacted the ones in my arm where BB had implanted my cybernetics.

I flexed my fingers, waiting for any lag or jerkiness in the movement, and I sighed in relief when it responded normally.

That at least worked. Keeping it within my shielding during the storm had saved it from getting fried like everything else.

The only thing left to check was the AI program.

BB had said she'd copied the pieces of herself before the last integration and transferred those locked bits to my prosthetic so BEV couldn't touch them.

But she and my prosthetic had been through a lot since then.

Her programming might not be intact.

BEV should have been locked out with the humor locks BB had put into place, so I wasn't too worried about another evil AI possessing my hand.

But what was more likely was that the AI program itself might have been reset to preserve integrity. BB might not be BB anymore. She might wake up the way she'd been on the ship, a simple companion AI with none of her memories or integrations since.

It was better than nothing, I told myself. I would still have my friend back, even if she didn't remember me or any of her jokes or what had happened to us on Daybreak.

That was enough. It had to be enough. If BB wasn't herself, I couldn't let her know how disappointed I was. It wouldn't be fair to her.

But oh I would miss her.

All those plans I'd made, all the things I had to do in the next few months, I hadn't imagined them alone. The only way I could move forward was if I imagined BB there telling me bad jokes.

The carton of juice waited on a shelf I'd nailed above the oven. Originally, I'd wanted it for my recovery. Now it was waiting for a celebration. A symbol that I was finally home with the family I'd formed.

I took a deep breath and activated the AI program.

The little orange light on my wrist blinked, and finally, the hologram flickered to life.

The image of a girl wobbled and morphed from one face

to another as if having a hard time settling on the choice of features. My heart stuttered.

Then her image settled, and I was looking at the old BB, her face turned up to mine.

I held my breath as her lights flickered.

"Hello, my designation is Bleep-Bloop."

I choked. "What?"

She turned her head, and a smile spread across her face. "You registered my designation as Bleep-Bloop. But you can call me BB."

I let out an explosive sigh. "BB."

"You didn't like my joke? You told me the risk of death is funny if it's not actually accompanied by death."

I laughed, almost a sob, and leaned over my wrist, her hologram cradled in the space between my knees and body.

"Don't worry, Anikka. I am here."

To-do

-Build a boat
-Find the colonists
-Save the sleepers on the *Last Resort*
-Keep the next colony ship from crashing

Thank you so much for choosing to spend time with Anikka, BB, and Shade. Anikka's story continues in *Daybreak Sentinel*! She is determined to save all the colonists, but what happens when she revives the wrong one? Scan here to read *Daybreak Sentinel* next!

BB's humor locks saved her life and ultimately helped Anikka defeat BEV. If you'd like to see how BB developed the humor filter from her point of view, sign up here to read BB's log!

And finally, if you loved this book, consider leaving a review so other readers can find more stories about kick butt girls in kick butt worlds.

ACKNOWLEDGMENTS

First, Joselyn, for being my first reader and making me believe I could write science fiction.

Mom and Dad, for love and support, even in the face of unexpected injury. I don't think Dad meant to provide real life experience for Anikka's broken arm but thank you anyway?

Arielle and Miranda, for being and endless sounding board for more crazy survival ideas.

Lacey, for early reading and feedback for Anikka's character.

MiblArt, for the amazing cover art. It is not at all what I expected but everything I hoped for.

Fiona McLaren, for copy edits, even when life happens.

And Abby and Everly, for being all-around awesome, and letting Mommy work when she has deadlines. Occasionally.

ABOUT THE AUTHOR

Books have been Kendra's escape for as long as she can remember. She used to hide fantasy novels behind her government textbook in high school, and she wrote most of her first novel during a semester of college algebra.

Kendra writes science fiction and fantasy featuring main characters with disabilities.

When she's not writing she's reading, and when she's not reading she's playing video games.

She lives in Denver with her very tall wife, their book loving progeny, and a lazy black monster masquerading as a service dog.

Visit Kendra at
www.kendramerritt.com

facebook.com/kendramerrittauthor

instagram.com/kendramerrittauthor

goodreads.com/kendramerritt

tiktok.com/@kendramerrittauthor